SHATTERED

A WIZARD'S WORK ♦ BOOK ONE

MARK FASSETT

RAVENSTAR PRESS
MONROE, WA

Published 2011 by Ravenstar Press
Monroe, WA
http://www.ravenstarpress.com

Designed by Mark Fassett using StoryBox software
http://www.markfassett.com
http://www.storyboxsoftware.com

Cover art by Joe Slucher
http://www.joeslucher.com

ISBN: 978-0615479996

For Wendy
Without you, this wouldn't
have happened

Don't take that to
mean that I'm
blaming you

CHAPTER 1

A MIDST AN ORANGE glow from the Weave-heated glass, Robert struggled to maintain his concentration.

Other activities around the lab kept picking at his attention. Gerard worked in one corner of the lab with a Weave designed to pull the heat out of water to create ice. Wallace sat at his bench, cutting and mixing ingredients for some future project. Angela, his most persistent distraction, was carefully pouring a reddish powder into a solution she was creating to fill the Focus Robert had already spent several hours preparing, for the third time. He wanted to catch her eye which hid behind a lock of raven hair, but she remained completely focused on her task.

Ignore her. You can't let her see you fail again.

With some effort, Robert pulled his attention back to his work. He found he'd let the flow of energie he fed to the Weaves he'd created falter, allowing them to weaken. He gathered up the energie required from within himself and fed it to the Weaves until they regained their proper strength.

He maintained a Weave surrounding each hand, like a pair of gloves. Another Weave, shaped like a bowl, floated above his workbench, anchored by several thin Threads of energie. He used his Weave-gloved hands to form the molten glass around the floating Weave so that it would eventually become a bowl.

From behind him, Robert heard the clop of boots striking the stone floor. He nearly turned around to see who approached, but caught himself before he ruined the Focus.

Don't look. It's just Monteous. Concentrate.

Robert knew losing his concentration now would result in disaster, as this was his last chance to get it right. Monteous had stressed, more than once, the need to complete it correctly by the evening. An evening that was little more than an hour away.

All that remained was to complete shaping the glass around the Weave, tie it off, and let it cool.

A bead of sweat rolled down his forehead and into his left eye. The salt stung, but he couldn't use his hands to wipe it away. He blinked the eye, shut it tight and even leaned his head off to the left to let the sweat drain, but none of his attempts worked. He resolved to try to ignore it. He was almost done. A minute at most.

His arms and hands shook with the ache of exhaustion as he kept rolling the glass up the Weave.

I'm almost there. Just need to roll it over the top and tie it off.

The molten glass finally reached the top of the form. He used his Weave covered hands to push it just a bit higher, then rolled that bit over the top to create a rounded lip that would hold the glass to the form while it cooled.

He tied the Threads off, one by one, and was about to tie the last when he caught movement out of the corner of his right eye and looked quickly in that direction. He looked back quickly when he realized what he'd done. Only a fraction of a second, but the damage was done. The form Weave began to unravel in front of him yet again.

To his surprise, it didn't unravel far before the Weave was taken from his control and knotted back together.

"Finish tying it off, Robert."

Robert heard the disappointment in Monteous's voice, but followed the instructions and completed the Work, tying off the remaining thread. He brought his hands together and merged his Weave gloves into a single Weave, then wrapped it around the outside of the Focus to protect the glass while it cooled.

Once he tied that off, he reached into his workbench and pulled out a wrought iron stand created specifically to hold the Focus. He set the stand under the Focus, then nudged the glass down until it settled in place on the stand.

With the Focus resting in its stand, its glow fading, Robert could finally reach up and wipe at his eye. Then he stole a look to his right to see what distracted him. Only Wallace, putting phials away on a shelf. Robert clasped his hands behind his neck and leaned back, staring at the rough timber that comprised the frame of the roof.

A hand landed on his shoulder and gave it a squeeze. "Much better that time."

Robert didn't want to look at his Master, didn't want to see the disappointment he knew would be there. "I still lost it. You had to save me."

"Yes, but you saved yourself on the first slip. Neither of your previous tries even came close to completion. You handled the four Weaves with little trouble. You didn't overheat the glass this time. The metals are in the proper alignment. You had sweat in your eye, which I thought for sure would cause failure, but you persevered and ignored it."

Robert glanced around the lab and found the other apprentices studiously not looking in his direction. He turned and faced his Master. "I still failed. You had to step in and help me at the end."

And I see the disappointment in you.

"But you nearly succeeded. With a little more effort, a little more concentration on the task..."

"I didn't succeed, though. It's the same every time. I can't shut out the world. I can't shut off my brain. I should be taking the tests now."

Monteous sighed. His shoulders slumped a little. "You're right, of course, Robert. You have the ability. You should be taking your tests by now. But you insist on worrying about your failures, and with that, I can't help you."

Robert sat back against his workbench and searched Monteous's stubble-encrusted face.

"I've tried everything I can think of to get you to see it another way. I can't make you. Until you figure out inside your own head what you want, there's nothing more I can teach you."

Robert's chest tightened. A sour lump formed in the pit of his stomach. *There's nothing more you can teach me?*

He watched Monteous appraise the rapidly cooling Focus one more time. Monteous clapped a hand on his shoulder once, twice, then walked off across the lab, heading to Angela's workbench. Robert wanted to shout, to question. *What's that mean? I'm still an apprentice, aren't I?* But he didn't voice those questions aloud. He didn't really want to hear the answer he feared.

ANGELA COULDN'T BELIEVE what she'd heard, but didn't look up from her work. The solution brewing in the apparatus in front of her bubbled and frothed as she fed more energie into the Weave that heated it. Each ingredient she added required bringing the solution to a specific temperature, and the solution was nearing the appropriate temperature for the wormroot extract. Looking up might cause her to overheat the solution and ruin all her work.

From what she heard, it sounded like Robert had already ruined the Focus. She couldn't imagine why else Monteous would be so disappointed as to tell Robert he had nothing else to teach him. History played its part in her assessment, too. "You need to concentrate, Robert. You need to focus more," was a constant refrain she heard throughout her time with Monteous.

There.

She stirred in a pre-measured dollop of the wormroot extract with a glass rod, then released the heating Weave, allowing the solution to cool.

She looked up from her work, and gazed across the room at Robert's bench. The Focus rested, to her eye, complete in its stand. Robert stood on the other side of it, his back to her. His shoulders hunched, his arms apparently crossed in front of him, he held his head with its close-cropped chocolate-colored hair bent forward and down, exposing his neck. Angela suppressed the urge to walk over and rub it.

"You're finished?" Monteous's voice intruded on her.

"Yes, yes I am, Master."

Monteous bent down and peered into the solution, then sniffed it.

Let it be right. The first time he trusts me on a project of this nature. I don't think I made any mistakes.

After a moment, he stood and faced her. "Good work, Angela. I can't detect any flaws."

She couldn't keep the smile from her face. This was the first time Monteous had trusted her to participate in a Work of this magnitude for a patron. A portal. Generally agreed to be among the toughest Works to create, and she'd played a part. Though she didn't yet have enough control over the elemental Weaves to create the Focus herself, crafting the solution satisfied her.

"Thank you. Is the Focus done? Are you going to open the portal tonight?"

Monteous glanced Robert's way for a moment before answering. "It is finished and you both did a wonderful job. I couldn't be happier."

"What about..."

"Opening it? Patience, Angela. I have to prepare a few things, and the Focus still needs to cool for a while. I'll open the portal tonight when I return."

"You're leaving?"

"Only to go to the market. I thought we ought to have some food before my work begins, and you four need time to clean this place up."

Angela looked around, and indeed, because of the work they'd done, much of the laboratory was in disarray. Her bench was covered with an accumulation of phials and containers. Rods, tongs, flasks, phials, crystals, books and other items were out of place. Angela knew Monteous liked the lab free of clutter when he worked.

She nodded, and Monteous went to a coat rack near the door and pulled on a thick heavy cloak. Addressing the room, he said, "Clean up. I'll be back soon. We'll cook supper, eat, then get paid."

He swung the door open, letting in a chilling breeze, and stepped out into the icy late-afternoon air. The door slammed shut.

As soon as the door shut, Angela heard Gerard. "Fouled it up again, Robert?"

"Go eat dung." Robert didn't even look around as he responded.

Gerard laughed.

Angela wanted to go over and hug Robert, tell him she believed in him. She couldn't let herself do that though. He'd want more, expect more, and she couldn't give it to him. Instead, she said, "Leave him alone, Gerard. The Focus is complete, so he obviously didn't foul it up."

"It took him three tries, though."

"So? Could you have done it at all?"

He scowled at her, then looked away. She knew he couldn't do it. She also knew he wouldn't risk crossing her. As much as she wanted Robert, Gerard had an interest in her. He'd shown it in dozens of ways, small touches, hints, even direct questions, though never in public.

His pride can't handle a public rejection.

Robert turned around, and faced her, his dark eyes deep pools she could fall into and drown. "Leave it. Angela's right. The Focus is complete, which is all that matters. Let's clean up."

And that was what drew her to Robert, despite his failures. He never gave up. If only she could follow through on her desire.

❈ ❈ ❈

ROBERT FELT QUITE a bit better after he'd eaten the pork and bread Monteous had purchased at the market. The bread was fresh, and the roasted pork warmed and refreshed him with each bite. The food restored much of the energie drained from him while creating the Focus.

The five of them sat around a large, well used, dining table in the kitchen. Monteous commanded the table's head, the rest of them arrayed along either side of its length. They talked as they always did. Despite a few glances from Monteous, the old wizard said nothing to him to indicate anything had irrevocably changed as a result of the incident with the Focus.

After the meal, Monteous sent them out to the lab again, directing them to retrieve their cloaks from the rack by the door on the way.

"Robert," Monteous said when they had all gathered in the lab, "please place the Focus in the center of the stage."

Robert went to his bench, picked up the Focus and its stand, and brought them to the far end of the lab. The "stage", as Monteous called it, was a raised stone platform roughly a dozen feet in diameter. One circular slab of granite, larger than Robert could cross in two strides, marked the center of the stage. Surrounding it lay smaller stones in a pattern organized to direct energie to the wizard working on the stage. Monteous had chosen each stone in the pattern for the properties it possessed, and not necessarily for aesthetics.

He stepped onto the stage and placed the Focus in the center of the granite slab. Angela followed him onto the stage carrying the flask with the amplifying solution. Robert moved out of her way so she could pour the solution into the Focus. As the clear liquid met the formed glass, it appeared to change color, becoming a deep violet.

"It changed color," Robert heard Wallace say.

"Correct, Wallace," said Monteous. "The solution reacts with the metals embedded in the glass. If it doesn't change color, you know you did something wrong.

"Now, off the stage, you two." He made a shooing motion at Robert and Angela.

Robert quickly left the stage, stepping in between Angela and Gerard. He knew Gerard had an interest in her. After Gerard's remarks earlier, Robert didn't feel like making it easy for him.

"There are three keys to successfully opening a portal," Monteous said. "The first is placing the matrix of metals into the Focus in the proper pattern so that you go where you want to go. The second is drawing enough energie from your body without completely draining yourself. You will still draw energie from other elements around you, but the primary component must be your own."

Monteous's gaze fell in turn upon each of the apprentices as he spoke, eventually coming to rest on Robert. "The last is that you must maintain your concentration and focus until the portal is open. Any slip, any at all, and the threads will unravel leaving you without a portal, and without the energie to make a second attempt."

"Master," Robert said. "If opening a portal drains so much energie from you, will you have enough left for any other Weaves once you've finished?"

"There's the trick. You have to balance what you take from yourself with what you draw from around you so that you have enough of your body energie, but not so much that you can't weave anything else. Also, remember that carrying a staff or a wand with you will allow you to create many Weaves that won't require much of your personal energie."

Monteous then went to the wall nearest the stage where he had an array of staves, and pulled down his personal staff. Monteous had created it from a six foot length of blackened wood, and adorned it with silver and gold filigree along its upper length. Emerald and sapphire stones were arrayed in a ring near the head. Robert knew an iron and copper core, twisted together, ran through its entire length. He could see many of the Weaves wrapped around and woven through the staff.

For a moment, Robert looked forward to making his own staff, the final test for entrance into the Guild, but a glance at the Focus reminded him of his earlier failure. *I'll never get my own staff.*

Monteous didn't leave him any time for dwelling on the thought. "Once I open the portal, the lab will be vulnerable to anything from the other side. I don't expect anyone to be there, but you should be vigilant. Get your staves and wands."

Robert went to get his staff, a plain, well-worn length of ash with an iron core. He returned to the stage first, as his bench was closest. Gerard had the farthest to go to get his staff. Angela came back with a wand before Gerard had started to return. Wallace never left. He'd been Monteous's apprentice for less than a year, and only recently mastered some of the fundamental Weaves. Robert thought Wallace's training with a wand would begin soon, but he knew it hadn't started yet.

When Gerard returned, Monteous said, "Gerard, if anyone tries to get through the portal, and they are not me, use whatever Weaves you must to keep them on the other side. Robert, if Gerard can't keep them from coming through, unravel the Weave."

"With you on the other side?" Robert asked.

"Yes. I can find my way home. I do not want strangers in my lab."

Robert nodded. He didn't like it, but if that's what Monteous wanted, it's what he would do.

Monteous rapped the heel of his staff on the stone twice, and all the lamps in the room went out, plunging them into darkness. "All right. Everything is ready. While I'm working, pay close attention to the threads and how I weave them."

They all nodded. Robert felt excitement race through his body. Watching Monteous work always held a thrill for him. His Master's skill was obvious to any wizard, and to most who could not even see a thread.

Monteous stepped back off the center stone, and raised his staff a few inches off the floor.

Robert slipped quickly into the vew, a sort of trance, a way of seeing, that allowed him to perceive Weaves and the threads that made them. He could see the energie that flowed from Monteous's staff, the draws from the stone in the floor and the air around him. But more than the energie from the environment, he saw what Monteous meant about the balance of energie from within.

The threads, in the vew, appeared as strands of light, different colors according to the energie source. Monteous folded them and wrapped them together, creating a thick, intricate rope that he fed to the Focus. The metals in the Focus reacted with the threads and spun them out into an upright elliptical field above the Focus.

Monteous put so much of his own energie into that rope that Robert could see how a mistake in gauging the necessary amounts could easily drain the wizard before he completed the portal. In that moment, he also understood why most wizards couldn't open a portal. *They'd drain themselves.*

The portal continued to take form above the Focus, and it grew until it was a bit taller than the height of a man. At that point, Monteous started another thread and this time, used it to wrap the edges of the portal. When the edge was wrapped, Monteous tied the thread and released it and the rope.

Robert slipped out of the vew, and without the threads of the Weave superimposed, could see the portal as it appeared to a normal: a window pane, hanging in the air above the Focus. The edges were indistinct, but the view through it was clear.

And through it, he could see darkened trunks of trees, a forest at night. Frost covered the branches and the ground. Cold air slipped through the portal to chill the room, and Robert understood why they'd been told to don their cloaks.

"Where does it lead?" Wallace asked.

"Shh. Try not to say anything while I'm away," Monteous admonished in a quiet voice, nearly a whisper.

Monteous peered through the portal for a moment, then turned to face them again. "The area looks clear. If it leads where it should, I should step through right outside the rear wall of an estate owned by a man who stole an artifact dear to our patron."

Robert nodded, and saw the others do the same. He gripped his staff a little tighter.

A mischievous grin formed on Monteous's face. "Here I go. Keep the room dark. We don't want light spilling into the forest and announcing the existence of the portal."

He turned and stepped through the portal, careful to step over the Focus and not disturb it.

Once he'd safely crossed to the other side, Robert saw him turn, enough to see Monteous's face again. The mischievous grin fell flat, and his eyes grew wide. "What are you..."

Robert started to move toward the portal, not quite sure what to do, but it was too late.

The Weave maintaining the portal's integrity unraveled. The portal snapped shut, shattering the Focus beneath it, leaving Monteous trapped on the other side.

CHAPTER 2

ROBERT STOOD AND lit some lamps in the room. His hands shook as he strung the threads to each lamp. Lighting them took longer than it should have.

Angela was the first to say anything. "What happened? Why did it close?"

"I don't know. It shouldn't have closed by itself, and I don't think it did."

Gerard spoke up. "It didn't. I swear I saw someone's energie undo the binding from the other side."

"Is that possible?" asked Wallace.

Robert nodded. "Sure it's possible, if a wizard was standing there. The question we should be asking, I think, is who did Monteous see? Who was waiting there for him? Who would know he was going to be there?"

"You're right," Angela said. "Who would know?"

"The patron would know," said Gerard. "He would know where the target was, at the very least."

Robert stepped onto the stage and bent down to examine the shattered Focus. His hands still shook, and he tried willing them to stop. "Does anyone know who the patron was?" The shards of the Focus lay scattered across the stone, Angela's solution, what was left of it, already evaporating. "Did anyone see him?"

He looked up and saw the others shaking their heads.

This is a disaster.

"I think it's obvious," he said, "that whoever Monteous was retrieving the object from knew Monteous was coming, and either had a wizard on retainer, or is a wizard himself."

"Do you think the patron was involved somehow?" asked Wallace.

"It's certainly possible. Until we know who the patron is, it will be impossible to know. And unless the he shows up here announcing himself, we may never know who the he is." Robert held his hands to his knees to steady them. "We can probably be certain the patron won't appear here if he was involved."

"So what do we do?"

Robert didn't know. He looked around the lab, and couldn't imagine living without Monteous, learning from him. *If we can't find him, that's exactly what will happen.*

While his mind worked at creating a plan, he started gathering up the shards of the Focus.

They could try to find the patron, and maybe figure out where Monteous was through him. But finding the patron was unlikely. Monteous never kept records of who he did business with. If they asked around and inquired of wrong person, whoever held Monteous might find out they were looking and seize them, too. *Or just kill us.*

So what else could they do? He held the glass shards in his hand, shifting them around with his fingers.

"If anyone comes by asking for him, we pretend he is away," he said. "Anyone."

He felt, more than saw, Angela kneel down next to him. "What do we tell them if they ask why?"

"That he's Working for a patron. Anything, really, that will keep people away."

"We won't be able to keep them away for long."

He turned his head to look at her. "Long enough for us to make another portal."

"But who's going to do the Work?" Gerard asked. "You?"

"Yes, I know how. I made the Focus." *Are you sure you can do it?*

"You almost ruined the Focus."

Robert nodded. *You failed all three times. Why are you so sure you can do it this time? What does it matter? I have to make it. None of the others can.*

"Can you do it Gerard? You can manipulate fire and lightning better than the rest of us, but those aren't what are needed for a portal. And Wallace doesn't have the experience yet. Angela..."

Angela interrupted him. "No, I can't do it. You're the only one of us that is capable of doing it, if you can keep yourself from getting distracted." She turned to face Gerard.

"I think Robert's right. Trying to open another portal is the only option we really have. The four of us can do it. We did almost all of the work to open this one, everything except the final Working."

"I just think we ought to tell someone."

Angela stood to face Gerard, and Robert stood to back her up. He knew he wouldn't win this argument with Gerard by himself, but if he let Angela take the lead, he thought she could convince Gerard.

"Who would we tell, Gerard? Who could help against a Master Wizard? The city guard?"

"But we don't know..."

"Of course we know. Only a Master could have closed that portal from the other side. Monteous was set up by the patron, or by someone who knew the patron was sending Monteous after the artifact. Opening the portal is our likeliest chance of finding out where Monteous is, and our best chance at getting him back."

"Couldn't you try to divine his location?"

"Of course I'll try to divine it, if Monteous left something here I can work with."

"Even if she could find him," said Robert, "making another portal is the quickest way to get to him. The portal could have opened anywhere — a hundred miles, a thousand."

Angela stepped up close to Gerard, and had to look up as he towered over her. "Look, we all know Robert's shortcomings," she said, and Robert winced, "but he will overcome them at some point, and now is as good a time as any to believe he will. None of the rest of us are capable of opening that portal, yet. While we're working on the portal, you and Wallace can see if you can find out anything about the patron. Maybe there's something around the Master's chambers that you can find that will identify the patron. Maybe we'll get lucky and the patron will come by on his own. We can't know, so we have to do what we can do, and one of those things is helping Robert attempt to open another portal."

Robert held his breath. He could see that Gerard was pondering what she said, even seeing the sense in it. Really, they were all still in shock. The idea that their Master, the head of the Guild and the greatest wizard currently practicing, could be snatched and held against his will, went against everything they had thought possible. Of course it was possible, but it was easy to forget when each day spent with Monteous and his absolute control over his energie and the amazing Works he created pointed to his ability to handle anything that came his way.

The silence from Gerard grew too lengthy for Robert to bear. "Gerard, let's just think about it overnight. We can't do anything right away, in any case. We have to get more materials, and some of us need to recoup our energie."

"No, you two are right. It's our best option right now. I don't like it, but you're right. Just don't screw it up, Robert."

"With that decided," Angela said, "let's clean this up and then get some rest. At first light, we'll get started."

✹ ✹ ✹

ROBERT LAY ON his bed, staring at the rafters. As the Senior Wizard, and probably the most renowned wizard in the Guild, Monteous's home was large enough that Robert had a room to himself. He was grateful for the privacy it afforded him as he allowed numbness and shock to take over.

He couldn't sleep. Every time he closed his eyes, he saw the portal closing, the Focus shattering, the door slamming shut on the rest of his life.

He rolled onto his side and stared at the four books he could call his own. They sat on the shelf next to a belt buckle that had been his father's, and a copper bracelet that had belonged to his mother.

The first of the four books was the first gift Monteous had ever given him, both reward and incentive for learning to read.

What's to become of me?

He had to shut his eyes.

What master will take me on? I can't stay focused enough to complete any complex Weave.

He thought back to the last conversation about the Focus that he'd had with Monteous. Robert wished he'd said something different.

The others won't have any trouble finding new masters.

Wallace had as much talent as anyone, and he was still young enough to be molded in any way a new master could want. Angela and Gerard still had a couple years before they could even consider taking their tests, and they were both capable.

They don't have my deficiency.

It was something Monteous had failed to train out of him. For whatever reason, he still lacked the confidence, the ability to concentrate on his task to the exclusion of everything else.

He opened his eyes again and stared at the bookshelf, looking at a book with its title stamped and gilt into the spine. "A History of Wizards in the Seven Kingdoms". Time and again, it had taken his mind off his parents. The blackened bodies, trapped in the fire that consumed the inn they owned, a fire started by outlaws, rebelling against nothing Robert could understand at the age of eight.

Monteous had given him shelter for his body, and with the book, shelter for his mind. He'd taken Robert in, and over time, Robert had come to see him as something more than a kind wizard, or a Master.

Monteous had become, intentionally or not, Robert's father in all but name.

One way or another, whatever it takes, Monteous, I will find you. I swear to anyone who can hear. I. Will. Find. You.

CHAPTER 3

THEY WOKE EARLY, the four of them, even before first light. Robert thought the others must have had as much trouble sleeping as he.

Monteous didn't keep cooks or servants, so they worked together on making breakfast. Robert could hear his Master's voice proclaim, "That's what apprentices are for!"

The apprentices were expected to take care of all of the menial chores: cooking, cleaning, going to the market for any and all sundries. And so they fell into making breakfast out of habit as much as anything else. It almost seemed to Robert that it was their way of avoiding the subject that none of them really wanted to broach. It kept the idea that Monteous was not there with them at bay.

They were fairly silent, too, voicing only the thoughts and requests necessary to get them through breakfast. And when it was done, and all the dishes cleaned and dried and put away, they all came back to the table and sat around it, silent.

Eventually, Robert had enough. "If we're going to find Monteous, we'd best be about it. Did anyone come up with a better plan?"

They all shook their heads, even Gerard, who Robert was sure would voice more opposition.

"Then we should write up list of the materials we need for the portal. As soon as we've got that list, someone will have to go to the market and purchase what we don't have while Angela works on trying to divine Monteous's location."

She nodded, but it wasn't very enthusiastic. In fact, Robert realized, none of the other three looked like they were ready to do anything at all.

"Why are you all so glum?"

They looked at each other, seemingly exchanging unspoken thoughts, until eventually, Angela spoke up. "We don't even know if he's alive."

Robert sat, stunned. He'd avoided that thought the entire night for fear it would unravel him. He needed Monteous to be alive. His life, as he'd imagined it, would never come to pass if Monteous was dead.

"I can't accept that," he said after a moment. "I just can't. Even if he is, we have to find out for sure. We have to know.

"Because, if he's not dead, and we just leave him with whoever abducted him..."

Robert could feel Angela's eyes on him, as much or more than he saw them. He couldn't help but look back, try to invite her in. *What is she looking for? What does she want? Whatever you're after, ask. I'll answer.*

"You're right," she said eventually. "We can't take the chance that he's sitting there waiting for help. We have to know, or we'll have to find another Master to take us on, and there aren't any that equal Monteous."

Wallace and Gerard nodded in agreement, and Wallace said, "I don't want to go looking for another Master. I like it here. What if I can't find one?" The distress in his voice was palpable.

"Don't worry," Robert said. "You, of all of us, would have no trouble finding another Master."

He tried to move the subject back to the original topic. "So, are we agreed to our course?"

They all assented — Gerard, it seemed, grudgingly. But it was good enough for Robert.

✸ ✸ ✸

NOW THAT THEY were agreed on a course of action, they took care of their individual tasks without much discussion. Robert made a list of materials they would need for the Focus, checked it against the stores of materials they already had, and made a second list of materials they needed to acquire. Angela was doing the same for the solution. Wallace was set to cleaning up the shards of the first Focus, and Gerard took on the task of searching Monteous's rooms for any hint of who the patron might be.

It wasn't long before Angela and Robert came together at her bench to combine their lists into a single shopping list. Angela's only listed a few items, but Robert's list was comprised of nearly everything needed for the Focus. Robert feared quite a few of the items on his list, the metals, especially, would cost more than they had.

"I don't know how we're going to get all these," Robert said.

"He's got to have some gold in his study somewhere."

"Which will be worthless to us if it's warded."

Just then, Wallace came up to them with the shards of the Focus. "Couldn't you get the materials you need for the Focus out of this — at least, the metals?"

Robert and Angela looked at each other, then Robert said, "I don't see why we shouldn't be able to get most of the materials out. We probably won't be able to reuse the glass, though."

"What should I do with it?"

"Put every sliver you can find on my bench."

As Wallace carried the shards to Robert's desk, Robert heard a loud shout, and then quick footsteps as Gerard came running into the lab. "I may have found something."

"What?" Robert and Angela asked in unison.

"A note, a scrap of parchment, really, but it has a name, the name of an inn, and a date about two weeks ago."

"What name?" Robert asked

"Demetrius."

"Maybe it is something. A meeting request?"

Wallace returned from Robert's bench and looked at the parchment. "We started work on the portal right after that date," he said.

"I know that inn," said Gerard. "It's near the Inner City market."

Robert nodded, then quickly went through his shopping list, scratching off everything he'd likely be able to recover from the Focus shards.

"Gerard, I think you and Wallace should make a trip to the Inner City, do some shopping, and see if you can find any trace of someone with that name while you're there." He handed the list to Gerard. "Maybe you could stop at that inn for some lunch, see if the proprietor knows anyone by that name."

"Do I really have to take Wallace?"

"I think two sets of eyes looking about may have better luck than one."

Gerard looked like he would say something more, for a moment, then turned to Wallace. "Let's go see if we can find this Demetrius."

❉ ❉ ❉

GERARD AND WALLACE left in search of the items they needed, as well as the person named Demetrius. Angela went off into Monteous's study to find something personal of the wizard's for use in trying to divine his whereabouts — preferably something he used or wore often.

Robert went to the stage, looked it over, ensuring Wallace had picked up every last bit of the Focus. Once he satisfied himself nothing of the Focus remained on the stage, he moved to his workbench.

He examined the shards of glass with their embedded metal flakes, and worked out a plan to extract them.

Tungsten and iron, if one were careful, could be melted out, but the other metals, they'd melt before the glass did. He decided he'd have to grind the shards to dust and chunks of metal, before doing anything else.

He reached underneath his workbench and pulled out a mortar and pestle, and commenced making dust.

Next, he spread the glass dust across his workbench into a thin layer. He pulled an iron rod from a drawer, and passed the rod over the dust several times, directing a different kind of energie through it each pass. The rod attracted a specific metal, dependent upon the energie he used. After each pass, he dropped the flakes into separate piles on his workbench.

When that was done, he spent a couple minutes sifting through the glass, making sure there weren't any metal flakes left on the table. Then, he pulled a crucible out from under his workbench and swept the glass dust into it. He set the crucible down and heated it into a molten mass using an oak rod. When it was one glob, he used the same rod to direct some of the heat in the glass into the air around them. It warmed the room a little, but cooled the glass enough that he was able to take the mass out of the crucible using some tongs and set it on his workbench. He probably couldn't use the glass for another Focus as it likely wasn't pure enough, but there were always little trinkets that could be made from it which one could sell to those looking for ways to ward off spirits or protect against specific types of magic.

The next task would be to remove any remaining glass from the metal flakes. To do this, he would heat each metal in the crucible until the glass melted, or the metal melted, whichever happened first, and then use another tool to separate the glass from the metal, lifting whichever was still solid out of the molten liquid. It was tedious, hot work, and tiring. But it would be worth the effort, as obtaining new supplies of the elements would be potentially expensive, and likely difficult on short notice.

As Robert reflected on the task ahead of him, Angela came back into the lab carrying a particularly ratty looking sock, and Robert had to stifle a laugh to keep from blowing his carefully set out piles of metal flakes off his bench and onto the floor.

"I hope that doesn't smell too awful," he said.

"Not so bad," she confirmed. "I think he wore it sometime this week, but it was sitting where it could air out, so the stink is mostly gone." She grew somber. "But if it could help me find him, I would not care if it smelled like rotting eggs and still contained his foot."

Robert nodded. He felt the same way. "Will it help? Will it be enough?"

"If he is warded by a Master, there is likely nothing here that would help. I would need hair or nail clippings, or even better, a finger or a toe — something of his flesh. But he's too careful and destroys all those useful items. There aren't any solid pieces of him anywhere."

Robert knew this was the case, but he'd hoped. Any Master of any stature would destroy clippings and any other pieces of themselves to keep them from being used against him by a rival. Threads directed through a fingernail or a hair could cause illness or injury, and was only one of the many hazards of being a Master. Apprentice's learned the tedious practice of destroying those pieces of oneself early.

Robert watched Angela for a moment as she pulled a wooden bowl and pitcher out from underneath her workbench, then set the bowl and the sock on top of the bench and took the pitcher in hand to the water pump and started pumping water into it.

He forced his attention back to his own work, and carefully, using a thin spatula, scraped up the first pile of metal flakes and dumped them into the crucible. Tungsten. This one was easy, really. A fairly large difference in the melting point between glass and tungsten. Hard to screw it up. Taking up his oak rod, he started to pull the energie through the rod, and from himself and everything else around him, and concentrated it into the crucible, centering it on the glass around the metal flakes, slowly raising the temperature.

And just as the remaining glass attached to the tungsten began to melt, he heard the announcement bell ring. Someone had come to the lab's front door. He looked down at his bench, realized there wasn't much that could be done about the state of it. It would be hard, he thought, for anyone to guess what he was up to.

He looked to Angela, and saw the sock and the bowl on her bench. Almost anyone could guess what she was about to do. "Angela, hide the sock. We don't know who it is, and we don't want anyone knowing Monteous is missing.

"Right." She hurried back to her bench.

The bell rang again, and Robert got up and headed out to the front door of the complex to open it. He hoped he could conceal Monteous's absence from whoever it was that had come to the door.

He peered through the spy hole, and, recognizing the visitor, had to take a minute to calm his breath. The man on the other side of the door was dangerous.

Just as the bell rang again, Robert pulled open the door, standing up as straight as he could. The man, dressed in a top hat and a long black wool coat that hung to his knees to keep the winter chill out, was taller than Robert by a good two hands. His mustache, black as the coat, was well kept and waxed, and his eyes were sharp and pointed as they looked down on Robert.

"I'm Orliss Kilore. I'm here to see your Master." Steam from his breath wafted up and around his head, almost like a fog.

"I know who you are," Robert said. And he did, too. Orliss Kilore was Monteous's closest rival among the Masters. "My Master is out on an errand. He won't be back for some time."

Robert could swear Orliss nearly smiled. "Out on an errand, is he? Could you tell me where to find him? There is an urgent matter that I absolutely must speak to him about."

"He did not say where he was going. He often doesn't when he is doing Work for a patron."

Orliss nodded, almost smugly. "Ah, he is out Working. Well, please tell him when he returns that there is an urgent Guild matter I must discuss with him, and would he be so kind as to contact me when he returns?"

"I shall let him know."

"Be sure that you do. Your eventual status as a Master may depend upon it, Robert." And with that, Orliss turned his back on Robert and took the steps down to the stone path that led back to the gate that bordered the street.

Robert quickly shut the door behind him, locked it, and then leaned his back against it. *What is going on?* He had to rest for a moment to calm himself. It almost seemed as if Orliss had come for something more than just talking to Monteous. It was a long moment before Robert realized what was really bothering him about the encounter. Orliss hadn't seemed at all surprised that Monteous was not available. *Did he know Monteous was missing? Did he have something to do with it?*

This last thought could not be easily put out of his mind. There had long been evidence of Orliss's enmity toward Monteous. Orliss coveted the first position, and had for longer than Robert had been an apprentice. Orliss also envied Monteous's skill. It was widely known that the two did not like each other. It was widely suspected that Orliss would do anything to replace Monteous as the Senior Wizard, if he could ever find a way.

And Orliss was the first person Robert had thought of who could close the portal from the other side. If only they could prove it. If only they could find Monteous alive and get him back without letting Orliss, or whoever had him, know. And if it was Orliss they were up against, Robert shuddered. Orliss was formidable, if not a match for Monteous on an even field. Orliss could easily best the four of them in a fight.

But if Orliss did not know, then who? Who had the power? Who had held a grudge? No, it had to be Orliss. Didn't it?

CHAPTER 4

WALLACE FOLLOWED GERARD out into the street. The morning winter chill seeped through his coat and into his muscles in just a few minutes, even though they were walking quickly. He always had to walk quickly to keep up with Gerard.

"Why does it have to be so cold?" he asked. He hated the winter.

"Cold?" Gerard laughed. "This is like spring in Risuk."

Wallace couldn't grasp that at all. "In Aretria, it's never this cold. I never even saw frost until I came to this place."

"Frost. In Risuk during the winter, the snow piles up taller than a man."

Wallace couldn't imagine that. "I've never seen snow."

"You will. It snows here, though not as much as home."

"I miss home sometimes. The grape fields, the trips to Seawatch to sell wine."

"You want to go back?"

"No. I've wanted to be a wizard since I could remember. I couldn't believe it when Monteous appeared at our home and told me I could go with him. I belong here, with Monteous..." He couldn't finish. The thought of Monteous missing, perhaps gone forever, stilled his tongue.

They continued walking in silence through the streets. Apparently, Gerard didn't want to talk about the possibilities, either.

They slowed as they approached the gate to the inner city. The guards at the gate stood proud, despite the chill that must seep through their armor. They watched every person that passed through the gate, keeping an eye out for the safety of the king and the courtiers and the merchants that lived in the Inner City.

"Why are we slowing?" Wallace asked.

"We don't want them to think there is anything amiss. Do you want to answer questions about Monteous?"

Wallace shook his head. "No."

"Neither do I, so we walk patiently, like nothing has happened."

"I just want to hurry because I'm freezing."

One of the guards put his hand out, motioning for them to stop. "Aren't you Monteous's apprentices? Where is the wizard?"

"He asked us to run some errands for him today. He said it was too cold for any sane wizard to be running around outside," Gerard said.

The guard laughed. "Isn't that the truth? Get on with it then."

And like that, they were in the Inner City. Wallace enjoyed coming to the Inner City. The streets were kept clean, and there were fewer vagabonds and cut-purses hanging around. The buildings were taller and better built, made of stone instead of whatever material came to hand. The Lords and Ladies in their carriages, no matter how fast they moved, always seemed to move with a bit more grace. Brought up on a farm, the first time Wallace had seen the Inner City, he had been unable to say much of anything. His eyes had grown as big as saucers trying to take everything in, and Gerard had laughed at the country boy. Wallace suspected Gerard's reaction was much the same on his first trip to the Inner City, but he'd never spent the time asking around to find out.

Now, however, he'd been to the Inner City enough that it no longer cowed him, no longer amazed him enough to make him want to stare at everything at once.

"What do we do first, Gerard?"

"We should get the materials first, I think. We could spend all day tracking down Demetrius. In fact, I think we'll get the materials, and then I'll send you back with them. Robert and Angela will want to get started on the Focus as soon as possible."

Gerard started walking toward the market, and Wallace had to hurry to keep up. "Is that a good idea? What if you run into problems?"

Gerard laughed. "What problems could I run into where you'd be more help than hindrance? I can take care of myself."

Wallace wanted to dispute his uselessness, but thought better of it. Gerard was right in many ways. He could take care of himself, perhaps better than any of the rest of them. But he also had a bit of a temper, which wouldn't help at all if things needed a little massaging. It would, however, do no good to argue the point with him. Robert and Angela *would* need the materials as soon as they could get them. They might even be ready for them before noon, and the sooner they got them, the quicker they could open another portal. *I hope it will be that easy — or easier.*

A few minutes later, as they approached the market, Wallace began to smell the food and treats that the various shop keepers made available. From foods as humble as freshly baked bread to various confections, pies, and sweetmeats. The quality of the food in the Inner City market was a significant step up from most of what was available in the Middle City, where they bought most of their food. Unfortunately, the the prices jumped significantly as well, perhaps even more than the quality warranted. Wallace figured it was just another reason Monteous didn't keep his lab in the Inner City.

Wallace didn't care, though. Not when he got to treat himself when they did visit the Inner City Market.

They rounded a corner, and the market opened up in front of them. The street they were on was split down the middle by an island of shops. The island ran a quarter mile or more before the separate halves rejoined each other at the end of the market. Every shop front was adorned with a carved sign as prescribed by the Council shop laws, and awnings woven with bright colors and fanciful designs protected the goods and the keepers from the brunt of the weather. Even on a cold cloudy day such as the current one, the awnings almost seemed to shine, despite the lack of sun.

Wallace saw that it was a busy day at the market. Throngs of people moved down the streets, examining the goods, stopping to haggle with shopkeepers, eating treats, hurrying without seeming rushed. There were too many people to rush.

"This is going to take a while," Gerard said. Wallace heard a note of annoyance in Gerard's voice. "Well, nothing for it but to get on with it." He pulled out the list and examined it.

"What's first?" Wallace asked.

"Some herbs. Gunnel, Rastiroot."

"Those should be easy, at least."

"Yes, let's hurry."

With a sudden move, Gerard walked off purposefully through the crowd toward the herb dealers. Wallace, taken by surprise, had to hurry to catch up to Gerard before he lost him in the crowd. Gerard stopped in front of a shop, kept by an older woman, thick around the middle, yet strangely thin in the face. She wore a friendly smile.

"Gerard, good to see you," she said. "Where's Monteous?"

"He's Working for a patron. He sent us to get supplies today. He said he was too busy to come."

Her brow furrowed. "Now, that doesn't seem like him," she said. And Wallace knew it wasn't. Monteous liked to buy his own supplies so he could verify the quality of the materials he was receiving. He brought the apprentices along, often, but never sent them alone.

Gerard recovered quickly, though. "It's not, and he didn't like it at all, but he said he needed Gunnel and Rastiroot, and he couldn't leave the Work."

"Well," she said. "That's just a shame. It is what it is, though. Let me see what I've got here."

And then they got down to looking at the herbs and haggling over how much. Wallace quickly lost interest, and started watching the people passing by behind them.

After a few moments of watching the courtiers and Lords passing by, he noticed what he thought was a man watching him, though the man quickly turned and walked away once he saw Wallace looking at him. He couldn't remember ever seeing the man before.

"Gerard, look, do you see that man walking away over there? The one with the red hood?"

"Huh," he said. "Can it wait? We're almost done."

"No, look quickly, before he disappears."

"Where?" Wallace pointed. "What about him?"

"I think he was watching us."

"That's ridiculous. Why would anyone be watching us? Let me finish this." And he turned back to the proprietor and resumed haggling. Wallace saw the woman look at him quickly, sizing him up, it seemed, then returning her attention to Gerard.

Wallace felt sure now, that the man had been watching them. And despite what Gerard said, Wallace didn't think it was ridiculous. There could be a very good reason for someone to be watching them, and no matter what Gerard thought, Wallace intended to keep an eye out. Anyone who knew Monteous likely knew who his apprentices were. And anyone who intended Monteous harm certainly knew who his apprentices were.

After a few moments, Gerard completed the purchase. He turned and grabbed Wallace's arm and pulled him into the crowd. He cut across the flow of people toward an alley that crossed the shop island. The alley was relatively free of people. When they'd reached a semi private spot, Gerard pulled Wallace around to face him.

"You need to be more careful about what you say and when. We're going to have enough trouble buying this stuff without the shopkeepers getting suspicious without you yelling out whenever you think someone is after us."

"But that man was watching us." Wallace couldn't believe Gerard didn't see what a problem that was.

"I believe you. It's no surprise we're being watched. Don't let on that you know, alright? Not unless we're in imminent danger. We have to keep it as quiet as possible that we're on our own. Keep an eye out. If you see him again, tap my shoulder or tug my coat. But don't shout it out for everyone to hear."

Wallace felt chagrin creep over him. Gerard had thought it

through after all, and Wallace had potentially made the shopkeeper more suspicious than she already was. If word got out Monteous was missing, he could only imagine the trouble they'd find themselves in.

"I'm sorry. I hadn't thought that far."

"Well, think about this. If they're here watching us, there's probably someone watching the lab. The only thing that's likely keeping us from being overrun by Monteous's assailants is that they have no idea what kind of wards he might have around the lab. They are probably unsure about our abilities, as well."

"And you wanted to send me back by myself?"

"Well, thinking of it, that may not really be the best idea, especially now that we know we're being watched, and they may know we're watching them."

"So what do we do?"

"We have to get the rest of the materials. And then, I suppose we'll have to take them back together, and I'll just have to go back out to look for Demetrius later."

"But shouldn't we go out together?"

"I can protect myself. Don't worry about that."

Gerard was right. He could protect himself from anything he could see. But what if he failed to see it coming — like Monteous? Something else concerned Wallace about Gerard's insistence upon looking for Demetrius alone, but he couldn't put his finger on it. Gerard's reasoning seemed sound, but something about it still felt odd.

"Can we go get the rest of the materials now? Are you satisfied?" Gerard asked.

Reluctantly, Wallace nodded. "Okay, let's go. Let's hurry, though. I don't like being watched."

"Neither do I."

"Here, take the herbs." Gerard handed him a burlap sack with the herbs in it, and then examined the list again. "Next are salts."

And off he went, heading through the crowd again. Wallace had to rush to keep up. Despite what Gerard had said, Wallace didn't think Gerard really thought there was much danger. Wallace, however, couldn't stop from swiveling his neck around like a Craybird, looking for the man in the red hood. He wanted a better look at the man to fix him in his mind so they could figure out who he was. Walace thought, perhaps, if they could identify the man, it could somehow lead them to Monteous. It certainly seemed obvious that the watcher did not wish to be watched himself.

One other time before they'd finished their shopping, Wallace thought he saw the red hooded man from a distance. He was gone almost as quick, and Wallace didn't bother to interrupt Gerard. He'd bring it up with Robert when they got back. Robert would listen.

ROBERT TURNED AROUND in surprise to face the door as it opened, and relaxed a bit when he saw Gerard and Wallace step through it. They were earlier than he expected. He wasn't quite done with recovering the metals, having one pile still remaining. Wallace entered after Gerard and carried a sack through the door, which he promptly set on his workbench.

"Someone was following us at the market." he said. The excitement and worry showed on his face.

"Following you?" Robert asked. "Why would anyone..." He broke off what he was going to say as the answer to his question dawned on him. "Were you followed here?"

"No," said Gerard, "But it hardly matters. If they know who we are, they know where Monteous houses us. It's hardly a secret."

"Of course. You think it's someone who knows where Monteous is?"

"Who else would follow us, but someone who wished Monteous ill? Anyone who knew anything and wanted to help would approach."

"What did he look like?" Robert asked.

"I don't know. Wallace saw him before I did, and I only ever got a look at the back of him, and he was wearing a hood."

"I didn't get a good look at his face either," said Wallace. "He was too far away, and turned away as soon as he realized that I saw him."

Robert went to the window and pulled the shade aside just a little. Enough, he hoped, that he could look out without being seen. He tried to peer through the grimy window, but could only see streaks of dirt. He'd have to get them cleaned soon. He took the cuff of his sleeve and wiped away some of the grime.

Beyond the low, stone wall surrounding the estate, people walked up and down the street, as they normally would. Every time a face turned toward the lab, he immediately wondered if they were looking for something, but inevitably, they'd soon turn away and continue on their journey. After a time, he concluded that no one in his view watched the lab. But that didn't mean no one watched. Just that he couldn't see them.

"We all need to be really careful," he said as he turned around and let the shades close behind him. "We can't let anyone know what we're planning, or even get an idea that we're planning something. We don't want to end up trapped like Monteous, or worse."

Everyone nodded in agreement.

Angela went over to the sack that Wallace had sent on the bench and opened it up. "Did you get everything?" she asked.

Gerard nodded. "Yes, I think we got everything. We got everything on the list, at least. Some of the shopkeepers were curious as to our Master's whereabouts."

"I should have thought of that," said Robert, as Angela started pulling items from the sack.

"Well, I think I covered it well enough. I told those that asked that Monteous was busy and we were acquiring materials for our studies as part of a lesson," said Gerard.

"Let's hope that was good enough."

Robert went over to the bench and started sorting through the items with Angela. She took mostly herbs and salts. The rest, three different types of silica and some dyes, Robert gathered up and took them to his bench, where he stored them in a container below.

"As soon as I get the last of this metal separated, I can get to work laying out the Focus. Two days from now, we'll open the portal and find Monteous."

"Unless I find him first," Gerard said.

"What do you mean?" Robert turned to look at him. He'd put his hand on the door handle.

"I'm going back to the Inner City to look for Demetrius. We didn't get a chance to stop at the inn while we were out."

"Do you think it's safe?"

"I don't think it's any less safe than sitting here for two days while you two work on the portal. They know where we are, if they wanted to try us. Besides, I can defend myself, and we might not have two days to wait. If there's any chance I can find him before you can finish the Focus, I have to try it, don't you think? After all, we don't even know if you can open the portal."

Robert had to agree, even though he didn't want to. Despite Gerard's assertion that he could protect himself, they were certainly safer in a group than split apart. But they had to do everything they could to find Monteous, even with the risk. And Gerard was right about the portal, too. Even though he could make the Focus, and he knew, technically, how to open the portal, he'd never done it, and no one considered opening a portal an easy task. Not even Monteous.

"Alright, but be careful. We need you here when we open the portal."

With that, Gerard opened the door and stepped out. A cold breeze blew in while the door was open, and Robert hoped it wasn't an omen.

Angela came up to stand beside him as the door shut behind Gerard, cutting off the breeze. "Do you really think it's safe?"

"No, I don't think it's safe," said Robert. Angela's raven hair mesmerized him when she stood close. "I'm not sure anything we do right now is safe, unless we do nothing. Gerard is right. We should try everything we can before we open the portal. What if they're waiting for us on the other side of the portal when we open it? We're even less likely to be able to defend ourselves than Monteous. Our only advantage is that they don't know when."

He didn't know if she heard the anxiety he felt in his voice, but she rested her hand on his shoulder as if she did. "You'll do fine. You'll open the portal and we'll get him back. I have every confidence."

He wished he did. All he saw was the life as he knew it coming to a close, and he could not see past that end.

"We better get to work," she said. "The portal won't open itself."

"You're right. Wallace," he said, turning to face the youngest apprentice. "Come here, you can help me with the last of these metals."

And like that, they were back to business, working with a purpose, on the thread of a hope that Robert really could open the portal.

CHAPTER 5

TWILIGHT SETTLED ACROSS the city, finding Gerard ready to head back to the lab. He'd visited the King's Rest, the inn named on the scrap of parchment. The proprietor claimed to have never heard of anyone named Demetrius. If Angela had been with him, she could have sensed if he was really telling the truth, but short of threatening to burn down the inn, Gerard didn't have many options for eliciting a different answer from the man.

So he'd left the inn and visited the other inns, asking about Demetrius. While on the streets, he searched for the man in the red hood, the man that had followed them earlier while they were in the market. He had no luck with the inns. He could find no trace of someone named Demetrius. Several times, however, he thought he'd spied the man in the red hood from a distance, only to have whoever he'd seen disappear as Gerard tried to close the distance between them. Unless he'd only imagined him, the man in red was very good at not being seen.

And now, with the sun setting, Gerard felt tired and frustrated. He'd wasted most of the day chasing after a name and shadows and could not think of a thing he'd accomplished.

I hope Robert and Angela made progress on the portal. If only Robert doesn't foul it up.

Gerard knew Robert had more innate ability than the rest of them. What he couldn't figure out is how Robert managed to fail so often, sometimes on the easiest of Weaves.

I don't understand why Monteous keeps him around. In Risuk, he'd be turned out to watch the goats. He failed twice on that Focus, and almost ruined it a third time. I sure hope he's up to the task.

Especially since I can't even find a man that's watching me.

As he reached the Inner City gate on his way back to the lab, the sun, what little of it was visible behind the clouds, dipped behind the mountains to the west, plunging the city into the night. The guards at gate were huddled as close to the walls as they could get, trying to stay out of the breeze.

A breeze Gerard hardly noticed. Gerard had spent his winters growing up with snow deeper than he was tall, and daytime temperatures that never rose above freezing for months at a time. Winter here was a season he looked forward to. The season he dreaded was summer, with its heat. He could never stay cool enough, especially in the lab with all the fires and other things going on.

He passed the guards, and moved into the Middle city where it was a bit darker. He wished, now, that he hadn't been so aimless in looking for the man. Being out after dark in the Middle City, while not exactly dangerous, especially for someone with his abilities, was not exactly safe. Cut-purses and other people with nefarious intentions liked to hang out in the shadows of the alleys, waiting for the easy mark. The guards would make their rounds, but not nearly as often here as they would in the Inner City.

He picked up his pace a bit, though not so much that someone might think he was hurrying.

Just as he passed one pool of light thrown from a window into the darkness spilling from an alley, a strong hand grabbed his shoulder and swung him around, slamming his face up against a wall. He tried to reach into his pocket for the cherry-wood rod he always kept there, but stopped as he felt steel against his throat, pressing in just so slightly.

"Don't even think about it," said the wielder of the knife.

Gerard let his hands drop. "What do you want?"

"Listen close and pay attention. You and your friends are neck deep in a fast flowing river, and you're heading for the falls. Whatever it is that you're planning, you need to stop. Monteous is in very grave danger, and you four will only get yourselves killed if you try to help him."

Gerard couldn't believe it. He'd been looking for this man all day, prepared to fight it out if necessary, and the man had caught him without even a struggle. *How could I have missed him?* And now, the man was threatening them. He knew something about Monteous, about where he was, what's happening, and Gerard could do nothing about it. Not yet, at least.

"Where is he?"

"You don't need to know. Now, go back to the lab and tell your friends to stop whatever it is they're working on. We'll take care of it. You four just keep to yourselves and wait."

Then the knife came away from his throat and the hand released its grip on his shoulder. Gerard turned around quickly, but the man had already disappeared. He reached up to rub his shoulder where the man had gripped him. He thought for sure he'd have a bruise there in the morning.

"What under Erie's Moon was that?" He couldn't figure it out. He'd thought the man was threatening them, but then he said "We'll take care of it." It almost sounded like they were going to attempt to rescue Monteous, whoever "they" were.

He reached into his pocket and took out the cherry-wood rod. He wasn't going to get taken like that again.

But he hurried quite a bit more now toward the lab, not worrying about how it made him look. He didn't know what to make of that confrontation, and he hoped Robert or Angela could figure it out.

❋ ❋ ❋

LINES OF WORRY creased Angela's forehead. "I tell you, I sensed something. Something frightened Gerard."

"That doesn't mean there's anything wrong. It's dark, and we don't know who is out there watching, perhaps waiting for us," Robert said.

"I still think we should go out looking for him as a group. What if he's hurt, or worse?"

"You said you sensed fear, not pain. Not anything worse. He could have been jumping at shadows."

"But..."

And just then, the door swung open violently and Gerard rushed into the lab, with the cold blowing in after him. Then he slammed the door shut and immediately went to the eye-hole and looked through it.

"Gerard!" Wallace shouted. Robert thought he almost jumped up in excitement.

Gerard shushed them with his hand behind his back. He stood at the eye-hole for a couple moments more, and then, apparently satisfied, slowly turned to face the rest of them.

"Someone followed you? Someone watching?" Robert hazarded a guess.

"No," he said. "Not watching that I can see, at least. Is there any food ready?"

"Yes," Angela said. "On the table in the kitchen."

"Alright, might as well sit down and eat while I tell you what happened."

He walked off toward the kitchen. Robert looked at Angela and could see she was puzzled, too. Quickly they followed him and took places around the table. Wallace came in after.

Robert watched Gerard stuff some bread and pork into his mouth and eventually swallow the whole mess. He took another bite of the bread, swallowed that, then began to talk.

"First, I went to the inn mentioned on that scrap of parchment, but had no luck. The proprietor either really didn't know Demetrius, or he lied to me. Maybe if Angela had been there, she could have figured out the answer to that question, but whatever the case, he wasn't there."

"It could be that Demetrius isn't his real name," Robert said.

"Entirely possible. In any case, I visited every inn in the Inner City always keeping an eye out for the man in red, while trying to find out if anyone knew a Demetrius of any sort, and found nothing."

"Then why all the commotion at the door? Angela tried to divine what was taking you so long, and she said she felt fear emanating from you."

Angela nodded in agreement.

"As I was heading back, I walked past an alley. Someone I couldn't see reached out and pulled me into it, putting a knife to my throat. He knew me, and somehow knew I would walk by that alley. He wasn't following me. He was waiting."

"So what happened? He obviously didn't kill you."

"No. He could have, but he didn't. Instead, he said we should stop our efforts to find Monteous. Said 'they'd take care of it.'"

"They?"

"They. He didn't explain more. At first, I thought he was one of the people that took Monteous, but now, after thinking about what he said, I'm not so sure."

"Did you get a look at him?" Wallace asked. "Was he the man that was following us earlier?"

Gerard shook his head, then took another bite of the pork. "No," he said around the pork, "I didn't get a look at him at all. He was very careful to keep me faced away from him the whole time."

Robert didn't know what to think. Stop looking for Monteous? He didn't know if he could do that. And if Gerard was right, then someone other than Monteous's captors knew he was being held. And if someone else knew, then who were they? What was going on? Could they be trusted to get Monteous back?

"Did he say anything else?"

"No. Just that we were in danger if we continued doing what we're doing."

And then Robert thought of the visit from Orliss Kilore earlier that day. Could that have been related? Did Orliss know?

"I should tell you," he said, "about a strange visit earlier today while you and Wallace were at the market."

"Oh?"

"Would you believe Orliss Kilore came by the shop today looking for Monteous?"

Gerard nearly choked on the bread that he'd just stuffed into his mouth. "*The* Orliss Kilore?"

Robert nodded.

"Did he say why he came? This would be the last place I would expect to see Orliss."

"He said there was urgent Guild business he had to discuss with Monteous. I don't know why I didn't think anything about it at the time. But you're right. I don't think he's ever been here before."

"If there's anyone in this city that would benefit from Monteous's disappearance," Gerard said, "it would be Orliss. That man has been scheming to become Senior Wizard probably since the very day Monteous won the position."

Robert felt the tension in his head growing into a headache — pain throbbed behind his temple. It was getting more complicated by the hour, it seemed.

"So, what do we do? Do we stop? Protect ourselves?" Robert couldn't believe he was asking those questions aloud. He knew his answer. He couldn't afford to stop, couldn't take the chance the man that assailed Gerard was lying to get them to stop.

Angela echoed his unspoken thoughts. "We can't stop trying to open another portal. We haven't any idea who the man that attacked you is working for. Was he lying? If he really is working toward finding Monteous, why didn't he tell you who he is?"

"But what if he's right?" Gerard asked. "What if we're involved in something that we can't even begin to deal with? This whole thing is getting out of hand, especially if Orliss is involved. He may not be the same level of wizard as Monteous, but he's close, and could probably take care of all of us together without much effort."

Robert thought Gerard voiced doubts they all felt. "What about you Wallace, what do you think?"

"I just want Monteous back."

"I think we all want that." Robert paused a moment, thinking through everything he could, trying to discern all the sinkholes that might open below them. They just didn't know who had taken Monteous, or who was warning, or threatening, them.

"I just don't think we can leave it up to anyone else. I know how to open the portal. We don't know who any of these people are, and we have no idea if any of them are really working to help Monteous. I think we should just keep to ourselves tomorrow, finish the Focus and the solution, and open the portal as quickly as we can. No one will believe apprentices can open a portal. If we can, we might just surprise whoever trapped Monteous, and that can only be good for our chances."

Robert swept his gaze around the table, trying to gauge the other apprentice's responses. He caught Angela nodding, and Wallace sitting a little straighter. Robert worried most over how Gerard would respond. They didn't need him to open the portal, but once they went through, his help would be essential. Gerard's facility with fire and lightning was the only real weapon they had. Robert could Work those same Weaves, but opening the portal would likely drain too much of his energie. It wouldn't surprise Robert to find himself unable to weave anything afterward.

And Gerard looked like he wanted to flee. His gaze flicked from them to the door and back again while his fingers tapped the table. It seemed to Robert minutes passed while he waited for Gerard.

"If that's what you want," Gerard finally said. "I think you're all crazy, but I'll go along. None of this sits well with me, and I do believe my attacker wasn't lying. We are all in danger if we continue."

Robert let his breath go. He hadn't realized he'd been holding it. *At least he didn't say no.*

"So," Gerard said, "where are we with the portal?"

"The glass is prepared. I should be able to have the Focus completed tomorrow evening."

"So we go through the portal tomorrow night?"

"Yes," Robert said. *If I can open it.*

"And what about Demetrius?"

"We forget about him for now. If we're successful tomorrow, Demetrius won't matter. If we're not, well, we'll deal with that after."

"What do you mean, 'If we're not'?" Wallace asked.

"What he means," Gerard said, "is that when we get there, Monteous might not be there anymore."

"Oh."

Robert wished Gerard hadn't given voice to that thought, but he resolved not to let it affect him. They were counting on him to not foul it up, which is what he'd really meant. *If I don't foul it up, then we won't have to worry about Demetrius.*

"Let's get some sleep," he said, trying to sound more optimistic than he felt. "We have a long day of Work ahead of us."

❋❋❋

ANGELA COULDN'T SLEEP. Her work during the day hadn't been at all tiring, and her mind wouldn't stop running in circles, imagining scenarios of failure and success, but mostly failure.

She threw off the heavy covers and shrugged into a thick robe to keep her warm, then left her room and went to the lab. Of all the places she would have listed as comforting before she became an apprentice, the last kind of place she would have imagined would be the lab. After only a few years, however, the lab held such a promise of potential, and memories of so many amazing things, it relaxed her even more than a walk through a garden.

A walk through a garden was about the least relaxing thing she could imagine.

In the dark, with the lamps all snuffed and the moonlight shining in through the windows, the lab wore an eerie, expectant cloak of shadows.

She sat on her stool at her workbench, and ran her hands across its stone surface. Once, it had been smooth and polished, but now, she felt each of the scars she'd inflicted on it through years of working and learning.

If Robert can't open the portal, if we can't find Monteous, we'll be separated. I'll be separated from this place.

She shivered at the thought. Of course, another wizard would take her in, but she doubted whatever wizard took her would take Robert or the others.

And I won't go home.

She heard the door to the lab open and shut, and turned to look. At first, all she saw was a shadow, and hoped it was Robert. She longed for his arms around her. *If he comes over and hugs me, I won't stop him.* And she realized the truth. She needed some comfort, even if she couldn't let it become more.

But as the figure stepped into the room, she saw Gerard emerge from the shadow, and her hopes died.

"Angela," he said as the door shut behind him.

"Gerard." She couldn't put any warmth into it.

"What are you doing in here?"

She turned back to her workbench. "Thinking. I couldn't sleep."

She felt him step up beside her, but didn't turn to face him.

"Do you think he can do it? Really?"

"Of course I do."

"Is that because you actually believe he'll do it, or is it for some other reason? Are you just saying it because you and he..."

What? "What do you mean by that, Gerard?"

"You're always taking his side, following along with whatever he says, wherever he wants to go. You're always looking at him."

"I am not." *I am not, am I? How did he notice?*

"Why don't you look at me? Aren't I worthy of interest? I'm the son of a Lord of Risuk. He's just an orphan. I could take care of you better than he ever could."

Anger flared in her, and she shot up from her stool to face him.

"Take care of me? Why do you think I'm here, Gerard? To be taken care of? I don't need to be taken care of."

"You aren't a wizard yet. None of us are. Without Monteous who are we to trust? Who is going to take us in? If you go with Robert, you'll be stuck wandering the small villages for the rest of your life, or worse, out of the Seven Kingdoms altogether."

He reached out and put his arms on her shoulders. "With me, you would be..."

Her rage exploded. "No one touches me!" She reached out with her hand and slapped him with all her strength.

His hands went to his face, and then something flooded his eyes. Anger or malice — she couldn't tell, but his body went rigid in front of her, and his voice spewed ice. "If you so much as hint that you want Robert instead of me, I will ruin you with him. I will tell him that you and I already spent intimate evenings alone together."

Her heart quavered, and fear replaced her anger. "You wouldn't dare."

He smiled a feral grin at her. "I would dare. If I can't have you, he won't have you either."

He turned and walked away, his hand still rubbing the spot on his face where she'd hit him.

She sat down on her stool and stared after him. *He wouldn't really, would he?* But she could imagine him following through. And if Robert thought she'd lain with Gerard, he wouldn't want her.

And even if I could prove Gerard was lying, the other... She couldn't even finish the rest of the thought.

No. I just have to help Robert free Monteous. It has to work, and things will go back to the way they were.

After a minute, she resolved to try to get some sleep. She couldn't sit in this room anymore, and she had a great deal of work to do in the morning.

Try as she might, she couldn't quite believe her life wasn't ruined.

CHAPTER 6

ROBERT AWOKE IN the morning to the smell of eggs and pork. He rolled out of bed quickly, surprised a bit that the others hadn't already roused him from his sleep. After dressing, he went to the kitchen, expecting to see everyone already at the table. He found only Angela, cooking.

She turned around as he entered. "You're awake. Breakfast is almost ready." A quick smile crossed her lips, but faded almost immediately. She turned back to the stove.

"Where are the others?" Robert went to the cupboard and began to pull some plates down.

"Asleep, I suppose. It's early yet."

He brought the plates to her, and she lifted the eggs and pork on to one of them. It looked to be just enough for the two of them. "Is that enough?"

"For the two of us. I doubt the others will be up soon. They can make their own."

Robert took the plates and set them out on the table, then turned to a drawer and pulled out silverware for the two of them. Angela took a place across from him as he returned to the table. He handed her a knife and fork, then went about dividing the food between them.

After sitting, he looked out the window for the first time and realized that the sun, were it capable of being seen through the gray winter cloud cover, would have just risen. "It *is* early, I guess."

"I couldn't sleep. Too much worry about today. Do you really think you'll be ready by tonight?"

Robert looked down at the plate of food before answering. "If I don't foul it up. If I don't get distracted."

She reached a hand across the table to him. He reached out and took it, not really sure he knew what it might mean. "I know you can do it, Robert." She gave his hand a squeeze. Her fingers were warm, supple. He could sit there all day holding her hand. "You made the Focus just a couple days ago. There's no reason you can't make another."

Robert wondered if she realized she'd just provided another distraction.

He looked into her slate colored eyes and found fear, or maybe sadness there. She'd never reached out to him like this before. He wondered if it was all for his comfort, or maybe, she needed comfort herself. After a moment of silence, though he felt he had to at least acknowledge what she'd said, affirm to her that he agreed with her, despite his doubts. "You're right, there's no reason I can't make another."

"Well, look at this!" Gerard's voice erupted into the room.

Angela quickly pulled her hand from his, hiding it behind the table, as if Robert's hand had become a snake. He tried to catch her eye, see what he'd done to cause her to pull away, but she'd turned to face Gerard.

"Lazy bones decides to wake up!" Angela's sharp retort surprised Robert. He hadn't heard her speak that way to Gerard before.

Gerard walked over and sat at the table, a grin stretching across his face, no doubt pleasure at interrupting whatever he thought was taking place between the two of them. "I haven't a lazy bone in my body. You two are up far too early. I smell breakfast."

"You'll have to make your own. Robert and I have work to do." She stood up.

Robert thought for a second about standing, too, but didn't. He hadn't yet touched his food, and he'd need the energie. His vow to find Monteous took precedence over finding out the cause of Angela's odd behavior.

"Gerard," Robert said, "I could use your help today. If I have to heat that glass all day on my own, I'm going to be too worn out to open the portal tonight."

Gerard looked at him, pondering for a moment, it appeared. "I thought only one person could be involved in making the Focus."

"I'm not so sure that's completely correct. I think you'd want only one person directing the energies, but I don't see why I couldn't draw some of those energies from someone else. If I don't get help somehow, I won't be able to open it tonight. I'll fall over before it's done."

"What about Wallace?"

Angela sat back down. "He'll need to be helping me. He's far better at powders and liquids than you, Gerard."

"And don't I know it. Are you sure you need my help? I was planning on continuing the search for Demetrius."

Robert took a bite of his eggs and chewed for a moment. "I don't think that's a good idea. Not if that ruffian you met last night is telling the truth. And if he's watching you, maybe he's someone to avoid crossing. We ought to just keep our heads down and get this portal open as quick as possible. I can't believe we have a lot of time to waste."

Robert looked to Angela, where he saw she was just pushing her food around on her plate with her fork.

"Alright, if you think I can help, I'll lend my help. At the very least, I'll keep a lookout so you won't get interrupted without some warning." Gerard smiled. "Do I really have to make my own breakfast, Angela? Yours smells so good!"

She looked down and studied it for a moment, then pushed it across the table to him. "It's yours. I'm not hungry anymore." She stood up and walked out of the room, slowing only momentarily as Wallace stepped through the doorway.

When she'd gone, Gerard scooped some eggs onto his fork, lifted them to his lips, then paused a moment. "So, Robert, what was that all about?" Then he popped the eggs into his mouth.

I wish I knew, he thought. He debated saying something, and ate a few more bites while thinking about it. While he thought, Wallace took a seat at the table across from Gerard.

"What are you talking about?"

Robert shook his head, then stood up. "Get some breakfast, Wallace. When you're done, help Angela. It's going to be a long day." He left the room, in search of Angela. Despite the need for energie, he had to try to understand her behavior, or he'd be distracted by it all day long. And that was no state in which to Work.

He found her at her bench, already pulling out the utensils, phials and other apparatus she'd need for concocting the fluid. As he approached, she appeared to be trying to look anywhere but at him, keeping her head down, focused on her equipment.

"Angela..."

She glanced up at him, then back at her work. "No, no, I'm sorry. I didn't mean..." She seemed to catch herself.

"Didn't mean what?" What had happened? Why was she so reticent to say anything when back in the kitchen, she'd been so concerned, inviting. She'd reached out to him. But for what?

She shook her head. A lock of her hair fell out of the wrap intended to keep it out of her work. Robert wanted to reach out and tuck it back in for her.

"Please, Angela. Why'd you leave, why'd you get so angry when Gerard walked in?"

She looked up at him then, and in her eyes, he saw something, a longing, or something else he couldn't interpret. "Robert, please. I'll tell you later, if things turn out well. I don't want to be a distraction to you, yet clearly, I have. It's nothing that won't wait until after we've opened the portal and have found Monteous."

He realized then what he saw in her eyes was a plea. A plea for what, he didn't know, but she needed his help somehow. He'd thought he'd known her, but maybe he didn't. First the hand at the table, and then whatever this was. "You promise? After we have Monteous back?"

She glanced over toward the door where, any minute, any second, he knew Gerard could walk into the room. What would an encore of his kitchen entry cause her to do? What had she been seeking? She looked back at him, her right hand moving slightly toward him almost of its own volition, but she kept it in check. "I promise. After we find Monteous."

He stood there for a moment longer, looking into her eyes, searching for some hint of what it was all about, and gave in after a moment. "Alright, tomorrow, after Monteous is back."

He reached out for the hand that had stirred, but she looked at the entryway, then pulled it out of his reach. "No distractions Robert."

"Right."

He turned away and walked over to his bench, trying to figure out how to concentrate on the Work he had to perform. His primary distraction, which before soaked him like a mild spring rain, now raged like a late summer thunderstorm.

ROBERT HAD JUST begun to sort his materials out on his bench when Gerard and Wallace entered the room. Wallace went directly to Angela's station and asked what he could do to help her, while Gerard spent a few seconds observing before making his way toward Robert. Robert tried not to wonder what Gerard was thinking, tried to block out everything that transpired that morning, and was somewhat successful, he thought. He hoped he could keep it up through the remainder of the day.

"So what do you need from me?"

Robert continued organizing his materials, not looking up while he spoke. "I need you to be open to me drawing energie from you. You know how Monteous taught us to block attempts to steal energie?"

"You need me to not block you."

"Right. Other than that, if I ask for a pair of hands, be ready to provide them."

"Done." Gerard turned away for a moment, as if making to leave, then turned back. "Are you sure you'll be able to open the portal tonight? Should we not wait for tomorrow?"

"Do you think we have time to wait?"

"If you try tonight, and you drain yourself, or it doesn't work for some other reason, it could be days before we could try again. I want Monteous back as much as you, but I think we — you shouldn't make the attempt until you've got the best possible chance to succeed."

"I can't help thinking that maybe we're already too late. I have to try."

They looked at each other for several heartbeats, silent. Robert tried to think of a way to to wait that didn't create more risk for Monteous, and failed. Gerard, well Robert had no idea what Gerard thought. His eyes sat unmoving in their sockets like crystals of ice. Robert looked away first, going back to the materials on the workbench.

"It's not on my head if you fail," said Gerard. "I'm going to go check around. See if anyone is watching us."

"Fine. Keep yourself open to me. You don't have to be right here. I'll try to draw only a little at a time, so you don't have to worry about my draining you." Robert looked up and saw that he'd been talking to Gerard's back.

Robert took a moment to reign in his annoyance. The tension in the room was tangible, something he felt he could reach out and grab hold of. If he didn't start concentrating on the Work, it would overwhelm him. He would fail himself, Angela, and Monteous.

He started by working through some breathing exercises Monteous had tried to teach him, slowing his breath down, becoming conscious of it, working to feel each part of his body, from his toes to his beating heart. He focused on his heart, slowing it, relaxing it. He built a mental wall between himself and the tension, the need in the room. He'd practiced building the wall for years, and still, he worried as he built it. His worry generated ripples in the wall, but it held. And as long as it would hold, as long as he could maintain it, he could Work. It only had to hold for the rest of the day.

One thing he hoped would help was that he'd made this particular Focus so recently. The steps were fresh in his mind, the outcome clearly defined.

He pushed all thoughts of Angela as far out of his head as he could, and committed himself to trying to avoid even looking at her.

By mid-morning, he had everything ready to start forming the glass.

He called Gerard over to him.

"I'm about to start forming the glass. I think I should start drawing your energie now, instead of trying to tap it when I'm in the middle of trying to keep everything together."

Gerard nodded.

Robert slipped into the vew, allowing him to see the energie that ran throughout the lab. The threads woven through every object, the patterns surrounding the other apprentices, woven to form shields to protect their inner energie from being drawn by an unfriendly wizard.

Gerard still held on to his energie shield.

"Gerard, you're still blocking."

A moment later, the pattern around Gerard shifted and grew loose, making his inner energie available and exposed. Robert drew a small thread from Gerard, and saw him shiver a moment as the energie left him.

"Feels strange," Gerard said. "Do I need to stay here?"

"Stay in the lab. I don't know if I can draw it through walls."

"Fine." Gerard walked away.

Robert took the thread from Gerard and started to weave it in with his own and feed it into the glass to start heating it. A few moments later, he was lost in the work.

A sandwich appeared on his bench at some point, and he took a few bites, but didn't stop working. He hadn't even seen who placed it there. He could feel the others around him working, but somehow, managed to maintain his concentration.

And then, as if the Focus appeared on its own, it was done and he relaxed, and the rest of the lab impinged on his senses again. And after a few moments, he noticed the others looking at him, and relief washed over him. His limbs went slack, and despite a feeling of fatigue in his muscles, he wanted to jump up and down and hug them all.

He'd done it. He'd subsumed himself in his Work, blocked out all distractions, and had created a perfect Focus. He didn't even have to look at it to know, though he looked at it anyway. Despite all the distractions, he'd overcome his implacable foe, rendering distraction harmless, at least for this day.

He looked right at Angela, and said, "I did it."

He received a smile in return. "If only Monteous had been here to see it."

Robert's elation grew shrouded by a cold shiver of worry. "If only we're not too late."

ANGELA HADN'T QUITE finished with the liquid yet, so Robert busied himself with cleaning up his bench and preparing everything for the portal attempt. Robert took some time looking through the tomes in Monteous's library, looking for insights on opening a portal and making it go where you intended. He found nothing that suggested any special trick to it. The destination was set by the pattern of the metals in the Focus, and Robert had matched those exactly to the original. If the solution was properly prepared, and the energie flows were directed into the Focus in the proper amounts, the portal would form.

It sounded simple on the surface, but Robert knew it wasn't. He'd seen the amount of energie Monteous had poured into the portal he'd opened, and it dwarfed anything Robert had tried on his own.

Wallace bounded into the library, his blonde haired head bobbing up and down. "Angela's done, Robert. It's all ready."

When Robert turned, he found Wallace grinning, and his eyes

flashing. He looked about ready to hop up and down. Robert turned back to the book. "I'll be there in a moment."

One last passage required his attention, and after reading it, he shut the book and stood up. His muscles ached with fatigue. The early rise and the day's Work were taking their toll already. He wondered if he could follow through and get the portal open before he collapsed.

I have to. None of the others are capable, yet. There lay the truth. If he couldn't do it, none of the others could, and Monteous would remain with his captors, whoever they were, assuming of course that he wasn't already dead. Robert tried not to think about that as he left the library and walked back to the laboratory.

When he arrived the others were busy preparing. Angela had her hands full of her apparatus, carrying it to the wash basin. Wallace was busy cleaning phials and beakers she'd apparently already brought to him. Gerard stood next to a window, peering out, looking, Robert assumed, for anything out of the ordinary. As he entered, they all turned to face him, the same question seemed fixed on each face.

Can you do it? Even though not one of them said a word, Robert heard the question anyway, and had to work to keep from shaking his head. Instead, he kept his head up and tried to project a confidence he didn't feel. Tried to hide the fatigue that already threatened to ruin him. They needed him to succeed. Monteous needed him to open the portal. What if he couldn't?

And then he shook his head. He couldn't think like that. He knew the consequences of following that thought to its conclusion. He looked to Angela, then. "Wallace told me you'd finished."

"Yes, it's done. " She finished her trip to the wash basin by unloading the apparatus on Wallace. "Are you ready?"

"As ready as I can be."

Robert went to his bench where the Focus sat, squat, clear but for the metal embedded in the glass. For all he could tell, he'd created an identical match to the one they'd used two nights ago. He picked it up and carefully walked it to the center of the stage and set it exactly where Monteous had directed the previous one be set. Then he stood back and stared into it, thinking through what he was about to do.

Fortunately, the process of opening the portal would be fairly quick. But he paled at the thought of the vast amounts of energie required, and what would happen if he failed to supply the proper levels of each type.

He heard his friends approach and looked up. Angela carried the solution in a leather gloved hand, Gerard had his staff with him, and Wallace held a long kitchen knife.

"What's the knife for, Wallace?"

Wallace looked down at it, and then shrugged. "I thought it could be useful."

"You're not going through. Someone needs to stay here and guard this side, be ready to close the portal if necessary."

"But I'm not..."

"You're staying here. It'd do us no good to go find Monteous, then come back to the portal only to find someone waiting for us here."

Wallace nodded, apparently relenting.

"Well, now's the time." Gerard rapped the butt of his staff on the stone of the stage. "I assume I'm going through the portal first."

Robert nodded. "I'll be exhausted, I suspect. Be sure you're ready to take care of anything waiting on the other side. I don't think we want to be surprised like Monteous."

"No, I'll fry anything or anyone I see."

"And Angela, wait before going through. Wait until Gerard has made sure the area is clear. You've got the job of searching Monteous out."

She just nodded.

Robert looked toward the windows. The sun had set. Beyond the shutters, he saw only blackness. "I guess it's time."

Angela knelt and poured the solution into the Focus, just as carefully as the previous time, and they watched as the color of the solution changed. Success, so far.

Angela looked up at Robert, mouthed the words, "You can do it," then stepped back, along with the rest of them, leaving Robert alone on the stage. The others stood just off the stage, waiting for him. Gerard was looking at Angela, and she was staring back at him, eyes cold as steel. Angela had tried to give him confidence, there. She had promised to tell him after, and she had risked something to mouth those words. What, he still didn't know.

"I guess this is it."

Robert pulled his staff from the wall where he'd set it earlier, then came back to stand where Monteous had stood. He stared down into the Focus, into the solution, and tried to shed every thought about anything that didn't pertain to opening the portal. He shut out the lab, shut out Gerard, shut out Angela, shut out the flickering of the lamps. He raised his left arm to shoulder height, steadied himself with the staff in his right, and then began to create the threads of energie, taking them from the stone, the air, his staff, and himself. He wound them into a rope, exactly as he'd seen Monteous do, and fed them to the Focus. His arms wanted to fall, but he wouldn't let them.

And the portal grew above the Focus, the energie swirling in it. He could feel it trying to fly apart, but he held the Weave together, just as he'd seen Monteous do. The edges wanted to unravel, but he restrained them. He poured more energie into the Focus and the oval above it grew larger.

Soon, he neared his limits. His knees wanted to fold. He wanted to drop his arms, but he needed them to control the shape of the portal. His breath grew shorter. His heart beat faster, pounding hard enough he thought he could hear it. Stars appeared in his vision.

Almost there. He kept pouring his energie out, pushing the portal larger.

When it was large enough to get through safely, he started another thread and bound the edges of the portal with it.

As he wrapped, the room grew darker. He could still see the portal, and he kept wrapping, but he could no longer see anything else. His legs were weak. The only thing holding him up was his grasp on the staff.

One more turn around the edge, and then he tied the thread off. He saw, for a moment, the darkness of a forest through the portal. *I did it!*

The room blackened completely, and he lost his grip on the staff. He felt himself falling, and something pounded in his ears. His last thought, before thought was lost. *I failed.*

CHAPTER 7

ANGELA JUMPED WHEN she heard the pounding on the door just as the portal snapped into place and Robert dropped to the floor like a bag of stones. For a moment, Robert held her attention. Was he alright? What happened? Had he drained himself? Had it been too much for him? She started moving toward him, reaching out, forgetting about Gerard and what he might say or do, until a muffled shout broke the spell.

"Open up!"

Someone was at the door, and she turned to see Gerard heading for the door.

She stopped her movement toward Robert and ran after Gerard instead. Wallace was still standing, rooted in place. She passed by him and grabbed Gerard's sleeve, pulling him around to face her.

"You're not going to let them in, are you?"

The pounding at the door was insistent. "No, I was going to give them a reason to stop pounding at our door."

She felt him pulling toward the door still. What should they do? She looked back at Robert, lying on the floor behind the portal, lifeless, perhaps. She couldn't tell. Wallace, she could see, was looking to her and Gerard, obviously unsure of what to do. And then, she focused on the portal, the open portal. A way out.

"Let's go." She pulled on Gerard as hard as she could, but he didn't move much.

"Go where?"

"Through the portal. We can escape through it, untie the Weave from the other side, or toss a rock through and destroy the Focus. Anything but stay here. They know we're trying to save Monteous."

And for some reason, that last bit did the trick. "You're right. We can just escape through the portal. They'll think we weren't here, as long as we can get out before they get through the door."

With that, he started moving quickly toward the portal, and Angela had to hurry to keep up. "Wallace, help me with Robert. We have to carry him through."

She thought about what they might need, and realized they wouldn't have any food, and she would need her staff. She didn't have the control over the elements that the others did, but any help was better than none. She pulled away. "I have to get my staff, and food to eat."

"No, no time for food. We'll figure that out. Grab our coats though, or we'll freeze to death."

"Right," she said, and ran off to collect what she could. Staff first, then the coats, which, unfortunately, were hanging near the door. If that door opened while she was there, they'd have her. She prayed it would hold longer than that.

As she reached the door, the man who had shouted through it shouted again. "You don't have much time. We know you're there, just come out and you'll all be safe. You'll be treated well."

He pounded on the door as she pulled the coats off the hooks, and she jumped back, but the door held. She knew the door should hold against just about anyone. Monteous's enchantments wouldn't be that easy to break, but he wasn't there to reinforce them either.

She ran across the lab, watching Gerard and Wallace struggle to drag Robert's limp body to the front of the portal. As she neared the platform, she thought she heard steel striking steel, knives, or swords. She looked through the unnatural opening for the first time, saw the forest beyond, and recognized it for the same forest she'd seen through Monteous's portal. Robert had succeeded, and her heart leapt up, until she looked down at him for a moment, then it fell again. His face was pale, ghost like.

She heard the steel again, which brought her attention back to the portal, and she noticed that something was different, and very, very wrong. Everything was tinged with orange and red, a dancing orange and red. The smell of smoke wafted through.

She was about to tell Gerard she didn't think it was a good idea to go through the portal, when any opportunity they'd had to escape through the portal was lost forever as two men, locked in combat, stumbled through it, right into her, knocking her to the floor. A body lay on top of her, crushing the breath out of her.

The man on top of her kicked out. For a brief moment that seared itself in her memory, she had a view of the portal as it collapsed on the second combatant. It severed his legs mid-thigh as it sliced shut. A scream from the man, blood everywhere, and then the man on top of her rolled off, freeing her.

She shut her eyes tight, trying to unsee what she'd seen, and tried to pull her legs into her chest, but found they were still trapped by something.

Her throat constricted. She knew she didn't want to look, knew it had to be the dying man.

They were all dead, she knew it. Their way out, gone. And she was trapped under a dead man.

"Drop it." Gerard's voice. She heard a blade fall to the floor, and opened her eyes to see Gerard with his staff readied in a combat position, and the man, kneeling with his feet under him, ready to spring up if necessary. The man wore a red cloak. She could see he wore a ring vest underneath.

"I'm not your enemy, Gerard."

Angela wondered how he knew Gerard's name, but only moments passed before it became apparent Gerard recognized the man.

"You, you're the man who held a knife to my throat last night."

"Yes."

Angela struggled to get herself out from under the now dead man, a house guard, she suspected. She sat up and started pushing on his shoulders, but the armor the dead man wore was slick with blood and she had trouble getting a good purchase on it with her hands. Her blood was racing, and bile threatened to force itself out.

"How can I trust you?"

Wallace finally noticed her plight and stepped over to help her out from under the dead weight.

The pounding on the door resumed, and the voice shouted through it. "Your time is up."

Frighteningly quick to Angela's mind, the man stood and wrested the staff from Gerard before Gerard even moved, perhaps before he had a chance to move. "They're at your door. We don't have time for this."

One last shove from Wallace and her together, and she was free. She stood as quick as she could. She could feel some bruises, but nothing worse. She looked down at Robert, saw he was still breathing, then turned to address the man. "You're right, they're at our door and we don't have much time. You also just destroyed our way out."

He turned his head enough to see her out of the corner of his eye, but he also still appeared to be keeping the other on Gerard. He must have assumed he was the bigger threat. "That was no way out. We slipped into the estate to find Monteous, but they'd taken him elsewhere and laid an ambush for us."

"An ambush. But that means…"

"Yes, they were waiting for you, or someone, to make an attempt at a rescue. If you'd been any quicker with your portal, you would be in their hands, or dead."

"So who are you?"

"Look, can we get out of this first, and I'll explain later?"

Tremors ran through her whole body, threatening to consume her. *Think, Angela. Monteous taught all those exercises. Lock away the emotion.*

She took her fear, imagined stripping it away and locking it in a box to keep for later. She willed her body to stop shaking. She slipped into the vew, and took the measure of this man's energie. Other than a strange arrangement of energie in the man's pocket, and a more ordered pattern than most normals, he was not shielded. She'd watched Robert drawing energie from Gerard. It didn't seem difficult. She could draw energie from this man, if she had to. It would be difficult to direct without a staff or a wand, but she could do it.

Having a plan helped calm her tremors. She motioned to Gerard to back off. With the plan came a realization. The man appeared to have no interest in killing them, not right away. He'd have already done so.

Seeing this, the man looked down at Robert and shook his head. "He's alive?"

"Yes, drained himself opening the..."

At that moment, an explosion of sound and wind flooded the laboratory. Papers, phials, and jars flew across the room, away from the door. Above the roar, a scream of agony. They were all knocked to the ground, and Angela covered her head with her arms, trying to keep the flying objects from striking her in the face.

When she dared to show her face again, she saw the intruder scrambling from window to window. He was back before she'd pushed herself to her feet. What was it with him? So quick. Almost inhuman.

"Well," he said, "that took care of the wizard that was with them. Looks like just hired help left. I don't suspect they'll be too eager to enter, but we have to get out before another wizard shows up."

Wallace and Gerard had stood and were brushing themselves off.

Gerard shook his head. "I don't think we should trust him."

"We could use his help." She felt herself shaking inside again. She was losing the battle to control her tremors.

"We don't need his help. With my staff, I can take care of them."

The man snorted, the ring vest jingling as he turned to face Gerard. "You can face ten swordsmen by yourself when you couldn't even protect yourself from me?"

"Ten?"

"Yes. In the front." He tossed the staff back to Gerard. Gerard managed to catch it.

Angela made the decision. "Alright then, we follow you, if you think you can get us out."

"I can get you out, if we hurry. Between us, they should be no problem if you can use a staff as well."

"I'm not good with elements, but I should be able to make us difficult to see," she said.

"That will work just fine."

She looked at her staff where it lay on the floor. It was nearly as tall as she was. *I won't be able to run with that.*

She went to her bench to get a wand. She wouldn't be able to direct as much extra energie as she could through the staff, but it was better than nothing. She only needed to confuse the minds of their assailants, if she could. "Wallace, Gerard," she said as she moved, "bring Robert."

"Leave him," the man countermanded. "We'll be captured or killed if we try to bring him."

Her tremors grew uncontrollable for a moment, just as she placed her hand on the wand, and she turned back to face them all, and she felt heat sweep through her. She clamped down hard on her tremors, stuffing them back in the imaginary box. From the moment he'd fallen, she'd feared they would have to leave Robert. "There has to be a way. We can't just leave him."

"We can, and we must. We have to fight and run. We can't do that dragging him along." He said it with such force that Angela knew he believed it, and would brook no more arguing.

I can't leave him here unprotected.

Her heart was already heavy that he'd drained himself to open the portal. *I should have helped him somehow.*

She looked around the room, searching for anything that might help her save Robert.

What can I do?

She heard the man order Gerard to check the windows, and then heard his steps as he approached her. "We have to go," he said, "now, while they're confused. I don't believe they will hurt him. You'll understand once I have the time to explain."

She wanted him to explain now, but then her gaze passed over a shelf, cleared by the wind of the glassware that had been on it. She had an idea, if there was room, if Robert would fit.

"Help me," she begged the man. "Drag him over by that shelf. I can hide him."

"We don't have time."

"We do, please." *Help me.*

He turned to Gerard, and she had some hope. "Do we have time, Gerard?"

"They're just standing around out there. It looks like they're waiting for someone."

The man said something under his breath Angela couldn't catch, then ran over to Robert. "Wallace, help me with him. Grab his legs."

The two of them dragged Robert to where Angela had directed, and placed him on the shelf. It was tight, but they managed to fit him in the empty space. The man, soldier, directed Wallace to trickle some water into Robert's mouth, and then Angela went to work.

She couldn't really make him invisible, but she could tie a Weave around him that would make anyone want to look away from that space. A Master Wizard who was paying attention would be able to see through it, but she was good at this kind of Weave. Anyone who wasn't really searching would just look past it. She had to hope that would be enough. She had to hope that Robert wouldn't wake up with someone in the room with him.

Quickly, she wove some air with her own energie and wrapped it around Robert. Once she tied it off, she heard the stranger speak under his breath. "Impressive." Then, louder, he asked, "Satisfied?"

She looked down at Robert, aching that there was nothing more she could do. "No, not really. We'll be back, soon, right?"

"We'll send someone back for him, if we can."

She gave in and turned away. "Alright. Lead on."

GERARD HEARD ANGELA say, "Lead on," and he shook his head. He turned to look at her, not believing that they were actually going to follow this man into this madness. At this point, he thought they were better off taking their chances with whoever waited outside. They couldn't really be in any danger if they went along nicely, could they? It was Monteous that they wanted, and the already had him. The stranger had been right. They shouldn't have meddled. They would have been left alone.

Now, going out to fight ten swordsmen? Sure, they were all capable of using a number of Weaves that could possibly help, but they couldn't fight swords. Not that many, at least. How could Angela think this stranger had the answer?

The stranger moved to stand next to him, motioning the others to follow.

Gerard felt uncomfortable with him standing there, so he peered out the window again, and saw the enemy, if that's what they were, arrayed around the entrance to the compound, ready to capture or kill them as they came out. They stood there, attentive, but apparently content to wait. The smoking remains of the wizard that had tried Monteous's wards still lay on the short stone-paved path that led to the street. Gerard shuddered at the sight. He'd never contemplated what would happen to anyone attacking Monteous in his home. He could only imagine the result if Monteous had been here in person to defend it.

A hand on his shoulder, and the stranger was gently pushing him away from the window. Gerard let it happen, even backed away quicker than necessary. He didn't want that hand on his shoulder. Something about it unsettled him. The stranger looked out the window and nodded in apparent satisfaction, then turned back to them.

"Angela, can you do for us what you did for Robert?"

Gerard looked over to where they'd taken Robert and didn't see him at all. Whatever she'd done, it was impressive.

"No, what I did for Robert would require you to remain still. If he moves, he'll be visible again, until he stops moving. I could, perhaps, draw a mirage between us and them, but I couldn't do it for long. They would see the air shimmering, and it would be difficult for them to pick out exactly where we are."

"How long?"

"A few seconds at most. I've been Working all day."

The stranger nodded, then addressed Wallace. "You stay back with Angela. You can't have been apprenticed long enough to be useful in this fight. Keep an eye out for anyone coming her way and shout if someone does. Find a knife. It will be better protection than nothing."

Wallace nodded, but his face paled a bit.

"Wouldn't a staff be better?" Gerard asked.

"He's not big enough. It would be too slow. I suspect they only want to capture you, so if he keeps the knife hidden, they'll likely get in close enough he can surprise them with it." To Wallace, he said, "Keep it hidden as long as you can."

Gerard grew tired of waiting. "So what do you want from me?"

"Something spectacular. I've heard that you're an elementalist."

Gerard nodded.

"Can you give us wind and fire?"

"I can give you fire. If Robert hadn't been leeching off me all day..."

"Gerard!" Angela's voice held anger in it. Gerard didn't care.

"He used my energie, then opened that portal. Now look where we are."

The stranger stepped between them. "It doesn't matter now. Fire will be enough. We need something big enough, scary enough, to make them want to flee. It doesn't have to be strong enough to do much damage. Stay behind Angela's mirage."

"I can do that."

The stranger turned back to the window. "No time to waste, then." He stepped away from the window and moved quickly to the door. Angela and Wallace followed right behind him, Angela with her wand ready, and Wallace trying to hide the butcher knife he'd somehow managed find while the stranger gave instructions.

Gerard hung back a bit. Did they really have to trust this man?

Couldn't they find another way? He racked his brain trying to find something, anything that would let him escape without following this soldier's orders. That's what he had to be. But, soldier for who?

No alternative came to mind. He couldn't figure a way out. He could always leave later — especially if Monteous was dead.

At the door, the stranger paused.

"When I open the door, Angela, put up the mirage. We'll need to move quickly. Gerard, throw your fire into their midst as soon as you're through the door. Once I've engaged them, the three of you run south for the Outer City. If we're separated, keep going until you're out of the city and come to the river. Stay off the road, and we'll meet near the ferry, but stay hidden. Don't approach the ferry."

"How will you find us?"

"Don't worry about that. I'll find you." He put his hand to the large iron latch on the door. "Ready?"

Gerard saw nods from his friends, and then the stranger jerked the door open and they committed themselves to whatever fate lay beyond.

CHAPTER 8

WALLACE'S KNEES STARTED to tremble as he approached the door, and his legs nearly failed him as the strange soldier put his hand to the door and asked, "Ready?"

Wallace had his knife in his hand, held down to his side and behind him in an effort to keep it hidden. It might be worth something, but if he had be objective, every man waiting for them had a sword, and likely outweighed him by fifty pounds or more. He knew he wasn't physically imposing, and he'd not been apprenticed to Monteous near long enough to be useful in a duel of Work and Weave.

No, like the soldier said, he would be best at staying out of the way, hiding and running. But they were going out there, among those men with who-knew-what orders.

He looked back toward where he knew Robert was hidden and wondered what Robert would have done.

I can't believe we're just leaving him here.

And then the door opened, and the soldier pushed through it. Wallace slipped into the vew for a moment, and he could see the Weave Angela had placed to obscure them from the enemy. It was invisible from this side to anyone not gifted and trained to see. From the other side, the air would appear to shimmer and everything behind it would be a blur. A person would see shapes and colors, perhaps, but nothing distinct.

He heard shouts from the swordsmen waiting for them, surprise and something else, maybe fear, in their voices. Maybe fear, but maybe just wariness.

Wallace saw several large ribbons of flame erupt among them, scattering them, causing some to fall to the ground. For certain, then, there was fear. No man wanted to fight a wizard throwing fire at him. Confusion spread among them, and Wallace saw a few of them break. Into that confusion, the stranger leapt, Wallace thought unnaturally fast.

In a near blink, the stranger stuck one soldier through the throat with his long bladed knife, stole that man's sword and used it to disembowel a second who took a long time to realize he'd just spilled his guts onto the cobblestones.

The stranger was shouting, even as he was planting his knife into the eye socket of a third man. Yelling, and finally, the words broke through Wallace's veil of shock. "Run, you idiots, run!"

Wallace needed no more encouragement. South. Out of the city, to the river. He ran, jumped the low fence to avoid the thick of the melee. He pushed his legs to move as fast as he could make them go to take him to safety.

After he was in the street, beyond the reach of anyone with a sword, and into the dark of the night, he heard footsteps behind him, and turned to see shadows, shadows he guessed were Gerard and Angela, losing ground to him, falling behind.

"Slow... Slow down, Wallace." A shout from behind him. Gerard. "They're not following."

Wallace took another look behind him, and saw, indeed, that they were alone running through the streets, and he slowed to a walk.

He didn't want to be caught out in these streets alone, not in the Middle City, and certainly not in the Outer City, where every sort of thief, cut-purse and murderer ruled the night.

As he slowed, the rush of fear and a burning in his lungs and muscles started to catch up with him.

"Damn, you're fast," Gerard said as he slowed to a walk next to Wallace. Angela came up behind them. Both of them were breathing louder and harder than Wallace thought he was.

Wallace nodded. He wasn't the biggest, or the strongest, but in the Feastday races he entered, he always won.

After they'd caught their breath, Gerard abruptly came to a stop. "Alright, we're safe for the moment. Are we really going to meet that guy at the ferry?"

Wallace pulled up and looked at him, then at Angela. She'd turned to Gerard, and in the shadows of the street it was difficult to see her face, but she cocked her head to one side. "What do you mean, Gerard? We agreed..."

"You agreed. I did nothing of the sort. I don't trust that man."

Wallace was confused. "Why don't you trust him? He helped us escape?"

"It's just too convenient — him finding me in the street, knowing my name, falling through the portal right after we opened it up?"

"After Robert opened it."

"Whatever, I just don't trust that he's on our side. Something big is going on here, and we don't know who's on our side, or even what side we're on."

Wallace pondered that while Angela and Gerard continued to argue. Monteous was kidnapped, maybe murdered, they didn't know. Why? What was he after when he went through that portal? They didn't know who this Demetrius person was, and the soldier or whatever he was, he appeared to be on Monteous's side, but Gerard was right. How would they know?

By the time he surfaced from his thinking, Angela and Gerard were near to shouting, Angela arguing for meeting the soldier and Gerard vehemently arguing that they should go in a different direction.

"Gerard, Angela..." They ignored him. He tried again, louder this time. "Hey..."

Finally, he stepped in between them, and Gerard exploded. "What do you think you're doing!"

Wallace held his ground, mostly. "Look. We don't know what's going on. You're right, Gerard," which mollified Gerard a bit. "But the only person so far that hasn't threatened us is that soldier."

"He told me we should stay out of it or we'd get hurt."

"But was that a threat, or a warning? We can't do anything until we figure out what's going on, and figure out who is fighting and what they're fighting over. Our best chance of saving Monteous, and now Robert, is finding out who this stranger is. We don't have to trust him." Wallace ran out of argument. If it didn't work, he didn't know what else he could say, but he felt he was right and hoped Gerard would listen to reason.

And then a shadow stepped out of the darkness and laid a hand on Wallace's shoulder, gripping it solidly, but without aggression. Wallace tensed and spun out of it. Gerard and Angela jumped back and Gerard brought up his staff.

"That's a well-reasoned argument, young Wallace. Gerard would do well to be swayed by it."

The tension went out of Wallace as he realized who spoke and that he wasn't in immediate danger.

"I will do nothing," Gerard said, his staff still ready, "until you at least tell us who you are."

"Fair enough. We are not in immediate danger here, though we should not tarry much longer."

Wallace turned to face the man as he stepped out of the dark shadows into the lamp light.

"I am Demetrius, a servant, of sorts, to your Master, Monteous."

Wallace felt hope and a surge of excitement, as well as confusion, rush through him. "Monteous never mentioned you."

Demetrius smiled. "There are many things that wizards don't tell their apprentices."

Gerard's voice still held more than a hint of skepticism. "Why were you meeting Monteous two weeks ago?"

"That, Gerard, I don't have time to explain, nor am I sure that I even should. My goal tonight was to rescue Monteous, which, unfortunately didn't go as planned. My secondary goal was keeping the four of you out of trouble. I seem to have failed there, as well. Could you help me at least meet my third goal?"

"Which is?"

"Getting you out of the trouble you have got yourselves into."

Wallace decided he had to speak. "Gerard, he's offered us no harm..."

"Offered you no harm. He held a knife to my neck."

You probably deserved it. Wallace gave up on Gerard and looked to Demetrius, glad to know the connection between them and the mysterious man, if not understanding it completely.

Voices erupted into shouts a couple streets over, and Wallace, along with everyone else, turned to look, though they could see nothing.

"We must go," Demetrius said, turning into the alley where the dark waited. "Come with me if you want to survive this night, or not. I'm done with trying to convince you, Gerard."

Wallace looked to Gerard, then made up his own mind and ran to catch up with Demetrius. Out of the corner of his eye, he saw Angela catch up with him. It seemed minutes, but was only moments, before he heard Gerard's loping steps as he, too, caught up with them.

Demetrius led them quickly through the city, using dark alleys, unlit streets, quick stops and detours to avoid guards, drunks, and other prying eyes.

Gerard, once, tried to ask another question, but Demetrius shushed him with a hand and a stern, hissed, "Quiet."

As they approached the gate that led from the Middle City to the Outer City, Demetrius slowed. He kept the party to the shadows, looking, Wallace thought, for any sign of their pursuers.

"If we're to be caught in the city, this is the place." Demetrius's voice was low, loud enough for just the three of them to hear. "Wait here."

And then he was gone, silently, into the night. Wallace strained to see him in the dark, and shivered. The cold had found its way into his coat. *My bones will be ice, soon,* he thought, and tried to wrap his coat closer around him. The cold wasn't as noticeable when they were moving.

Long moments passed before Demetrius reappeared, stepping out of the shadows near the gate, and approached the guardsman standing there. They exchanged words, and then something, money perhaps, changed hands, and Demetrius summoned the three of them from their hiding place.

Wallace didn't wait for the others to decide. He moved quickly out of the shadows toward the gate, and heard Angela close on him. He looked back once and saw Gerard trailing them.

As he crossed the courtyard, Wallace thought he felt eyes watching him. The lamplight around the edges kept it well lit. Anyone hiding in the shadows would have little trouble picking them off with an arrow or a crossbow bolt.

Demetrius still waved them on, urging them to hurry, and Wallace picked up his pace, almost running. When he reached the gate, Demetrius ushered him through it, and Angela and Gerard as well, then followed with a quick thanks to the guardsman.

The Outer City, along the main thoroughfares was well lit. Elsewhere, darkness and gloom abounded. The poor, the wretched, the down on their luck, they lived in the Outer City. The businesses here catered to them. The streets were dangerous to everyone, and the guard patrolled only the main routes to the city. Everywhere else, thieves, thugs, and assassins ruled.

Wallace had traveled through the Outer City only a few times, always while the sun rode the sky. As they passed through, he imagined ill-washed thugs waiting in every pool of shadow and made sure he stayed close to Demetrius. Even Demetrius kept to the lit streets, though on their edges.

"Stay with me," he had said as they embarked on their trip through the Outer City. "Don't stray, and we'll be fine. Groups aren't generally accosted."

Wallace had no trouble following that order. Neither, it seemed did Gerard.

As they worked their way to the edge of the city, Wallace was grateful for the cold. It held the smell of the place down. During the summer, he knew the smell of human waste, rotting trash, and the stench of the corrupt was overwhelming if you were not prepared for it. Now, the cold and keeping his nose buried in the collar of his coat made it bearable.

Just about the time he thought they'd never be quit of the Outer City, they came upon the outer wall and the gateway to the outside world, guarded only by the tenements on either side of it. Soon, they were out of the squalor and into the fields surrounding the city.

A weight lifted from Wallace, one he hadn't realized was there. "We're free."

"Not yet, young Wallace. We must cross the river and find our allies. Only then, will we be safe for a time."

"For a time?" Angela had been quiet for quite a while, and her voice surprised Wallace.

"Yes, long enough, I think, to explain what's going on, and hopefully create a plan to free Monteous and Robert while keeping you three safe."

"Let's go, then," said Angela. "I'm going to freeze just standing here."

"Yes, you're right. Follow me."

And he turned off the road, hopped a low, wooden fence, and began trekking across the barren fields. The three apprentices quickly hurried after.

"Why are we cutting across the fields?" Wallace asked when he'd caught up to Demetrius.

"Ignoring the fact that it's shorter, we're less likely to be caught if we're not on the road."

"But these fields are barren. There's nowhere to hide," said Gerard.

"Agreed. However, they will be looking for us on the road. The clouds also work in our favor. No moonlight or starlight will reflect from us. Away from lamps, we might as well not even exist." He lowered his voice to a whisper. "And if we are quiet, there will be even less reason for them to look our direction."

Wallace didn't need to be told twice.

It was difficult, though, to keep silent. The ground, frozen hard, held potholes and ridges that grabbed at toes and snatched at heels, causing Wallace to stumble a great deal. More often, he thought, than Demetrius. With every stumble, a grunt or a muffled cry of surprise threatened to escape his lips. He heard noises from Angela and Gerard, as well. With every noise, the fear they'd be heard and captured threatened to overwhelm him.

After what he thought was perhaps a mile, he was so tired of almost turning his ankle and having to hold his breath just to be sure he couldn't hear any pursuers, he wished he could just return to the lab. He wished everything would go back to normal. He'd just begun to start moving beyond the basic Weaves most new apprentices learn, things like lighting candles and making small warding trinkets and minor draughts. He yearned to be intimately involved with the Works Monteous had Robert and Angela helping with. He had been looking forward to it.

And now it was all gone, swept away through the portal and out the door by people he didn't know, and they were being hunted for no reason he could fathom. And Robert, he was still back there, lying on the shelf. What would happen to him? What would happen to all of them? Wallace kept trudging across the empty fields, though. What other choice did he have? None he could see.

After what felt like hours of stumbling across the fields, he saw some low trees in the distance, shadows of trees, really, and he knew they'd reached the river.

Gerard stepped up close to Demetrius. "Aren't they going to be looking for us at the ferry?"

"It's possible, I suppose, but we're not going to use the ferry. A friend has a boat upriver."

Thus, the real reason for traipsing across these fields, Wallace thought.

As they approached the middle of the last field they'd have to cross, Demetrius brought them to a halt. "Stay low, stay here, and stay quiet. I'm going to scout the road." And then he moved off, quickly and quietly, much like a cat, or well, like something that didn't make any noise and flowed over the ground at a pace just shy of an all-out run. Soon, Wallace lost him among the shadows.

Wallace knelt on the ground and huddled as close to it as he could without laying on it. The frozen earth quickly leeched warmth from his knees and shins, and after just moments, he wanted to stand again, but the thought that someone might be watching kept him from it.

Angela was sitting on her feet, one hand on the ground to keep her balance. Gerard was behind them, where he'd stayed through most of the trip across the fields. Wallace didn't understand why Gerard held so much distrust for Demetrius. As far as he could tell, Wallace didn't see anything strange or untrustworthy in the man's behavior. He'd gotten them out of the laboratory with ease, it seemed. All of them but Robert, but there'd been little choice. And it was clear that Monteous knew him. Why else would his name be on that parchment. Whether Demetrius was the patron, or a "servant" as he claimed, Wallace didn't know, but there was a connection, and it seemed a good one.

He heard Gerard creep up between him and Angela, and turned to look at him. Whatever time Gerard had spent climbing mountains or whatever where he was from, he'd never learned to move quietly.

"I think we should leave, now, while he's gone."

Angela's head turned quickly to face Gerard, and Wallace could have sworn he'd seen her eyes flash silver, despite the lack of moonlight. "Why? Where would we go?"

"There's got to be someone else we could go to. Orliss, for instance. He's a Master Wizard. He'd know what to do."

Wallace couldn't believe he'd just heard Gerard suggest Orliss. Apparently, neither could Angela. "You think we can trust Orliss? He and Monteous have been at each other's throats for years. There's no way he would help."

"I'm not talking about help. He'd take us in, all of us, I'm sure, and we could continue our apprenticeships."

"No." Wallace was glad to hear the same word cross Angela's lips at the same time it had escaped his.

"You've got to accept reality. Monteous is probably dead, by now. No one could hold him this long against his will."

"No, apprentice. Monteous is not dead." Wallace nearly jumped up, he was so startled by Demetrius's voice. Somehow, the man had managed to sneak up on them.

"I would know," Demetrius continued. "I'll have to inform him he needs to work on teaching you to listen to those who politely request that you stay quiet when you're being hunted.

"And, Gerard, if you think, that you would be better off with Orliss, go now. I'm not interested in trying to save you from the dragon if you're just going to run back to that snake."

Gerard hung his head, chastened, it seemed. When he looked up, it was difficult to tell in the dark, but Wallace thought he saw some sort of resolve replace the reluctance that had marked the hours since they'd left the lab.

"Good," Demetrius said. "The road is clear. Follow me and stay close."

In a crouch, he ran off across the field, surprising Wallace that he'd run at all, but Wallace quickly jumped up from the ground and ran after him, keeping as low as possible while trying not to trip over the rough ground.

Quickly, they were at the fence and clambering over it and crossing the road. Wallace kept turning his head left and right as they crossed, looking for shadows of pursuers, expecting at any moment to hear shouts and steel sliding out of scabbards or arrows flying overhead, or worse.

But they crossed the road and moved into the trees lining the rivers edge with none of what he'd feared coming to pass.

Demetrius stood, then started making his way upriver through the trees, following the river's edge closely. Wallace had a hard time keeping the low hanging, leafless branches out of his teeth. He wished for some moonlight, or even just starlight, or just a tiny little firestick light, anything to lift the darkness a little so he could avoid the trees.

Only five or so minutes passed, though it seemed to Wallace like hours, before they came to a clearing. A small cottage squatted a good fifty paces from the black, flowing river, defined by lamplight from the two windows Wallace could see. Demetrius put his hand out, motioning again to stay where they were, and then he crept up to the door of the cottage, staying in the shadows as much as possible. Wallace saw him knock on the door, lightly enough that no sound could be heard from where Wallace stood. Soon, the door opened. A handshake, some gestures towards the river, and then Demetrius started on his way back and the door closed behind him.

Only a moment later, the lamps dimmed, though they weren't put out entirely. Just as Demetrius reached the three of them, the door opened again. An immense man stepped out into the darkness and headed toward the river, disappearing as he passed out of the glow cast from the windows.

"Come," Demetrius said, "my friend will take us across the river."

He turned, and Wallace found himself following quickly after, glad to be out of the woods.

As they approached the river, Wallace gained a real appreciation for just how large Demetrius's friend was. He towered over Gerard, who no one would call short, and he was as large around as three normal men combined. When he saw the boat the man was preparing to launch, Wallace couldn't imagine the boat would hold the man, let alone the rest of them, without foundering.

"I know what you're thinking, young apprentices." His voice was the sound of rocks grinding together. "But fear not, the boat will hold us all. You will not be getting wet this fine night." And then he snorted a laugh that sounded like it hurt.

The big man bent over and pushed on the bow of the boat, shoving it in to the river, stern first. When it was most of the way in, he rasped, "Everybody in."

Demetrius clambered in, then held his hand out to Angela, which she took, and he helped her in. Then, Gerard pushed Wallace forward, and Demetrius was giving him a hand into the boat as well. Angela moved toward the stern, and Wallace followed her, after looking to see if Gerard was going to climb into the boat, or slip away to go who knew where. Gerard refused Demetrius's hand, and climbed in on his own.

Then the big man pushed the boat even further into the water, until the bow just rested on the bed of rock underneath the river's edge, and climbed in himself, rocking the boat far less than Wallace would have imagined. He moved past Demetrius and Gerard, took a seat near the middle with his back to the prow. The oars were stowed next to him, and he pulled them out and set them into the locks. He gave a couple pushes with the oars, and they were free and floating in the river.

He spun the boat around and put himself to work, pulling them with great, huge strokes across the river.

In what seemed like no time at all, the boat nudged up against the far bank. Gerard wasted little time climbing out. Demetrius followed him.

Wallace let Angela go forward, first, and as she passed the boatman, she said, "Thank you for your help..."

"You're welcome, Miss. If ever you need across the river, call on ol' Ergin any time."

Demetrius turned around at that and looked at the big man. "Do you think that was wise?"

"I don't think it can hurt, them knowin' my name. If they be captured, things will be all sorts of wrong, regardless. I think it's better they think me a friend, don't you? You just do your job and take care of 'em, and it won't matter one bit whether they know my name."

Wallace saw the shadow of Demetrius's head shake. "It's your thick neck. Come on, Wallace. We need to let this big fool go back to pretending he's just a fisherman."

Wallace wasted no time climbing past Ergin, whispering his own thanks, and jumping out of the boat onto solid ground.

Demetrius motioned them on. "Into the forest. Not much farther, and we'll be safe for the night."

Wallace hoped he was right. The rest in the boat had given his body a chance to relax and start complaining to him that it was past time for sleep. But he ignored it as much as he could and placed one foot in front of the other, following Demetrius up the bank and into the forest, hoping for a warm bed at the end of their trek.

CHAPTER 9

ONE MOMENT, ROBERT felt himself falling, and then he found himself looking up at the underside of a shelf. His body couldn't move — fatigue battled desire and won. For what seemed like hours, but might have been minutes, he stared up at the shelf above him, trying to remember how he'd arrived at his resting place.

What was I doing? He'd obviously done something extremely strenuous. He felt like his body weighed as much as one of those immense, gray, horned beasts that arrived with the traveling menageries.

He decided to at least look around, and turned his head to the side. The movement rewarded him with an achy head and swimming vision, almost as if a Weave hung between him and the room. He closed his eyes, and after a moment, the pain ebbed just a bit. When he felt comfortable that he could open his eyes without having his head split completely apart, he found himself looking through a blurry veil. He tried to look through it, but could see nothing but vague shapes. A quick glance above him, and he realized the shelf above was not blurry at all. Reassured that his eyes were fine, he concluded it must be a Weave, but the reason eluded him. He tried to slip into the vew, but his eyes wouldn't make the transition. He really needed more sleep.

He couldn't sleep however, and he couldn't move. He thought about calling out for help, but something stopped him, some nearly imperceptible feeling of danger.

And then, one of the shapes beyond the veil moved.

"How long do we have to sit here waiting?" Robert didn't recognize the voice.

"Waiting?" asked a different voice, further away. This one had iron in it. "We wait until Orliss says we're done here. He's sure they will be back."

They? Who are these people? Where am I?

"Why's he so sure? This place is a mess, and they know we're looking for 'em."

"Only three of the apprentices left, and none of them were the one he was wanting. He says that one'll come back."

They left? Angela, Wallace, and Gerard left?

"Then who was the fourth one with 'em? That's the guy I want a piece of."

Fourth? Who was with them?

"Some hired hand, I suspect. Nobody worth following."

"I want his head. He hacked Grun apart out there."

"We stay here until Orliss says otherwise. Now shut up. This other apprentice won't enter if he hears us in here jawin' away like shop-keepers."

And then Robert remembered enough to deduce how he'd come to be lying on this shelf, behind a Weave that was obviously hiding him. He remembered the portal first, the energie drain, beginning to black out as he tied off the portal at the last second, and hearing something that sounded like pounding.

Someone must have come to the door. Who, he figured, must have been Orliss, or some of his hired thugs. For some reason, the others had carried him here and hidden him on the shelf. The Weave had to be Angela's. They'd left, somehow, and some other person had come in and hacked apart this thug's partner in the escape.

He still had questions he couldn't anser. Where would Angela and the others go? How did they escape, and who had helped them? Did they go through the portal? Robert thought it likely. It would be the easiest way. But where, exactly, did that portal lead? Monteous had worked out the design of the Focus himself, not trusting Robert with the location — perhaps not trusting anyone, for now obvious reasons. Someone had still found out despite his caution.

And that someone, Robert now felt sure, was Orliss. Robert certainly wouldn't put it past Orliss to have set the whole thing up in the first place.

So they left him. Orliss's thugs were staked out in the laboratory, waiting for Robert to come back, and he was trapped here, his friends gone, unable to move for several reasons, not the least of which was the fatigue in his limbs.

I must have drained myself opening that portal.

The portal. I opened it. I actually pulled it off, one of the hardest Works for any wizard to finish, and I did it.

If he'd done that, he could certainly find his way out of this mess, couldn't he? He just needed to think, and rest. Lots of rest. And try not to make noise. Concealment Weaves could be made to block sound as well as obscure vision, but without having created this Weave, he couldn't know for sure what it could do. He guessed, though, that Angela wouldn't have had enough time or energie to create it to block sound. He'd just have to hope, if he fell asleep, that he wouldn't snore.

But before he allowed himself to fall back asleep, he set himself to making a plan. Orliss wanted him, for some reason, and didn't really care about the others. Why would Orliss want him? Why would Orliss kidnap Monteous?

I'm just an apprentice? Why would he want me?

WHEN SHE EMERGED from the forest and saw her destination, Angela had to admit she could not have been more pleased. Centered in a clearing, stood what looked, to her mind, like a fortress. She knew it wasn't. It was just a walled estate, but after the night she'd just had, stone walls were welcoming walls. The glow of fires and lamps emerged from doors and windows and reflected off walls. She could see the shadows of guards among the parapets.

Demetrius had been right. They would be as safe here, for the night, as they would be anywhere.

As the four of them approached the gate, a small panel flipped open, and eyes peered through it for a moment. The panel slid shut as quickly as it opened, and Angela heard a large wooden thud which she took to be the drawbar being lifted. Soon, the left hand side of the gate opened just enough to let them pass through one at a time.

A man in armor came running up to Demetrius, and embraced him roughly, clapping him on the back. To Angela's eyes, he was of a height with Demetrius, but thicker and stronger. In the flickering light, she thought his slightly thinning hair might have been red once. "Demetrius, you did make it out!"

"I did, though not perhaps the way you might have guessed."

The man laughed. "You shall have to regale me with your adventure, but later. First, you must introduce me to your three..."

It was Demetrius's turn to laugh. "Apprentices."

The man's eyes grew wide.

"Yes, Ivron. This is Angela," he said, gesturing toward her, "Wallace, and Gerard. Three of Monteous's fine apprentices. Apprentices, this is Ivron, Lord of Antimonch, and this manor."

"That is good news, good news. How in the Seven Kingdoms did you manage to get from that trap, into the city to pick up these three? Wait, where's the fourth?"

"We had to leave him behind. I'll explain why later. We need to send someone to Monteous's laboratory to help Robert. He may not be discovered yet, and we may still have a chance to extricate him."

"Yes, of course. Georg, Horuth!"

Two men came running in response to Ivron's call. "I need you to go to the city, and keep an eye on Monteous's place. One of his apprentices is still in hiding there..."

"On a shelf," Demetrius interrupted.

Angela saw a puzzled look cross Ivron's wide face before he continued. "We need to try to retrieve him before he is discovered, or apprehended. Try not to get noticed this time."

The one on the left elbowed the other. "'t was all his fault."

"Just go, and hurry. We can't lose him. This night has already seen too many failures."

They both nodded, the gate opened again, and they slipped out through it. It closed behind them, and two men slid the bar back into place.

Angela wished them speed and luck. The decision to leave Robert there still had her stomach turning over each time she thought of it.

Ivron clapped his arm around Demetrius's shoulder. "Now, let's go find some food and fire to warm ourselves, and you can tell me how you came to be in the city when you should have been twenty miles the other direction from here."

Ivron led them off to the manor toward the rear of the compound. It stood large and imposing, but many of the windows were lit, suggesting warmth and rest awaited. Once they were inside, Angela shrugged off her coat as she found the manor was indeed well heated. A servant, dressed smartly in gray, appeared to take the coat from her. He gathered the coats from the others as Ivron led them to the dining room where servers were already placing food on the table.

She wondered how the food could be ready so quickly. Apparently, she'd wondered aloud, as Ivron spoke to her, "We have had men coming in all evening, returning from the debacle that was our effort to retrieve Monteous. We have had the fires stoked and food ready to feed them as they arrive."

He turned to Demetrius. "So, how did you manage to be in the city?"

Despite everything, Demetrius somehow managed to laugh before answering. "I managed it a bit unceremoniously, I must admit. I was engaged with a very good swordsman, after the residence had been set aflame and we were being driven out. I saw a portal open, and I had a feeling these apprentices," he swung his arm about, indicating the three of them, "had managed to open it. I maneuvered so that I was in front of it. My opponent rushed me, and I fell into the portal with him right on me. We landed on this fine young lady here. I kicked away the Focus, shattering it and the portal, which closed upon the legs of my opponent."

At this point, Angela turned to her food, now knowing the truth of how she'd come to end up playing the cushion for Demetrius.

Demetrius continued to talk with Ivron about their escape from Monteous's workshop, and Angela tried to shut most of it out. The memories were still too vivid, especially the parts about leaving Robert, and she had no interest in reliving them so soon. When her stomach felt full, she asked about a room and a bed, and Ivron called over one of his servants, a young woman who appeared little older, if any, than Angela.

"Please," he said to the servant, "guide this lady to her room, and run a bath for her if she wishes."

"A hot bath?" Angela asked.

The young woman nodded. "Oh yes, after what you've been through, I should think so. A hot bath and a warm bed, and I'll get those clothes cleaned up for you and have them ready in the morning, as well."

"You're very kind." Angela couldn't believe her luck.

"Lord Ivron," she said. "Thank you so much for your hospitality. I don't know..."

"It's nothing," he interrupted. "Just call me Ivron, and get yourself taken care of."

She didn't know what to say. She was so tired she just nodded and said, "Thank you."

She motioned for the woman to lead, and left Gerard and Wallace still eating at the table. She heard Gerard start to ask a question, but she had no interest in what it might be.

The maid kept sneaking glances at her as they went up a flight of stairs and down a hallway into a room larger than any she'd ever had to herself. A fire was already burning in the fireplace, warming the room which was sheathed in a dark wood paneling. A large, inviting bed took up most of the wall across from the fireplace. A door led past it into another room where she could spot a tub.

"It's been a long time," she said to the maid, who was shutting the door behind her.

She quickly moved past Angela, toward the bath. "Come, come, let's get you cleaned up and into bed. You look exhausted."

Angela followed her in, where the maid helped her undress and slip into the bath that was already heated. While she wasn't paying attention, Ivron must have instructed his servants to prepare rooms for her and the others.

The hot bath eased the tension from her muscles, and she relaxed into the tub, trying to forget all that had transpired that evening. She needed a moment of peace. But a gnawing fear for Robert and Monteous wouldn't let her relax more than a moment.

The maid began to massage her shoulders. "You are so very tense."

"I've had a rough couple of days."

"Do you need an ear?"

Angela thought about it for a moment, and couldn't imagine talking about what had happened with a stranger. Few would understand, and she wasn't sure she even understood.

"Maybe later, I don't know. I mostly need to sleep."

The maid didn't say another word, other than those necessary to help Angela wash and rinse. When she was done, the maid helped her dry herself, and provided her with a night-gown, then went with her and tucked her into bed. She went back to the bath, and came out carrying Angela's clothes, then went around the room snuffing the candles, leaving the fire in the fireplace as the only light in the room. It had burned down while she'd bathed, and now gave off a warm orange glow.

The maid went to the door, still holding Angela's clothes. "I'll have these washed and ready for you in the morning. If you need anything during the night, pull on that cord there, and someone will come and help you with anything you need."

Angela didn't know what to say, and could think of nothing more elaborate than "Thank you."

The maid curtsied. "It's my pleasure. Sleep well."

She left, and Angela closed her eyes, trying not to think about Robert and how she'd left him there, alone. Despite her exhaustion, sleep took a long time to overcome her worry.

CHAPTER 10

GERARD DIDN'T SLEEP well. Dreams of Angela, naked, next to him, metamorphosed into dreams of Robert in a grave while someone threw dirt down on top of him. Gerard blinked, and found Angela sharing the grave with Robert, covered to their necks in dirt, and Gerard himself held the shovel that filled the pit. He blinked again, and Gerard found himself and Monteous in the grave with Robert and Angela. Orliss stood above them all, laughing, as he shoveled in the last bits of dirt, which spilled into Gerard's mouth causing him to cough and gasp for air.

Gerard sat up in his bed, his heart pounding in his chest as if he'd just run up Blisterwind Pass. Sweat dripped from him, in spite of the chill that had invaded the room while he'd slept. Only coals remained of the fire that had warmed the room when he'd stumbled in, guided by one of Ivron's servants. The coals shed only the tiniest bit of light into the room. Through the frost-tinged windows, he saw darkness still blanketed the world.

He ran his hand through his hair, massaging his scalp, and tried to slow his heart. It had only been a dream.

Angela. He wished he knew where her room was. He assumed it was close by, but he couldn't just go knocking on doors just. He suspected she wouldn't welcome him anyway.

I was such a fool. He didn't know what he was thinking when he'd threatened her with that silly lie. Sure, Robert seemingly had every advantage over him when it came to Angela. It was no excuse for his behavior. *Mother would strap my backside if she knew.*

Angela had slapped him, and he could sometimes still feel the sting. "I would dare," he'd said. The thought of how Robert remained Monteous's favorite, despite his failures, and how he won Angela, had stripped him of his good sense. He still couldn't stomach the idea of Angela at Robert's side. He'd never stomached losing. It didn't make what he'd done right.

His mistake, he was sure, fed the first part of the dream. The rest was pure fear that everything was falling apart, and that he was responsible. He certainly felt responsible.

And then, Demetrius. Gerard knew now that Demetrius was what he claimed, or at least, when he'd asked Ivron how he knew Demetrius, Ivron had confirmed what Demetrius had told him. Gerard still didn't trust the man. Something about him just didn't seem right. He was too quick, knew too much. Gerard didn't want to accept that he was just that good.

"Uggh." He swung his legs out of the bed. "I'm going to go crazy lying here."

But what could he do? He remembered they'd taken his clothes to clean them. He had only the robe that hung beside the bed. He reached over and pulled it from the hook and wrapped it around himself. Then he saw the cord hanging from the wall in the dim light. They'd said he could pull it at any time. He reached over and gave it a good yank.

He walked over to the window and peered out through the frost-covered glass. He could see only the torches along the outer wall. The sky was too dark to be nearing sunup.

Quicker than he'd anticipated, he heard a knock at his door. When he opened it, a servant was waiting.

"How may I help you, sir?"

"Could you get my clothes? I can't sleep, and I'd like to go outside and take a walk."

"I will go see if they are ready."

"Thanks. Oh, would you know what time it is?"

The servant nodded. "Yes, it's just past the fourth hour."

"Thank you."

"Sir," the servant said, and turned to leave. Gerard shut the door behind him.

Sunup was still a few hours a way.

He wanted to do something. Strike back at whoever had put them in this position. Ivron and Demetrius seemed to want to blame Orliss. Certainly, Gerard could see how Orliss might be inclined to try kidnapping Monteous. He'd heard Monteous talking on occasion about how he'd thwarted some scheme or other that Orliss wanted the Conclave to pass. Could Monteous have just stonewalled Orliss one too many times? Or was this something different?

He opened the door when the servant knocked. The servant had his clothes, folded, underneath a tray that held some warm biscuits and some tea. "I thought you might like something to eat."

The biscuits did smell good. Gerard admitted the servant, who took the tray and set it on the small table near the far wall. The servant then set the clothes on the bed. Gerard held the door open for him.

"Is there anything else I can do for you, sir?"

"No, I think I'll be fine."

The servant left the room, shutting the door behind him. Gerard walked over to the table and picked up one of the biscuits and started eating. He rinsed it down with some tea that warmed his insides, then went to the bed and dressed himself. He took his staff from where it leaned against the wall, and made his way out of the room, down the hall and the stairs, then to the front door.

A guard stood watch by the door. He nodded as Gerard went out.

Gerard decided to walk the perimeter of the compound, just to give himself time to think. He still hadn't figured out what to do. He didn't want to stay here with Demetrius, and he knew now that Orliss wasn't the answer, but the problem. Going home crossed his mind. He missed his family, but if he went home, he'd never take the tests and would never become part of the Guild. *And my father would throw me out almost as soon as I arrived.*

He walked the perimeter of the compound, passing men who stood atop the wall, watching the forest. He walked by stables, a barracks, and several other outbuildings. This place, he realized, was built to withstand more than bandits. The stone walls looked thick, solid, and well maintained. The doors appeared to carry nearly as much bulk as the walls.

As he approached the front gate, he came upon another building that looked, if at all possible, stouter than the rest. And in the dim light cast from the various lamps around the courtyard, he could see the Guild symbol above the doorway. He walked up to it, and was about to knock on the door, when a voice from behind him said "It's empty."

Gerard turned around to find Demetrius there.

"Why are you following me?"

"I wasn't following you. I saw you from across the courtyard, and came over to ask if all was well."

"No. Nothing is well. Why is it empty?"

"Reuy, the wizard to whom it belonged, perished this evening when Ivron found him to be a traitor."

Gerard was shaken. "Traitor?" Was Demetrius implying that he thought Gerard would do that?

"Someone told Orliss we were coming, and Orliss had Monteous moved before we arrived. For some reason, Reuy was reluctant to go with us, but when Ivron pressed him, he came anyway. When we were set upon, he was one of the first to die."

"You killed him?"

"No. Orliss, or one of his cronies, silenced him, before he had a chance to warn us of the trap. An assassin's bolt through the neck will even kill a wizard."

Gerard hissed, and looked around into the dark.

"Relax, you should be safe here. There are enough watchmen. Let's go back inside. It's cold out here."

Gerard went with him. He didn't see another choice, but he intended to come back and look in that laboratory.

He shuddered as he realized he'd nearly knocked on the laboratory door without looking for protective Weaves. If Reuy were a traitor, it was highly likely he left something nasty protecting the entryway.

For the first time, he wished they hadn't left Robert behind. He could help look for any protective Weaves the previous occupant had set. Angela could help, but he wasn't sure she'd help him do anything. And Robert was more experienced than any of them.

I can't believe I almost knocked on that door. One of the first things he'd been taught as an apprentice was to respect another wizard's laboratory, for his own safety, if for no other reason. And he'd forgotten.

Demetrius interrupted his woolgathering. "Gerard, what were you doing out here?"

"I couldn't sleep. Figured I'd come out here, let the cold clean out my thoughts."

"Did it work?"

"I don't know," said Gerard. "What are we going to do? Do we even have an idea where to search for Monteous?"

Demetrius waited a moment before answering. "I don't know for sure. I suspect we will try to retrieve Robert, first. We know where he is, and we know that he's in danger. After that, we need to find other Guild members that are allied with Monteous. They are spread throughout the Seven Kingdoms, and without Monteous here, it will be difficult to know exactly who we can trust.

"Also, there is a Conclave soon, I think in a week or so. The Guild will elect the next Senior Wizard, then. It wouldn't surprise me if that is what this is all about. Orliss wants the seat, and a wizard must be present in order to be considered. If Monteous is absent, he will lose his seat, and it's likely that Orliss will claim it."

"Even if everyone is told that Orliss has kidnapped him?" Gerard asked.

"Even so. The rules state clearly that you must be present to be considered. The other members of the Guild will demand proof that Orliss has kidnapped Monteous, and right now, we don't have any."

"That's why he wants us."

"Yes. That is exactly why you must be kept from him."

Gerard didn't quite know what he thought of being a pawn in this game the master wizards were playing, beyond being sure he didn't like it. Trusting the wrong person could wind up with him dead in an alley somewhere, or worse, where no one could find him.

He thought back to his dream, and realized it might have been trying to tell him more. *I need to start helping, or I'll end up buried with the rest of them.*

"Demetrius, I can't trust you. I don't know anything about you, other than what you've told me." *And you've humiliated me twice, three times.* "If you go back for Robert, I'm coming with you. If you really are who and what you say you are, you'll need me." *And if you're not, I'll take you out.*

"That will be up to Ivron, but I agree. As we are currently short on full wizards, your help could be useful. Go back to bed, and I'll wake you and we will talk when it's light."

Gerard nodded. "When it's light." Then he turned and made his way back to his room.

✵ ✵ ✵

WHEN ROBERT WOKE again, he didn't feel like he'd slept long, but found most of his energie restored. His stomach felt hollow, and he knew he'd need food soon, or he'd drain himself just moving. First, though, he had to figure out if he was alone.

He turned his head, as slowly as he could, to try to view the room. The veil still pretty much blinded him to detail, but it looked brighter. The shapes that had been men were no longer where they'd been, but that didn't mean much. They could have, and likely did, move. But to where?

Robert resigned himself to waiting for a while. He hoped Orliss's men would move or make a noise. He hoped it would happen before his empty stomach started growling and gave him away.

Several minutes passed, and he still hadn't heard a sound or seen any movement. He wished whomever had laid him here had thought to leave him with a staff or a rod. Something he could use in his defense, or as an offense. *While I'm wishing, I might as well wish they'd taken me with them.*

Slowly, he moved his aching muscles, pushing his head through the veil, just far enough to see clearly around the room.

What he saw dismayed him. Broken glass covered the floor, benches and chairs lay on their sides where they'd overturned. It would require a week to clean up, or longer, once Monteous was back.

He looked at the floor near him, hoping something he might be able to use had rolled near him, but his luck, if that's what had kept him hidden so far, had run dry. Nothing of use was in reach, and he feared all the rods had been taken. If a wizard had ransacked the laboratory, he would have certainly taken those things.

What he didn't see, were the pair of guards he'd heard talking the night before. *Maybe they left.*

And maybe they left a steaming turkey dinner waiting for me.

He eased his legs out over the floor, and lowered his feet to the ground. He couldn't sit up without disturbing the shelf above him, so he rolled his body over to let his knees contact the floor. Doing so put him in a precarious position for a moment, but he managed it without falling from the shelf. From there, he brought the rest of his torso out.

He knelt for a moment, feeling a little dizzy. He needed food as soon as he could find it, but first, he needed something he could use for protection. He did not doubt his enemy, or enemies, waited nearby.

After a moment, the dizziness passed, and he was able to get to his feet. He tried to work out the likeliest place a rod would be hiding. A metal rod, iron if he coud find it, would be best. *Any metal will do.* Something he could use against the knives or swords they would have.

He decided he'd search his bench first where he knew, if they had not been taken, he'd find metal rods of various types. He stepped carefully among the shards of glass and bits of metal strewn across the floor. A misstep could shatter the larger pieces, announcing his presence to whoever might be listening. After maneuvering around the wreckage, he arrived at his bench. It lay on its back, the drawers accessible, but several of them had been removed, their contents tossed about the floor.

The rods had been in the top drawer, which remained in the bench. He hoped whoever had gone through his bench had decided the rods were worthless. He hoped it hadn't been a wizard, but even then, an iron rod was worth little more than the knife it might have made. He started to draw the drawer out, and almost immediately, something tumbled about inside it, then fell into the interior of the bench. The noise in the silent laboratory, rang loud in his ears, and he stopped withdrawing the drawer and waited for the inevitable shouts of men coming for him.

Tense moments passed. He heard nothing but the normal noise of the city as it awoke. When he thought it safe, he resumed pulling the drawer up and out. He managed to finish its removal without any more thuds or bangs. He set it on the overturned bench, where it became apparent why he'd made no more noise. It was empty.

Robert wanted to groan. Whoever had emptied the bench was thorough. They'd taken all of the rods.

He looked down into the hole where the drawer had been, but it was dark enough, he couldn't see what had fallen out. He knelt by the bench, and reached down into the hole, casting around with the tips of his fingers at the bottom, hoping to find whatever had fallen out.

His fingertips grazed the top of a cold piece of metal. He delved into it with a bit of energie, and felt relief. They'd left the iron rod. He could not fathom why, though the others were far more expensive. Why not take them all? Who cares. He pushed his hand a little farther into the bench and put his hand around the rod. He started to draw it out, then heard from behind him the crunch of boots on broken glass.

Robert flipped his head around to find a man, not four feet away from him, holding a sword pointed at his face. "Hold it right there. I'm s'posed to bring you in live, like, but it won't bother me none to bring you dead."

Robert stopped moving as requested, but he already had the rod in his hand.

"Where will you be taking me?"

"You just never mind that. Pull that arm out of there real slow, like."

Robert did, as slowly as he could, so he could guage the energie flows he needed. Using the energie of the iron rod, he started to wrap the sword with a Weave, so his would-be captor couldn't wield it against him. When the Weave was finished, he would run. He would run as fast as his drained body would allow.

As he finished wrapping the sword the man held, he pulled his hand free of the bench, then tightened the Weave on the sword and scrambled backward, away from it.

The man shouted in annoyance and surprise as his sword refused to move.

Robert turned and ran out through the back door of the Laboratory, into the small garden Monteous kept. Behind him, the man shouted for help.

Now he was free, but he wouldn't be able to run far. Even the minimal Weave he'd placed on that sword had taken a lot of effort.

He scrambled over the stone wall behind Monteous's complex, and into the street beyond. Where could he go? Who did he know? Who would help him? Wherever he went, it had to be close by, somewhere he could reach before he collapsed again.

Robert looked over the wall and saw the swordsman, pursuing through the garden without his sword. He decided he had to find food. A kitchen or an inn. He turned north and ran for all he was worth, turned left, turned another corner, ran a bit further, then ducked into an inn he recognized. He checked behind him, his pursuer hadn't followed him around the last corner, before ducking into the entryway, out of breath.

The common room was nearly empty, this early in the morning, but the innkeep was ready to serve anyone walking through his doors, or down from his rooms. He greeted Robert nearly as soon as he'd entered.

"Can I help you, young Master?"

Master. Robert realized he still carried the rod openly in his hand. An easy way to identify a wizard. The innkeep looked a bit nervous. His eyes kept twitching down to the rod, and then back up to Robert's face. Most common folk didn't feel entirely comfortable dealing with wizards. It wasn't dislike, as much as uncertainty. Strange things had a way of happening near a wizard.

"I need food," Robert said in between trying to catch breaths. "And some privacy."

"Of course. This way." The innkeep strode off, appealing with his hands for Robert to follow.

He led Robert to a private dining room near the rear of the building, which was well-appointed for an inn of the Middle City. When he'd seated Robert, he said, "Is there anything in particular the Master would like?"

"Just bread, meat, and water."

The innkeep bowed and left, shutting the door after him.

Weariness washed over him as he relaxed into the chair. *I'll fall out of my chair soon if he doesn't hurry with that food.* He tried to think of what to do next, but his mind felt as empty as his stomach.

The innkeep returned quickly, bringing freshly baked bread and some pork on a platter that Robert guessed was the inn's best. *One of the benefits of being a Master.* The innkeep waited for Robert to look over the fare before asking "Does it meet your approval?"

"Yes, this is just fine."

The innkeep ducked out the door, and Robert attacked the meal with little regard to propriety. He began to feel better almost as soon as the first bites slid down his throat. Within minutes, he found himself wiping the plate clean with the last of his bread.

Sated, he considered his situation.

He held no illusion that he'd escaped his captors. They would be looking for him, and searching buildings nearby. It may take a little while, he thought, if they had to round up some help, but he hadn't the faintest idea how many of Orliss's men had been watching Monteous's laboratory, or how many waited close by.

He also had no idea where Wallace, Gerard and Angela had gone. Were they captured? Escaped? Dead? He cut short that line of thinking. They had to be alive, or at least, Angela had to be alive. He couldn't imagine her dead.

He needed money. Being a Master had got him fed without showing coin, but that wasn't the safest way for him, right now, of getting things he needed. Shopkeeps and innkeeps still required coin for their goods and services. Of course, pretending to be a Master was a sure way to ruin his chances of ever becoming a Master.

No. He needed solutions that didn't involve him pretending to be a Master.

He also needed a staff.

And if he was ever to find Monteous, or the others, he would need a laboratory.

His head sunk into his hands as he realized he had no idea how to acquire any of those things, and that Orliss's henchmen were likely closing in on him by the minute. There wasn't a chance in Hecae that the Innkeep would keep his mouth shut. Not when he found out Robert couldn't pay him.

CHAPTER 11

"MISS ANGELA, MISS Angela."

A voice in a dream, she thought. But no, she was being shaken gently. She rolled over, and through gummy, half-open eyes, found the maid from the previous night looking down at her.

"Don't you ever sleep?"

"Not when there're guests in the house, Miss. They're waitin' for you."

"Waiting?"

"Yes, my Lord and your friends that you came in with. They said to fetch you down quick."

Angela sat up slowly. The room was cold, the bed, so much warmer. "Why do they need me up in such a hurry?"

"I don't know, Miss, but breakfast is waiting. My Lord is never one to lounge around 'til mid-day when there is work to be done."

Angela stretched her arms to the ceiling, trying to get her muscles to work. Then, she stood, and her bare foot pressed down onto something sharp. She bent over and picked it out from under her.

Glass? She held it up so she could see it, and saw some metal flakes embedded in it.

"Did you step on somethin', Miss?" asked the maid.

"A piece of the Focus," she replied, turning it in her fingers. It reminded her of Robert.

"A piece of what?"

Angela ignored her. She didn't want to explain. *It must have hung up in my clothes and fallen out when I took them off.*

Her clothes. "Where are my clothes?"

The maid didn't flutter even an eyelash at not being answered. "I'm sorry, but your clothes were ruined. The blood stained them. None of it was yours, was it?"

Angela shook her head. "I don't want to talk about it. What shall I do for clothes, then?"

"The Lady of the house offered this." The maid went to a chair where Angela saw what looked to be a very expensive, light purple dress. The maid held it up for Angela to see. *I haven't worn something like that since before...*

"I can't take this."

The maid's eyes grew wide. "You must, you must. The Lady insists!"

She nodded her assent. "Fine." Gerard and Wallace would laugh when they saw her in it. Apprentices did not wear outfits this fine, and she'd been quite happy to never wear a dress like that again.

Angela set the shard on the nightstand.

"Would you like me to get take care of that?"

"No," she said sharply, then softer, "No. It's important to me." *It's my only connection to him. I hope he's still safe.*

When she was satisfied the maid wouldn't throw the shard away, she slipped out of the night-gown. Once free of it, the maid helped her into the dress. Angela was glad for the help. She could never reach the buttons on her own.

As soon as it was on, she heard the maid say, "We must do your hair."

"No," she said. "I don't think there's time. Lead me to them please." If there was news about Robert, there was absolutely no time.

"At least let me tie it back. Come, let me show you."

The maid took her to an immense, but beautiful armoire in the corner of the room and opened one of the doors. Inside hung a mirror, and when Angela stepped in so she could see herself, she agreed. She could not allow a dress this nice to be disgraced by the tangled mess her hair had become.

"Can you fix it quickly?"

"Only a couple minutes."

She ushered Angela to the bath where she found a comb and a brush and teased out the worst of the snarls with a deft hand. Angela worried that the quick work would produce a tender scalp, and found herself amazed when the maid put the comb down. She'd felt little pain at all. The maid escorted her back to the mirror, and Angela gasped. The last time she'd had the opportunity to look in a mirror wearing a dress like this, she'd been a child. But now, the young woman reflected back at her could fare well when held up against any of the ladies fanning themselves in the markets of the Inner City during the spring and summer months.

"Imagine," the maid said, "what I could do if we had time for makeup. You are really very beautiful."

Angela reached her hand up to her hair, stunned by what she was seeing.

She shook herself. She didn't have time to stand staring at herself in a mirror. They were waiting for her, and she had to find out what they were planning to do about Robert, if she could.

"Thank you. I would love to see what you could do, but I really must find out why I'm needed."

WHEN ANGELA ENTERED the room where they'd dined the previous night, all eyes turned toward her, and she had to resist shying away from the attention. Instead, she forced herself to stare at Gerard, daring him to say anything. He looked like he might choke, and she thought if he didn't breathe soon, he'd probably pass out.

She held in a laugh. It was good to see him incapable of speech.

Ivron stepped up beside her, took her hand and guided her to a seat across from Demetrius. "You look lovely, dear. Far more alive than you looked last night."

She nodded slightly. "Thank you. Your maid has been good to me."

"Apparently, so has my wife. Sit, eat, and we will discuss where we go from here. Perhaps we'll even explain to you three what this is all about."

She now noticed the eggs, ham, biscuits and jam on the table. A plate had been set for her. A server emerged from a hidden alcove and filled her plate with food, inquiring as to her wishes as he went.

She looked around and saw that the others had mostly finished eating.

When the server finished, he returned to the hidden alcove. The food, still warm somehow, smelled like the elaborate breakfasts she remembered eating as a child, and invited her to start eating it.

Gerard apparently had managed to get over his anoxia. "What is this about?" he asked.

"I suppose that's as good a place as any to start," said Ivron. "You may or may not know, but it is unusual for a wizard to take on so many apprentices at once as Monteous has done."

Angela nodded. She knew of no other wizards with more than one apprentice.

"There are reasons and reasons for it. Ultimately, money is the root of it. Many wizards believe adding additional wizards to the Guild rolls will diminish their earnings.

"As a whole, the Guild likes to keep the number of wizards to what they consider a manageable number — no more than two or three wizards per city. Even fewer in the countryside."

Demetrius laughed. "The countryside takes care of itself, with the prices most wizards charge for their Work."

"True. What this means, however, is that there are generally fewer than one hundred full wizards in the entirety of the Seven Kingdoms.

"To keep it that way, apprentices are generally approved only for the well-known, connected, and powerful wizards, and then, only when a wizard has passed away, or they near the end of their life, usually fifteen years or so before they're expected to fade."

"Do you three know all this?" Ivron asked.

Angela looked up from her food. "I've heard the numbers, but not the reasons."

"The reason is greed, pure and simple. Fewer wizards means more money for the ones that are practicing."

"So why does Monteous have the four of us?"

"Because he believes keeping the number of wizards so low creates two problems. First, it strangles the total sum knowledge of wizardry in the Seven Kingdoms. Second, it puts us at risk of invasion by our enemies."

Gerard broke in. "What? I don't understand."

"First, the fewer wizards we have, the less research they perform. Wizardry, Monteous claims, is not a static body of knowledge, but something that should be encouraged to grow. He thinks additional research can result in more wealth for the Masters rather than less."

"What about our enemies?"

"Wizardry is not just the province of the Seven Kingdoms. The lands outside our boundaries have their own magics, and those magics are often supplemented by apprentices that fail their tests, the hedge wizards and the like that can't make a living in the Seven Kingdoms. Eventually, Monteous believes, some of our enemies may grow more powerful than our own wizards. At that point, even if it's just through sheer numbers, our Kingdoms will be overrun."

Angela couldn't believe what she was hearing. Not really. "The Seven Kingdoms has been the dominant power on this continent for generations."

Demetrius shook his head. "Has been is right. Monteous, however, believes that it might no longer be the case, and that's what this fight is about. Monteous has lobbied the Guild for years to take on more apprentices. For the last decade, he's been Senior Wizard, and has managed to bring a number of wizards to his side.

"However, the Conclave meets again this year, in about a week. They will elect a new Senior Wizard, and Orliss intends to be that wizard."

"Why don't we find some of the other wizards that are with Monteous and tell them what's happened?" Angela asked.

"Because it won't matter. All candidates are tested to determine their ability, and they only perform the tests during the Conclave. Normally, the strongest wizard generally wins the vote. If Monteous can't make an appearance to take the tests, Orliss will prove strongest.

"However, if we could prove Orliss murdered Monteous to keep him from appearing, we could, perhaps, keep Orliss from the seat. But any other means short of murder won't keep him from winning if Monteous is not there. It will be assumed that Monteous must no longer be the most powerful, if he cannot escape from captivity."

"Why hasn't Monteous told this to any of us?"

"I couldn't tell you. Perhaps he had hoped to change the Guild rules before any of you were put to the test. He believed he was getting close to having enough votes. But if he doesn't appear, it will likely all have been for nothing, and I suspect that the days of the Seven Kingdoms as a sovereign entity will be few."

They all sat quiet then for a moment, thinking their own thoughts. In the quiet, while she thought about the consequences of not finding Monteous in time, Angela thought she heard the front gate open and shut. But she ignored it for the moment. "If Monteous doesn't win the election, what are our chances of passing the tests?"

"If Monteous doesn't win re-election, your chances of even getting to take the tests are slim. Since he already had Robert for an apprentice, he flouted Guild rules to take you three on."

A soldier burst into the room behind her, his breathing heavy and labored.

"My Lord, Robert has escaped Monteous's Laboratory."

Angela turned around. "What?" Her heart seemed to want to break a hole in her chest.

"Robert managed to escape the Laboratory. At least, we think it was him"

Demetrius jumped out of his chair. "Where is he? Is he here?"

The soldier, Georg, Angela thought, dropped his shoulders a bit. "No. We lost him when we intercepted the men chasing him. Horuth stayed behind to look for him. He could have gone anywhere."

"No, I don't think so," said Demetrius. "He will be very tired, still, and probably as hungry as three men after a day without food. He will, for a time, remain near the Laboratory."

Angela stood up. "We should go look for him."

Ivron waved her back down. "Don't go getting too far ahead of yourself, my dear. We can't go sending too many soldiers into the streets in the daytime, nor is it safe for you to be entering the city. Horuth is a fine tracker, and he knows the city."

She sat again, disappointed, and then her thoughts turned to that piece of the Focus she'd stepped on in her room. Robert had made it. "If only I had a Laboratory and a scryer's glass."

Gerard slapped the table. "Angela, we have a Laboratory!"

Angela turned to look at him, but saw the frown cross Demetrius face. "No, Gerard," Demetrius said. "It's too dangerous. You've no idea what kind of traps might be on that building. Don't forget what happened to the wizard that tried to force his way into Monteous's lab."

"Was your wizard in Monteous's league, Ivron?" Gerard asked.

"No, no he wasn't."

"Then let us go look. The three of us together," he was including Wallace, "ought to be able to see any traps he placed. What do you think?"

Ivron seemed to ponder for a moment. "Reuy wasn't exactly a force of nature, and we hurried him out pretty quickly. Would he have had time to set anything?"

Angela turned the idea over and over in her head, until she came to a decision. "Are either of you wizards? No. We've been trained to look for these things by the best wizard in the land. We should go see, at the very least. If we can get in, and find a scryer's glass, I can pin-point Robert, and no one will have to search. I might even be able to send a message to him."

"You think you can do this?"

"I'm confident I can find him."

She got reluctant nods for a response. She turned away before she let her face betray her real feelings. She could do it, if they got in, if they could find a scryer's glass, and if she could find something of Robert's to use as an Origin allowing her to create the link necessary to find him.

❈ ❈ ❈

WALLACE FOLLOWED EVERYONE out the door and across the courtyard. He really didn't know why he was going, beyond the vain hope that he might be able to help. So far, he felt pretty useless. He had no idea what he could see or do that the other two couldn't.

Sure. Gerard was limited to essentially elemental magic, but in that field, he excelled. And Angela, she was the best of them at the scryer's arts, illusions, shields. Except where she was actively opposed, if she couldn't see something, it likely wasn't there. Wallace knew she had recently worked with Monteous on overcoming opposition, as well.

No, they didn't need him to help them break into this dead wizard's Laboratory.

But he followed anyway.

It was even colder than the night before, he thought. And there was something in the air. The clouds above loomed heavy and gray. He suspected snow would soon arrive. It was cold enough, he was shivering even in the thick coat he'd donned before they left the warmth of the Manor.

He saw their destination across the courtyard as soon as he stepped out. A long, low building, with a black tile roof which would likely prove resistant to the occasional overeager blazes to which some wizards were prone. Few windows were cut into its stone walls.

Hanging above the door, however, was the unmistakable Guild symbol. Two lightning bolts, crossed through a ball of fire.

Even as he crossed the courtyard, Wallace started looking for Weaves. The others would likely see anything first, but he needed the practice. Any excuse to use anything he knew, and searching out the Weaves of others was among the first things he'd been taught. It took a long time to master, Monteous had said. "And it's crucial, my lad, to staying alive in this dangerous world, if you are a wizard."

They came to a halt a few yards from the building. He stepped in near Angela and Gerard to listen, but for several moments, they said nothing.

Then Demetrius stepped up beside Angela. "Do you see anything?"

"There is a general Weave that is often used to keep people from being too eager to enter a wizard's Laboratory. It's not dangerous, but it helps people decide that they don't really need to see the wizard today. It's of little use against another wizard, though."

Wallace saw it, wrapped around the door and across the windows. A light Weave, easily penetrated by anyone with the willpower to persevere against it. He noticed something else, too. Something he hadn't seen before.

But Angela had already seen it. "There's a second Weave, as well. This one is aimed at wizards, but it's poorly made, intentionally or not, I don't know. It will be easy to unravel. If a wizard were to walk through it unaware, which is unlikely, it would wrap itself around him and cut off his access to the energies around him."

Wallace found himself nodding. Nasty if you were running into battle against another wizard, but not fatal if you weren't. Just uncomfortable. He could even see where to start pulling on the threads to unravel it. Angela was right about its quality.

"Was he in a hurry?" Wallace asked himself.

"What, Wallace?" Angela asked.

"I just wondered if he was in a hurry when he made that Weave."

Ivron, from behind them said, "We did hurry him out of here. He was really reluctant to come with us."

Angela shrugged and began to pull the threads apart, one by one, until the Weave unraveled. Wallace watched carefully. Monteous had warned him many times about taking care unraveling a Weave. Carelessness could cause the Weave to fall apart, releasing its energie in an explosion that could kill the wizard, or worse. But Angela pulled each thread precisely, and Wallace watched the energies being released into the world in a controlled fashion.

Despite the fact Wallace knew the delicacy of the work, Wallace found himself wishing Angela would hurry. Fingers of cold had found their way through his coat. He wanted to get inside.

But she didn't hurry, and her careful work paid off eventually as the last thread of the Weave vanished.

"Now, for the other Weave."

This one was quicker, and easier, but Wallace still paid attention. If he'd learned anything from his parents while growing up, it was that paying attention to the details while making wine was crucial to getting the flavor you wanted. Monteous had commented on several occasions about his attention to detail.

Wallace understood you could never know when you might miss something crucial. With wizardry, it wasn't just the flavor of the wine at stake. It could be your life, or the lives of the people around you.

But Angela was deft at unraveling the Weaves.

When she finished with the second Weave, Gerard walked quickly up to the door. "Shall I open it?"

"I don't see anything else. Do you Wallace?"

Wallace looked again, but could not see any Weaves, and said as much.

"Alright," Gerard said, and then pushed open the door.

The room beyond was dark. For a moment, Wallace thought he saw a shimmer around the inside of the door frame, but it quickly faded. He stared hard at the door frame, using every trick he knew, but could not make the silvery shimmer he'd seen reappear.

He thought he'd better say something, anyway. "Uh, Angela? Did you see anything when he opened the door?"

"No, did you?"

"I thought I saw something. A silvery shimmer around the door frame."

"Do you see it now?"

"No. It was there only a moment."

Demetrius quickly stepped in front of them both, blocking their way to the door. "I can't let you go in."

"What do you mean?" Angela asked. "There's nothing there."

"In Monteous's absence, I'm charged with your safety. And if young Wallace here thought he saw something, I'm inclined to believe he did see something. If there is one thing I know about magic, I know you don't go playing around with it if you're not sure what it is."

Gerard stepped up. "Look Demetrius, the three of us know what we're doing, far more than you do. It's likely what Wallace saw was residual energies from the other Weaves. If that's not what he saw, and was instead another Weave, he should still be able to see it. Once you see a Weave, you can always see it."

"What I know is that the three of you are apprentices, still, and don't know everything yet. The wizard that lived here passed his tests long ago. He may not have had the power of Monteous or Orliss, but I'm sure if Wallace saw something and now doesn't, there's an explanation for it, and we might not like that explanation. I won't let you three go in there."

Wallace watched Angela's face grow red, and she stepped up into Demetrius's face. Her voice was low, but strong and steady. "You made me leave Robert there on that shelf. He could be anywhere, could have anyone chasing him. I'm not going to let a chance to find him get away from me."

And then she walked right past Demetrius, fast enough and forceful enough, even in the dress she was wearing, that Demetrius could do nothing to stop her.

Wallace stared as hard as he could at the doorway, trying to recall whatever he'd seen. He hoped he was wrong, that he hadn't seen anything other than residual energies.

Demetrius turned to run after her.

By the time he turned, and by the time Wallace saw the Weave spring across the door right as Angela stepped through it, it was far too late for his shout to save her.

For a long moment, she hung suspended in the doorway, and then fell slowly to the ground, gracefully. Wallace would have said unconscious. The Weave, its power spent, dissipated. Wallace rushed to her side, brushing past Demetrius. Gerard reached her nearly as quickly, and they rolled her over so that her face was no longer on the floor.

Wallace watched her for a moment, saw her chest rise, and let out the breath he hadn't realized he'd held in. She was alive. Unconscious, but alive.

He looked around the room, and didn't see any other Weaves. They had a Laboratory, and likely all the tools they needed, but Angela's condition fell squarely on his shoulders. If he'd only been fast enough, or sure about what he'd seen.

He felt Demetrius at his shoulder. "Let's get her inside where she can be warm, at least. It is safe to move her?"

"It's safe. The Weave is gone."

"What did it do to her?"

"I don't know. If Robert were here, he might know. Is there another wizard you can trust?"

"Not without Monteous's guidance. His supporters were reluctant to be public in their support."

Ivron stepped up to help carry her. "Then we shall just have to hope she recovers on her own, or that we can find Robert another way. Demetrius, sometime soon, you're going to have to tell me why he's so important."

"Once he's back in our care."

The four of them lifted her, and carried her across the courtyard and back into the manor, and up to her room where they lay her on the bed. The maid shooed them out. "Go find a physician, at the very least."

Ivron and Demetrius went off to do just that. Gerard turned to

Wallace then, as they waited out in the hall. "Why don't we go invest-igate that Lab?"

Wallace peeked into Angela's room, then nodded. All he wanted was to crawl into a deep, dark hole and disappear. The lab sounded as good a place as any.

CHAPTER 12

DESPITE HIS FULL belly, and the energie it had already given him, what Robert really wanted was a full day of rest. The fatigue still lurked just below the surface. Any lengthy Work or Weave would wear him out. But he felt far more capable than he had just a half hour ago.

He pushed his plate aside and let his thoughts turn to figuring out what to do next. He didn't know where Angela and the others had gone. He didn't know where Monteous was. He didn't know what the whole thing was about. And he didn't know where to go. He didn't even have a lab to work in to try to figure these things out.

The innkeep chose just that moment to burst in the room. "You are no Master!"

Robert stood quickly, knocking his chair backward, and grabbed the rod off the table. "What are you talking about?"

"You told me you were a master, but you're just an apprentice." His face was red with embarrassment or fury. Robert couldn't tell.

"I never told you I was a master."

That stopped the innkeep dead, for a moment. "You came in, waving that rod."

"I did, and I can use it." Robert thrust it out in front of him, in what he hoped was a threatening gesture. The innkeep didn't have any metal on him for Robert to use it against, but he didn't imagine the man would know the difference.

It was quickly obvious that he didn't. "Please, please, no."

Robert thought of something. "How did you know I wasn't a Master?"

"A soldier just came in looking for you, describing you. He called you an apprentice."

Robert's heart jumped. He could feel his pulse quickening. "Is there another way out?"

"Not past the soldier. He saw me come in here. He knows you are here."

Robert needed time to think, and he needed to see this soldier. See if it was the one chasing him. Of course, there could be many soldiers looking for him.

He motioned with the rod for the innkeep to move over against the wall, and the innkeep slid past him, staying as far away from the rod as he could. He was looking at it like it was a snake, or a sword.

Robert went to the door and opened it slightly, trying to peek out, hoping the soldier wasn't too attentive.

But when Robert cast an eye over him, he saw that he'd been wrong and the soldier was very attentive, and he was heading for the room. At least, Robert thought, it wasn't the one that chased him out of the Lab. Maybe this one would fall for the same trick.

Robert stepped off to the side of the door, trying to give him the best chance to run out of the room. If he could just get the soldier far enough into the room, Robert could slip out the door, and shut it, give himself a little chance to escape, maybe heat the handle so that it would burn anyone trying to pull it open.

Whatever he did, he'd have to do it fast.

"Innkeep." He motioned to a chair with the rod. "Sit."

And then, the soldier did something Robert did not expect. He knocked. Politely.

"Who is it?"

"I'm Horuth."

"I don't know you."

"Of course you don't. May I come in and explain?"

Very polite for a soldier, especially one trying to capture him, or worse. It was strange and unnerving, is what it was, and Robert didn't like it one bit. But, he told himself, anyone trying to take him would just bust through the door. They wouldn't have knocked. *Is someone trying to help me?*

Robert stepped back away from the door, almost across the room from it, before he answered. "Open the door slowly, and draw no weapon."

Horuth did as he was told. The door opened slowly, slower even, than Robert had wanted, and then the soldier stepped into the room with his hands up, showing they were empty. He shut the door with his boot.

"So, who are you?"

"I'm Horuth. I'm a soldier attached to Ivron Meningale, who is a friend of Demetrius, whom you may know, and the Master Wizard Monteous Roarke, who I am sure you do know."

Demetrius. That name. The name on the parchment scrap. *What's going on?*

"Why are you here?"

"If you are an apprentice named Robert, I'm looking for you."

"And why would you be looking for me?" Robert wished the soldier had volunteered the information.

"Ivron sent me to look for you, to keep you out of the hands of Orliss Kilore, and to bring you back if possible."

"Really?" Robert, for the first time, dared to hope something might go right.

"Well," he said, and then a contrite look stole across his face, "not exactly. We were supposed to watch and see what happened, and bring back news if possible. But you managed to escape the lab on your own, so we followed, and took out the two thugs Orliss had left at the lab as they tried to follow you."

Robert relaxed a bit, letting the rod fall to his waste. "So I'm safe here."

"For the moment, perhaps. They will come looking, however."

The Innkeep spoke up. "You're not staying here."

Robert looked at the innkeep with the angriest face he could muster. "Sit down." The innkeep did just that, and just as quickly.

"Come sit for a moment," Robert said. "We don't have to continue to stand."

"I'd rather not."

"Fine. Do you know where my friends are?"

"Two young men, younger than yourself, and a young lady?"

"Yes."

"They were with Ivron and Demetrius when Ivron sent us to watch for you."

Demetrius... that name again. Where had he heard that name? And then it came to him. The parchment. They'd been out searching for him. How had the others come to be in his company? He knew what he had to do now.

"Could you take me to them?"

"I probably should. The City Guard don't particularly care for dead men in the streets, and we left a couple of 'em there."

"No reason to wait then." Robert took his coat from the chair he'd hung it on and pulled it on.

The innkeep stood. "What about my money? You owe me for the food."

Robert turned slowly, anger rising in him. He could feel his hand wanting to shake. He looked straight at the pudgy, balding man, looked him right in the eyes and held him there for long moments before saying anything. Robert saw the sheen of sweat on the innkeep's forehead thicken.

It will start rolling off in drops if we stand here any longer.

Robert tried to keep his voice even despite his anger at the man. "I think we are even."

"But..."

"You sold me to this man for nothing. You get nothing."

"He's a friend to you." The man cowered back. "He came to help you."

Robert stepped toward him, raising the rod. "But I didn't know him, and you certainly didn't know. You were just angry at me for your own mistakes. You would have sold me to my enemies just as easily."

The man sat back in his chair. Drops of sweat rolled down his face. "What do you want?"

"It's not what I want. It's what you want. If you would keep your inn, you would be wise to keep your mouth shut. If I find you've told anyone I was here, I will return and make you wish you'd held your tongue." *What am I saying? Threatening the man? If Monteous heard me...*

"I... I promise." The innkeep's voice cracked as he spoke. No one took a threat from a wizard lightly. Not even if the wizard were an apprentice. Common folk used stories of angry wizards to frighten their children into behaving.

"Look, if you keep quiet, Monteous will pay you double what I owe you. If anybody asks, just tell them you don't remember seeing me. Whatever is going on is bigger than either of us. I'm just a pawn. You don't want to be involved."

The man nodded, and Robert turned his back to him. He worked to quell his anger. It wasn't easy.

When he noticed Horuth again, Robert saw something in his face, something had changed. Robert couldn't tell if it was respect, or fear.

He hated himself in that moment. Monteous had drilled into him the proper uses of their powers, as well as improper, and Robert knew his behavior fell into the latter category, even if he hadn't actually done anything to the man.

Horuth opened the door, and looked out into the common room, using a hand to keep Robert from going out first. "If I'm to keep you safe," he whispered, "I go first." And then he led Robert through the door.

Robert turned back to look at the innkeep as he walked through the common room, and the innkeep still sat in the chair. Robert suspected the man would sit there until long after Robert and his guide left the inn.

❋❋❋

ROBERT FELT AMAZED at how easy their exit from the city seemed. They stopped first to purchase a cloak that would not announce Robert as a wizard's apprentice. Then Horuth brought Robert to a stable where Horuth had left his horse. There, they purchased another horse on Ivron's credit, and rode out. Robert hunched over on the ride, trying to keep his face hidden as much as possible.

Robert felt sure Orliss would have someone at the gates waiting for him, but no one blocked their way. Horuth suggested that maybe Orliss expected one young man alone and on foot, not two men on horseback. Robert allowed as how that might be the case.

But in his heart, he felt it was too easy. He was constantly looking for Weaves, or a Work. Something might tell Orliss where he was without having to have men do it. Robert couldn't see anything obvious. He kept looking however.

As they exited the City, they kept to the road. "We'll cross the river on the ferry," said Horuth. "Then we'll head northeast to the estate my Lord keeps in the forest."

"Do you think it's safe there?"

"It's as safe as anywhere. My Lord keeps a fairly large garrison there when he's visiting."

"He just visits there?"

"Yes, my Lord Ivron is from Antimonch. He keeps the estate here for when he has dealings in the City."

"I've never been to Antimonch."

"It's beautiful when the sun rises over the ocean, and you can hear the surf rolling in, and taste the salt on the wind. I miss it whenever we have to come inland."

"I shall have to visit one day."

"Maybe that visit will be sooner than you think?"

"I don't think so. There are probably still years ahead of me before I can go where I will."

"Years?"

"I'm nearly done with my apprenticeship, if I can pass the tests."

"And then aren't you free to make your own way?"

"Hardly. Once the tests are passed, you get additional training from the Guild before they let you join. Until you join, I'm told the members keep the applicants busy with innumerable chores, to test your conviction."

"You would think finishing your apprenticeship and passing the tests would be a good indication of your conviction."

"Apparently, it's not."

They rode in silence for a while after that, having little more to talk about. Horuth knew nothing about Angela, Gerard and Wallace, save that they were at the estate when he'd left the previous night. Robert had asked about Demetrius, and Horuth told him he only knew Demetrius and Ivron were friends, and that Ivron and Monteous were friends. Robert thought that might make Demetrius and Monteous friends, but he resigned himself to not knowing until after he arrived.

Finally, they approached the river, and the small group of buildings built near the river to service the ferry. Robert made to urge his horse into a trot, but Horuth put a hand out. "Wait, something's not right here."

Robert looked again, and saw what Horuth was talking about. Several armed men stood near the ferry. A couple of them, having seen riders on the road, were already watching them. Robert knew what they were doing there.

"They're looking for me."

"You're right. Can't you do something to take care of them?"

"If I had a staff, I could probably work something up, but all I've got is this Rod, and it can't guide enough energie to do anything to all of them at once."

"Then we have to run, north."

Robert saw up ahead that a road ran north along the river, probably half the distance between the ferry and where they stood. On horseback, they could get to the road before the men at the ferry. *But what if there are more of them, or they have bows?*

"Can we make it?"

"If we run now. Fly!"

Robert urged his horse to run as fast as he could, and the horse took off. He heard the hooves of Horuth's mount pounding the ground behind him. The soldiers started shouting and running toward them. None appeared armed with bows, or they weren't really interested in killing him. Whichever was the case, Robert felt grateful for that bit of good fortune.

Robert saw they'd make the turnoff easily ahead of the soldiers. But then the soldiers started pointing and shouting. They turned and ran back to the ferry, apparently realizing at nearly the last moment their quarry would turn away from them.

Horuth shouted at him. "Keep going! They're going back for their mounts!"

In moments, Robert and Horuth reached the turnoff and started down the north running road. They left the soldiers behind them, still running back for their own horses.

"We'll have some time. If we can get far enough ahead, we'll make it across the river before they can catch us."

Robert said nothing, and concentrated on guiding his horse. He'd learned to ride when he was young, but he was out of practice. Being an apprentice wizard didn't lend itself to spending lots of time on horseback. The two horses pounded their way down the road.

Eventually, Horuth told him to slow, and appeared to Robert to be looking to the side of the road for something.

"What are you looking for?"

"There is a marker that will lead us to a friend in the woods. He will take us across the river, though we'll have to leave the horses with him."

Soon, he motioned to Robert. "There it is." He pointed. All Robert saw was an innocuous array of stones at the side of the road that appeared to him to be randomly tossed to the ground.

"The stones?"

"Yes. Dismount. We'll have to lead the horses."

Robert dismounted, and followed Horuth, who was leading his

horse through the brush into the forest beyond. The brush looked impenetrable, but a few feet into it, Robert broke free onto a trail that appeared to lead down toward the river.

They walked for several minutes, and then, Robert smelled something. Woodsmoke. *Someone lives out here.* The smoke grew thicker and thicker, though, as they made their way down the trail. He thought it was too thick to just be someone's fireplace.

He'd just about decided to say something when they broke into a clearing. In front of them, the cottage that had stood there, probably intact only hours before, was a smoking ruin.

CHAPTER 13

A HEAD OF ROBERT, Horuth quickly mounted his horse and spurred it to gallop for the ruin. A chimney still stood, and the stone walls, for the most part, remained upright, but the roof had burned away.

When Horuth reached the gutted cottage, he jumped off the horse and ran around to what Robert assumed was the front, and Robert lost sight of him. Robert picked up his pace, urging his horse to go along with him. He didn't like being out of sight of Horuth in this clearing. Whoever had done this could still be around. Robert had a hard time believing it an accident.

As he approached, he took hold of the reigns of Horuth's horse so that it didn't go wandering, and then lead both horses to the front of the cottage.

What Robert saw nearly made him sick. A large man lay on the ground in front of the house. His fingers, the ones that remained, appeared broken. His torso was bare, and everywhere upon it, were the marks of knives and boots. The man's eye sockets stared up at Robert, empty.

Robert turned away, bent over and put his hands on his knees. His stomach wanted him to vomit, but he refused to give in to it.

Horuth came up beside him. "We have to leave. They tortured him to find out where your friends went — or as a warning."

Robert stood up a bit and looked to Horuth. "Do you think he said anything?"

"He was a strong man. I would like to believe he held his tongue, but..." Horuth shook his head. After a moment's pause, he said, "They burned his wife alive inside the cottage."

"Why? Why would they do this?"

Horuth shook his head. "I do not know. Powerful men do whatever they wish to get what they want. Good common men like myself, like Ergin here, we can do little about it. We must go. They will not be long."

"Where do we go now?"

"We go down by the river. He has a boat there. We can use that to take us across. We'll have to tie the horses and send someone back for them."

Robert looked back at the man on the ground, a man he didn't know, tortured and killed, in part, because of him and his friends. *Does this fate await us all?*

Robert had to clench his fists to keep them from shaking. He resolved then, that it would not be his fate, or the fate of Angela, Wallace, or Gerard. *I'll do whatever it takes to make you pay for this, Orliss.*

Robert turned to mount his horse, and found Horuth already in the saddle.

Horuth put the palm of his hand to his forehead and held it there while he looked down at his friend. "Sleep well the long sleep, Ergin." Then he looked back over his shoulder at the woods from where they'd come. "They come. Ride!"

Robert needed no further urging, and sent his horse after Horuth's, pounding down the slope to the river. He looked back, and saw Orliss's men mounting their horses to give chase.

When they came to the edge of the river, Horuth led them right to the boat, and jumped from his horse. "Help me push this thing into the river."

Robert jumped down and put what strength he had into pushing the boat into the water. Too slowly, it seemed, it moved. Robert once turned to look back, but Horuth growled at him. "Don't look back, just push."

Right when Robert began to worry that they would never make it, it got easier and easier as the stern of the boat hit the water, and then they were running and the boat was all the way in the water.

"Jump in."

Robert splashed through the icy water. It spilled into his boots and soaked his pants. His first jump fell short, held down by his inundated boots. He gave it another jump, and managed to pull himself into the boat. He could hear the horses of Orliss's men thundering down the hill.

"Stop," one of them yelled.

Horuth kept pushing and grunting, muscles bulging, until, at the last minute, he jumped into the boat, and they were away, floating down river.

"Help me with these oars."

Robert helped him settle the oars in the locks, and Horuth took a position toward the center of the boat. "Sit. Get down in case they shoot."

"You know how to make this thing go?"

"I've seen it done."

The horses carrying Orliss's men splashed into the water, but by then, Robert and Horuth had floated too far out into the river for the horses to follow.

One of the men held out his sword, waving it at Robert and Horuth. "We'll find you, apprentice, wherever you go!"

Robert pulled out his iron rod and held it below the edge of the boat, so the soldier wouldn't see it. He made the same Weave he'd made earlier, wrapping it around the soldiers sword. It went much quicker now that he had some energie to work with.

But this time, instead of just holding the sword in place, Robert pulled on the threads of the Weave, yanking the sword from the soldier's hand, and then spun it around, pointing it at the soldier's neck.

"You tell Orliss," he shouted across the widening gap, "you tell him to release Monteous, or he will be wishing by every crown in the Seven

Kingdoms that he had been the one in that cottage up there when you set it ablaze."

Robert floated the sword to him, across the water, and dropped it into the boat. The soldier watched them for a bit, then turned and ordered his troop back to the road.

Horuth laughed a grim sort of laugh when they'd gone. "That was a neat trick, Robert. Could you have done it to all of them?"

"One at a time."

"Ah, well. You know, it probably wasn't very wise to threaten him."

Robert thought about it, and decided he didn't care. "You're probably right, but over the last few days, my Master has been kidnapped, I've been attacked, chased, seen people I don't know tortured because of me..."

Horuth looked him straight in the eye. "Don't go thinkin' that last. It's not because of you. Orliss wants something, and you're in the way. Ergin got in the way too."

Robert nodded. "Alright. Orliss is still going to pay."

"Right you are. But it will take more than me and you to make it happen."

The boat nudged up on the other side of the river, and they got out and pulled the boat up out of the water. Robert's legs and feet, everything below his knees, were freezing. He hoped wherever they were going, would have a fire and a place to rest.

"How far is it from here?"

"Only a couple miles through the forest."

"Won't they know that's where we're going?"

"They might suspect. But we should be safe enough."

Horuth set off into the forest, and Robert followed behind him. Robert had changed, something about opening that portal had changed him. No matter how angry he'd become in the past, he'd never let it get so far out of hand that he would threaten people. But he'd threatened two men since waking that morning. He thought about it all during their hike through the forest, and could only come to one conclusion. Whatever had happened, he had to control his anger. Anger was dangerous. Wizardry required complete control.

I controlled it for so long. I thought I conquered it.

Robert thought back to the time just after Monteous had taken him in. Robert remembered his frequent outbursts. Often, Monteous urged him to remember that wizards who lost their temper when something went wrong never lived very long.

Robert started running through the control exercises Monteous taught him, hoping they would help.

WHEN THEY APPROACHED the estate, Robert understood why Horuth thought they'd be safe there. It looked more like a keep. It would take a good sized force to assault it, and few beyond the King had such a force to call upon.

As soon as the sentries recognized Horuth, the gates opened for them, and shouts could be heard urging a runner to bring Ivron.

By the time they entered, and the gate shut behind them, two men were exiting the manor and heading straight for them. They were of an age, older than Robert, but not so old that there was any gray in their hair. Their manner, however, couldn't have been more dissimilar. The one on the right held himself like a Lord, and probably was the Lord of this estate. Robert guessed that one was Ivron. The other was thinner, and held himself almost as if ready to fight or flee, even here where they were supposedly safe.

That one, as soon as he saw Robert, and Robert was sure that it was himself who was his focus, broke into a grin and a run almost immediately. If forced to guess, Robert would have said the man was relieved to see him. It struck Robert as odd, since he'd never seen the man before.

The man slowed as he neared Robert, and then held out his hand.

Robert took it. Wiry as the man looked, his grip was strong. "Robert. I am glad that you made it here."

Robert pulled his hand free. "I'm sorry, but I don't know who you are."

"Of course. Forgive me. My name is Demetrius."

This made sense, but also made Robert wary. "So you're Demetrius. Were you Monteous's patron. Did you set him up for that kidnapping?"

"No, no. I'm not his patron. I've been in his employ for longer than you've been his apprentice, since before he rescued you."

"How is it that I've never seen you or heard of you before?"

The other man, Ivron, finally made his way to them. "Because, Robert, wizards have networks all across this land that keep eyes on various things, mostly on other wizards. They don't trust each other, and they use men like our friend Demetrius to cause their rivals consternation." He clapped his hand on Demetrius shoulder.

"I'm hurt that you would describe my profession in that manner." Demetrius laughed. "I would swear to the King himself that Monteous has never used me that way." He turned back to Robert, and then looked him up and down. "You look like an icicle. We can talk about this inside. Also, there are other things we need to discuss, and it's much warmer by the fire."

Ivron looked at Horuth. "You come, too. I need to hear how you managed to get out of the city with him."

The manor was warm indeed. Ivron led them to a sitting room where he passed out some brandy and urged them to sip before they started talking. Robert glanced at Horuth, who looked like he felt a bit out of place. The man clearly had never held crystal goblets before. He looked like he was trying not to crush the one in his hand.

When they'd all taken chairs, Robert found himself sitting across from Ivron. Demetrius sat to Robert's left, Horuth to his right.

Ivron seemed to study Robert for a moment. "Before we get to Demetrius's ancient history, I'd like to hear how you got out of the city. Georg told us you escaped the Lab on your own, so we know that part."

Robert couldn't decide where to start. Fortunately, Horuth began to talk, reporting everything from finding Robert in the inn to buying the horses, to running from Orliss's men at the ferry. When he started to detail Ergin's murder, his voice grew cold, and Robert thought he might stop. But Horuth pressed on through until he told of Ergin's wife's death.

Demetrius interrupted at that point, anger wild on his face. "I'll have that man's testicles and nail them up where everyone can see them." Robert felt the same way, even still. Apparently, his own resolve to avenge Ergin's death was more than just momentary anger. He'd have to think about that.

Horuth waited a moment, to make sure Demetrius had finished, then related the rest of the tale, including the part where Robert Worked the sword from the leader of Orliss's thugs and threatened the man with it. Robert caught Demetrius smiling at that. Horuth then finished his tale with an account of the trek through the forest.

When he was done, a maid came into the room and brought dry trousers and socks for Horuth and Robert. She left and Robert and Horuth changed into the dry clothing. The maid came back soon after and took the wet clothes from the room. Robert hoped she hadn't been watching him change.

When they sat back down, Robert realized he hadn't seen Angela, or the others. "Horuth said my friends are here, but I haven't seen them."

The two men looked at each other, and Robert suddenly got worried. Neither of the two looked like they wanted to talk. Eventually, Demetrius lost, and turned to Robert.

"There is a Laboratory in the yard that belonged to a wizard that betrayed us when we went to try to rescue Monteous. Gerard and Wallace are out there taking inventory."

"What about Angela."

"When they tried to enter the Laboratory, it seemed they were very careful in checking for Weaves. She removed two of them. The three of them thought there were no more. But when she stepped through the door, she collapsed."

Robert's body tensed, and his heart raced. The last time he'd felt this, his parents... He refused to finish the thought. "She's not dead." *She can't be!*

"No, she's not dead. She appears to be in a very deep sleep. She breathes, and her heart continues to beat, but she doesn't move or respond to anything."

Robert stood quickly. "Can you take me to her? I need to see her."

"Do you think you can do something for her?" Ivron asked. "We still need to discuss the situation we're in."

"Please, take me to her. I might be able to help her. You don't need me here."

"No, Robert, we do need you here. There are things you need to know." Ivron paused.

Robert stood, waiting.

"But I can see," Ivron continued, "you probably aren't going to be able to think straight until you've seen her."

Demetrius stood, and led Robert out of the room. Ivron didn't follow, and kept Horuth with him.

Robert followed Demetrius up the stairs, wishing he would hurry, but Demetrius seemed immune to the mental shoves that Robert kept throwing at him. The hallway Demetrius led him down was decorated with a dark paneled wood, trophies of various animals from the hunt, and several paintings. Robert ignored it all.

Demetrius stopped at a richly carved door and pushed it open. Robert pushed right past him, practically running up to the side of the bed.

Angela lay there, her raven hair spread off to one side, thick blankets pulled up to her chin keeping her warm. Her eyes were closed, and she was breathing slowly and evenly. He barely noticed a different maid, who had been sitting in a chair on the far side of the room, stand up and walk to the foot of the bed.

"She just lies there, not moving."

Robert bent down close to her, took in the color of her skin, and looked for any little marks or tags. Monteous had told him about

Works that could be attached to the tips of projectiles like darts, and would remain behind in the victim after the dart was removed.

But he found no holes, no indication that anything had happened to her at all.

Robert looked up for a moment, staring across the room. Whatever Weave or Work that held her, it was small and not very powerful, or he would be able to feel it. He should be able to feel it, to see it when he looked for it.

Was she drained? Had the wizard somehow drained her power? He didn't think so. That would be an incredible Weave, and Robert had never heard of such a thing even being possible. There were ways to drain others, but any apprentice learned to guard against that early.

He turned to Demetrius. "You said Gerard and Wallace were out in the Laboratory?"

"Yes."

"Could you take me to them? I need to see what this wizard had in his Lab. There may be Works in there that will let me uncover whatever he's done to her."

"You think you will find something there?"

"Possibly. Whatever Weave he set seems to be intended to stop an intruder without killing them. You have to be able to see a Weave to undo it. None of the normal ways of seeing the Weave are working, so it would seem to me that he's got a Work there that will let us see it."

Whether I can use the Work is a different question entirely.

"Follow me, then."

CHAPTER 14

WHEN ROBERT ENTERED the Laboratory, Wallace greeted him with a shout and a grin. "You made it out! We didn't know if you'd be found and captured while you slept."

"Angela's Weave was good. They didn't see me at all, though they certainly acted like they expected me to return there for some reason. They kept men there all night."

"How did you escape?"

"Why don't we talk about that later." He didn't want to talk about it at all. The vision of Ergin's corpse was still fresh. He thought it would haunt him in his sleep for the rest of his life.

Gerard stepped over and grabbed Robert's hand, then surprisingly, gave it a good warm shake. "It's good to see you. Did you see Angela?"

"Yes, that's why I'm down here. There's got to be a Work or something down here that will let me see whatever has trapped her in her head."

"Trapped her in her head? I thought it was just that she'd been drained. She looked just like you did after you opened the portal."

"No, she's not drained. It doesn't seem like a real sleep to me. Her color is good, her breathing steady. I think it's something else. Did either of you see anything when it happened?"

"Wallace thought he saw something around the door frame for a moment before Angela entered..."

"And neither of you believed me."

Gerard glared at Wallace. "Neither of us saw it, and it was gone, we thought."

Robert looked around the room, looked at the doorway. "Arguing about it won't wake her up."

The Laboratory was smaller than Monteous's, but it was organized much the same way. Beakers and phials and other apparatus on shelves. A workbench stood, centered toward one end, a stone "stage" near it. This wizard had never had an apprentice.

"Tell me what you've found in here so far."

"Mostly the same tools we had in Monteous's lab. There are some books here that Monteous didn't have, but there are quite a few that Monteous had that aren't here. Other than that Weave that got placed on Angela, I'd think he was a pretty minor wizard."

"So no odd looking Works?"

"Oh, there are more than a few of those. I don't understand what most of them are for."

While they talked, Demetrius strolled around the room.

"Demetrius, how soon do you think before Orliss sends his henchmen here? How much time do we have to search this place?"

Demetrius cocked his head sideways a bit, apparently in thought. "It would depend on if those men figured out you were coming here or not. Ivron is fairly well known, and it's known that he's a friend of Monteous. If they managed to get my name out of Ergin, then it could be tonight, or never. They may just post sentries to try to catch us if we leave. It suits his purposes to have us locked up here, though I think he would prefer to have you in hand, Robert."

"Why is that?"

"He knows now, or suspects, I would think, that you can open a portal."

"That won't do us any good here, I don't think. We need certain materials for that."

"He won't know you don't have them. It'll come down to what he thinks is the greater risk. Trying to take this estate and failing, or your ability to walk right out should he decide to trap us here."

"What's the shortest time, do you think, before we'll know what he's going to try?"

"I'd say a few more hours. He probably already has a scout out there watching us right now."

"Why don't you see if Ivron will join us down here? If we need to discuss our strategy, let's do it here while I search for a way to help Angela. We'll need her." *I need her.* She'd looked so vulnerable up in that bed.

Demetrius gave him a bow and hurried off. *What was that about, I wonder?*

"Wallace, Gerard, you should start going through the books you've never seen before. Just browse through them quickly, looking for anything that might refer to the condition Angela is in and what you saw happen."

They nodded. "And you?" Gerard asked.

"I'm going to look through this place like you two did. Maybe I'll see something you didn't. And if I find nothing, I'll join you with those books. I don't think we have much time."

The three of them went to work. Gerard started pulling books from the bookcase, then handed them to Wallace who took them to the workbench and stacked them up. When there were nearly a dozen books on the stack, they each took one and began to skim through them. Robert hoped they'd find something quickly.

He turned his attention to the Works that lined one wall.

Most of them, he recognized from either reading about them, or from making them with Monteous. A scryer's glass, various types of focuses, some metal, others glass or wood, a bottle that would hold a dozen times its volume in liquid. But, there were a few that he didn't recognize, and he collected these and brought them to the workbench.

"While you're looking through those books, keep an eye out for these items. Perhaps we'll find out what they do."

A knock on the door interrupted him just as he was about to start looking through the apparatus. He went to the door and opened it to find Ivron and Demetrius standing there. Robert ushered them in.

"You knock on doors of your own estate?"

"Is it a good idea to walk in on a wizard?"

Robert laughed. "Of course not. You might wind up with singed hair, or worse, as something else entirely."

"Exactly. So I knock. Have you found anything?"

Robert sighed. "Not yet, but we've only really just started. I've got Gerard and Wallace looking through the books we don't recognize. We might find something.

"Would you mind me asking you a question or two about this wizard?"

"Go ahead. He's not here to get upset about it."

"The three of us, after looking around here, sort of got the impression that he's not a very powerful wizard."

"No, he wasn't, at least not that I knew."

"Did you know he was working for Orliss? I'm assuming that's what you meant when you called him a traitor."

"No, I didn't know. He warned Orliss we were coming, and I only found out about it when we arrived at Orliss's estate."

"Orliss's estate?"

"Oh, right. You don't know yet."

Robert listened as Ivron filled him in on the disaster at Orliss's estate that more than likely also lead to the ambush at Monteous's Laboratory. At the point where he told about Demetrius stepping through the portal, Robert interrupted him. "Okay, so it would seem, Demetrius, that perhaps our opening of the portal was fortuitous in that it not only saved your skin, but allowed you to save ours."

"That's one way to look at it," said Demetrius. "Perhaps Orliss knew you were going to open the portal and he sent his men to try to stop you from doing it. Perhaps, if you'd done nothing at all, as I suggested, he wouldn't have sent men to get you."

"Perhaps. Did anyone tell you that we had a visit from Orliss the day before we opened the portal?" asked Robert.

"No. Maybe you're right, then. Sounds like he might have been after you all along, though why he didn't just take you then..."

"We'll have to ask him before we kill him."

Robert saw Gerard and Wallace look up at him as he realized what he'd just said. Surprise was about the least of the emotions that crossed their faces. *I don't care what they think. Orliss took Monteous from me, and now, he's taken Angela, too.*

"It may just come to that, but let's concentrate on getting Monteous back, first."

Robert realized he'd strayed far from his goal. "First, we need to help Angela. Unless you have another wizard around here, we're going to need her help. To get Monteous back, we need to find him, and she's the best of us at scrying."

Ivron motioned for Demetrius to follow him. "Let's leave these three to their search. If we can avoid sending scouts to every possible location that Orliss might have Monteous, we need to try, and these three can't do what they need to do with us interrupting them. We can't make real plans until we know where he is."

When they were out the door, Robert went back to looking through the various apparatus the previous resident of this Laboratory had kept around, and he didn't see anything unusual.

He returned to the bench, and picked up a book that lay on the unread pile. "Find anything yet?"

With his nose still buried in a book, Wallace said, "No."

Robert started flipping through the book he'd picked up, looking at every page, but only quickly, reading captions and bits and pieces that looked like they might hold some promise. As he read, he realized that many of the Works and Weaves described were among the list of Works and Weaves that were proscribed by Guild law. One he stumbled across would allow the maker of the Work to compel the target to do whatever the wizard wanted, even at great distances. Another could make a person appear to have been killed, but would leave them alive inside their body, feeling everything that happened to them, but unable to do anything about it.

He finished that book, finding nothing that matched the symptoms Angela was showing, and picked up another.

Wallace looked up from his book to examine the Works arrayed on the bench, picked one out and set it aside. It looked much like a portal Focus, only flatter and wider, and with strips of metal embedded around the edges.

Robert looked up. "Is that something that looks promising?"

"No, just setting it aside because it's not what we're looking for. It lets you communicate with its sibling over great distances."

"I wonder why Monteous never showed us that one."

"The solution used in making it work requires human blood."

"Human blood?" Robert felt sick.

Wallace nodded. "And not just a drop, either."

Robert wondered no longer. Monteous was set against any works that required human blood, unless it was the blood of someone you were trying to save. One of the major reasons the Guild existed was to stamp out Works like this.

Gerard looked up from his book. "I bet I know who has the twin."

Of course. "That's how they communicated. That's how he knew they were coming for Monteous."

"I wonder if Ivron knew the work that his wizard was doing in here."

"I wonder where he got the blood."

"The City isn't far. There are any number of beggars in the Outer City that would never be missed if he killed them."

"Whatever the case, at the moment, it's not going to help Angela." Robert went back to skimming through his book.

An hour passed. They'd skimmed through about three quarters of the books, and discarded most of the Works on the bench, when Wallace asked, "Do you really think there's something in one of these?"

Robert understood how Wallace felt. He had noticed the beginnings of despair in himself. He worried they might never find anything in the books to help them remove whatever Weave held Angela. But he had to keep at it. She would die of thirst or starvation, if the Weave didn't kill her first.

"We'll find something."

But fifteen minutes later, he slammed down his current book. "How are we supposed to fight this stuff if we don't even know about it?"

Wallace said, "Why would we have to fight it? No one is supposed to use it."

"But someone did use it, and if we'd known about it at all, Angela might have been able to defend herself."

Then Gerard's head popped up quickly from the book he was reading and he scanned the few remaining Works. And when his eyes stopped moving, he reached out and grabbed a small piece that looked like a magnifying glass. However, instead of the typical magnifying lens, this lens was cupped. The glass was so cloudy it was practically black.

Gerard looked at it, then went back to reading his book, glancing up at it every few seconds or so.

Robert was too anxious to wait for Gerard to say something on his own. "Did you find something?"

"I think I found what we're looking for."

Robert's despair fled, and he dared to hope.

Gerard set the book down and spun it around so Robert could read it. "Here, look."

There, on the left page, a picture of the Work Gerard held in his hand. On the right, a description of how to make it, and below that, a description of how to use it. Robert read it through twice, committing it to memory.

He held his hand out to Gerard. "May I have that?"

Gerard handed it to him, and he brought it up to his eye and looked through it. He could see nothing but the cloudy interior of the glass.

"Is that it?"

"I think you're right. This is what we're looking for."

They looked at each other for a moment. Then they were out the door, running across the courtyard, coats forgotten in the Laboratory in their rush to try the Work on Angela.

They ran up the stairs, Robert in the lead carrying the odd glass, Gerard and Wallace trailing behind. He rushed into Angela's room. The maid, who had fallen asleep in the chair, jumped up with a scream as the door slammed open. Robert ignored her and strode to the bed, then knelt to get a good look at Angela.

She appeared weaker, though it had only been a few hours. Her skin was pale. Something was strangling her life force, and he now had the means to see it, if the Work he held in his hand was the right glass.

He held the glass up to her head, sent a bit of his personal energie into it, and the near black glass cleared. Through it, he could clearly see the Weave that had wrapped itself around her brain, turned itself inside out so it could not be seen, and cut Angela off from the use of her body.

Now that he could see it, though, it was simple, if delicate work, to undo the Weave. The book had said, if he wanted, he could choose to release only a portion of the Weave. You could free just the parts that let the person talk, or hear, or allow any combination of body usage.

Robert set to freeing her completely. One thread at a time, he pulled the Weave apart, careful to keep it from collapsing. As he pulled apart the last of the threads, she immediately started breathing more rapidly.

Demetrius came up behind him, and clapped him on the shoulder. Demetrius must have entered while he was picking out the Weave. "You have done it?"

Robert stood. "Yes, I think I have. But Gerard deserves the thanks. He found it."

Demetrius turned and grabbed Gerard by the shoulders. "Well done, Gerard."

Robert would have sworn Gerard's faced turned a bit red.

Demetrius swung back to Robert. "Do you think it will be long before she recovers?"

"I don't think it will be long. The Weave sort of turned all body control thoughts back in on her. It wouldn't allow any of her senses to send her anything, nor could she control anything. She already looks like she's gone into a more normal sleep.

"I'm going to stay here, if you don't mind. I want to keep an eye on her."

"The maid can do that."

"I know. But if something goes wrong from here, the maid couldn't help. I'd rather stay until she wakes."

And then he swayed a bit.

"Are you well?" Demetrius asked.

He was still not fully rested, he realized. And he hadn't had anything to eat since that breakfast at the inn.

"Is there any way I could get some food sent up here while I wait for her? I haven't eaten since this morning."

Demetrius finished the thought. "And you still haven't fully recovered from being drained, have you."

"No, I don't think so."

"Why don't you sit in that chair. I'll have some food sent up."

Robert started making his way over to the chair that the maid had been sitting in when they entered the room. It was near the fire, and looked comfortable.

Gerard spoke up. "I think Wallace and I will go back and finish leafing through those books to see if we can identify the remaining Works."

"Good idea." He sat down in the chair. It was as comfortable as it had looked. He could easily fall asleep in it.

And then, everybody left, and he leaned back in the chair. Moments later, he'd fallen asleep. When the food arrived, the maid quietly placed it on the table near him and left.

SOMEWHERE, SOMEHOW, IN the middle of her dream, the barrier had lifted. Freedom returned after what seemed like ages of captivity. One moment, she was pounding on the barrier, pushing at it, screaming with all her might. The next, she could pass right through where it had withstood her every effort.

Her normal dreams returned, and she accepted them as a comfort despite the nightmares they sometimes brought. She knew these. The other had been unnatural.

When she awoke, she felt more relaxed and refreshed than she had in days. For long moments, she didn't even open her eyes, reveling in the feeling of being whole and out of whatever cage had trapped her for so long.

Eventually, Angela opened her eyes, and found herself staring at a ceiling she couldn't immediately place. It was paneled in dark red wood. The wood reflected what must be firelight, as the rest of the room seemed fairly dark. She closed her eyes and opened them again. The ceiling seemed a bit familiar, as if she'd seen it once or twice, but it wasn't her room in Monteous's compound. And the bed, the bed was too soft to be hers.

Then, like a flood, it all came back to her. She was at an estate in the forest, Ivron's estate. And the room, the room was where she'd slept that first night. *What happened? I went out to look at that lab, we took care of the wards, and I started walking in...*

Her mind recoiled a bit at the thinking of what had happened next. She didn't want to remember it. *I wonder how I got here.*

Then she sat up and looked around. There was someone, asleep apparently, in the chair, but in the low light, she couldn't see whoever it was very well. She leaned over to the nightstand and used a thread of energie to light the oil lamp that rested there. Better.

She swung her legs out over the side of the bed, and set them down on the floor. One of them came down on something soft, and she looked down to find someone had left a pair of slippers there for her. She slipped them on, as the floor was cold to her bare feet. Someone had also dressed her in a night-gown. She hoped it was the maid.

She stood, slowly, and found her legs weak and unsteady. She ignored them.

She saw a robe hanging against the wall near the bed. She pulled it off its hook and slipped it on, tying the belt tight around her. She picked up the lamp, finally, and started to make her way over to the chair her sleeping watcher occupied.

As the ring of light cast by the oil lamp slowly moved over the sleeping form, she quickly began to hope, and picked up her pace. And when the light finally revealed Robert's face, she couldn't keep herself from erupting in a squeal of joy.

"Robert!" She wanted to jump up and down, run over to him and hug him, but in her weakened state, all she could do was shuffle more quickly.

Robert woke up and looked quickly around the room, until his eyes focused on her. She lowered the lamp until he could see her face.

He smiled that warm smile that she loved. "Angela, you're awake."

He stood quickly, and came to her then, and hugged her in an embrace she'd longed for, hoped for, and couldn't allow to happen. But she let him this time, for she so wanted that hug. After what she'd done to him.

And then, after a moment, she pushed him back a bit. "How did you get here? Did they go and rescue you?"

"No, I escaped Monteous's Laboratory on my own. Thanks to your Weave. It was yours, right?"

"Yes."

"I don't know how long I slept, but it restored enough of my energie that I could use it to escape." And then he stopped. "Do we have to talk about this now? I came here and found that you..."

"That I was stupid?" And as she thought about it, she realized she had been stupid. She shouldn't have ignored Wallace.

"No, that you were dying. When we'd figured out how to remove the Weave that held you, I came up here, and even in the few hours it had taken us to search, you had grown far weaker. In fact, you still look a little weak. Do you need to sit down?"

"Yes, that would probably be a good idea." Robert took her hand and guided her to another seat near the one where he'd been sleeping. As she took steps, she realized her legs wouldn't hold her much longer.

Once she was sitting, Robert went back to his chair, and she sighed inside about the loss of his touch. But she forgot it as she saw the food on the small table in between them. Her stomach rumbled as if it were hollow.

"Is this for me?" she asked.

"I think it was for me, but you may have it."

"We'll share. How long was I out?"

"I don't know, exactly, unless you know the time."

She shook her head. Her mouth was full of bread. The food was cold, so it had been here awhile.

Robert looked at her then, and there was something in that look that was different than all the other times. She couldn't place her finger on it, but it stirred her heart. "Angela. I really do have to thank you."

In between bites, she said, "Thank me?"

"The Weave you made was brilliant."

Her guilt wouldn't allow her to accept the praise. "I left you there. If..."

"They never knew I was there. If you hadn't done that, Orliss would have me for sure. After what we found in the Laboratory here, I'm not sure I would enjoy his company."

"But..."

"No, Demetrius explained to me what happened. You really had little choice. Don't beat yourself over this. You did the right thing, and it worked. I'm here, you're here."

She couldn't take more, so she tried to change the subject. "What did you find in the Laboratory?"

"He had a lot of books that I've never seen. None of us have. We also found several Works we don't understand."

"Well, that shouldn't be a big surprise, we're only apprentices."

"But Monteous, if he'd ever used them, if he knew about them, he should have had examples, right? He's the Senior Wizard, after all. This guy here, he was a very low rank wizard. Why would he know about things Monteous didn't?"

She suspected she knew the answer, but didn't want to voice it.

She didn't have to. Robert did it for her. "Most of what is in those books, I suspect, are proscribed Weaves, and the Works, I'm sure they're proscribed, too."

"But how can that be? Why wouldn't Monteous teach us about these things?"

"As an apprentice, we don't need to know them. Once you pass the tests and become a Guild member, there is still quite a bit of training left. I've never been told what the training consisted of, but it wouldn't surprise me if it included instruction on proscribed Weaves and Works, at the very least so Guild members would be able to defend against them."

"It would make sense. You wouldn't want someone who didn't pass the tests running around knowing those things."

She put some cold ham in her mouth and started chewing. And while she chewed, she looked at him, watched his eyes, while he watched her eat. She saw something there that she'd never seen before. A determination, a concentration, a commitment. He'd changed in these last few days.

He'd opened a portal. Only the most powerful of the wizards could do that, and he'd done it. She'd overheard Monteous talking once to a visitor whom she hadn't known, about Robert. "He'll be among the best of us, if he can ever control himself." Angela hadn't really believed it was possible. Robert had more mishaps than any of the other apprentices, and he'd been with Monteous years longer.

But, he'd opened a portal. He'd escaped the lab on his own. And he'd saved her life.

While she was watching him, something shifted, and some of the old vulnerability came back, the uncertainty, and she wanted to go sit next to him in his chair, hold him close, and make that uncertainty go away.

But she couldn't. If Gerard walked in? If he said what he'd threatened to say? She'd never see those looks from Robert again. And it wouldn't matter if Gerard wasn't telling the truth, because she knew the truth. And the truth was too close to the lie. Robert would never approach her again. No man would, if they knew.

So she sat in her chair and ate, and let the silence grow longer, until finally, she had to break it. "What are we going to do now, then?"

He sat back in his chair. "I don't know. I suspect we'll meet with Ivron and Demetrius in the morning and find out what they think is best. It all hinges, though, on being able to find Monteous."

Of course it would. This meant, in a way, it might hinge on her. If only they had something of Monteous's that had more essence of him than the hair she'd tried before. It had been away from him so long, it had lost much of the connection.

They sat and ate in silence until the sky outside the window began to lighten. She had been trapped in that Weave for quite a long time, it turned out.

CHAPTER 15

THE MAID KNOCKED lightly on the door, startling Robert from a reverie.

He felt so grateful Angela had survived the nasty trap. Despite appearing nearly out of energie, she seemed little worse for it. He'd been thinking about how she'd hugged him warmly when he'd stood. Much of the time after the conversation had fallen off he spent wondering if he'd imagined her hug. He wondered if relief at being alive spurred her hug, or if some other deeper feeling played a role.

Whatever warmth had been there initially, she'd shut off, and he had noticed. She'd deliberately pulled away from him. Whenever he caught her in a smile that seemed warm, something happened in her head and the smile thinned.

His musings however, were interrupted by the maid's knocking, and Angela's subsequent acknowledgment and request for her to come in.

"Sir, Miss, if you are recovered, Lord Ivron has requested your presence in the dining room."

When Angela stood, Robert noticed she seemed a bit steadier on her feet. The food must have helped.

"I'll need clothes." Then she turned to Robert and looked at him.

"Yes, I'll see you downstairs?"

Angela nodded, and he turned and left the room, passing by the maid on his way out.

"Robert?"

He turned back.

"Thank you, again."

Was the warmth there? He thought it might be. "You're welcome."

And then he turned and left. She was far too confusing.

Another servant waited out in the hall. "If you'd come with me, we'll get you a quick wash and some clean clothes."

"Do we have time?" The door closed behind him.

"Yes, there is plenty of time."

The servant turned down the hall, obviously expecting Robert to follow, so Robert did.

When they reached the room that had apparently been designated for him, and he had not yet slept in it, he caught his reflection in a mirror and realized how much of a mess he was. He was surprised Angela hadn't thrown him out of the room at first sight.

The servant was efficient, the water had already been drawn and heated, and a half hour of scrubbing and rinsing later, as well as a new set of clothes, Robert felt more normal than he had in days.

He was led by the servant to the dining area, to find Ivron, Demetrius, Wallace, and Gerard waiting for him. Angela must still be doing her hair or something. If he had learned one thing from his mother, it was that women always spent at least twice the time a man would getting ready. Why that was, he'd never know, but his father claimed his mother would start to ready herself for a ball hours before his father would. And she would still make them late.

He shook his head to clear the thought. How had he come to let thoughts of his family stray into his head? He'd banished them long ago.

Demetrius gestured to him. "Sit and eat, Robert. I hear that Angela is up and awake."

"Yes, she is," he said as he sat down at a place that had already been set. The table had several platters on it, with breads, salted pork, eggs, and some dried fruits. The servant offered some of each, and he accepted it all. Hot tea was offered, and he agreed to that, too.

"She's doing well, then."

"It seems so, though she was a little weak at first."

"Good. Eat, eat. We'll talk when we're all done eating."

Robert set to eating, and was well on his way to finishing his meal when Angela finally arrived. He didn't see her come into the room, as his back was to the doorway.

He knew something was up when Demetrius stood. "Angela, you are even more stunning today than you were yesterday, if that's at all possible."

Robert spun in his chair quick enough to catch her blush. Not having known how she looked yesterday, Robert couldn't vouch for the veracity of Demetrius statement beyond the fact that he'd never seen her in anything other than apprentice work clothes. The dress she was in framed and accentuated her in a way that he had only imagined, and had never even thought to see. Her hair was up, pinned in place with precision, and the rigors of the previous day had been artfully masked.

"Thank you, Demetrius."

He'd never imagined when he stared at her from across the lab that she could look so stunning. He could only believe, now, that she might never be his. Dressed like this, she could attract a man with far more status than that of a mistake-prone apprentice.

But she had hugged him this morning. Maybe that meant something. It had to.

He set his fork down with the food still on it, stood up, then pulled out the empty chair next to him. He would, at least, be a gentleman.

She seated herself in it, then said in a quiet voice, "Thank you, Robert."

When he'd seated himself, he looked across the table and saw Gerard wearing a strange, appraising look on his face. He had eyes only for Angela.

A sideways glance showed Angela staring at Gerard with a dark look, almost as if daring him to say something.

A servant rushed up and helped Angela fill her plate, and she took her eyes off Gerard long enough to address the servant's questions.

When the servant departed, Ivron spoke. "Now that everyone has gathered, the first topic we need to tackle is why we're all here."

Gerard took his attention away from Angela. "We know why we're here. Orliss."

"Yes, but do you understand why Orliss has done what he's done? Some of you do, I know. But the others, especially you, Robert, need to know.

"Orliss seeks the Senior Wizard position in the Guild. We think, beyond mere ambition, he is trying to ensure that the current apprentice training situation does not change. Monteous wants more apprentices. He sees a threat from outside the Seven Kingdoms that only training more wizards will help combat. Orliss likely sees only that Monteous wants to decrease the ability of the Guild members to charge exorbitantly for their services."

Robert thought about it. Something lurked at the back of his mind, but he couldn't pin it down.

Demetrius took over from Ivron. "That's why he captured Monteous. There is a Conclave a few nights from now, and if Monteous is not there, he will not be eligible to continue as the Senior Wizard. Also, at this meeting, they are scheduled to vote on Monteous's proposal that a school be created to train apprentices, and that the numbers be increased substantially."

Robert got excited about that. *A school. What would that be like?*

"But if Monteous is not there to champion the proposal, it will fail, if it is even brought to a vote."

"How can that be? Wouldn't someone else bring it to a vote?" Wallace asked.

"It's a very controversial measure. Only someone of Monteous's standing in the Guild could bring it to a vote. Monteous or Orliss, or perhaps a couple others. But most are more interested in maintaining their status, or moving up. They wouldn't risk proposing something like this. A wizard's standing in the Guild affects a great number of things. Most wizards would do anything short of using the proscribed Works to maintain their position."

"Wait, wait." Robert now knew what had been bothering him. "Gerard, did you tell them what we found in the Laboratory?"

"We didn't have the time."

Or didn't want to.

"What did you find?" Ivron asked.

Robert took a long breath to calm himself. "Your wizard had several texts filled with the patterns for proscribed Works and Weaves..."

"That doesn't mean he used them."

"True, but he also had several proscribed Works among his belongings."

Ivron looked shocked. "This cannot be. He was a traitor sure, but you're saying..." He sat back in his chair.

"We think he used one of these Works to communicate with Orliss, or whoever it was he told that you were coming for Monteous."

Demetrius looked at Ivron. "If what they're saying is true, then there may be much more at stake here than merely who is Senior Wizard."

"Orliss wouldn't go that far, would he?" Ivron seemed to want to resist the idea. Robert only wished he knew what idea he was resisting.

"If he's using proscribed Works, then there's no telling how far he would go. You don't know him, Ivron. He's a scheming whoreson and lusts for power. Monteous and I never thought he would resort to proscribed Works. If he's done that, is his ultimate aim just the Senior Wizardship?"

"Excuse me," Angela said, "but what are you worried about?"

Ivron and Demetrius looked at each other, for a moment, and then Ivron apparently gave in. "Might as well, they're in it, whatever it is."

Demetrius sighed. "I told you I was Monteous's agent. And I am. But in the past few years, I've gone farther afield than just the Seven Kingdoms. There are other powers beyond our borders that covet what we have. The one deterrent has been the Wizard Guild. No one state has ever been able to find enough powerful wizards within its borders to even give it an even chance in trying to take some of the Seven Kingdom's wealth.

"In the past few years, Mrongil, through treachery or some other means, has managed to incorporate its neighbors into the territory it governs. Monteous sent me there to see what I could discover, and what I found worries me. While the numbers don't yet rival ours, Mrongil has increased the number of wizards at its disposal. And the wizards are all under the direct control of the Mrongil Crown."

Robert had a hard time digesting this. "If they don't have our numbers, than what is the immediate problem?"

"Imagine what would happen if a large number of our wizards refused to fight? Or worse, what if they fought for Mrongil? What if Orliss had been paid to quash Monteous's proposition to train large numbers of new apprentices while Mrongil continues to increase its own numbers?"

Silence reigned. Robert was stunned. He could see his friends were, too. That one of their own could even consider such a thing, that large numbers of the Guild members would consider not protecting the Seven Kingdoms left his stomach feeling sour.

Gerard broke the silence. "So now, in addition to finding Monteous, we have to somehow stop Mrongil from invading?"

Ivron cleared his throat. "Fortunately, if we can find Monteous and get him to the Conclave in time, the problem of Mrongil resolves itself, or is at least postponed for several years."

"Yes," Demetrius said. "With Monteous at the Conclave, Orliss will not win the Senior Wizardship, and any plans Mrongil had for using Orliss should be disrupted."

Robert finally felt like he had wrapped his brain around the problem. "So, the real issue we're facing here, then, is how we find Monteous. Right?"

"Yes. How do we find him, and then, how do we free him."

Robert heard footsteps pounding up the steps to the front door of the manor, and then the front door open and shut. Ivron looked to the entryway, waiting for whoever was coming. They didn't have to wait long.

A soldier came in, out of breath. He had a gash across his shoulder, and he was favoring his right arm.

"My Lord," he said.

"Trin, what is it? How were you hurt?" Ivron stood and went to him, concern obvious in his eyes.

"I was set upon in the forest on my way back from the City. Men have the estate surrounded."

"How many?"

"I could not get a full count, but if they were arrayed around the entire estate in the same fashion as the point where I made my run through their blockade, I would say fifty or sixty, at least."

"Did they have any wizards with them?"

"I didn't see any, My Lord."

"They let him in," Demetrius said.

"I agree. I'd be willing to bet they won't let anyone out, though." Ivron patted Trin on his good shoulder. "Thank you, Trin. Go get that shoulder looked at."

Trin bowed. "Yes Lord." He turned and left. Ivron went back to his seat.

"If we had the materials," Robert said, "I could make a portal."

Demetrius laughed, a sort of unbelieving laugh that Robert hoped wasn't directed at him. "Are you sure you'd want to try that again? The last two times, it's led to disaster."

"If it would help rescue Monteous, then yes, I'd try again."

"We still have to find him, don't we?" Gerard asked.

Ivron nodded. "Yes, that's still the crux of the problem. Finding Monteous. Let's solve that first, before we go on to the other problems before us."

"Well," Demetrius said, "I don't think he's likely to be hidden at any of Orliss's personal estates. We did manage to burn his closest estate to the ground, and I can't imagine he'd hold Monteous in the city. Orliss probably needs to keep him close, though."

"Where could he keep him that would be close enough?" Robert asked.

"A supporter's estate, I suspect. Someone who is close to Orliss and is completely trustworthy. All the powerful wizards keep estates near the City. He could be at any one of them."

Robert looked at his friends. *What can we do to find Monteous?*

"Angela," Demetrius said, "could you scrye him out?"

"We tried that," she said. "I couldn't find him even with a piece of his hair. Someone was blocking him."

Something clicked in Robert's head. "Orliss, he showed up the day you tried that. He knew. Monteous was close enough that day that Orliss was shielding him."

"Of course. He followed my search back somehow."

Demetrius leaned forward across the table, and looked at Angela. "If you had something more strongly tied to Monteous than a piece of his hair, could you find him?"

"If I'm not being blocked. I don't know what we'd have that's more strongly attached to him than a piece of his hair would be. And I still wouldn't be sure I could see through whatever barrier Orliss has erected."

"Let me worry about distracting Orliss," said Demetrius. "As long as you're sure you can find him."

"Gerard, there was a scrying bowl in the Lab?" Angela asked.

Gerard nodded.

"If there are no shields, I'm sure I can find him."

"Ivron, I figure if I take Gerard here, and a couple of your best, we can break through their line. The High King needs to know about this threat sooner, rather than later. It's gone far beyond just wizard infighting."

Ivron considered for a bit before responding. "Do you think it's safe to take Gerard with you?"

"I need his talents. He may be an apprentice, but he's a far stronger Elementalist than the vast majority of the Guild wizards. He was instrumental in getting us out of Monteous's Laboratory, and, considering what we've just discussed, I don't think anyone is very safe anymore."

Ivron tapped the table with his forefinger. "Gerard, I can't make you go. You're not part of my household, nor does Demetrius hold your allegiance. If you want to go with Demetrius, I'll wish you luck and strong magic. If you want to stay, I'd be more than happy to have your help defending my estate."

Robert looked to Gerard, and found Gerard looking at him, as if asking a question. Robert had no idea what question Gerard asked, though. Then Gerard looked at Angela, his face wearing a confusing mask of expectation and something else. Then something seemed to settle inside, and he spoke. "My father always told me that important men became that way by doing important things when they were required. He said a man did not always have the luxury of knowing ahead of time what was important and what was not."

Gerard rapped his knuckles on the table a couple times. "He never told me what to do when there were too many important things to be done at once. Finding Monteous is what I yearn to be doing, but my gifts lie elsewhere. If Demetrius thinks I will be of help, I'll help him."

Ivron slapped his hand to the table. "I agree, then, Demetrius. Orliss appears to be a threat to the Seven Kingdoms, and King Everance needs to be prepared. I'm assuming you think your exit will be the distraction Angela needs."

"That's what I'm hoping. My thought is to have Gerard sow some confusion among the men Orliss has stationed around us, giving us the chance to slip out. And hopefully, Orliss is paying attention."

CHAPTER 16

EXCITEMENT COURSED THROUGH Gerard since the first mention of him going with Demetrius. He still found it difficult to completely trust the man, but a chance to meet the King, a chance to matter, these were things for which he could set aside that distrust.

If he had to admit it to himself, it wasn't really distrust. Just plain jealousy. Which also had been something his father talked with him about, many many times.

Now, as he stood near the gate, he worked at readying himself for what was to come. *Am I doing the right thing? Shouldn't I stay and help find Monteous?*

He quashed that line of thinking. *This is the right choice.*

But he knew snow was coming, soon. If they didn't hurry, they'd be easy to track.

"Demetrius," he called out.

Demetrius was in conversation with Angela across the yard, and Gerard saw him hand her something, which she looked at in the palm of her hand, then quickly pocketed in the long coat that Ivron had given her to wear.

Ivron had given him a warmer coat than the one he'd worn during their escape from Monteous's compound. He'd also provided Gerard with some thicker leggings and some sturdy boots to help defend against the cold during their trip to the city.

Demetrius turned away from Angela, and made his way across the yard.

"What is it Gerard?"

"We're going to have snow, soon."

"That's not good news. It will make us easier to track."

"Do you think they will track us far?"

"I hope they will track us far enough. Have you ever used a sword?"

Gerard shook his head. "Growing up, we used short spears to hunt bear and mountain goat, and we trained with them for defense as well, but never swords. They're far too heavy to lug around when you're climbing mountains. I have some experience with knives, though, if you have an extra one."

"I'll go find you something, and then we'll go make some noise."

Robert approached him. There was something different about Robert, he seemed more confident, more focused. Gerard didn't really know what to make of it. He'd always envied Robert his abilities, but had never understood why Robert couldn't concentrate.

"Robert," he said.

"You're really going."

"Someone has to. I can't help you find Monteous, anyway."

"But if we find him," Robert said, "we'll need your help in rescuing him."

That was the irritating thing about Robert. He always seemed to try to make everyone feel important, even when it was obvious they were not. "If you find him, you'll have my help. I don't expect Demetrius will want to miss the rescue."

"No, I expect not. Be careful, then. You're no wizard, yet."

Gerard laughed. "Neither are you. But you opened that portal. It's my turn to see what I can do."

They shook hands then, and Robert turned and walked over to where Angela was standing next to Ivron.

As he stood there watching her, and watching Robert, he realized he'd have to do something to remedy the chasm he'd created between them. It had just been jealousy, his threat, and he'd never really have carried through with it. At least he didn't think so. He just hadn't been able to deal with the idea that she preferred Robert over him.

At home, he'd always been second choice. His brother destined to inherit his father's estates, and he, he'd been sent off to study to be a wizard. But he'd never be a full Master. He just didn't have enough control over the other disciplines.

And he hadn't liked it when Angela had obviously chosen Robert over him.

But Robert had been nothing but good to him. All he'd done when he'd made his threat is caused Angela to hate him. He needed to apologize to her, but he could never do it while Robert was there.

No. He'd wait until after he came back, when he could find Angela alone.

His musings were cut off when Demetrius came back, flanked by a pair of soldiers leading four horses. He also noticed Angela and Robert approaching.

"Angela is going to make the same Weave across the door that she did when we were leaving Monteous's compound," Demetrius said. "Robert will help her, and they've promised to keep it in front of us as far out as they can.

"As soon as you can see their line, I want you to light them up like you did before, though if you can, do it in more places than just one. Spread it out so that it causes confusion and terror. As soon as I ride, follow me as close as you can. We want to break through in spectacular fashion."

Gerard nodded that he understood.

Demetrius handed him a knife, and Gerard held it up to examine it. The blade was a foot long, thin but solid, and well made. "Thanks," Gerard said, and slipped the knife into his belt.

He took the reins of one of the horses from a soldier, then slipped his staff into a loop on the saddle typically used for holding a lance. He hoped the movement of the horse wouldn't break his concentration at a crucial moment. He'd never tried creating Weaves on horseback.

Then, they were all mounting, and once astride the horse, Gerard pulled his staff from the loop.

Gerard saw his first snowflake.

Demetrius apparently saw it too. "Time to go. Angela?"

Gerard slipped into the vew for a quick moment and saw the Weave she was creating, and as they opened the gate, it hung, shimmering across the gap. Demetrius urged his horse forward, through the gate, and Gerard followed. The shimmering wall moved forward with them as they entered the clearing outside the stone walls of the estate.

Then, they were outside, and Demetrius started picking up the pace. The Weave in front also kept moving forward. The two soldiers that were coming with them formed up on either side of Gerard. They were charged with keeping him alive.

Gerard figured they'd crossed half of the clearing when he noticed that the Weave was beginning to unravel a bit. He guessed she'd be able to cast it only a little farther while still maintaining its structure.

Demetrius called out, then. "Ready, Gerard!"

Gerard looked through the Weave, and saw movement in the tree line. Someone was waiting for them, getting ready for them.

"Ready!"

He started marshaling his energie. Focusing it into the staff. He wished the day were warmer, so he could pull more energie from the air, but wishing would not make it so.

And when Demetrius shouted "Now!" Gerard was ready.

Using the staff as his focus, he unleashed all the energie he dared, conjuring fireballs among the trees wherever he saw movement. He heard men screaming, in that moment, but didn't let up. Burst after burst he sent into those trees, trying to clear the area of the men that would undoubtedly chase them after they passed through.

The Weave in front of them collapsed, and Demetrius kicked his horse into a gallop. Gerard did the same, and had to stop Weaving, just to stay on his horse as they charged down the road and into the trees.

He heard screaming to either side of him. His escorts slashed at men on foot as they tried to slow the four of them.

Moments later, they were through, the screams and shouting behind them, and then gone. All he heard were the hoof-beats on the road as they ran, the trees whipping by him. The snow, falling harder now, spotted his face. He pulled his hood down tight, trying to keep his ears and face warm.

He just wished he knew how Demetrius was planning to cross the river.

They pounded down the road that way for quite a while, opening up as much distance as they could from any pursuit. Eventually, Demetrius slowed and led them into the trees, away from the road.

The snow fell rapidly now, even among the trees, and the horses blew large quantities of fog in the frozen air. The winter made their going through the forest easier, as all the ground level plants had given up much of their foliage. Gerard still had to struggle at times to keep low hanging branches out of his face and eyes.

Soon, they broke out onto a hunting trail, and they were able to move more freely.

After an hour or so, they came to a little clearing that had obviously been used as a campsite on more than one occasion, and Demetrius brought them to a halt.

The snow on the ground was more than a couple inches deep and blanketed everything.

"Gerard, what's your guess on this snow? Is it going to let up soon?"

"I don't think so."

"How do you tell?"

"There's an energie to the weather, much like a Weave, but looser. If you've studied them enough you can get a sense of what's likely to happen. These clouds, the cold, is all coming down from the North, and the pattern of the energie in the clouds seems to indicate this is just the beginning."

Demetrius snorted. "That's not what I wanted to hear."

"If you don't mind my asking, how are we getting across the river?"

"We're going to go south of the Ferry. There are other towns farther south where we should be able to find passage across."

"What about Ergin's boat?"

"If I thought it would still be there, we would take it. But knowing they saw Robert and Horuth cross with it, one of the first things I would have done is destroy it. I would also post sentries in the area."

Gerard brushed off some of the snow that was collecting on his saddle. "There's no other easy choice? This weather is going to get worse before it gets better."

"No, no easy choice. How do you like being a wizard, Gerard? That's all I hear from Monteous. Never an easy choice."

Gerard had heard Monteous utter that same comment a hundred times, always under his breath. He'd never understood why Monteous said it, but he was beginning to understand now.

"Let's get going before we freeze," said Gerard.

"Right. There's a point at which we'll have to cross the road that leads to the ferry. We'll want to be careful there. About an hour past that point, I know of a small farm whose owner I am friends with. If we can make it there without attracting attention, maybe I can convince him to let us weather the storm, at least for the evening."

"Anywhere that's warm."

Demetrius spun his mount back around and goaded it down the trail. Gerard and the soldiers followed quickly after. Gerard had no desire to spend any more time out in this storm, no matter how much it reminded him of home. In part, *because* it reminded him of home.

THE GATE SLAMMED shut as Angela felt her Weave falter, and the explosions of fire began to erupt among the trees. Regardless of how much she detested him, Gerard was still the best of them with elemental Weaves.

She felt her knees wobble. Time to go sit down somewhere and study the crystal Demetrius had given her.

"Robert, let's go to the Laboratory."

He looked at her, and immediately, a frown crossed his face. *Can he see my weakness?* If he could, he said nothing about it.

"Right, we have our own work to be about."

He put his arm around her and started helping her toward the Laboratory. He didn't say anything, of course. But he had noticed.

She thought about pushing him away. She didn't want him to turn that ill-advised hug from the night before into something more than she could give. His arm around her felt warm and comfortable, though, and helpful.

Angela felt weary. She'd pushed the Weave as far as she could, and held it up until her energie was nearly gone. It probably had been a mistake to ignore Robert's offer of aid.

In order to enter the Laboratory, Robert had to release his hold on her, and she wished he didn't have to. Once inside, he led her over to the workbench and pulled out a stool for her to sit on. She'd have to put a stop to that, but not right now. She was too tired.

Angela looked around the Laboratory. It didn't look much different than Monteous's lab. She wasn't sure what she'd expected, but she had figured someone dabbling in proscribed Works would be easy to discover. She said as much to Robert, who was pulling another stool over to the other side of the workbench for himself.

"I suppose, if we had passed the tests, we might have an easier time picking out the differences. We only noticed because we didn't recognize some of the books and the Works. Reading through the books, it became obvious. If we had known those books, or known of them, maybe we would have seen it. But you're right. It's hardly the lair you would expect of someone who commits murder to obtain some of their materials."

Angela shuddered. "It makes me wonder about the real purpose behind the Weave that captured me. What would he have done with me?"

"Fortunately, we'll never have to find out."

"Yes. Fortune was certainly with me that you managed to escape and get here in time to help."

She watched him close his eyes momentarily, and when he opened them again, she saw a little bit of excitement instead of dread.

"Alright, let's see it."

"See what?"

"I saw Demetrius hand you something before they left."

"Ah." She pulled it out and set it on the bench between them.

"What is it?"

She looked at it sitting there, and wondered what it really was. It appeared to be a translucent white crystal, the length of her ring finger. A sort of soft pulsing glow emanated from its center. "I don't know exactly what it is. Demetrius said it was a Work Monteous gave him long ago. It was supposed to be a way for Monteous to call Demetrius home, wherever he was in the Seven Kingdoms."

Robert picked it up and turned it over and over in his hand, examining it closely. "How was it supposed to call him back?"

"Demetrius told me it would start glowing like it's doing now. He said it had never glowed until the night Monteous was captured."

"Do you suppose it could lead us to him?"

"Demetrius hopes it might work better than the hair we tried, and I believe it might. Monteous had to put his energie into it when making it. He might even be trickling energie into it right now to make it pulse."

Robert's brow furrowed. She could see he was thinking about something, studying the crystal deeply. After a moment, he stood up and held the crystal out in front of him and spun in place slowly. He made about two revolutions, then came to a stop, a huge grin on his face.

"What, what is it?" she asked.

He held the crystal close to her. "Look at the Weave inside."

She did look, focusing inside, on the pulsing light. Around it, embedded in it, she could see the Weave, contained by the outer crystal layer that was the work.

"I see the Weave."

"Now, watch as I turn it." He proceeded to slowly spin the crystal in his hand, and she watched closely. The Weave inside didn't turn.

"It stays oriented in one direction. It doesn't turn with the crystal."

"Yes. Why do you think that is?"

After a moment, she saw it. "It *is* connected to Monteous. It's oriented on him!"

"Right."

And then her hopes sagged. "There's no way to tell which direction he's in. It's the same all the way around."

"Wait." He moved around the bench and came up behind her, putting his arms around her. She wanted to melt into them. He helped her stand.

Robert held the crystal out in front of her, and snuck his head over her shoulder so they could both see the crystal. He started to spin her, holding the crystal out in front. For a moment, it felt like dancing. She missed dancing.

"Now, watch the Weave as we spin. Tell me what you see."

She watched, trying to ignore the feel of his body up against hers. "It's the same." And it was for a moment. But as they turned, she saw something, a single end of a thread that was different than the rest of the Weave. It extended beyond the pattern just a bit, and was very small. It was pointing West, across the river.

"I see it — a little nub of a thread. You don't suppose..."

"That it points to him?"

"Yes. You think it does, don't you."

"I hope so."

She turned in his arms to look at him. He was too close, taller, her eyes right at his lips.

No, no. I can't think these things. She backed away, and ducked out under his arms to get away from him. He looked confused, but said nothing. "How do we know for sure? It could be pointing directly at him, or directly away from him."

"We don't know. The only way to really be sure is to somehow scrye him out and see if the direction is the same."

"There's one problem. We lack anything of Monteous's to use as the Origin." As she said this, she went to go sit down on the stool that had originally been Robert's. Her legs were tiring, and she didn't want to get too close to him.

"We can't use this, can we?"

"We could, I think, if we wanted to risk destroying the Weave."

He shook his head. "If we could only be sure which direction it pointed, this could lead us to Monteous without alerting Orliss that we're looking for him."

What could they do? *Maybe we made a mistake staying behind.*

If they'd known about the crystal, they could have left with Demetrius and Gerard, and tried following that thread wherever it lead, instead of being stuck in here with a winter storm about to unload its wrath upon them.

She looked around the Laboratory. Apparatus, shelves, Works, books. Books.

"Did you read everything in these books, Robert?"

"No, I stopped when I found the Work to help you. Gerard and Wallace may have read more."

"I wonder if Wallace saw something in one of these books that might help us out."

"I don't know. Maybe I should go get him."

"Would you? Bring Ivron and lunch, too, and maybe wood for the fire. And, could you bring me one of the books you haven't read, please? I'll get to reading it while you're rounding everybody up."

Robert brought her a thick book, set the crystal on the bench in front of her, wrapped himself up, and then, just before heading out, turned to look at her. He just stood there, and she looked back. She felt guilty for confusing him, but it was better than the alternative. Having him hate or dismiss her after Gerard tells his lie.

"I'll be right back," he said, then he opened the door, and wind and snow rushed through it as he slipped out. The storm had already started, and Gerard was out in it.

Gerard. If he only knew how close his threat was to the reality she wanted to forget, she didn't think he'd have issued it. But then, she'd have had to admit it to him. And she wasn't about to tell anyone.

The pulsing of the crystal caught her eye, and reminded her of her task. She opened the book and started reading.

It wasn't long before Wallace opened the door, letting even more snow and wind blow through the Laboratory. They were alone for a moment.

Immediately after he'd managed to shut the door, she said, "Wallace, I haven't had the time to apologize."

"What?"

"I need to apologize for yesterday. I should have listened to you."

"It's nothing."

"No, it's not nothing. You saw the Weave, and we dismissed your worries because you're the youngest of us. It almost got me killed."

His face went red. "Thank you."

And then he turned and went to the bookshelf and pulled out several books. He brought them to the workbench, and immediately took the other stool. He reached out and picked up the crystal.

"So this is what we're looking for?"

She nodded.

"I didn't see anything like it yesterday. It could have been in the books Gerard read."

"But he's not here."

"Right. I guess I should get those out, too."

Right then, the fire cracked. "You know which books Gerard read?"

"Of course. You know, though, there's all this stuff we've never seen. It makes me wonder."

"Wonder what?"

"Wonder whether every Weave and Work is known and written

down for us to follow. Someone had to figure them out at some point, right?"

His question reminded her of how quick Wallace was at learning things. She tried to think back to why she'd ignored him, and could only put it down to worry about Robert. Her mother had once told her that love made one do stupid things.

And then Angela stifled that thought as quick as she could. She did not love Robert. She was just worried because she felt guilty about leaving him behind. That was it.

"Angela?"

She forced herself to focus on Wallace. "Right. Let's just hope this one is in here somewhere, and can tell us how it works."

The door banged open again, and this time, Robert and Ivron came through it carrying what looked like lunch.

Once they'd shut the door on the blizzard outside, and unwrapped their bundles on the hastily cleared bench, she found warm loaves of bread, cheese and smoked venison. Ivron also produced a pitcher of hot water and everything else needed for tea. One thing she could say about Ivron and his estate. They ate well here.

"So Robert tells me you've found something interesting about that item Demetrius left with you," Ivron said around a large bite of bread.

"Well, Robert found it."

"Never mind who figured it out. Just tell me what you learned."

"We think it could lead us straight to Monteous."

Ivron's eyes went wide. "Like a compass?"

"Yes, more or less."

"Why didn't Demetrius let us in on this secret before?"

She took a sip of her tea before answering. "He doesn't know, I'm sure. He can't see what we can see, so Monteous would have no reason to tell him. He thought it was only a signal to come home."

"May I see it?"

Wallace held it up for him to see.

"Interesting. The light coming from it?"

"It's from the Weave inside. Did Robert tell you what our problem is?" One thing she didn't want to do was try to explain how the crystal worked. She didn't know, yet.

"Not in any detail."

"I'm concerned, if I use the crystal as an Origin for scrying, it might destroy the Weave inside."

"Which you think might be pointing directly at Monteous."

She nodded.

"Let me see if I understand this, then. You could use the crystal to potentially find out where Monteous is right now and possibly destroy it in the process. If he is moved, we may not be able to find him again."

Ivron reached and took the crystal from Wallace, and held it in front of his face, slowly rotating it back and forth. "Or we could go out and search for him using this crystal directly, and have it lead you to him, even if he moves."

"That's it."

"Well, I don't think we want to make another mistake with this thing, do we?"

"Another mistake?"

"I'm sorry. I've already made far too many mistakes. Hiring that wizard, the ill-conceived attempt to rescue Monteous, and now letting Demetrius run off without you three."

"I'm sorry," she said. "I don't understand."

"If we had known about this crystal, I would have sent you with him. You could have figured out where Monteous was just by moving at a tangent to where the crystal pointed for a while. Now, I don't have anyone else I can send with you."

"We're not going anywhere right now," Robert said.

"No. This storm is going to keep us all here, and even if it wasn't, I don't have any protection I could lend you. I can't take the chance, unlikely though I think it is, that our enemy would leave this keep alone if I let any more of my soldiers go."

"So what should we do?"

"I don't think the crystal should be used to scrye for Monteous until we have no other choice. Do what you do best. Look through these books. Learn what you can learn. Maybe you'll find something useful while we wait out this storm. And if we're lucky, Demetrius will be back in a couple days with some help from King Everance."

"Is that likely? I thought the King stayed out of Wizard Guild business, including feuds."

"He does, until it risks the security of the Seven Kingdoms, at which point, he will take whatever measures he deems necessary." He held up his tea, as if to toast. "Here's to King Everance deeming us necessary."

Angela lifted her teacup to Ivron's.

"Now," Ivron said, "If you'll excuse me, I must inspect the fortifications, such as they are. Later, after you tire of reading these dusty books, Angela, you must visit with my wife. She has been badgering me for a visit."

"I'd be delighted to visit with her. After all, she lent me this lovely dress. It's the least I can do."

"Good! After dinner, then."

He opened the door, letting in another blast of cold air and snow. He pushed out into it, pulling the door shut behind him, leaving her alone with Robert and Wallace.

Deep in her heart, though she didn't want to admit it to herself, she wished it was just Robert.

Robert looked at her, and said, "Do you think he's right?"

"I don't think we're going anywhere, so scrying for Monteous right now is a waste of time."

"Well, I haven't had much time to look at what else is here. Have you Wallace?"

Wallace shook his head. "No, my nose has been in these books the whole time."

"I wonder what materials this wizard had in stock."

Angela suspected she knew what he was thinking. "Why would a low level wizard have the materials for a portal Focus lying around?"

"Why wouldn't he? Most of them are fairly common, and they're all used in other Works."

"But we don't even know where Monteous is. Even if we could make a portal, we couldn't put it anywhere near him."

"You're right. However, if we could make a portal, we could leave here with Orliss none the wiser, and Ivron wouldn't have to send a large escort with us." He started moving away to a chest of drawers that was against the wall. "You two keep looking through those books for anything about the crystal. I think Ivron's right. We don't actually need to know when we start if it's pointing at him or away from him. We just need to watch it as we move. And we need to get out of here."

Angela wanted to believe in him, so she stuck her nose into one of the books and started looking for answers.

CHAPTER 17

BY THE TIME Gerard caught sight of the the farm to which Demetrius had led them, the sky had grown dark. The slog through the early snowfall had become a trudge through a blizzard, a two hour ride turned into six, and Gerard felt frozen from head to toe. His mind wanted to spend time comparing this blizzard to what he was used to at home, and all he could keep thinking was that at home, they were smart enough not to try to travel in the middle of a blizzard.

Not that the four of them had much choice.

Before they'd even reached the road Demetrius had mentioned, the snow was half a foot deep, and they had already fallen well off the anticipated pace. Demetrius was sure they weren't being followed any further — no hired thug would think about trying to track someone through the storm. But, he also was sure there was no place closer than the farm to wait it out.

They'd stopped more than once where Gerard had set fire to a dead log so they could warm frozen hands. The warmth never lasted long enough, but it kept the frostbite away. Gerard tried to do what he could for the horses, as well, but the best thing for them would be to get to the farm and into a stable.

Privately, he wondered if they'd survive. He wondered if any of them would survive.

The road, when they'd reached it, had been deserted. Gerard had asked if maybe they could just head to the ferry from here and cross.

Demetrius had snorted at that. "I wish we could. The ferry won't be running, though. Not in this weather."

So, they'd trudged on through the snow, pushing the horses as much as they dared. The snow fell so thick at times that visibility was little farther than a horse length. They had to go slow just to stay within sight of each other.

By the time the fence that marked the edge of the farm came into view, Gerard's ears and nose stung from the cold, and it was all he could do to keep his eyes open. The snow angled in on him, blowing right across his face.

"Here we are!" Demetrius shouted through the storm.

Gerard felt a small surge of excitement run through him at the thought they'd soon be warm, and he sat up a bit to see their destination.

The farm was small, surrounded on all sides by forest. In the snow, with dusk coming upon them, he could barely make out a farmhouse and a small stable. He hoped there was room for the horses.

They followed the fence around the field, skirting between it and the edge of the forest, until they came to a horse-path that led them between a pair of fields and right to the stable. Demetrius signaled for him to dismount, which Gerard did gratefully, and told the soldiers to stable the horses.

He leaned into Gerard. "Come with me."

Gerard followed him to the farmhouse and up the steps.

Demetrius knocked on the door, and it cracked open almost immediately, as if someone had been watching.

The door popped open wide, and Gerard saw a middle aged man, thin and wiry, and obviously used to physical labor. "Demetrius!" He smiled openly. "Come in, come in! What are you doing out in this mess?"

Demetrius stepped through the door, and Gerard followed quickly, and the man shut the door.

"Owen," Demetrius said. "Could we impose on you for the night? There are two more out stabling our horses."

"Of course, of course. It'll be tight, but no man should be out in this weather. Moma, come, come. Demetrius is here with some friends!"

"Demetrius?" A woman's voice from around the corner, husky and vibrant. And then she came around the corner. She was stout, and her hair was pulled back. She smiled when she first saw Demetrius, but it turned to a look of concern as she came closer to Demetrius and Gerard.

"You poor dears, you need something hot in you! Nina, put the tea on." Her voice was even louder in person, and it echoed through the house.

Gerard heard footsteps coming up onto the porch outside, and a knock at the door. Owen slipped past him to open the door.

Moma looked at Owen, frowning. "There are more? Why didn't you tell me Owen? Nina, make that two pots, and hurry."

"Yes, Moma," came a young sounding female voice from somewhere within the house.

"Come in, and get settled." Moma waved them in to the larger living area where there was a fire in the fire place. "We don't have much room, but it's certainly got to be better than traveling through that weather."

"Get those coats off so you can warm up. Owen, come help me get 'em some blankets. They're all nearly frozen!"

She spent some more time getting them all settled in front of the fire so they could warm up, and quickly, Gerard's fingers and toes started to thaw. And then she said, "I have to go work up supper, and find out why it's taking that girl so long with the tea.

"Owen, why didn't you tell me we were going to have company? If I'd of known, I could've had the food all ready."

"I didn't know, Moma."

"Well, you just make sure they're all warm and there's no frostbite on 'em. We don't need 'em losing fingers and toes in our home."

Gerard saw him look to Demetrius and roll his eyes as his wife passed out of the room and into the kitchen.

"So," Owen said when she was gone, "How is that old fool, and what brings you out here?"

Demetrius sighed. "The old fool went and got himself captured. We're out here trying to rectify that situation."

Owen's eyes went wide. "Captured? How did someone manage that?"

"That's something I'd like to know. What I do know is that they somehow tricked him into opening a portal to one of Orliss's estates and they were there to capture him when he went through."

"You think Orliss did it?"

"We suspect so."

Owen just nodded. Then he gestured to Gerard and said, "And who is this young wizard here?"

"That's Gerard. He's one of Monteous's current apprentices."

The girl's voice came from right behind him. "You're an apprentice of Monteous?"

"Nina, just the tea. There'll be plenty of time to talk to him later."

"Yes, pa."

And then she stepped around and he saw her for the first time. She was pretty, though not perhaps as pretty as Angela, but there was something else about her, too, that he couldn't put his finger on. She looked to be only a couple years younger than he, and no taller than his chest.

She handed him a steaming cup of tea, and he took it gingerly, wrapping his still warming fingers around it as much as he dared, hoping to speed up the thaw. He smiled at her. "Thank you."

She smiled back, and there was something in it, a question, or a promise. "You're welcome." Then she moved on to the others.

Owen said, "Young Gerard, you will have to watch yourself with Nina."

"Pa!"

"She has a soft spot in her heart for any young man that might happen by and promises to take her away. I'll give you all the money I've got if you promise to take her away." He laughed as he said it.

"Pa, you don't have any money."

"Oh, right. Well, watch out for her, Gerard. She keeps talking about running away to be a wizard, and I wouldn't put it past her to latch on to you."

Gerard looked at Owen, then Nina. He caught her sneaking a glance back at him while she filled a cup for Demetrius. What would Angela think if he came back with Nina hot on his heals? She'd probably hate him even more than she did already. *I really do need to settle that with her.*

"She won't want to be coming with us, not now."

Owen laughed some more. "You don't know Nina."

Nina practically growled. "Why wouldn't I want to be coming with you?" She finished filling the last of the cups as she said this.

"Because," Demetrius said, "there are some very mean spirited men chasing us. Their intent, I believe, is to bury us in a snowdrift." Then he turned to Owen. "In point of fact, Owen, our being here may endanger you and your family."

"Nina, go help Moma with the supper."

"But pa."

"Go."

She slunk out of the room, without another word, and Gerard watched her go. She did watch Gerard as she left, and smiled at him right before she had to turn away. Gerard promised himself, if Nina didn't go with them, he'd have to find a reason to visit again.

Once she was out of sight, Owen turned back to Demetrius. "Just how much danger? You don't think they could have followed you through this storm, do you?"

"It's doubtful, but I worry. They tortured Ergin and burned his wife alive because he helped us across the river."

Owen looked stricken. "Ergin was a good man. What could Orliss want that would possess him so?"

"We don't know if Orliss sanctioned that savagery, or if it was just the result of hiring those particular thugs. However, some of the wizards in Orliss's camp have resorted to using proscribed

Works, and there is indirect evidence that Orliss has engaged in them too.

"As for what he wants, it seems obvious that he wants to be Senior Wizard. What we don't know the answer to, however, is why. We suspect there's even the possibility that he has plans to overthrow the Seven Kingdoms."

"Why would you suspect that?"

"The use of proscribed Works is supposed to be an automatic expulsion from the Guild, as well as from the Kingdoms. I can only imagine why Orliss would use proscribed works. He must think he's somehow protected himself from expulsion."

Owen stomped his foot on the floor. "The only way he doesn't get expelled is if he is in charge, or if the rules change."

"Right."

"This is a fine mess, Demetrius. So what are your plans?"

"Try to get across the river, and back into the City, and get an audience with Everance."

"Do you think he will listen?"

"I hope he will. He's been a good patron for Monteous at times. I think he would be interested in knowing what's going on."

"He's kept out of Guild politics, even more so than his father did."

"I know, but if we are right, this extends far beyond Guild politics."

Gerard just listened to the two men discuss the life he'd lived for the last few days. And after a few minutes of it, with the warm tea in his belly, and the fire in the hearth keeping the room warm, he leaned back and closed his eyes. His bones were tired, and his rear was sore from riding the horse for so long. He'd ridden before, but never often, and never for as long as they'd trekked through the snow. He really just wanted to go to sleep.

"Gerard," Owen said, and Gerard lifted his head to see what he wanted. "How'd you get mixed up with Monteous?"

"My father. I'm the youngest in my family. In Risuk, if you are youngest, you don't stand to inherit anything. My father's business was running caravans from our home to Stradetra. He met people during his travels, and one of them, apparently, was Monteous. I don't know how my father and he got to talking about me, but one summer, Monteous came back with my father and tested me. He offered to have me as his apprentice."

"He does have the knack for finding the talented ones."

"Pa, supper's on." Owen's wife's voice rang throughout the small farmhouse.

"Let's go eat," Owen said, springing up from his chair much quicker than Gerard expected.

Gerard had to push himself out of his own chair. As he approached the table in the next room and saw the food laid out on it, he began to register the smell, and his stomach rumbled. There wasn't enough space to seat them all at the table, so they filled plates with food and took them back to sit by the fire. Nina filled a plate of her own and sat near him. He caught her stealing glances all the while she was eating.

The conversation turned away from business, and on to other lighter fare. It was obvious to Gerard that the two men knew each other well. They talked to each other, mostly ignoring Gerard. The two soldiers, Gerard still did not know their names, sat by themselves and talked.

"Do you know why Pa thinks I'll chase after you?"

Nina's voice, and her question, were unexpected, and Gerard looked to see her staring at him, her plate empty. He wasn't sure how to, or even if he should, respond, so he said nothing.

"It's because Monteous came and tested me once."

"He did?"

"He said I had some talent, but that it was too weak to ever give me a good chance at becoming a Guild member. I was heartbroken. All I'd ever wanted to be was a wizard."

"Why?"

"Growing up, Monteous was always stopping by. My father worked for him when he was younger, and they became friends. I think, in a way, my father still works for him. Monteous was so full of mystery and surprises. I wanted to be just like him.

"When he told me he couldn't take me on as an apprentice, I wanted to cry, but I didn't. I still remember what he said to me. He said, 'I'm working to change that. Anyone with any talent should be trained.'"

Gerard tried to imagine what his life would be like now if Monteous had said to him that he could not be trained, that he had some power, but that he'd never know how to use it. Try as he might, though, he couldn't imagine it.

Then he said, "You know, I think that's one of the things we're trying to do."

"What?"

"There's a Guild Conclave in the next few days, and we're trying to make sure that Monteous is at that meeting. I think they were going to vote on new rules for taking on apprentices, as well as for who's allowed to join the Guild. At least, that's what I've been able to glean from all the talk around me."

Nina's eyes lit up. "That would be wonderful."

"Shh. Don't tell your Pa, or anyone else I told you, and don't get your hopes up. One of the reasons we're here is that there's a lot of opposition."

"That's why we're in danger."

"You heard," he said.

"It's a small house."

"Still..."

"Don't worry. I won't say a thing." Then she got an appraising look. "Tell me about yourself, Gerard. I want to know everything."

"Everything? Why ever for?"

"Because there's not a lot to do other than talk, with this many people in here." She leaned closer to him. "And so far, I like you."

Gerard looked away from her for a moment, and caught Owen smirking at him, almost like he was saying, "I told you so."

And for whatever reason, when he turned back to Nina, he opened his mouth and everything came out. They spent a long time talking that night. After a while, he was sorry he'd have to leave when the storm let up.

ROBERT WENT UNREWARDED in his search for materials. Most of the key metals were in the cabinets, but tungsten was missing, and some of the materials for the fluid were also absent. It wasn't a surprise, just strangely upsetting. He wanted to try another portal, this one made to take them directly to the City so they could join Gerard and Demetrius.

Even more disappointing, after hours of searching through the tomes, they'd come up empty as well. When Wallace closed the last volume without finding a description of the crystal, the three of them sat at the bench for several minutes, each lost in thought.

"I'm tired of this," Robert said, finally fed up with thinking about it all. "I'm going back up to the manor. I want to talk to Ivron, find out what I can about his previous wizard."

"I'll come with you," Angela said. "I need to meet with his wife."

"What about you, Wallace?"

"I'm going to stay here and study these for a while longer. I might find something useful, or at least learn how we can protect ourselves against some of the things Orliss knows how to do."

Robert was happy to let Wallace do as he said. Wallace was studious. Robert had never cared as much for the studying.

They bundled up, preparing to head out into the blizzard. When they were ready, they opened the door, and found the snow was drifted against it.

"It's only getting worse," Robert said as the snow fell into the room.

Wallace had to come over and push on the door to close it. As they walked across the courtyard, the snow found its way into his boots. They hunched over against the wind and the driving snow, and went in the direction they knew the manor rested. They couldn't see it through all the snow.

When they reached the steps, they were covered in snow, making it tricky to ascend them, but they made it up without slipping. Robert hurried Angela, and then himself, through the door and into the manor. Somehow, they managed to allow only a little snow to follow them into the foyer.

As they brushed themselves off, Ivron came down to greet them, and his wife followed soon after. Despite her age, she was beautiful, a good match for the dress she had loaned Angela. Robert guessed she had been positively striking when she was younger.

Ivron performed introductions. "Robert, Angela, this is my wife Marena."

"How do you do?" Robert said, an echo he heard from Angela.

"Marena, these are the Wizard Apprentices Robert, and Angela."

"Welcome to my home. I'm sorry I didn't get a chance to greet you when you arrived, but you all arrived at such odd hours and under such strange circumstances."

To Robert, she looked truly sorry she had missed them when they'd first arrived.

"Thank you for your hospitality. Your home has been an unexpected pleasure."

She moved to take Angela's hand. "You are a beauty, aren't you? And a wizard as well. Absolutely amazing. Come with me. You and I must take some tea together before dinner, and then we will all dine." She turned to Ivron. "No meetings tonight, my husband. I want some time to get to know our guests."

"As you wish."

Robert watched as Marena led Angela away, immediately asking her a half dozen questions before giving Angela a chance to respond. Robert didn't hear all of the questions or any of the answers, and he felt quite sure it was intended that he not.

"Come, Robert. Let's go sit by the fire and have some rum. It will take off the chill. Is Wallace going to join us soon?"

"I don't think so. He wanted to continue researching those books."

"I shall have to send someone to take him some food and make sure he has enough wood for the fire."

Robert soon found himself submerged in a comfortable leather chair with his right hand holding a glass of rum. He didn't drink much. Being a wizard required almost all of your wits nearly all of the time. However, his first sip of the rum warmed him deep inside, and he settled in to get warm inside and out.

After a couple minutes of sipping in silence, Ivron resettled himself and attracted Robert's attention. "You haven't said whether you found any information regarding that crystal."

"We didn't find even a mention of something similar."

"Did you discover anything useful?"

Robert leaned his head back in the chair and stared at the ceiling. "We discovered quite a few things that we aren't able to do, either because we lack the materials, or the Works and Weaves are proscribed."

"Did you have any idea your wizard was involved with that kind of thing?" *I can't believe I'm talking to a Lord like this.*

"How would I have known? Wizards are all secretive. They guard their knowledge and what they do as closely as anyone I've known. I've been in there, but the books all look like books to me, and everything else is, well, just wizard stuff. I had no idea he'd turn against me like he did."

"Do you know when the Conclave is supposed to be held?"

"It's held Midwinter's Eve, so we've got two days to find Monteous and get him there. When we find Monteous, he will know where."

"It would have to be in the city, wouldn't it?"

"I wouldn't think that likely. Too many eyes, too much chance of being spied upon. A hundred wizards converging on one place in the City? No, I think the Guild probably has estates or a Guild hall somewhere."

Robert tried to think back over his years with Monteous. The old wizard had never been very forthcoming when it came to the Guild. Whenever Robert asked about the Guild, Monteous would tell him, "You won't need to know that until you pass your tests." So Robert's knowledge of things like the Conclave was limited to just about the same knowledge that any non-Guild member had. Obviously, some people like Ivron knew more, but that was, in a way, expected of a Lord.

And when Robert thought about previous Midwinter Eves, he couldn't remember one where Monteous had been present, nor could he remember large numbers of wizards in the City. Of course, nothing said they had to arrive on foot or horseback or in a carriage.

"I've been thinking, while we were out in the Laboratory. We need to be out searching for Monteous. Staying here feels like we're wasting time."

Ivron nodded. "It is wasting time. I'd hoped you could discern where Monteous is, and then we could go rescue him, but things never work out like I plan. And now that we have a probable way to find him that doesn't rely on a method that might alert Orliss to our search, this storm rolls in and we can't do anything. I've never felt so impotent in my life." He emphasized this last by slamming his fist onto the arm of the chair.

Robert didn't know what to say to that, so he just sipped his drink and stared into the fire. And after a while, his thoughts drifted back to Angela. She was so confusing. One moment, she's hugging him, holding him close, and then another, it was as if she was trying to keep her distance. He felt sure it had something to do with Gerard. She always grew quiet when Gerard came into the room, withdrawing into herself in a way. He couldn't figure it out.

"Tell me about yourself, Robert." Ivron startled him out of his thinking.

"What do you want to know?"

"Where are you from? How'd you come to apprentice for Monteous?"

"I came to Monteous when I was young, younger than most apprentices, but I wasn't really an apprentice then. He rescued me during the uprising in Vanarth."

"I remember hearing about that, the uprising. Bad for everyone involved. If you don't mind talking about it, How'd he rescue you?"

"I don't remember a whole lot, mostly the fires, the screaming. I remember hiding in a stable among the hay bales. And then this man, Monteous, came and sat with me, soothed the fear in me somehow, and asked if I wanted to come with him. I asked him where my mother was, if he could take me to her. I remember tears in his eyes when he told me that my parents were dead, our home burned. So I went with him. I didn't think then, to ask him how he knew my parents, nor have I asked him since."

"I think you should ask him when you get the chance. I've known Monteous a long time. He never does anything without purpose. He was there to rescue you for a reason."

"What reason could that be? I can't imagine he was there just for me."

"It wouldn't surprise me if that was exactly the reason why he was there. Has he ever told you anything about your potential?"

"He's never said anything beyond, 'If you want to pass your tests, you need to concentrate!'"

"Did you know that Orliss is particularly interested in you, above all of your friends?"

"No." Robert sat up, then. "Why would that be?"

"Demetrius told me that Monteous expects you to succeed him in the Guild."

"Succeed him?"

"As Senior Wizard. Monteous apparently believes your potential to be greater than his, greater than any wizard in a generation."

Robert couldn't quite believe that. Monteous had never, to his memory, said anything of the sort to him. All he'd ever been was patient when Robert made mistakes for lack of concentration.

"But how could Orliss know?"

"You've met Orliss, have you not?"

"Of course."

And of course was all the answer Robert needed to piece it together. A wizard could gauge the ability of other wizards just by watching the energie flows surrounding them. He had even done it with his friends. He knew where each of them stood. The only thing you never knew was exactly where you stood in relation to others. You couldn't see your own energie flows. Robert imagined that after years of seeing lots of other wizards at the various Conclaves, one could have a good idea of where everyone stood, and become a good judge of whose power was greater, and by how much.

"So Orliss sees me as competition."

"Not immediate competition, I'm sure, and he may see you as a potential ally."

"Is that why you're telling me this now?"

"If you know why Orliss wants you, if he happens to get you, you'll be able to fight him, or at least defend against his attacks. There is nothing worse in warfare than a lack of knowledge of the enemy. And if you know what the enemy thinks of you, he's that much easier to outmaneuver."

Robert stood up. He had to walk around to think about this. The idea that Monteous thought him to be potentially more powerful than anyone in the Guild seemed like wild speculation. Monteous had never said anything to make him think he was better than the others. But as he paced back and forth, the rum working on him, he realized that the projects Monteous gave him, they were always the hardest. They were always just beyond what Robert himself thought he could do.

And I opened a portal on my own.

"I wish I had another wizard to talk to. There are some questions I really need to ask. Do you know any we might be able to contact?"

"Not that I could trust. I'd thought I could trust the last one I contracted with."

"Right. It all comes down to rescuing Monteous."

A servant ducked into the room at that moment. "My Lord, dinner is ready."

"We'll be right there. Send someone to Wallace out in the Laboratory. Invite him in, or bring him food, if he wishes."

"Yes my Lord."

Ivron stood and set his empty glass on the side table. "Well, Robert, shall we head to the dining room?"

"Yes. Eating sounds like a good idea right now."

ANGELA ALLOWED MARENA to guide her up to a small sitting room. A window with a view of a garden, now covered in snow, was irresistible. A pair of chairs flanked a small table that had a steaming pot of tea and cups already prepared. A plate held a couple of small, steaming buns that looked delicious.

"Sit down," said Marena. "Have some tea and a bun."

Angela picked the chair nearest her and sat down. It faced out toward the window, and the light from the lamps in the room illuminated some of the snowflakes coming down. Marena took the other chair and poured some tea for each of them.

"You must tell me what it's like being both a woman and a wizard."

"I'm not a wizard yet, just an apprentice."

"Of course, dear, but you're far more wizard than I will ever be."

Angela took a sip of her tea. It was hot and tasted of mint. "To tell you the truth, it's about all I've ever known since I was thirteen. Monteous showed up, and my parents bundled me off with him straight away."

"It's just been Monteous taking care of you since you were thirteen?"

Angela nodded.

"It's no wonder, then, that you came dressed in those clothes. You really are beautiful, you know. You do yourself a disservice dressing that way."

"What's wrong with them? They are what we wear around the Laboratory."

"They're not at all flattering, dear. How would you ever expect to attract an appropriate man wearing them?"

"Attract a man? We wear them because they won't interfere with our Work." Attract a man? She already had two that were attracted to her. One she wanted, another one not. And it was a man that got her placed with Monteous in the first place.

Something in her face must have given her away, though. "Oh, you already have a man picked out. One of your fellow apprentices?" Marena was perceptive. "It's the one with my husband, isn't it? Robert, I think?"

Angela must have nodded her head or something, for Marena kept on going. "He is handsome. Does he know of your interest?"

"No." She hoped not. It was hard enough as it was to keep pushing him away. If he knew, she'd not be able to keep him away, and keeping her secret would be doubly hard.

"Let me tell you what you must do, if you want to attract him. Obviously, you can't come right out and tell him. You have to drop little hints. Smile at him when he's looking at you but don't let him know you notice him watching."

Angela had to stop this. "I can't let him know of my interest."

"Why ever not?"

How much should she say? Anything at all? She wanted to like this woman. She hadn't had a woman to talk to since she was a child. She'd only been home twice since she'd been Monteous's apprentice, and neither time had she wanted to talk to anyone. Her parents blamed her mistake for their misfortune.

"Listen honey, whatever it is, I can help you with it. I'm not a vapid old woman that only thinks about men."

Angela decided she'd trust this woman. She couldn't tell anyone else, and she needed some advice from somewhere, or she'd end up going crazy.

"'If he ever found out about my interest, he'd eventually discover why I'm studying to be a wizard, instead of married to a rich Lord, and then he'd leave. I can't stand the thought of him knowing these things, or the idea that he might toss me away like my family did."

Marena's eyes opened wide, and then narrowed as she ferreted out the reason. "There was already a man, wasn't there."

Angela hung her head. "I thought he loved me. He brought me flowers and fruits, he was handsome, a friend of a great number of Lords. He was exciting and gallant. And I just had to be with him.

"Then, one early summer night, during a wedding celebration for one of my cousins, he invited me out to a secluded part of the estate, and..." She couldn't say the words.

"He used you, didn't he?"

Angela nodded. She could feel tears on her cheeks as she remembered. It hadn't been nice or wonderful or anything. She'd felt dirty and abused.

"When I went to my parents, I thought they would help, that they would make it all better, but all they did was blame me for the whole thing. I didn't know, but they'd arranged a marriage to the son of a much wealthier family than ours, and I'd destroyed their hopes." She put her hands in her head, the tears flowing freely like they hadn't since Monteous had come to give her some hope of a better life.

She felt hands on her, rubbing her shoulders. "Angela, it was not your fault. Men who do that sort of thing are a blight on the lives of women."

"My parents confronted him, after, and he blamed me for seducing him. And they believed him."

Marena dug in a bit more as she worked Angela's shoulders. "Not all men are like that, and not all men would blame you for something that was clearly not your fault. How do you know Robert is one of those men?"

"I don't, but I just couldn't live through him tossing me aside."

"Angela, look at me." Angela felt Marena's hands move to the sides of her head, gently guiding Angela to look. There was understanding in Marena's face, and something else, the look of someone who loved a challenge. "There are things a woman can do to a man that will make him love her so much, that he will overlook even this. You are beautiful enough, and powerful enough, that if you want him, you can have him. You just have to ensnare him so that there is no possibility of escape or thought of leaving, no matter what you do."

"But..."

"You're no longer the girl you were. You're a wizard, and you're a woman, and if that doesn't make a combination of power that can overwhelm a man's heart, I don't know what would. Trust me. Once I decided Ivron was going to be mine, he never stood a chance."

"I'm not a..."

"Wizard? Virgin? It doesn't matter. You will be a wizard, regardless of your protestations that you aren't. The other thing, you have three choices. You can lie to him and live with it, or you can tell him the truth, or you can just not worry about it and see what happens. If he never asks, you'll never have to tell."

"I could never lie to him."

"No, I understand that, and I wouldn't recommend it, either. Lies result in more lies and vicious, ugly marriages."

"Marriage?"

"Forget I said that, but ultimately, that's what you'll be after, I assume, with Robert, or with someone else. Trust me, though. Lies are a poisons that destroy relationships."

"I can't just tell him the truth, either."

"Of course you can. You only risk him walking away. But that leaves you with the option of not telling him, and hoping he doesn't find out some other way. Imagine, for instance, you took him to visit your parents. Would they remain silent?"

"I'd never visit my parents." She couldn't imagine ever returning home.

Marena's eyebrow raised at this. "Are you sure? Not even to gloat? To show them what you've become?"

It would be nice, she thought, to go home and show them what she'd become. Even nicer if she could bring someone home as her husband, someone they would admire. Gods, she couldn't not tell Robert, if it came to that. She'd have to tell him before she ever took him to meet her parents.

She sunk her head into her hands. "Everything I do risks losing him."

"It's a problem, sure. But you don't even have him yet. You're putting the carriage before the horse."

And she was. Angela recognized that. She wanted him to be hers. The man, no — the wizard, he'd become, and he was so nice to her, so polite and thoughtful. He never had a harsh word, nor was he sneaky, like Gerard.

Gerard. He wasn't here. But. Maybe Marena had an answer. "There's one more reason I can't let him know I'm interested."

"Another reason?"

"After I told Gerard I wasn't interested in him, Gerard threatened to tell Robert that he had already had me."

"Dear, that's just spite and jealousy talking. It may even just have been impulse. He may have no intention of following through with it. It isn't true, is it?"

"No!"

Marena smiled. "Good. At least you don't have to worry about that, too." She stood, putting hands on Angela's shoulders again. "Do you want to find out if you can get your man?"

"I'll have to tell him."

"Of course, dear. But you don't have to tell him tonight."

"I'll have to tell him before Gerard returns."

"Yes, probably. But that's up to you. First, you've must figure out if he's interested in you, and I can certainly help you ensure his interest. Do you want my help?"

Do I really want to do this? Her hands trembled at the thought. Her whole body felt wrung tight with anxious tension. But Marena was right, wasn't she? If she wanted Robert, she'd have to let go of herself. She'd have to risk losing him. Was it worth it? She didn't know. But one thing she did know. Once Robert passed the tests, she might never have another chance to find out. And if they never got Monteous back? If Orliss won? If Orliss really was working against the Kingdoms?

She looked up at Marena. "Yes." It was all she could muster, for the moment. But it was the right step, even if it scared her more than just about anything ever had. She was prepared to risk reliving the pain that sent her to Monteous.

"Good. Stand up. Let's go ready ourselves for dinner."

CHAPTER 18

ORLISS STARED OUT his window and silently cursed the weather. The blizzard had taken him by surprise, which normally wouldn't have happened, but he'd been so busy, and Monteous's apprentices had proved resourceful, or too damned lucky for words.

And now, the mercenaries he hired were caught out in the blizzard, most of them likely dead by morning, or so cold as to be useless at containing that trumped up Lord Ivron and Demetrius.

At least Monteous was safely under control, miles from the city under the protection of three of Orliss's closest allies in the Guild. Orliss wished he could just kill that damnable man, but if he did that, he risked losing the support he had. Monteous was too well respected. If Monteous died, and any rumor, or truth, escaped indicating that he was responsible, Orliss could very well find himself hanged by his allies.

Silas had even warned him. That odious man had the gall to bar him from killing Monteous. "If Monteous dies, we will not sit you as Senior. It is enough that he is absent from the Conclave."

And for what they knew, it was enough.

So Monteous had to live, at least until the seating was over, and the vote on Monteous's preposterous proposal to train more wizards.

"How long will this last?"

Orliss didn't even turn to face Boreth, the ambassador from Mrongil. The man had been his guest for two days now, here to see that his money was put to good use. Orliss hated him near as much as he hated Monteous, but could do nothing about it. Yet. "It may be over by morning, or it could last three days. It is difficult to know."

"Will it delay the Conclave?"

"Weather will not delay a Conclave."

"I must say, Orliss, that I am worried. You haven't proven very adept at corralling those apprentices."

Orliss felt anger grow in him. He gripped the window sill to keep himself from turning around and letting loose all of his frustrations on the Ambassador. Orliss needed him yet.

"The apprentices are of little concern. They are contained at Ivron's estate."

"But didn't one of your allies reside there? Didn't he have a Laboratory?"

"Yes, but they are apprentices, and we have the estate surrounded. There is little they can do from there."

The Laboratory did worry him a bit. If those apprentices found some of the Works, and understood what they were, there could be problems, and they would have to be dealt with. But they were apprentices, and apprentices should not know any of those Works.

There was one other bit that worried him, which fortunately, the Ambassador had not yet learned. Demetrius had escaped, and was free to cause trouble. Hopefully, he was caught out in this blizzard, too, and would freeze to death. But Orliss didn't trust his luck to be that good. Demetrius was out there, somewhere, and as soon as the blizzard let up, Demetrius would cause trouble for him.

"They will be free to go as soon as the blizzard lets up, you know."

"I know. But Monteous is hidden, and they have no way of finding him in time. I have three wizards watching over him, and the Conclave begins in two days."

"I hope, for your sake, that you are right. The Emperor doesn't take kindly to failures."

Orliss lost control of his anger at that moment. He grabbed his staff that was never far from his person, and whirled to face Boreth. He wrapped energie around the man and started squeezing. "You are in my house, in my country, in the Kingdom that I will rule. You watch your words, or you will find yourself never returning to your Emperor. I'm sure he will be sad to hear you lost your life to bandits in the countryside."

"I am... sorry... Master.... Orliss..." He barely got the words out.

Orliss kept squeezing him for a few moments, to drive the point home, then released him. "Leave me."

Boreth bowed, then turned and left without a word.

Two days. He had to keep Monteous hidden for those two days, plus at least two more, depending on how the Conclave voted. He went back to staring out the window. If only he could banish his greatest fear the way he banished the Emperor's puppet. He should have done something about Monteous's oldest apprentice when he'd had the chance.

But the Weave around Monteous's laboratory was dangerous. It had proved lethal to the wizard he'd sent to get the apprentices out.

Even so, it had been a mistake not to try. Given the energie that apprentice controlled, he needed a strong master. Not someone weak like Monteous.

I need to find that apprentice.

ROBERT AND IVRON were walking across the foyer when Angela appeared at the top of the sweeping staircase. Robert stopped almost immediately, and had to work hard to keep his mouth from gaping. He had thought her beautiful before, but standing at the top of the stairs, she looked like a princess. Her hair had been washed and curled and cascaded down onto bare shoulders. There was something about her face, too. Makeup? She never wore makeup. The dress she wore wrapped her close around her breasts, exposing just enough skin to muddle his brain, while hiding enough to remain decent.

He barely even noticed when Marena stepped onto the landing behind her.

"Robert, what do you think?" Angela asked.

He couldn't drive any words out of his mouth, as they were stuck in the back of his throat.

She laughed. "You can breathe, now." And then she started down the stairs.

Robert heard Ivron chuckle next to him. "I think you are going to have an interesting evening."

The two women reached the bottom of the stairs, and Marena stepped up to her husband and gave him a kiss, then slipped her arm through his.

Angela stopped in front of Robert. "So, what do you think? Really?"

"I think I have never seen anyone so beautiful as you are right now." And then he grimaced, wishing he'd said something more eloquent.

She stood on her toes and kissed him on the cheek. "Thank you," she said, and then snuck her arm through his, mimicking the Lord and his Lady.

Robert's heart pounded in his chest. He stood there, with her arm through his, feeling her close to him. It reminded him briefly of the hug they'd shared, but this was different somehow. This was deliberate. *Why now?*

Ivron and his wife started off to the dining room, but Robert stayed where he was, rooted in place by his confusion and shock.

"Are we going to eat, Robert?" There was a joy in her voice he'd never heard before. She was enjoying him being off balance. Or maybe something else, but he couldn't figure it out.

"Uh, sure." And he stepped forward to the dining room, her arm firmly wrapped through his.

Once they were in the dining room, she disengaged, and waited for something. After a moment, Robert realized what she waited for, and he pulled a chair out and helped her seat herself. Once she was settled, he went to go seat himself across from her, but she caught his hand, stopping him. She patted the chair next to her. "Sit here."

He looked to Ivron, saw him smiling, then caught a similar smile on Marena's face as the circled the table to take seats across from Angela.

If she wanted him to sit next to her, he wasn't going to argue, especially since it seemed Ivron and Marena were involved in whatever plan Angela had cooked up.

The servant that had informed them dinner was ready stepped in. "My Lord, Master Wallace has decided not to join you for dinner and elected to take his meal in the Laboratory instead."

Ivron nodded. Robert, however, wondered if Wallace's absence was part of the plan. And whatever plan was it?

For months, she'd played coy with him, and it had only gotten worse these past few days. She'd do something to make him think she might have interest in him, only to quickly turn and be cold as a stone in winter.

His thoughts were interrupted by the first course of the meal arriving. A warm, spicy smelling soup that had his mouth watering almost immediately. He took a spoon and started ladling it into his mouth.

"So Robert," Marena said, "Angela tells me you've been with Monteous a long time."

He nodded, not knowing where she was leading him. He felt sure she was leading him somewhere.

"Would you mind greatly if I asked how long? Wizards do interest me so."

Robert glanced at Angela. What were they talking about that this would come up? "I've been with him since I was a boy."

"Isn't that early? I didn't think wizards took apprentices until they were thirteen."

Robert again looked at Angela, and this time, he thought he caught her looking at him. He tried to remember, but he didn't think he'd ever told her how early he'd been with Monteous. The memories weren't exactly something he liked to talk about.

"I wasn't an apprentice the first few years. He was more like a foster father."

Marena's eyes softened, before she asked the question he knew was coming. He'd answered Ivron, but he wasn't sure he wanted to answer Marena, not with Angela here. She'd grown up wealthy. What would she think if she knew where he'd come from? Vanarth had not exactly been a wealthy town.

"Then something happened to your parents?"

Robert looked then at Angela, and she was looking back at him. This time, she did not turn away. He decided he would say as little as possible, and was about to speak, but then Ivron spoke up. "Marena, this is a subject best not discussed here."

Robert saw Marena look at her husband, then nod. "I'm sorry for prying, I did not mean to be so rude."

"It's alright."

They sipped their soup in silence for a while after that. When their soup was done, a new course was placed in front of them, this time a plate of meat, sliced into strips, and it smelled wonderful to Robert.

Eventually, Ivron put his fork down. "Angela, I know Robert is soon to take his tests. How long until you take yours?"

"It's not so much a length of time as the speed at which you progress. I'm doing well, I think, though not so well as Robert does. It will likely be a few years, yet."

"You seemed to do well getting Demetrius and Gerard out of here."

"That's one of the types of Weaves I'm good at. There are other areas where I need quite a bit of work."

Throughout the conversation, Robert kept sneaking glances at Angela, and saw nearly every time that she was sneaking glances at him.

When the meat was done, the servants brought a cake for dessert, topped with berries that they somehow had managed to keep fresh.

Angela apparently wondered, too. "How did you manage to keep the berries good into the middle of winter?"

Ivron laughed, but it was a dark laugh. "One of the things my late, traitorous wizard was good for was keeping berries frozen. Marena loves them on cakes. I was able to give her what she loves. Now, I fear, I will run out and we will no longer have berries during the winter."

"When we find Monteous, maybe we can find a way to make a Work that will keep your berries frozen, to repay you for all your help." Robert saw that Angela was looking right at Marena as she said it.

"That would be wonderful," said Marena.

But the mood in the room grew somber at the mention of Monteous, and another silence ensued while they finished their cake.

Marena stood up. "I refuse to have this evening be spoiled by thoughts of the outside world. Husband, call for the harper. I want to dance."

Robert froze. *Dance? I hope she doesn't want me to dance!* He'd never danced since joining Monteous, and he'd certainly never danced like he expected Marena wanted to dance.

Ivron crooked a finger, and when his servant appeared, Ivron said, "Have Luos meet us in the great room, and have him bring his harp. Marena wants to dance."

"Come, come," Marena said. "Stand up. This will be far more fun than sitting here at the table moping."

Robert grimaced inside. *More fun until I trip and fall and embarrass myself.* But he stood up, and when Angela lifted her hand to him, he helped her stand, too. When he tried to let go of her hand, she held on and wouldn't let go. *Why?*

They followed Marena into the great room, and it was a room designed for hosting parties. A large area in the center was clear for dancing, and there were a few small tables around the walls where people could sit and talk quietly. Luos, Robert assumed, was on a small riser to one end of the room, readying his harp.

Robert leaned in close to Angela and whispered, "I've never danced before."

She giggled. "Then this will be fun, as I haven't danced since I came to Monteous. We will just have to try to avoid stepping on each other's feet and falling over."

"But I don't know what to do."

"It's easy. You put your left hand on my hip, and your right hand in my right hand, and then move with the music. And try not to step on my feet."

"If you say so."

"Robert, if you need an example, just watch Ivron and Marena."

He looked then, at the Lord and his Lady, and saw what they were doing, and he stepped into Angela and tried to mimic Ivron's stance. The harper started playing almost immediately, and Angela took his hand, and placed her right arm on his shoulder, and they began to move, and it was easy, somehow. He let the music flow around him like it was a Weave, and just followed what it asked him to do.

After a few moments, Angela leaned in closer. "You dance wonderfully, for someone who doesn't know how to dance."

Right then, she was so close, and he could feel the curves of her as she leaned in. He wanted the dance to last forever. He had no idea why she was so interested in him tonight, when in the past, about the time she seemed ready to tell him something, to acknowledge feelings for him or something, she drew away like she was afraid of him.

He knew how he felt about her. If he could just figure out what it was she was afraid of.

But for now, the dance would be enough.

ANGELA ALMOST COULDN'T believe she was here, in the grand hall of this estate, dancing with Robert like a Lord and Lady. His dance was fluid, like the music. Natural, despite the occasional misstep. She never wanted to let go of his hands, nor wanted him to remove his hand from her waist.

After hearing the aborted attempt to find out about his past by

Marena, she was curious to know what had happened. She'd known he'd been with Monteous since he was a boy, but she'd never found out why. Robert never spoke of it, and she hadn't had the time or the reason to really try to figure it out. She also hadn't wanted to risk him, or anyone, finding out why she was there. Monteous had said on their arrival, "All your secrets are yours to share or not as you desire." And he'd kept to that.

But now, she knew she had to reveal her secret. Marena was right. After feeling Robert in her arms, she knew she had to tell him, somehow, had to trust him. Doing nothing at all was as good as letting him go. But she trembled inside at the thought of opening that wound up to him.

The harper started a third song, a slow piece that let them stay close together. *Marena must have said something to the harper. Well, now, or never.*

"Robert."

His eyes moved so that he was looking into her own, right, it felt, into her soul. She didn't know if she could go through with it. *But I have to, or I will do nothing and I will never have him.*

"I've wanted to tell you something for a long time," she said, "but I've been unwilling to risk the consequences."

"Consequences?" She could feel his heartbeat racing though him. His hand was growing sweaty. Or was that hers? She couldn't tell.

"Yes." And then her tongue froze. She couldn't say the words that were on her lips. Not yet, not until she knew for sure whether he felt the way she did. But it was so brazen for her to say the other. But...

"Hang me for being forward," she said. "I've seen you, how you look at me, always happy to see me, and never a bad word in my direction. Are you interested in courting me?"

His eyes opened wide, and his mouth wider, like he wanted to say something, and his steps faltered and he nearly stepped on her right foot as he stopped dancing. But no words came out. She'd surprised him, and she wanted to laugh, but held it in.

"Robert?"

He came out of it then, and said, "Yes," as if testing the temperature of the water with his toe. After a moment, it seemed he liked the temperature. "For as long as you've been with Monteous."

"Why have you not asked me?" She pulled him back into dancing with her.

"I was unsure if you'd be interested. One moment you'd seem like you would be, then another, you'd pull back like you had no interest at all."

Her heart felt all fluttery. "I've been interested in you, too."

"But then why?"

And here she was, on the edge of the abyss. Did she step off, and hope something caught her? She was breathing rapidly, and she forced herself to calm down.

"Did Monteous ever tell you why I came to be his apprentice?"

"No. He's always maintained that, once you're an apprentice, where you came from is of no matter."

"Well, promise me one thing."

"What?"

"That you will keep what I'm telling you a secret, and that you won't leave me here on the dance floor alone, no matter what you think of me after."

He smiled the smile that she loved. "That's two things."

"Just promise."

His face grew solemn. "I promise."

Angela told her story then, how she'd been tricked, and her family lied to, and essentially cast out, until Monteous came for her, and as she told it, she watched Robert's face grow hard and grave. He said nothing until she was finished. Her heart was beating so fast she felt faint. The tension in her head felt like it was going to rip her apart.

And then, he did what she didn't expect. He stopped dancing and pulled her close and hugged her tight. The tension flowed out of her, along with the tears that ran down her face, taking the carefully worked makeup with it.

He whispered into her ear. "My family was poor. We lived in a small town called Vanarth. I loved my parents and thought I had a good life. And then, there was an uprising, and lots of the townsfolk were killed during the attempt to crush it. Monteous found me and saved me, and told me my parents had both died."

Angela could feel him shaking in her arms.

"That your parents believed this bastard over you, that they worry more about their wealth than the well-being of their own, it sickens me. How could they do that to you?" She pulled back a bit to look into his eyes. Through her tears, she saw rage and compassion in his.

"Monteous is right, though. Whatever we were before, it is in the past. We are wizards, first and foremost, and whatever your parents may think, I am not going to be turned away by something done to you against your will."

All the tension left her, and she could barely hold herself up. If Robert hadn't been holding her, she would have sunk to her knees.

"You were worried I'd cast you away, too?"

She nodded her head against his chest.

He hugged her close, the strength of his arms pressing her into him. "I won't ever cast you away."

"There's one more thing I have to tell you."

"Something else?"

"Gerard. He..."

"You were with him." She felt him stiffen, but just a little.

"No, I wasn't. But he threatened me that if I ever went with you, he would tell you that he and I had been intimate."

"But I would have heard the lie. It would be easy to expose the lie."

"Yes, but it would have exposed the rest."

"And you worried about me finding out about that. Oh, Angela, how much time have we wasted?"

She looked up at him. "I don't care. I just don't want to waste any more."

She separated from him and got herself in position to dance. "Let's not waste any more of this music, either."

He joined her, and they danced long into the night, neither of them noticing when Ivron and Marena departed.

CHAPTER 19

GERARD AWOKE, EARLY in the morning, to find the snow had stopped falling and the wind had eased. The clouds above still looked angry and full. Owen's wife fed them a quick, hot breakfast. Soon after they finished eating, they prepared to leave.

As Gerard was about to step out into the cold, Nina emerged from her room. She wore a heavy coat, and had a pack strapped to her back and a bow over her shoulder.

Her father apparently saw her, too. "What do you think you are doing, Nina?"

"I'm going with them."

"You are not going with them."

Gerard stood where he was, trying not to draw attention to himself.

Nina stamped her foot. "Why not?"

"It's too dangerous. You don't know what they're facing."

"And you do?"

Owen put his hands on his hips, settling in like a rock. "I know quite a bit more about it than you do, Nina."

Nina took a breath, and stared at her father for a moment. "The fate of the Seven Kingdoms may be at stake, and you want me to sit here and do nothing."

Gerard thought he caught a flicker of a smile on Owen's face. Pride, perhaps. "That's exactly right. I need you here. You're not some big dull-witted swordsman."

At this point, Demetrius stepped across the room, bent down and whispered into Nina's ear. Gerard couldn't catch what was said, but whatever it was, it mollified her.

"Fine," she said. "I won't leave with them."

Gerard couldn't decide whether he was disappointed or relieved.

Demetrius came over to him and laid a hand on his shoulder. "Let's go. Time's wasting."

Gerard followed Demetrius out into the cold, where he found the horses saddled and waiting. The snow around the door had been shoveled away. Piles of it lay off to the side.

Nina came running up behind him and grabbed his coat to turn him around. He found himself looking down, and she stood up on her toes and kissed him quickly. Her lips were warm, and softer than he'd imagined. He found himself longing for a repeat.

"You better come back," she said.

"I will."

"Promise me."

It wasn't hard to promise her. He was already looking forward to more conversation and kisses. "I promise."

Demetrius laughed, and Gerard heard Owen snickering, too.

"What?"

"I warned you," said Owen.

"Time to leave, Gerard," said Demetrius as he climbed on his horse.

Gerard turned and left Nina to get on his horse.

He looked back as they left, their horses stepping gingerly through two feet of snow. Nina stood in the snow watching him go, and he reflected back on the previous evening.

Their talk had lasted long into the night, and he'd found himself talking about his entire life. Eventually, the discussion had somehow come around to Angela, and what he'd done.

Nina had looked at him then, disapproval in her eyes, when he'd told her what he'd threatened. "Gerard," she said, "that's beneath you and you know it. You need to apologize to her first thing, or I will have nothing to do with you."

It had been easy to agree, for he'd already decided the same thing, but the look in Nina's eyes had been enough to convince him not to delay. She might not be a wizard, but he would never want to cross this woman.

Once they entered the trees and he could no longer see her, he faced forward again. He would come back for her. No matter what happened, he'd hold to his promise.

Without turning to face him, Demetrius said, "Don't be surprised, Gerard, if we find her following us before too long."

Gerard urged his horse to catch up with Demetrius. "What do you mean?"

"I've known that girl quite a long time. When she makes up her mind to do something, she does it. She may not have the innate power that you or the other apprentices do, but the rules that keep her from being trained are poor rules. She would make a formidable wizard, I think. Her will is as strong as anyone I've known."

"What will we do if she shows up?"

"She'll come with us, of course. She can shoot well. I've seen it." Then he turned to Gerard and laughed. "If she's decided you're hers, I think you are in for some interesting times."

Gerard chose to ignore that last. He didn't know how to respond in any case. "What's our plan, then?"

"We continue on to the bridge farther south, and cross there, if they haven't guarded it too strongly. Hopefully, they won't be expecting us to travel that far."

"Do we have enough time?"

"The Conclave is in two days. If we can make good time, we should be there about this time tomorrow. If another storm comes in, or if this snow thaws, we'll have trouble."

They rode in silence, then, for quite a while, each of them keeping their thoughts to themselves. Georg and Horuth didn't talk much either.

When Gerard heard the sounds of a horse quickly approaching from behind, he looked to Demetrius for direction, but Demetrius shook his head and smiled. Moments later, Nina pulled up in their midst, dressed for the weather, and sporting an unstrung bow across her back.

"Hello, Demetrius," she said.

"Nina. I'm surprised you weren't along sooner."

"Pa suspected I would leave. He made it difficult to pack."

Demetrius turned his horse back to the trail. "On our way, then. We don't have much time."

Gerard couldn't believe Demetrius hadn't even argued with her, but then, maybe he was right.

She pulled up next to Gerard, and he heard the two soldiers snicker. She leaned over to him and said in a quiet voice, "You're not getting away from me that easily, Gerard." Then, she leaned back and urged her horse forward to catch up with Demetrius.

Gerard was left without even the chance to respond. Nina was nice, and he certainly wanted to see more of her, but she acted like she'd claimed him somehow. He felt the urge to turn and run quickly the other way, but he didn't. Something told him she'd follow if he tried to leave, and he still had to help stop Orliss.

ROBERT WOKE TO a pounding on his door.

"Robert, Robert, wake up."

It was Ivron. Robert turned and looked through the window. Dawn was just breaking, if the light through the window was any indication. The fire was just coals.

"Come in," Robert said. "I don't think it's locked."

Ivron poked his head in. "Get dressed quickly. The storm has freed us from our jailors. We must leave before they return."

Ivron ducked out and ran down the hall. Robert swung his legs out from under the warm covers and into the cold morning air of the room. "He could have sent someone to stoke the fire, first."

But he didn't let that delay him, and quickly put his clothes on and got his things together.

When he'd made it down to the dining room — *Ivron surely doesn't expect us to leave without breakfast* — he found food already on the table and Wallace just filling his plate.

Robert sat and scooped eggs and bread onto his own plate. "You didn't come in last night."

Wallace looked up from his food. "The books that wizard had are fascinating."

"Did you find anything about the crystal?"

"No, but there are Works in them that can do amazing things. It's a shame that most of them are proscribed."

Robert was about to say something to Wallace about staying away from those books when Angela arrived and he quickly forgot what he was going to say as she turned his head to the side, and planted a kiss on his cheek.

"Good morning," she said as she sat down. Robert brought his head back to the table and looked at her.

She was smiling as if she had not a care in the world, and Robert thought back to all the tension at the start of the previous night, and how it melted away. And he smiled.

"Did I miss something last night?" Wallace asked.

Robert looked at Angela, and she looked at him, and they both broke out laughing. It was good, and Robert was glad the days of confusion seemed to have been left in the past.

Then, Ivron arrived and sat down and immediately filled his plate.

"We have to leave quickly," he said, "so eat up. The quicker we can get across the river, the more time we'll have to find Monteous and formulate a plan to rescue him."

"How are we going to cross? Won't they have the ferry guarded?"

"I doubt they'll have too many men standing around outside in this weather. We should be able to cross with little incident, especially since I'm taking the largest portion of my guard. The rest will go with my wife to stay with an ally further east. I will leave this place bare until this is over. We don't have much time, and we won't be coming back."

"So what happened to the people surrounding us?"

"They either left, or froze to death in the storm. I'm assuming they were paid mercenaries, and probably left."

They ate quickly, and were soon out in the snow, wrapped in the warmest clothes Ivron had available. The courtyard swarmed with men and horses, preparing to leave the estate.

Robert and Angela ducked inside the Laboratory to grab useful items. Robert picked up some metal rods, as well as some knives and a short wand that the previous owner had left. It wouldn't be as good as a staff, as he wouldn't be able to run as much energie through it, but it would be better than nothing at all. He wouldn't have time, or the materials, to create a proper staff with iron end caps and specialized metals embedded in it. He also picked up the crystal, which Wallace had left on the work bench. He held it up, and could see the Weave still pulsing inside. He tucked it into a pocket.

Angela retrieved her own wand, and quickly sorted through the powders and herbs in the Laboratory, picking out things she would need and stashing them in small pouches intended for travel. Robert didn't pay much attention to what she took, but he assumed she intended to be prepared to give Monteous any aid she could.

She came over to him, put her hands on his shoulders, and made him face her. "Whatever happens, thank you for understanding. I was so terrified." She pulled him close, put her hand behind his head and pulled it to her, then kissed him. Her lips were soft against his, and warm, and he slipped his arms around her and pulled her tight against him. It seemed to last forever, while not lasting near long enough.

By some unspoken mutual agreement, they separated, and he looked into her eyes as they sparkled in the light coming through the windows. "Thank you," he said, "for telling me. I was so confused."

She laughed. "Marena says you're supposed to be confused." She followed it up immediately with another kiss so he couldn't respond, and then pulled away, and headed for the door. "They're waiting for us."

Robert thought knowing how she felt about him might be worse than not knowing, but didn't think he should say that aloud. He quickly glanced around the Laboratory, seeing if there was anything else he should take, and couldn't find anything, then followed her out into the cold of the courtyard.

They made their way through the horses and the men to where Ivron was standing next to Wallace, who held the reins of one horse. A stableman stood near them, with two other horses, which Robert immediately assumed were for him and Angela. The stableman passed off the reins of a large black gelding to him, and the reins of a smaller brown horse to Angela.

"Are you ready for this?"

The fog from their breath obscured everything. "No, but it doesn't seem we have much choice."

"It's going to be a cold ride. Keep your heads covered."

Ivron turned to face the rest of the crowded courtyard. "Mount up!" He promptly mounted his own horse.

The rest of them mounted their own horses, and soon, they were formed up. Ivron, Wallace, Angela and Robert sat their horses behind a vanguard. The rest of the soldiers that were going with them lined up behind them. Robert counted twenty in all. A small group would be staying with Ivron's wife, to leave soon after and take her east.

The gate opened wide, and the party rode out through it in pairs, the vanguard riding quickly forward to ensure the way was clear. A worry that it was a trap, and they were all going to get slaughtered after they were through the gate gnawed at Robert as he passed out of the courtyard and into the open, but by the time he cleared the gate, the vanguard was at the tree line, and he could see that the forest was empty.

As they entered the forest, Wallace dropped back to talk with him. "Why am I going along? I feel so useless."

Robert remembered when he first started his apprenticeship. He recalled long hours of reading, cleaning, learning to see the energies and manipulate them. It took him years to even be able to light a candle. But he didn't tell Wallace that. "You're not useless."

"How so? I can't do much of anything."

"Who saw the Weave that ended up trapping Angela?"

"I did."

"See, you're not useless. Neither Angela, nor Gerard saw it, but you did. I want you to be our lookout. You've always been perceptive. You learn quickly, and you may be able to see things easily that we would have to really search for." He ducked his head under a low hanging branch, heavy with snow. "If you see anything, and I mean anything at all that looks strange, I need to know."

Robert could see the posture of Wallace straighten a little as he thought about what Robert said. "I can do that."

"Also, if we have time, I'll help you start working with the wand. We'll need to find a sapling and carve it for you, and it won't have anything special beyond the properties of the wood, but it will be something you can focus with."

"You'd do that?" The excitement in his voice was obvious.

"Yes. We'll need all the help we can get, I think, to get Monteous back. I don't know if we'll have time to make you any good with it, but since we don't have any books for you to study, we'll have to make do."

"Thanks, Robert."

"Okay, now I need to go talk with Angela."

"Are you and her..."

"I hope so. Now go."

Wallace pulled ahead, leaving room for Angela to move up beside him.

"I heard what you told him."

"About what?"

"Are you really going to start him on wands? You might get in trouble for that."

"You heard that. I know I could get in trouble, but I don't care. I think we're going to need every possible advantage we can find to free Monteous. He's ready, anyway."

"But you're not a Master yet."

She was right. Apprentices weren't allowed to teach, except under the guidance of a Master. "What if it might make the difference between rescuing Monteous, and letting Orliss become the Senior Wizard? I think Monteous will cover for me."

"I suppose you're right. Keeping Orliss from prevailing is worth the risk."

They rode in silence after that. The trees sheltered them from the wind, for the most part, and they weren't riding fast, but the cold still bit at his ears and his face He pulled his hood tight around him. He hadn't realized what it would be like, having Angela at his side, knowing that she had feelings for him. It kept him, he thought, far warmer than he would have otherwise been.

CHAPTER 20

B Y MID-MORNING, WHEN Gerard followed Demetrius across the river into Shortbridge, there were still very few people moving about, and it had started to snow again. Shortbridge was laid out essentially on one road that led right up to the foot of the bridge. Most of the buildings were constructed primarily of wood, with the forest near, and were limited to a single storey. The one exception was the inn, which had a second floor of rooms. Demetrius suggested they step inside to warm up for a bit before they turned north on the road to the City.

Gerard quickly assented, welcoming the idea of being warm for a few minutes, and perhaps a chance to get some food into his belly. It was already taunting him despite the breakfast they'd eaten before they set out.

They tied their horses to the post in front of the inn, and Demetrius led them inside.

Gerard's eyes took a moment to adjust, coming from the snow into the fairly dark common room, but as they did, he saw a well kept establishment. He didn't know what he'd expected, but the place was clean, warm, and inviting. There were several guests sitting at tables spread around the room, talking, and probably snowed in. A fire roared in a large fireplace, and the smells of warm bread and spiced meat came from the kitchen. Stairs descended from the second storey to the rear of the common room.

They seated themselves at a table as close to the hearth as they could get, which wasn't all that close. The tables immediately surrounding it were occupied. Demetrius took the chair with the best view of the room, and Gerard sat next to him, getting perhaps the second best view of the room. He slid his staff onto the floor under the table so that it would be out of the way during the meal. Nina sat on the other side of him, boxing him in against Demetrius. Georg and Horuth sat across from them, a blockade against the rest of the room.

A waitress came to their table, a towel in her hand, an empty serving tray in the other. "What may I get for you?"

Demetrius ordered for them all. "Some warm bread, whatever meat that is hot, and some tea for each of us."

"I'll be right back." She turned and left.

Gerard took some time to look around the room while trying to avoid eye contact with anyone. The patrons mostly appeared to be merchants. They would likely have left the inn were it not for the snow. No one looked particularly dangerous, nor did he see anyone who looked particularly interested in anyone other than the group they sat with.

As he started to take in the view beyond Nina's seat, he became aware of her studying him. She smiled when she noticed his slight start at being watched.

What did she want? The talk the night before was nice, and he liked her, and had planned on going back. The idea that she'd followed him here, that she was chasing him, he didn't know what to think about it. He did the chasing, not the girls. It was unsettling to think about, and unsettling to have her eyeing him like a wolf sizing up its prey.

"Why did you follow us?"

She laughed. "You don't know why?"

He could come up with several guesses, but he didn't want to state the most likely one out loud, so he shook his head no.

At which, she smiled even wider. "You don't like being chased, do you?"

"It's not right."

She poked him in the shoulder. "Who is to say it's not right? I live on a farm. You know what I see? I see dogs, cats, cattle. The female goes into heat and the males come running. The males think they're in charge, but who's really in control? Hmmmm? It's no different for us. Do you think your Pa ever did anything your Ma didn't want him to do without getting into a whole heap of trouble?"

He tried to think back, and no, he couldn't think of a time his father wasn't doing exactly what his mother wanted. He decided to remain silent.

"Of course not. So why did I come after you?"

"Because you're in charge."

"Right, Gerard. I'm in charge, and I've decided that you are mine. I don't care how long it takes to make you come around, but come around you will."

"No wonder your father was so eager to see you go," Gerard muttered under his breath.

She laughed again, and it was music to his ears. "I heard that."

He looked to Demetrius for help, but Demetrius was quick to say, "Don't look to me for help. You were the one that spent all last night talking to her. Didn't you hear Owen warn you about her?"

The waitress saved Gerard from having to answer by showing up at their table with the food and the tea, which Gerard was eager to dig into. The outside of his body had started to warm, but the inside needed the tea. The food wasn't anything special. It wasn't horrendous, either. The meat turned out to be seasoned mutton, which Gerard had not eaten in quite a while.

The waitress waited for some coin, which Demetrius dug out of his purse, and then left. Once she was gone, Demetrius said, "Eat quickly. We must be on the road again soon if we are to get to the City by nightfall."

Gerard didn't hesitate to follow the instructions.

When he'd eaten about half of his mutton, he heard someone walking down the stairs from above, and he turned to look. The man's face was lined with age and framed by a short, thin, mostly gray beard. But something caught Gerard's attention, and on a suspicion, he trained his sight on the energie surrounding the man. Visible energies surrounded everyone, but for most normal people, they flowed in chaotic fashion depending on the person's mood. This man's energies were ordered and under control.

He leaned over to Demetrius, and whispered, "The old man coming down the stairs. He's a wizard."

"I know."

"You know?"

"Yes, I know him. Don't worry. We're in no immediate danger."

Gerard was confused. "Why not?"

"He doesn't sit very high in the Guild, and he's always been friendly to Monteous. Now, be quiet."

"Demetrius."

The voice came from behind Gerard, and he turned to find the man at their table.

"Erin, it's been too long."

"Yes, yes it has. Do you mind if I join you?"

Gerard thought it didn't exactly sound like a request, but more like he expected to be allowed. Demetrius waved Georg out of his seat, and Georg stood, taking the last of his food with him, moving to a table nearby. Horuth looked around the table, then quickly gathered his plate and went to sit with Georg.

Gerard felt the old man's eyes on him, probing him. He wondered what they saw. Erin looked to Nina, then, but not for as long. "They stay?" he asked.

"Yes, they need to hear what you can tell me, if you can tell me anything.

Gerard was surprised at Nina being included.

"I can't tell you much."

"What can you tell me?"

"I've been contacted no less than three times, pressured each time to vote against Monteous."

"Do you know who contacted you?"

"I have my guesses. They weren't very subtle. Monteous will be there won't he?"

"I don't think he intends to give up his seat. He still wants to change the rules on apprentices."

Gerard continued to eat, thinking through the implications of Demetrius skirting the truth. Demetrius apparently didn't trust this man, or maybe there was something else going on.

The old man rubbed at his beard. "That's good to hear. There have been rumors."

"Rumors?"

"You haven't heard them? There are rumors that Monteous has decided not to attend."

"I hope you didn't believe them."

"If I believed them, do you think I would be here? I had to hear it from someone as close to him as I could get at this time of year."

Demetrius leaned back in his chair. "He hasn't told me of any change of plans, and the issues on the agenda are far too important to him. I can't imagine he would miss it."

Then the old man looked straight at Gerard again, his eyes practically boring holes in to his brain, digging around. "Are you going to introduce me to the young apprentice here?"

Of course he knew, just like I knew he was a wizard, Gerard thought.

"This is Gerard. Gerard, this is Erin Soughty, Wizard of the Guild."

"Good to meet you Gerard." The wizard's eyes still held his.

"Good to meet you, Master Erin." Gerard tried to break his gaze away, but he couldn't. The Master may be physically frail, but his command of himself and his energies still had strength.

"What are you doing out and about? I've never heard that Monteous lets his apprentices roam around the countryside, especially not with rogues such as Demetrius."

Demetrius coughed. "Monteous had me take him on a small errand, delivering something to a patron. Monteous felt there wasn't enough time to deliver it himself and still prepare for the Conclave."

"Aah, and the girl?"

"A protégé of mine."

"She has some of the talent."

"But not enough, so Monteous bade me teach her what I could of my work so that she would be near at hand if he could get the rules changed."

Gerard tried to keep his visage immobile to cover his shock at hearing Demetrius lie to the wizard. He feared he might give away the lie. Gerard would have to ferret the reason out of Demetrius as soon as he could.

"Do you like the work with Demetrius, girl?"

Nina surprised Gerard by answering. "Yes, actually, I do."

Demetrius regained Erin's attention. "I'm really sorry, Master Erin, but we must be going. We have a long way to ride before night-fall."

"Of course, of course. Don't let me stop you." He placed his hands on the table and pushed himself up, slowly, so that he was standing. "A pleasure to meet you all." He turned and walked over to the bar.

Gerard looked at Demetrius, and Demetrius said, "Later. We need to go." Then he stood.

Gerard reached under the table and picked up his staff, then moved to follow Demetrius to the door. He was followed by Nina, then the two guards, out into the cold where they quickly got on their horses and started riding north toward the city.

Once they were out of sight of the town, Gerard pulled up next to Demetrius. "Why did you lie to him about Nina and me? Isn't he an ally of Monteous?"

"He votes for Monteous, and with Monteous, generally. If you re-member, though, he said he'd been pressured. If he thought there was any chance Monteous might not make the Conclave, he might cave in to that pressure before the Conclave begins."

"But if Monteous shows up..."

"If Erin switches sides, others might follow. We can't allow him to think there is real substance to those rumors. This way, I hope, he will spread positive rumors among his own allies. The Guild is fractious. Alliances change quickly, sometimes for very little reason."

"Why is that? I always thought the Guild was essentially one entity."

"It is a single entity, made up of individuals, and the system by which it is run is based on personal power and seniority. If it weren't for the very real profits to be made by individuals, the system might work to preclude rapid shifts in coalitions. But since there are so few Guild members, alliances change quickly based on external forces, particularly where money is likely to be made."

"And Monteous thinks that by allowing more apprentices, and ultimately, more Guild members, that might change?"

"Yes. If members have to work together outside, it might eliminate much of the current snake pit of alliances and make it easier to get things done."

Gerard struggled to get his head around it. "Do you think it will work?"

"Who knows? Someone has to try something. No one in the Guild can get anything done at all, these days, and there remains the threat from outside. That has to be dealt with."

Demetrius pushed his horse to move faster, and from that point, the group rode in silence, each thinking their own thoughts.

WHILE THEY'D RIDDEN south from the estate, Robert kept pulling the crystal out and checking it, and the thread continued to point west across the river. And as they rode toward the river, it kept pointing west. He felt certain it pointed to Monteous, that it was an indication of a link, but how far did they have to go, and what would the find when they got there?

Any thoughts of warmth were long gone. It snowed on and off as they rode, light dustings, mostly, but a good indication that there was little chance the weather would warm and the snow would melt.

The vanguard rode ahead quite a distance, but kept in sight. Robert thought it almost wasn't necessary. Only crazy people, or those desperate as themselves, would be out in this weather. But perhaps Orliss was equally as desperate. Would his men be out in this weather? Maybe caution wasn't entirely unwarranted.

Angela stayed next to him during the ride. They exchanged glances and smiles, and each brought joy to his heart he'd never anticipated feeling. Whatever concern he'd had seemed to have flown away following her unexpected and amazing revelations.

He leaned over to her. "You know, the man who caused you to be here, I don't know whether to turn him into a frog, or to thank him."

"Thank him?" She looked at him, squinting. "Why ever would you want to *thank* him?"

"If he hadn't done what he did, and I know it was an awful thing for you to have to go through, but if he hadn't, you wouldn't be with me right now."

"That's sweet of you to say, Robert. But mostly, I just want to kill him." A fire burned behind her eyes, anger that ran deep.

"Oh, no. I'm sorry Angela, I didn't mean to..."

"Don't be sorry Robert. I have nightmares to this day about it. You couldn't have known. Honestly, it's probably best if we never speak of it."

He nodded. "Alright." And he resolved right then to never again broach the subject.

A few minutes later, the vanguard came riding back. Ivron put up his hand to halt the column, and spoke over his shoulder. "We've reached the ferry."

He rode ahead to speak with his returning soldiers. After they'd talked for a few moments, Angela leaned over to him. "What's taking them so long?"

Robert shook his head. "I don't know. I hope it's nothing to delay us."

After another couple minutes, Ivron returned to the column, and the soldiers headed back down the road toward the ferry.

Ivron came to Angela, Robert and Wallace. "We have a bit of a problem. My men say the ferry is on the other side of the river, and there appear to be two of Orliss's men watching it. You can bet others are nearby. There's an inn near the ferry, and it's likely Orliss's men are there keeping warm. A good shout from either of the two lookouts would bring the rest running, making it very difficult to cross. I've sent the three men to beg the ferryman to bring the boat across, and they likely won't attract anything more than curiosity from the watchers, but I dare not bring the rest of us to the shore. We could try to bring them down with archers, but it's quite a distance, and it's difficult to be sure of catching a man in the throat with an arrow."

"What do we do then?"

Ivron held his hands out toward them. "I was hoping you might have an idea. You're wizards, after all."

Robert looked to Angela and Wallace. "Any ideas?"

They both shook their heads. *What can I do?* The sword trick wouldn't work, he could only really control one sword at a time, and that wouldn't keep them silent, unless he killed them with it. He didn't think he could do that. Monteous had taught him that Weaves should only be used against others in self-defense, or in protection of the Seven Kingdoms as sanctioned by the Guild. He didn't think killing them with their own swords fit either of those descriptions.

But what else could he do?

But, maybe... "Can you get me close enough to the river to see them, without me being seen?"

"What do you have in mind?"

"I'm not sure yet if I can do it, so I don't want to get your hopes up."

Ivron sighed. "You wizards are all so secretive. Come on."

He turned his horse around and led them down the road.

"What do you have in mind, Robert?" Angela asked.

"We've practiced wrapping Weaves around things and moving

them. How different could it be to wrap a Weave around a man and keep him from moving?"

"But there are two men."

"Yes, that's why we need to see where they're at. If they're close enough, I can probably get them both. If they're too far apart, though, you'll probably have to take the other one."

She shook her head. "I don't know if I can, or how long I would be able to maintain the Weave."

"I'm sure you can."

"Robert, I don't have your strength."

"Let's not worry about it until we see what we're up against."

Minutes later, Ivron stopped the column again and signaled for one of his men, a short soldier with a scar on his right cheek, to come forward.

"Thean, take the men right to where the road bends, just where you can see the river, and wait there for the ferry. When it docks, bring the men to the river as quick as you can ride. Have seven of them ready to board the ferry. The others should have their bows out, ready to put shafts into any of Orliss's men waiting for us to cross."

"Yes, my Lord."

Then, Ivron climbed down from his horse. "Are you three ready? From here, we need to hike through the woods. The forest hugs this side of the river, so we should be able to get quite near to the shore, but the woods are too dense for the horses. Thean will take them with the others."

Thean signaled some soldiers to come up and take their mounts.

Robert climbed off his horse, happy in a way to be out of the saddle, even though it meant trudging through snow up to his knees. Angela and Wallace were soon standing in the snow, as well.

When they were all dismounted, Ivron wasted no time leading them into the forest south of the road. He cut a path as near to the road as he could while making the best time he could. Further in, the underbrush diminished, and the snow wasn't as deep, thanks to the shelter of the trees. Robert didn't have much trouble trudging through the snow, but Angela and Wallace struggled, even though they followed in his footsteps. The snow reached nearly up to the middle of Angela's thigh.

They had to work to keep up with Ivron, who seemed to enjoy the trek. It wasn't long before Robert wished he could have come up with a plan that did not involve trekking through the snow-covered underbrush. He'd thought he was cold while riding the horse. Now, with the snow melting into his leggings and chilling his boots, he could only think of sitting in front of the fire at Ivron's estate.

Sooner than he expected, Ivron motioned for them to stop, and pointed. About a dozen feet in front of Ivron, Robert could see the forest's edge, and the water flowing past it, dark and cold.

"Angela, Wallace, stay here a moment. When I wave to you, come forward. Robert, follow me closely, and try to stay down and behind the brush. When I stop, you stop and don't move. We're going to sneak up to the edge of the river, hopefully without being noticed or falling in."

Here, near the river, and under cover of the forest, the snow wasn't quite as deep, and Ivron crouched fairly low and started moving forward, keeping trees between him and the river wherever he could. Robert did his best to follow Ivron's example. They moved from tree to tree, and eventually, Ivron led them to a spot almost on the river's edge, roughly three feet from the water, just behind a large snow-covered shrub. Ivron looked around it, and then pulled back.

"Peek around the edge of this bush. Try not to disturb it. We don't want the snow falling off and exposing us or attracting attention."

They switched places carefully, and then Robert snuck his head out from under the cover the bush provided.

The distance across the river here looked to be only two hundred yards or so. He could see the ferry, already nearly three quarters of the way to their side of the river. Where Robert and Ivron were hiding was probably twenty feet from where the ferry would land. Ivron's men had apparently succeeded at enticing the boatman to cross. Four linesmen worked the ropes, and seemed none too happy.

What he was most interested in were the two men on the other side of the river, armed with swords and enveloped in heavy cloaks. They were stamping their feet and rubbing their hands together. They were close enough to each other, he thought maybe he could constrain them both. If he couldn't — he needed Angela, just in case.

He said to Ivron, "Have Angela and Wallace move up. I need her, in case something goes wrong."

Ivron turned and waved them forward.

Moments later, they were behind the bush, too. Robert looked again and saw the ferry was almost docked. They'd have to take care of these two quickly.

"So what do I do?" Angela asked.

"When you look around the bush, take the one on the left. Wrap a Weave around his head, like it was a box you were going to lift. It should keep him from going anywhere. I'll do the same for the one on the right."

"They won't be able to breathe."

He hadn't thought of that. It might work to their advantage, though. "When he passes out, let the Weave go."

"And me?" Wallace asked.

"Watch for wizards. I don't know if they'll have any there, but you told me they sent one after you the night you escaped from the Lab. It wouldn't surprise me if there's another waiting in the inn."

"And when my soldiers are across the river," Ivron said, "get to the landing. You'll cross with the other half of my men."

Robert pulled out his wand, and looked back at the landing. The ferry was just nudging up against the dock. "Ready?"

Angela pulled out her own wand and went to the other side of the bush. "Ready." Wallace crawled around Robert so he could get a view of the inn.

Robert picked his target. "Now."

He pulled energie from the trees and bushes around him, as well as himself, and directed that energie through the wand and around the head of the soldier on the right. The man immediately reached up for his mouth, clawing at it. Robert noticed his partner turn to look at him, and saw him say something.

Is Angela late? Or is she having trouble controlling the Weave over the distance?

And then, that soldier also reached up to his mouth and tried to pull whatever was holding him away from his face. The two soldiers thrashed in place, silently.

Ivron jumped up and ran for the ferry. Robert heard the horses galloping to the dock. He risked a glance toward the dock and saw Ivron handing the ferryman coin for the passage while ten of his men led their horses onto the ferry.

Robert looked back at his man. Even from this side of the river, he could see the man's face turning blue. His struggling was growing weaker, as was the struggling of the soldier Angela held. He could see the face of the man she held turning a similar shade of blue. He hoped no one decided to peek out the door of the inn.

He wanted to ask Angela how her energie was holding up, but he didn't want to risk breaking her concentration, or his own, for that matter.

He glance at the ferry again, and found it moving back across the river. A few minutes and they would be across, but the man he held would be unconscious before then. His struggles had already slowed, and he hung near limp in the air from the Weave.

"I don't want to kill him," Angela said.

"You don't have to. Just slide the Weave down around his chest to hold him up once he stops struggling."

Robert did just that to his own captive once the soldier stopped moving. The man's head immediately lolled on his chest. He was unconscious, or dead. Robert hoped for the first.

Angela's had stopped struggling as well, and he saw that man's head slowly droop as well. "I don't know how long I can hold him up," she said.

"Just a few minutes, if you can. Enough for them to land. They don't want to have to fight their way off the ferry."

The ferry was now about half way across the river. The ferryman appeared agitated. He was talking to Ivron, and pointing at the two men he and Angela held. Apparently, he'd noticed they weren't behaving normally. It'd be just their luck if he refused to ferry the rest of them across.

"I can't hold him any longer," Angela said, right as her captive dropped into the snow. The snow was deep there, and Robert could no longer see the man. Hopefully, he wasn't visible from anywhere else. If anyone went looking for him, they might assume he'd wandered off.

"Do you see anything, Wallace?"

"No. I haven't seen anyone even peek their head out."

His prisoner was starting to move. At least he wasn't dead.

The ferry landed, and Ivron and his men stormed off it. Two went for the men Robert and Angela had incapacitated. Robert released his hold on his captive, and the soldier fell into the snow next to his companion. The two of them were quickly pulled from the snow, bound, and gagged.

The ferry started making its way back across the river.

The rest of Ivron's men spread out around the inn, staying mostly out of sight, waiting. Ivron was doing everything possible to avoid a fight.

Robert waited until the ferry crossed the midpoint of the river. "Time to go," he said, then followed Ivron's path through the forest and back to the road. He heard Angela and Wallace behind him.

They emerged onto the road as the ferry was landing, and accepted the reins of their horses from the soldiers that held them.

The ferryman watched as they boarded, a dark look on his face. His eyes moved constantly, until they came to Robert. The ferryman looked down, then quickly away as if frightened. Robert looked down to find what frightened the man, and saw the wand still in his hand.

"C'mon, I ain't got all day." The man said, clearly trying to take what little control of his situation that he could.

When they were aboard, the rope-men started pulling, and the ferry began its journey back across the river. The horses didn't seem to care for the movement of the ferry under their feet. Robert reached up to try and soothe his unfamiliar mount.

Wallace, at that point, tugged on Robert's coat. "Robert, look."

He looked across the river, and saw a soldier coming out of the inn. He hadn't yet closed the door, but was already looking around. Robert guessed he was searching for the two guards that had now disappeared behind a snowbank.

The soldier noticed the ferry, and the soldiers on it. He pulled his sword from its scabbard, shouted back into the inn, and then charged toward the landing.

Men boiled out of the inn behind him, pulling swords out and rushing, quickly as they could through the snow. Robert counted eight. Fewer than Ivron had on the shore, but, he realized, it would only take one of them to break through and cut the thick hawsers holding the ferry. It would send them down the river out of control.

Ivron and two of his men stepped out in front of the landing from where they'd been hiding, blocking, for the moment, direct access to the ropes. His other eight men surged out from their concealment to ring the onrushing group of soldiers.

The soldiers came to a stop as they realized they were surrounded, but only for a moment. One of them, a large man with a thick beard, yelled out, "Break through!" and then charged toward Ivron. The rest of his men followed, and it was quickly obvious that, though surrounded, the were not cowed. Apparently, Orliss's hirelings, weren't run of the mill brigands that could be thwarted merely by the sight of trained soldiers.

The ferryman yelled to his rope-men, "Stop pulling!"

Thean, the soldier Ivron had placed in charge of this group, pulled his sword and pointed it at the ferryman's substantial belly. "Keep going. Those men will cut the ropes. Do you want to be left to float down the river?"

The ferryman quickly reassessed his options and his order. "Pull!" He started chivying his men to pull faster.

The big, bearded mercenary was almost on Ivron, and Robert felt useless. *What can I do?* They were maybe sixty feet from the dock, and it might as well have been a mile. He wished Gerard were here with his staff to send fireballs into those men and scatter them. That much energie would consume Robert's wand.

The snow was flying up in front of them, though, and that gave Robert an idea. Quickly, he used a Weave to bind the snow that was already in the air, and forced it higher, flinging it into the faces of the oncoming men as they ran, partially blinding them.

The big man stumbled as he came to Ivron. Ivron's sword swept out and caught the man on the side of the head. The man fell into a heap and slid past Ivron in the snow. Robert, from the ferry in the river, could see the bloody stain on the snow. Two more of Orliss's men fell in similar fashion to the swords of men on either side of Ivron.

Their enemies now numbered only six.

Robert kept weaving the snow into the air. The six tried to abort their charge, but two had come within reach of Ivron and his men and couldn't save themselves. Ivron's sword took one man in the throat, and the other man had his legs cut out from under him.

A third soldier lost his footing in the snow and fell to the ground on his own. The remaining soldiers managed to stop themselves and remain upright. One of them looked around through the flying snow, and saw they were clearly outnumbered. He dropped his sword into the snow and thrust his hands into the air. The final pair quickly followed his lead.

Robert released his Weave allowing the flying snow to fall to the ground. Ivron directed his men to bind the four uninjured soldiers, and move them off to sit with their previously captured compatriots. Another of Ivron's soldiers was dealing with the one mercenary they'd cut down at the knee. He apparently still lived.

The ferry slid into the dock, and the rope-men tied it off. When it was his turn, he led his horse off the ferry onto solid ground, and went to where Ivron stood, directing his men.

"So, what do we do now?"

"One of these men needs a healer. He will probably lose his leg, if he survives. The others, we can't have them following us, or going to Orliss to tell him what happened."

"You're going to kill them?"

Ivron laughed. "No, not if I can help it."

"Robert!" Wallace's voice.

"What?"

"Up by the inn."

Robert looked, and saw a man in a red cloak coming out of the inn. Swirls of energie surrounded him, controlled in a way that only one group of people ever controlled their energie.

He started to raise his wand, but it was too late. He couldn't move. A wizard. He tried to find a thread in the Weave that held him that he could loosen, but the Weave was complex.

"Don't bother trying, young apprentice."

"How do you know I'm an apprentice?"

He laughed. "No real wizard would have allowed me to do to them what I have just done to you."

Robert looked around, and realized no one was moving except the strange wizard. Even, he noticed, the ferryman and his workers.

"Who are you?"

"Who I am is of no concern to you. I'm only, shall we say, an old man, passing through."

"How can you control so many Weaves at once?"

The old man lifted a finger and wagged it in Robert's face. "Who's to say it's many Weaves? Who are you to be asking so many questions, anyway? I'm the Master here. Answer my questions."

"You haven't asked any."

"Ah, true. I haven't. So, I shall ask. Who's your Master, and why has he let you out to play in the snow?"

"You don't know who I am?"

"Should I?"

"I suppose not." For some reason, Robert felt better with the idea that the wizard didn't know who he was. It meant that he likely wasn't working with Orliss, or with these men. "My Master is Monteous Roarke."

"Ah, Monteous. He's always been such a rogue. He was fun to watch in his younger days." He paused for a moment, pondering something. Robert wished he'd get on with it. He was getting cold now, following the heat of the recent action. "He is not here?"

"No, I was going to him when we were attacked by these men."

"It seems you did all the attacking." He waved his arm around at the men lying on the ground and those bound.

"They were waiting for us. They've been trying to capture or kill my friends and me for the last few days."

"Interesting times, yes? What did you do to them that they so sincerely wish to capture you?"

"We did nothing. They work for Orliss, who is trying to keep Monteous away from the Conclave so that Orliss can take the Senior Wizard seat." *Why am I telling him this?*

The old wizard nodded. "Orliss. He's always been ambitious." And then, another pause. "Guild politics. You'll be better off if you stay well clear of them. I certainly do."

"The politics came to me."

"Of course they did. Now, Robert, the reason I stopped this whole lovely dance. Your Weaves are strong, and you were clever. I especially admired how you suspended those two men from across the river. These buffoons never suspected a thing. But you could be so much better."

"Huh?"

"Monteous has brought you along far too slow, I think. You have strength, and skill, but you haven't yet learned to harness your greatest abilities."

Robert was indignant. "Monteous is the greatest wizard in the Guild!"

"Yes, he is. I could teach you more, however. Come to me when you are ready to quit this Guild business and really learn how to use your skills.

"Until then, be careful and keep watch. Guild business can be nasty, as you have found out. When you find Monteous, tell him I said hello."

"How would I find you? I don't even know your name."

"That," the wizard said, "will be your first test."

The old wizard waved a finger, and vanished. Robert stumbled a bit as the Weave holding him loosened. He looked around and found everyone else free, too.

"Robert, where'd he go?" Wallace asked. "He was just up there by the inn, and now he's gone."

"The wizard?"

"Yes. He was a strong one, too, as much as I could tell."

"He walked over and talked to me. Didn't you listen to him?"

Wallace shook his head. "What? No. He was up there, and then he vanished."

Robert looked around then, and everyone else, except Wallace, was pretty much engaged in what they were doing before.

"What are you two talking about?" Ivron asked.

"There was another wizard here. He put us all in a Weave, and he came down and talked to me for quite a while. Did you hear him or see him? He was standing right in front of you."

"No, nothing." Ivron looked at him a little strangely.

As Robert realized what the wizard had done, his appreciation for the power of the old wizard grew. Somehow, he'd put the rest of them in stasis or something, while holding Robert in place, and then winked off as if he'd stepped through a portal, without the use of one. *What kind of power did he have to accomplish that? Why isn't he Senior Wizard?*

"Well, I guess it doesn't matter." Robert said. "He didn't do anything to help or hurt us."

"Keep an eye out, all three of you. If you see him again, warn me. We don't know who he's working for, and we're in a very precarious position right now."

"He implied he wasn't working for anyone," Robert said, fairly certain he was right.

"Just the same, stay vigilant."

Robert nodded, and the others assented.

Ivron had some of his men bury the dead bodies under a distant snowbank. He had others take the prisoners back to the inn. When he returned several minutes later, the prisoners and two of his own men were absent.

"What did you do with them?" Robert asked.

"We tied them up in the cellar and I paid the innkeep to stay silent. I'm leaving two of my men to make sure it happens."

Ivron ordered everyone to mount, and Robert climbed into his saddle. When they were up, Ivron came up beside Robert.

"Where's that thing pointing?"

Robert pulled the crystal out from his pocket and held it up, examining the Weave.

"West," he said, using his other hand to point down a road which lead out of the town.

"Then west we ride."

In the moment it took Robert to put the crystal back in his pocket, the vanguard had moved out ahead of them again. He maneuvered his horse to fall in beside Angela, trailing Ivron and Wallace. The rest of the soldiers formed two columns behind them. Robert couldn't help but feel some excitement. That the crystal pointed down the road seemed a portent. It had to lead them to Monteous.

CHAPTER 21

A S THEY RODE into Ferry Town, all Gerard could think of was getting some more hot tea and warming himself, but as they approached the inn, Demetrius immediately appeared agitated and wary.

"There was a fight here," Demetrius said.

"Where?"

Demetrius pointed towards the ferry dock. "There's blood all through the snow. We should skip the inn and keep moving."

Nina immediately interposed herself into the conversation. "I'm cold, and I need something to warm me."

"Nina, we don't know who is in the inn. We don't know what happened by the docks. Orliss is looking for us, and I'm positive he would have men waiting here for us."

"No, let me go in. They don't know I'm with you."

"We'll be safer if no one goes inside."

"You said we don't know what happened. We need to know, don't we?" Then she jumped from her horse and ran to the door. "I won't be but a moment." Then she ducked inside.

Demetrius looked at Gerard then, resignation in his eyes. "You had to bring her along."

"What? I didn't bring her along. She came on her own."

"She came because of you. If you hadn't been so chatty with her last night..."

Nina abruptly returned. "There are two soldiers inside, but no one else. They're dressed like Georg and Horuth."

"Lots of soldiers dress like Georg and Horuth," Demetrius noted.

"I mean, they've got *that* insignia on them," and she pointed to the design embossed on Georg's coat.

"Ivron's men?" Demetrius immediately climbed down. "I wonder what they're doing here. Horuth, watch the horses and yell if you see any other soldiers. Georg, Gerard, come with me. There's something odd going on."

Gerard climbed down and tied his horse to the hitching post, then followed Demetrius and Nina into the inn. Georg entered behind.

The two soldiers had been seated across the inn, in a position where they could keep watch on the door. Their swords were out and accessible, and they seemed prepared for trouble. Gerard thought he recognized them from Ivron's estate.

They stood up as the party entered the room, and silent stares were replaced with grins as they recognized Demetrius and Georg.

"What are you two doing here?" Demetrius asked as he clasped hands first with one, then the other.

"Guarding some buried treasure."

"Buried treasure? How did you even get here?"

"Seems during the storm, Orliss's men up and left, or turned into icicles, so we just rode out."

Demetrius waved them back to the table, and motioned for the innkeep, who was standing behind the bar watching them warily, to come over. "We need some tea, and I'd like to sit while I hear this story."

They all sat around the table, and when the innkeep was off fetching their tea, Demetrius said, "First, I'd like to know whose blood is out there in the snow."

"Oh, that's from the mercenaries who were tryin' to keep us from crossing the river. Half of us managed to get across before they figured we were here, thanks to the young wizards. When they did find us, they rushed Ivron, and he took out two of them, and two more went down in the melee as well."

"The buried treasure?"

"Them that lived."

"So, where did Ivron and the wizards go?"

"They all went west. Left me and Otho here to watch 'em 'til sunrise, then go east to catch up with the lady, if he hadn't come back for us."

"Demetrius," Gerard said. "Do you think they found Monteous, then?"

"It would seem like it."

Gerard stood up quickly, "We need to go after them!"

"Sit down, Gerard. Drink your tea. We can't go after them yet."

Gerard sat back down. "Why can't we go after them?"

"We have our own mission to attend to. The King must hear what we suspect. He must be able to prepare a defense against Mrongil."

"But Monteous, if we can rescue him in time..."

"Whatever happens with Monteous, we cannot guarantee his rescue. If we follow the others instead of carrying out our own orders, we guarantee the King will not be prepared. Our duty is to The Seven Kingdoms."

Gerard leaned back in his chair and clasped his hands across his eyes. All he wanted to do was save Monteous, and go back to being an apprentice.

He felt a comforting hand on his shoulder. Nina leaned into his ear, her breath warm and exciting. "Wherever you go, I go."

It was reassuring and frightening at the same time. This girl, he felt like a mouse being chased by an alley cat. He wanted to help free Monteous, but at the same time, he knew Demetrius was right.

"I can't make you go, Gerard, but I must deliver the message to the King, and I will not help you find the others."

Gerard hated it. "No, you're right. I'll go with you. Promise me, though, we find the others after we've delivered the message."

Demetrius smiled. "Of course. I wouldn't dream of missing that confrontation."

Georg took some tea and bread out to Horuth while the rest of them finished theirs. Once they were finished, they stood, said goodbyes, and left the inn, warmer, fuller, and determined to pick up the pace.

They rode out of Ferry Town as fast as they dared make the horses go. It was mid-afternoon, and would be nearing dusk by the time they came to the City. Gerard hoped they could arrive before nightfall and manage to see the King immediately, instead of having to wait for morning.

THEY FOLLOWED THE road for several hours. Robert pulled the crystal out every few minutes, hoping to see a change in the direction of the thread, but it continued to point west.

The road wound its way through rolling hills. Every now and then, they'd pass a farmstead, or an estate, but the land, under the heavy blanket of snow, seemed nearly barren. Robert knew there were fields where they grew most of the wheat and other grains used to feed the City. When the fields were not awash in snow, there would also be sheep, goats and cattle in some of these lands.

"How far do you think they would have taken him?"

Ivron looked back. "No telling. I hope it won't be much farther. We'll need shelter soon."

Robert looked around, and he realized it was near dusk.

He pulled out the crystal again, and held it up, as he had done so often. It took him a moment to realize that he couldn't see the thread. It pointed in a new direction. He turned his horse out of the column and spun it around until he saw the thread again. It was pointing east, and a bit to the south toward a fairly tall hill.

"Ivron, Monteous is back there." Robert pointed in the direction the thread indicated.

Ivron brought the column to a halt, then rode up to Robert. "We passed him? How could that be? I didn't see anything over there."

"Behind the hill?"

"There would have to be smoke, if someone lived there."

"A wizard could hide the smoke. All I know is that the crystal now points back that direction."

"Let's go find out, then," Ivron said, and gave his mount a kick, sending it off the road toward the base of the hill. Robert followed, watching the crystal, and it never wavered in its direction. Angela and Wallace followed, as did Thean and another soldier.

Robert started looking for Weaves. If they were hiding the smoke, there would have to be a Weave somewhere. He couldn't find one, though.

At the bottom of the hill, Ivron slowed and dismounted. Robert followed his example.

"We need to climb this hill carefully, and keep low as we reach the top. If there's someone watching, we'll be very visible in the snow."

Robert looked up and understood Ivron's concerns. A few small, emaciated trees dotted the hill here and there, but nothing they could hide behind. They would be completely exposed at the top if anyone was watching. For a moment, Robert thought maybe Angela's obscuration Weave could help, but realized the the wizards keeping Monteous captive would be able to see it. "Should I come?"

"Yes, you, but probably not the others. Too many heads will only make us more visible."

Ivron started up the hill, and Robert followed him.

The snow made the hill slippery. Robert fell to his hands and knees more than once, plunging his face into the snow. As they reached the top, the slope leveled out somewhat and the climbing became easier.

When they were about to crest the hill, Ivron dropped to his knees, and motioned Robert to get down. Together, they crawled up the remainder of the slope until they could see over the crest.

Robert barely kept himself from gasping aloud when he saw what was beyond the hill. A small estate was nestled in a hollow, surrounded on three sides by hills. A lane led from the far side of the compound, through the hills, and curved around, probably leading back to the main road. The snow had obscured the lane.

The estate was really just a collection of buildings. A modest home stood closest to Ivron and Robert. A stable stood just beyond the home to the left, and a couple other outbuildings mirrored it on the right creating a courtyard. There was no wall, to speak of. Only a low, probably stone, barrier barely visible beneath the mounds of snow.

He slipped into the vew and sucked in his breath, stifling the urge to exclaim.

A large Weave covered the small valley, maybe more than one. He wasn't sure of its purpose, but guessed it protected against scrying. There seemed to be others around various parts of the estate, wrapping the flues, the doors, and the windows. The wizards here were expending a great deal of energie to keep this place hidden.

He saw another set of Weaves moving across the ridges, one of which he barely caught out of the corner of his eye before it could collide with him. He dropped himself quickly into the snow to avoid it.

"Down," he whispered.

Ivron immediately fell to the ground and was obscured by snow.

"Why am I down?"

"They're using Weaves to watch for intruders. One of them nearly caught me."

"Do you think they know we're here?"

"It's possible, but I would think we'd have been attacked already."

"Let's get off this ridge."

They slowly backed down from the crest, until they could stand without being seen. They descended the hill as fast as they could without tumbling.

Angela was waiting for him when he got down. "So, what did you see?"

"He's there. I'm sure of it. However, they're expending a large amount of energie to keep it hidden. There are detection Weaves, as well. We were nearly caught in one. There's got to be more than one wizard there. Did you see any guards, Ivron?"

"No. In this weather, it doesn't mean much. They're probably all inside staying warm, depending on the wizards to alert them to trouble. Stupid, really."

"What are we going to do, then?" Wallace asked.

Ivron glanced upwards toward the top of the hill, and started rubbing his chin with his hand. "Well, I'm not sure how to fight multiple wizards, and we don't know how many, if any, soldiers there are in the compound. I wish Demetrius were here. I'd send him in closer to scout around."

Robert looked at Angela. Her face was flushed from the cold. "That obscuration Weave, it's got to be an active Weave. You can tie off alarms and triggers, but to keep someone from poking through when scrying, someone has to maintain that. Whoever that is should be tired.

"We won't know what kind of traps are on the doors, so we need to entice whoever is inside to come out, or unravel the Weaves. The problem with unraveling the Weaves is that we'll be vulnerable while we pick them apart."

"They will probably have Monteous hidden in the main house," Ivron said. "I think we should split my men. I'll take half through down the lane on the opposite side of the compound and try to draw whoever we can away from the house.

"The rest will climb the hill with you three," he said, indicating Robert and the other apprentices. "When we've acquired their attention, descend into the valley and attempt to enter the house.

"Hopefully, you will find Monteous and escape with him before they know he's gone."

Excitement pulsed through Robert. They finally were going to free Monteous, the man who had raised him since childhood, and they'd thwart Orliss's plans, whatever they were. Angela's eyes were bright, too, excited.

Robert said to Wallace, "You and I will keep a lookout for wizards while Angela removes the Weaves. Watch the doors for additional Weaves, like the one that caught Angela back at Ivron's keep. If one of

Orliss's wizards has resorted to proscribed Weaves, there's no telling how many others have."

Wallace nodded.

Thean stepped up to Robert. "I'm coming with you. Anything I should know?"

Robert thought about it. "Mostly, keep your men spread out. If they're too close to each other, they'll make an easy target for a wizard."

"It will be harder for us to protect you."

"It's a risk, but you can't really protect us from a wizard."

"Of course."

They busied themselves getting the horses staked out at the bottom of the hill. The group going in the front would ride theirs. The hill was too steep for the horses to climb, though, so Robert and his group would be without.

As Robert's group prepared to climb the hill, Ivron rode over to him. "Are you ready for this?"

"I don't have much choice, do I?"

"You three could stay down here."

"What happened the last time you tried to rescue Monteous without the support of a wizard?"

"Nothing good." He spun his horse around. "Time to go then. Get Monteous out of the house and back to this side of the hill. We'll try to meet you in the house, but if we're held up, make sure you get Monteous out. Don't wait for us. He needs to be at the Conclave tomorrow."

"I don't even know where it is."

"Monteous will know."

Then Ivron headed off, calling his men to follow. Robert paused a moment, taking in his little group, Angela, Wallace, Thean, and eight other soldiers. They were about to put themselves up against an unknown number of wizards and mercenaries. Robert realized in that moment he would kill if he had to. These people were surely responsible for much of what had happened to him, and to the people around him, during the last few days. These people bore at least some responsibility for the gruesome torture and murder of Ergin by the river.

He could do this. He had to do this.

Thean said, "Shall we go?"

Angela and Wallace both nodded. Robert said, "Yes. Let's climb this thing."

The group of soldiers spread out, ten or so feet apart as they climbed to the top of the hill. Angela was on Robert's right, Thean on his left, and Wallace was on the other side of Thean.

When they reached the top, they crouched down behind snow drifts, and waited. The clouded sky had darkened further. Whoever was in the house had started some lamps burning. Robert pulled the crystal from his pocket and checked the Weave. It pointed right to the house.

What if I'm wrong? What if the Weave inside the crystal doesn't point to Monteous?

He shoved the thought into the dark corners of his mind and buried it. If Monteous wasn't in that house, Orliss had won.

Minutes passed, and nothing happened. He began to worry that something had gone wrong, that Ivron had run into resistance skirting the hills. Just as he thought to ask Thean about it, he heard the thunder of pounding hooves echo through the valley.

Ivron and his men raced into the courtyard of the compound carrying flaming torches and brandishing their swords. One rider pulled to one side and tossed his torch into the stable. Other torches went through the windows of the other outbuildings. Mercenaries rushed out of the house in twos and threes. Ivron tossed down his torch, and others did so as well, and charged the men streaming out of the house.

Thean stood then. "It's time to go."

The rest of them stood, and started down the hill, going as fast as they dared while still maintaining their footing. A detection Weave caught him as it passed over, and hoped it didn't matter. The wizards should already know they were under attack. If Ivron's plan had worked, all of the mercenaries had abandoned the house, and their approach would be free of physical protection.

The rush down the hill was frantic. He saw Angela slip and fall, but he was moving too fast to stop and help her. Out of the corner of his eye, though, he saw her get back up and continue on. A couple of the soldiers fell and rolled down the hill in the snow.

The battle in the courtyard was still raging when the roof line of the house blocked it from view.

As they reached the bottom of the hill, they set up in a semi-circle around the rear door. While Angela worked at the Weave on the door, Robert watched for wizards, and looked for traps. Wallace looked like he was doing the same. The kid seemed to be able to see Weaves that the others could not, and Robert hoped that would be protection enough against the proscribed Weaves.

He took an occasional glance at the Weave covering the door, and saw that it was coming apart thread by thread. Angela really was good at this sort of thing.

He had to deliberately resist urging her to hurry. One mistake pulling a thread and the Weave could unravel all on its own, with any number of dangerous outcomes. It would take as long as it took.

While he searched for any signs the wizards inside were paying attention to them, he listened to the clamor from the far side of the building. Shouts and screams of men, the ringing of sword on sword, the clang of sword on armor, echoed throughout the valley. The light of the flames from the burning outbuildings and stable flickered against the snow.

The last thread fell from the door, and as far as Robert could tell, it was free of residual Weaves or hidden traps. He looked at Wallace, who nodded.

"It's clear," Robert said to Thean.

Thean motioned to one of his men, a hulking giant, taller than Robert. The man stepped back and ran at the door, knocking it in. They'd already discussed trying to pick the lock and concluded they wouldn't have enough time.

The man crashed through the door, tearing it from its hinges. Lightning like fingers of energie encased him immediately. Inside, a wizard stood with a staff, directing bolt after bolt of energie at the writhing soldier. Robert quickly used his wand to wrap a Weave around the wizard's staff and separate it from its owner. The staff flew to Robert's hand, just as he saw a knife fly through the door from Thean's extended hand and pierce the wizard in the shoulder.

Using the newly acquired staff, Robert wrapped the wizard's head in a Weave as soldiers rushed into the house. The first one in jumped over the fallen soldier and his sword separated the wizard's head from his body.

Robert released his Weave, and nearly gagged at the sight of the head falling to the floor. He closed his eyes for a moment, and tried to forget the vision, but it persisted, even behind his shuttered eyelids.

Someone slapped him on the back. "Come on, you can do that later." Thean's voice.

Robert opened his eyes. Two soldiers were pulling the fallen soldier out of the way. Only two soldiers and Angela and Wallace remained with him outside the house. Angela's face looked green, and so did Wallace's.

Come on Robert, time to find Monteous.

He tucked the wand away into a pocket, and brought with him the staff he'd just acquired. He couldn't see it clearly, but in his hand, it felt finely carved. It was a real wizard staff, not one made for an apprentice. With his other hand, he pulled out the crystal, and held it up where he could see its Weave. He went into the house, carefully ignoring the decapitated wizard on the floor.

The door opened into the kitchen. The thread from the crystal seemed to point off somewhere to the right. There was a door in that direction. Two of Ivron's men were standing next to it, eyes directed through it.

"Which way?" Thean asked.

Robert pointed to the right, through the door, and Thean stepped ahead of him.

"Do you think that's a good idea, you leading?" asked Robert.

"Someone has to, and it won't be you."

Thean led him through the door, and they came out into a short hallway. There was a door on the right, and a door at the end. Robert guessed that an opening on the left led to the main entry. Thean held up as they approached that opening, and someone bumped into Robert from behind as he stopped. It was Wallace.

An idea struck Robert. He dug his wand out of his pocket and handed it to Wallace.

"Quick lesson on using a wand. Gather all of the energie that you can, and use the wand to direct it at your target. You won't be able to do anything complicated, so don't even try. Just point and send your energie through it."

Wallace nodded. "What if..."

"Don't worry about what if. Just do that. It'll hurt anyone in the way. It might destroy the wand in the process, but if you have to use it to protect yourself, don't hesitate."

Thean turned around. "There's no one through here."

Robert heard sounds of fighting in the courtyard, still. Fewer, though.

He held up the crystal. "It's pointing to the door at the end of the hall."

And then Wallace pulled him back by his shirt. "There's a Weave on that door."

"A Weave? I don't see any Weave."

"I can see it. It's faint and red. It's pulsing a bit."

"Where's Angela?"

"Here." Her voice came from behind Wallace.

"Can you see the Weave?"

"I don't see anything."

"I could try to knock it down." Thean said.

Robert shook his head. "We have no idea what it does."

"Wait," said Wallace. "I know what it does, or at least, what it is. Whoever made that used blood to create it."

"Blood? It's a proscribed Weave."

"Yes, it was in one of the books." Wallace was staring intensely at the door. "The blood helps to hide it."

"Why can you see it?"

"I don't know."

"Can you unravel it?"

Wallace squinted, and after a few moments, said "I think so."

"'I think so' is not good enough, Wallace."

"Is Monteous behind that door?"

"That's where the crystal points." Robert wasn't sure Wallace could do it. But if Wallace was the only one of them that could even see it, did he have any choice?

"Then I have to try, don't I? I've been essentially useless until now. Let me try."

Robert looked into Wallace's eyes, trying to tease out whether Wallace could succeed. Wallace had only been with them for a year or so. He'd only recently mastered basic Weaves.

Thean put a hand on Robert's shoulder and leaned into his ear. "If he thinks he can do it, let him. We could be running out of time."

"Alright. Wallace, come here by me. Everyone else, back down the hallway."

Wallace stepped forward, and nearly everyone else moved back, all but emptying the corridor. Angela was still with them, though. Robert didn't want her here, instead wishing her back in kitchen, out of harm's way.

When he was sure they were safe, as sure as he could be, he turned with Wallace to face the door.

"Just take it slow. Unraveling a Weave is something you do with patience. Try to find where the threads are tied, and pick at one of the knots, making sure you hold the end of that thread. You don't want it to snap free."

The energie that always surrounded Wallace coalesced, and he could see Wallace was using it to manipulate what would have to be threads, but were invisible to Robert.

Robert could only hope Wallace knew what he was doing.

WALLACE FELT EVERYONE backing away as he stepped up next to Robert. The Weave on the door shone to him with a dark red glow that had a way of wanting to deflect attention from itself. It was almost as if it was taunting him. *But that couldn't be, could it? No Weave has a mind of its own.*

But then, he still didn't know much. He sure didn't understand why Robert and Angela could not see it, but he could. *Is there something different about me? Or something else?*

"You really want to do this?" Robert's words broke in on his reverie.

Wallace didn't see that he had a choice. He nodded his head, though. He'd have to start soon.

"Just take it slow. Unraveling a Weave is something you do with patience. Try to find where the threads are tied, and pick at one of the knots, making sure you hold the end of that thread. You don't want it to snap free."

Wallace knew all this. Monteous had gone over the basics, and he'd practiced on many small, simple Weaves. The one in front of him was as complex a Weave as he'd seen.

He searched for thread ends, the knots, and found four of them. But the threads were intertwined.

"I see four threads here, and they're not just anchored to the door, they're anchored to each other. I'm not sure I can remove just one at a time."

"Remember, someone put it together. You can take it apart. You only need to find the pattern."

Wallace nodded, and started looking for a pattern. After a few moments, he hadn't found it by examining just the threads, so he brought his focus out of the threads and onto the Weave as a whole. He saw the pattern almost immediately.

If I can hold two threads at once — yes, it should work.

He started picking at the first knot, holding the thread taught. The knot loosened and he started unwinding the thread until it was blocked by another thread. He started on the knot, now trying to hold both threads at once. It was difficult, but he still could pick at the knot.

When that knot loosened, and he had control of both threads, he continued unweaving, pulling them through and about each other and the remaining threads. At times, he had to slow, as it seemed he was fighting two live snakes instead of threads in a Weave, but he managed to get them under control each time.

A drop of sweat rolled down his forehead and into his eye, and he quickly wiped it away with his hand.

And then, he was at a third junction of threads, and he had to untie the third knot, while maintaining his control over three threads. Again, he picked at a knot and managed to keep control of the three threads.

When the third thread finally loosened, all three threads actively fought him as he tried to untangle the Weave. They seemed to be pushing toward him, away from the door. He held them back, pushed them where he wanted them to go.

He felt his chest shaking with the effort and energie he was expending to control the threads. So close.

He came to the fourth and final knot. He just had to control the threads a little longer, manage the fourth one, and then it was done. He attacked the fourth knot while putting everything left over into controlling the four threads.

"Wallace, what's wrong?"

He couldn't answer. The fourth knot was tricky. It didn't want to come loose.

"Wallace." Robert's voice was full of worry. "Wallace. I can see the Weave. What are you doing, you can't hold that many threads at once while unraveling it!"

But I am holding all four. If only that fourth knot wasn't so stubborn.

In a beautiful and terrible explosion of light, the threads came loose, and he lost his grip. They reached out for him, red threads, straight as arrows now. The first one pierced him through his heart, its energie infusing him. The second one, through his eye, and he knew pain. He tried to grab at the other two, but his grasp was clumsy. One went through the other eye, to meet with its mate in the back of his brain, while the fourth entered through his mouth.

The one in his chest wrapped around his heart and squeezed. He could feel it in his chest, coiling around, constricting. His heart slowed. The threads in his head just seemed to be writhing around.

He fell to the floor, but didn't notice because he died before his body came to rest.

CHAPTER 22

WHEN ROBERT COULD finally see the threads, he could tell that Wallace was struggling. "Wallace, what's wrong?"

Wallace didn't answer, though.

"Wallace," he said again. "Wallace. I can see the Weave. What are you doing, you can't hold that many threads at once while unraveling it!"

It wasn't just the number of threads Wallace was trying to control. These threads looked unlike any he'd ever seen, and they seemed to be actively fighting against Wallace. They wanted free, almost as if they were alive.

In that moment, Robert saw the last knot come free, and Wallace lost control of the threads. One after the other, they aimed themselves for Wallace's body, penetrated it, and disappeared. Wallace stood there for a moment, then collapsed, the life fading from his eyes as his body fell to the ground.

He didn't want to believe it, though, and fell to the ground with Wallace.

"Wallace!"

He tried to feel for a heartbeat, but found nothing. Angela knelt down beside him, and placed her hand over his mouth, then shook her head. Tears dropped from her cheeks to the floor, some landing on Wallace.

Robert grabbed hold of him and shook him, but it made no difference. Wallace was gone. Robert knew the blame could clearly be cast at his own feet.

"We shouldn't have let him try. There had to be a better option."

"No," Angela said. "We couldn't see it. We couldn't have known what it would do."

"I saw it at the end."

"It's not your fault, Robert."

Thean knelt down next to them. "You did what you thought was right. It is best not to think further than that. We still need to find Monteous."

Robert looked up at him. The face he wore was caring and understanding, but unyielding, too. "You've had friends die."

"Many times. It happens in battle. Mourn him later. We need to find the wizard."

Thean was right. He didn't want to believe it, but he heard the sense. He took the wand he'd only just given Wallace and put it in a pocket. He pulled himself to his feet using the staff.

He'd only just started to turn toward the door when he saw it open, and a wizard come through it, but it wasn't Monteous.

Robert didn't hesitate. He poured all his anger and sadness into the staff, and directed it at the wizard. A hundred threads of energie poured forth from the staff to engulf the wizard. The wizard tried to throw up a quick defense, but failed, overwhelmed by Roberts rage. The wizard dropped the staff he held, fell to the ground and curled into a ball.

Robert kept feeding energie through the staff, even after it was obvious the wizard was dead. The wizard's death wasn't enough. It would never be enough.

"Robert," Angela's voice. Her body stood next to him. Her hands touched his shoulders. "It's done, Robert."

He cut the flow to the staff, then turned and buried his head in Angela's shoulder. His body ached, his chest was constricted, his eyes teared. He hugged her as hard as he could, and she hugged him back.

He couldn't stop the sobs as he whispered into her ear, "I killed Wallace."

"No, you didn't. Orliss did. Orliss and these wizards. You didn't use proscribed Weaves. They did."

Robert said nothing. He knew she was right, but he hurt to his bones. There had to have been some other option.

"Come on," she said. "Let's find Monteous and get out of here."

He gave her one more hug, then pulled away.

"The girl is right, Robert."

Orliss will pay. He resolved to himself that he would make Orliss pay. Maybe not now, Orliss still had too much power. But some day, if given the chance, Robert would make Orliss would rue this day.

He felt Angela sneak her hand into his, and he grasped it, feeling the warmth. He needed that right then, and it gave him strength.

They walked together to the door at the end of the hallway where the wizard's body lay charred and smoking. Robert stepped over the corpse and into the room.

The room was filled with plain furniture, but well made. In one of the chairs, his arms tied down, Monteous sat, waiting. His face was purple with bruises, but a smile crossed it as he recognized Robert, and then he slumped into the chair.

"Monteous!" Robert rushed to him, dropping the staff to the floor. Thean stepped around him and severed Monteous's bonds with his knife.

The Senior Wizard looked up at Robert. "I just need some rest. They haven't let me sleep. I'll be fine in a couple days."

"Can you walk?"

"With help, I think." He tried to stand, but fell back into the chair.

Thean signaled for two of his men to come help the wizard.

A commotion from the door caused Robert turn to see Ivron step into the room. He was covered in blood from head to toe. "Monteous, old friend. It is good to see you."

"Ivron. Thanks for finding me. I was beginning to think no one would come."

"It wasn't I that found you. Robert accomplished the finding."

"Robert?" The wizard looked at Robert with an appraising look.

"Demetrius had a crystal he said you gave him. I found the Weave in it, and I followed it to you."

"So you've met Demetrius? What crystal did he give you?"

"Monteous," Ivron interrupted. "We need to get you out of here. I've got men going to bring the other horses."

"Yes, yes. We can talk later after I get home and get some sleep."

Ivron stepped over and took the place of one of his men. "There's no time for later. We have to get you on a horse, and then to the Conclave."

Some of his vigor returned at that, for a moment. "The Conclave is so near? How many days have passed? I've lost count."

"The Conclave starts tomorrow night. Do you know where it is?"

"Of course. Where are we?"

The two men's conversation faded as they rounded the corner out of the little room.

Something bothered Robert. Monteous had left with Ivron, and had nearly dismissed Robert as soon as Ivron had appeared. "He still thinks of me as the apprentice that can't do anything," he mumbled.

Angela apparently heard him. "How would he think anything else? He doesn't know you opened a portal, he doesn't know anything that any of us have done."

"I didn't even tell him about Wallace."

"Ivron will tell him. We should go."

She pulled him, then, toward the door, and he followed. *Everything is all wrong.*

GERARD FOLLOWED DEMETRIUS into the City just before dusk. Nina had fallen back, but he could still feel her eyes on him.

The main road had been mostly cleared of deep snow. Due to the cold, it was mostly empty of people as well. They made their way quickly through the Outer City, and through the Middle City. They passed through the Inner City gates and wound their way through to the gates of Sendep Keep, the seat of power of the King of Kings.

Gerard had never been through the gates of the keep. They towered above him, and were constructed of timbers as big around as a man. They stood open, but an iron grate, as equally impressive as the gates, kept the City folk from intruding at night. A dozen of the King's Guard were stationed near the gate, dressed in chain mail, blue livery, and helmets with tall crests of indigo dyed horse hair.

As they approached the gate, a guard came forward, and held up a hand to stop them. "Your business?"

"I'm Demetrius Nirel, and I'm here at the request of Lord Ivron Meningale with urgent news for the King."

"You will need to come back in the morning."

"I am in the employ of Senior Wizard Monteous Roarke. The news I bring cannot wait until morning. Morning may be too late."

"Too late for what?"

"Let me at least talk with the King's Hand. Let him decide whether the King should hear what I have to say."

The guard looked like he was weighing his options. "Stay here." He ran to the grate and called through it. Another of the King's Guard, Gerard suspected his superior, came to meet him. A discussion ensued, and the new guard directed several looks at Demetrius and the rest of them.

"Do you think he'll let us through?" Gerard asked.

"We'll get through. It's just a matter of getting past the guard to someone with authority. The King's Hand knows Monteous and me. He'll get us in."

Several minutes passed, before the guard came back to them. "Wait here. He will be down in a few minutes." Then he stood in between them and the gate, blocking their way as if he thought they'd ignore his command.

Gerard wished the King's Hand would hurry. He needed to warm up. His ears felt frozen.

Nina brought her horse next to his. "Have you ever met the King?"

"Why would I have?"

"You're Monteous's apprentice. Everyone knows Monteous does the King's Work. You must have met him sometime."

He rubbed his hands together, trying to warm them up. "The King never comes to the Laboratory. I've never even seen him up close."

The King's Hand appeared at the gate moments later, then came out through a man-sized door in the iron grate. As he approached, Demetrius dismounted from his horse. The King's Hand was average height, thin, and as he came closer, Gerard saw his face wore a gray beard, trimmed close. His head, uncovered, was bald, and steam rose from it in the cold.

The King's Hand didn't stop until he stood nearly in Demetrius's face. "Well, well," he said. "Demetrius. What brings you calling at this hour?"

"I have news the King needs to hear, of events with potentially dire consequences."

"Can you tell me?"

"I'd rather not say it out in the open, but I can give you a hint."

The King's Hand nodded. "I understand. What can you tell me?"

"The Conclave is tomorrow."

"Yes, I know. That doesn't tell me why I should interrupt the King's meal."

"Monteous is missing."

The King's Hand's face turned to steel. "Missing? The King will want to know that. Come with me."

He motioned for the grate to be opened enough to let the horses through, and then led them through the gates and into the keep.

Stable boys came to take the horses as the party dismounted, and then the King's Hand led them across the courtyard.

"Is he taking us to the Hall of Audiences?" Gerard asked Demetrius in a whisper. He had always wanted to see it. Stories of its interior sparked his imagination, but with the way the buildings in the Keep were built, he had trouble telling one from another. They were all built

252 of thick stone

of thick stone and had few windows. A holdover from the nearly constant warfare of the Seven Kingdom's past, before they had been brought together under a single ruler.

"No. He's taking us to the King's residence."

The King's Hand ushered them inside. A guard station was near the door.

"I'm afraid you will need to leave your weapons here."

Demetrius pulled out his sword and set it on a table near the door, then pulled knives from several places on his person, and laid them on the table, too. Nina laid down her bow, then pulled two knives from inside her coat. She set them next to the bow.

"You will need to leave your staff."

Gerard started. "Huh? Oh, right." He leaned his staff up against the wall.

"Your men at arms shall stay as well. We can find them something to eat and get them warmed up."

"Of course," Demetrius said. "Georg, Horuth, don't relax too much. Be ready to ride."

The two men nodded.

"Alright. I must go inform the King. I shall return soon."

While they waited, Gerard inspected the room. It was essentially rectangular, and made of stone. The floor, however, was a mosaic map of the Seven Kingdoms. Tapestries from each of the Seven Kingdoms hung on the walls, each of them detailing different scenes from the struggles that led to the creation of the Seven Kingdoms. Scenes of war, deprivation, and conciliation.

The King's Hand ducked his head back into the room. "Follow me."

Demetrius went to him, and Gerard quickly followed, with Nina right behind.

The King's Hand led them down a hallway, then down another corridor, and then to another door. He stopped there, and turned to face them. "Don't make me regret this, Demetrius."

"I'll try not to."

The King's Hand opened the door and led them into the room.

On entering the room, which turned out to be a moderately large dining hall, Gerard saw that the austerity of the outer room and corridors contrasted greatly with the elaborately furnished living quarters of the King. The room was warm, a large fire burned in an even larger fireplace. Artwork of all kinds adorned the walls. The floor had been laid in an intricate mosaic of wood and stone.

The King was seated at his table, eating some sort of roasted bird. The Queen sat next to him, and the two young Princes, neither more than ten years old, sat across from him. He looked up as they entered, then waved them over.

Gerard followed Demetrius over to the table, then stood next to him as he stopped at the end.

"Sit, Demetrius. You and your friends. Sit and eat with us."

Demetrius sat down, slowly. "Sit," he said quietly to Gerard and Nina.

Gerard took a seat on his left, reluctantly. *We don't have the time for this.* Nina took a seat next to Gerard. The King motioned for food to be brought to them, and servants quickly set plates in front of them.

"So, Demetrius, what brings you here on this cold evening? Uri said something about Monteous gone missing?"

"More accurately, he was abducted."

The King dropped his fork. "Abducted?"

"I'm sure you're aware of the rules of succession in the Guild."

The King nodded.

"If Monteous is not at the Conclave tomorrow, he will lose his position. Someone managed to lure him into creating a portal, then abducted him as he stepped through it."

"Do you know who?"

"Orliss."

The King snorted in disgust. "Of course. He'll be a pain in the neck. But you know I can't get involved in the succession. The Articles of Founding forbid it."

"I know. I wouldn't be here if that were the entirety of the problem. You didn't ask how he was abducted."

"It makes a difference?"

"It does. How would you imagine anyone could abduct Monteous?"

"I can't. I always thought Monteous was the most powerful of wizards."

"You wouldn't be wrong if you were discussing Guild-approved Works and Weaves. Lord Ivron and I figured out where he was, and we tried rescuing him, but someone alerted Orliss. We arrived at the estate where Orliss was holding Monteous, but Monteous wasn't there. We were ambushed. Someone had told him we were coming."

"Who?"

"The wizard in Lord Ivron's employ. He was killed in the fighting. We did manage to save Monteous's apprentices from being abducted, or killed, though, and this one," he pointed at Gerard, "found some rather interesting items in the wizard's Laboratory at Lord Ivron's estate. This wizard was communicating with Orliss via proscribed Works."

The king stabbed his fork into the table, leaving it standing upright. "Orliss wouldn't."

"He would, if he was being paid, and if it would get him what he wants."

"I'm still not clear on why I should be involved," said the King. "Why would a wizard of the standing of Orliss risk being caught using proscribed works? It would mean expulsion from the Guild."

"Your Majesty, we suspect he is being paid by Mrongil."

"To what end?"

"Invasion. They are collecting wizards, training them. They do not yet have enough, but if prompt measures aren't taken, they will soon surpass our numbers. Monteous wants to increase the number of apprentices that we train, and was going to bring it to a vote at the Conclave. Orliss is being paid to keep that from happening."

"Treason." The King's eyes reflected the fire from the hearth, highlighting his anger. "I see now. You are sure?"

"I'm as sure as I can be. No other reason makes any sort of sense."

Gerard ate the meal in front of him, not really paying attention to what it was he was eating. He knew he had to eat, but what the King decided was far more important that the taste of the food on his fork.

"You, Apprentice, what is your name?" The King was looking right at him, burning eyes, probing.

Gerard dropped his fork. "Gerard, your Majesty."

"You found these proscribed Works?"

"Yes, your Majesty. He had many books of vile recipes." Gerard didn't know if he should say more.

"And it is your opinion these somehow came from Orliss?"

"I'm certain the wizard and Orliss communicated using one of them. Where this wizard got them, I don't know."

The King's eyes remained on him for a moment more, then moved away, leaving Gerard free from their scrutiny.

"Demetrius, I'm trusting you on this. Your evidence is shaky, but the consequences are too great to ignore. You know what will happen if you are wrong."

Demetrius nodded. "I accept them."

"That's not your responsibility," said the King, shaking his head. He stared at the table for moments that, to Gerard, stretched far too long. Gerard began to worry their mission would fail.

"Uri," the King said eventually. "Get Lord General Sibon. There is a traitor in our city, and I mean to have him in custody this night."

Gerard leaned over to Demetrius. "Does this mean we may leave now?"

Demetrius shook his head. "I'm afraid not."

"But Monteous..."

"We'll have to miss that fight. If we have a chance to take Orliss tonight, it should be done."

CHAPTER 23

ROBERT LEFT HIS horse with the stable master outside the inn, then stumbled inside. Ivron was already there, arguing with the innkeep over custom. Robert found a chair at an empty table and sat down, weary to the bone from exertion, cold, and sorrow.

He hardly registered Angela as she sat down next to him. His sight was still overcome with the repeating vision of Wallace as the threads pierced him and he fell to the ground. No matter what anyone said, he couldn't imagine how Wallace's death was not in some way his fault.

They'd strapped Wallace's body, along with the other six of Ivron's men that had died in the assault, to empty horses. The ground was too hard to bury them, and they would not decompose in the cold. Ivron had soldiers outside taking the bodies from the horses and laying them in a cart Ivron had purchased. They would cover them with canvas until after Orliss had been taken care of, and then they would hold a funeral for them all.

Monteous entered the inn slowly. His face was a mass of bruises and cuts, his robes stained with dried blood. He limped on his left leg. He searched the room for someone, and then made his way over to Robert's table, in visible pain. Every step looked to be a chore. Robert wanted to get up to help, but his muscles wouldn't move.

Monteous took the chair across from him and sat down, settling himself with care. "Ivron tells me things about you I find hard to believe, Robert."

Robert sat up a bit. "Such as?"

"He tells me you opened a portal, that you saved Angela from a trap most certainly proscribed, that you were instrumental in finding, and rescuing me."

"Did he tell you I killed Wallace?"

His Master's eyes dropped to the table for a moment, and when they came back up, they brimmed with water. "It was not you that killed him. Orliss is responsible. You did what you thought was necessary at the time."

"But he was so..." Robert buried his head in his hands.

"Yes, he was young, and he was inexperienced. But he could see the Weave, where I understand neither of you could. It's not your fault you've never been trained to see them. It's just a trick, in a way, but it's something we don't teach until you've passed the tests to leave your apprenticeship and join the Guild. I am curious how he saw it."

"Ivron's wizard had many books filled with proscribed Weaves. Wallace studied them far more than any of the rest of us."

"He was always studious. I'll have to visit Ivron, I guess, and take care of those things. They shouldn't be lying around." He seemed to be lost for a moment. "Oh, forgive me, there. I'm tired. In any case, Robert, it's not your fault."

Robert felt Angela's arm slip around his back and pull him close.

Monteous smiled. "I wondered when that would happen."

Robert couldn't suppress his shock. "What?"

"You've been mooning about her ever since she came to us. And Angela, it's been obvious to everyone you saw something in Robert. I never understood what was stopping you."

Her face turned red. "He knows."

"Ah, I see. Well, good. That's out of the way then." He put his hands down on the table, and watched them as he fidgeted with his fingers. "Did you really open a portal?"

Robert sensed there was something important in the question, beyond the question of his ability. "Yes, I did open it. But between creating the Focus and opening the portal on the same day, I drained myself and blacked out."

Monteous brought his head up and looked directly into Robert's eyes. He felt like Monteous was trying to peer through them and into his memories. "You opened the portal the same day you made the Focus? You made the Focus in a day?"

"We didn't have much time. We were trying to rescue you."

"How did you find the energie? Creating the Focus alone, in one day, should have been enough to keep you from even making the attempt at the portal."

"I borrowed power from Gerard. He didn't have anything else to do."

"Impressive. Really. Maybe Orliss did you a favor my boy. I've thought you had those capabilities in you since before I saved you from that dreadful uprising. I've spent this whole time trying to get you to concentrate, to focus, to leave your distractions behind you when you Work. And you move from struggling apprentice to accomplished wizard in a matter of days."

Robert couldn't believe it. Monteous had never praised him to such a degree in the entire time he'd lived with him. Always before, it was, "Good job, but you can do better."

"Thank you."

"Don't thank me, Robert. You've had it in you all the while. You will take the tests as soon as this business with Orliss is finished."

Robert knew he should be excited about the idea of the tests, but the mention of Orliss ruined it for him. "What are we going to do about him?"

"We? Well, hmm. Why, we go to the Conclave, of course. It would be better if we can find Demetrius before we go. His testimony would be useful."

"You're taking me to the Conclave?"

"Of course. You and Angela. It is your testimony that will be his undoing. You, Ivron, and Demetrius. It should be enough to keep him held until we can visit his estates and get the proof."

"Where is the Conclave?"

Monteous laughed, and it looked like it hurt. "Where? It's where it always is. Only the doors change place."

"When do we go?"

"In the morning, after I've slept. I haven't slept in days. You two get some sleep as well. You will need all your wits at the Conclave, especially if Orliss makes any sort of trouble." The old wizard stood and left the table, and made his way across the room to the innkeep who promptly found someone to lead him to a room.

Angela pulled him tight. "You know, Robert. Every hour since we shared our stories, I can't help but look at you and be glad that I let Marena bully me into it. If she hadn't, I would still be sitting across the table from you, and I would not have seen the way Monteous looked at you, proud like a father whose son has just done something impossible."

"He has never spoken that way to me in all the time I've known him. It hurts that it took all this happening for me to learn what he spent years trying to teach me."

"He is proud that you learned it, no matter how it came about, I think. Come, we should get some sleep, too."

Robert didn't want to move though, with Angela's arm around him, so he said nothing, and she didn't pull away. He leaned against her and thought of Wallace and Monteous and all that happened. They didn't go find beds until much later.

ORLISS KILORE STOOD, unbelieving, at his workbench. He stared down into the bowl, the bowl that should be showing Monteous, bound and helpless. All it showed him was an empty room.

He teased the bowl to reveal the hallway, and there on the floor, face down, lay Trilech's body. The door to the room where Monteous had been held, stood open. Teased some more, the bowl showed the kitchen where Uden lay, his head separated from the rest of his body. In the courtyard, the bowl displayed dead soldiers everywhere, the buildings burning, and Pruitt's body, which was missing an arm and had an ugly wound near his heart. His eyes were open, but no life remained.

How could this happen? How? How had they found him? How had those apprentices — it had to be them — managed to defeat three full wizards?

He wanted to strangle whoever was responsible for this. How did they even find Monteous? That Weave should have blocked all scrying. The Weave on the door to his room? Someone should have died entering that room.

This on top of his men at the inn gone missing. Well, not missing. They'd been routed. The blood in the snow had not been cleaned up. It was a disaster. Those men he'd had at Ivron's estate. Cowards, all of them. They were in a forest. Burn some wood to keep warm. Instead, they'd fled, taken his money and fled, and he had little idea of their whereabouts. Hopefully, they froze to death in the storm.

A knock at the door interrupted his internal rage.

"Who dares interrupt my work!" he yelled through the door.

The door opened, and Boreth strode through it. "I'm not hearing good news, Orliss."

"What news are you hearing that makes you think you're any less likely to die when you interrupt me and something goes wrong?"

"That the men you had at the ferry were slaughtered. That there were Weaves involved."

"How did you hear this?" *Did he have other agents nearby?*

"I have sources. I'm not so alone here as you think."

Orliss frowned. Boreth was far more confident than two days ago. His sources?

"It's a minor setback," he said. *How can I salvage this? Monteous is free.* "They still won't be able to find Monteous." He started moving toward Boreth, slow steps.

"A minor setback? You have no idea where those apprentices are heading. Maybe they're coming here. They surely suspect you."

A few more steps. He'd need to hide any obvious connection to Mrongil from anyone that came looking, especially Monteous.

"Of course they suspect me. It's part of the game, though. A long held practice of the Guild." His hand slipped into a pocket in his robe, and he wrapped it around the small, cold hilt of the knife hidden there. *No Weaves. Nothing to make them suspect me.* "The Senior Wizard is expected to be able to overcome the difficulties that are placed in his path. Outright murder is frowned upon, but detainment is within the rules."

"But if they find him and break him free, this whole scheme will collapse. We'll be set back years."

He slipped the knife up his sleeve, then put his arm around Boreth. "Come here, let me show you Monteous." He walked Boreth over to the bowl.

"Yes, that would be good to see."

When they reached the bowl, Orliss said, "Bend over it, look straight in." Orliss slipped the knife out of his sleeve and spun it around in his palm, all while his arm still rested around Boreth's shoulder.

Boreth did as Orliss instructed, unwittingly exposing his neck.

"I don't see anything."

"Just a moment, I need to bring it back into view."

The door to the Laboratory swung open again. "Master Orliss, the King's guard is at the gate. They have declared that you be placed under arrest for treason."

Boreth looked up, then, and Orliss jabbed the knife into his neck, severing an artery. Blood sprayed out of the wound when Orliss removed the knife. Orliss held him down over the bowl, letting the blood drain into it.

"I think it's time we leave, then. Get my things ready. I need to clean up this mess."

Orliss brought his lips right down near Boreth's ear. Boreth's struggles were quickly diminishing.

"Don't worry, Boreth. I will succeed, and your King will be pleased.

I can't, however, risk anyone finding out right yet how strong my ties are, or to whom they lead."

CHAPTER 24

GERARD AND NINA rode behind the Lord General and forty of his men, following them to Orliss's home in the Middle City. Demetrius, Georg and Horuth rode next to the Lord General, who had suggested that "the boy and the girl" should stay behind. He had meant, Gerard felt sure, they should stay at the keep. He'd said, "I'm not staying here," and Demetrius quickly agreed.

Demetrius had then said, "But you should probably stay back. Orliss is nearly as powerful as Monteous, and I don't think you'd fare well against him in a fight."

Which had made sense, and thus he, and Nina, were stuck in the rear.

When they reached the street Orliss's home was built beside, Gerard got his first look at Orliss's dwelling. Where Monteous kept his home modest, and his Laboratory, although larger by far, constructed of common stone, Orliss's home was endowed with marble columns, multiple turrets, and manicured gardens. Orliss displayed his power and wealth in ostentatious fashion. As they approached the building, Gerard saw stained glass windows and hand carved marble ornaments adorning every available corner.

He also saw that there were men at the gate, armed with swords, shields ready.

The Lord General stopped at the gate, and the column came to a halt. In the sudden quiet, he could hear the Lord General's voice clearly. "I'm here by order of the King, and do hereby declare that

Master Wizard Orliss Kilore is to be placed under arrest for suspicion of treason. Anyone found aiding him in any way shall also stand accused of treason, and will suffer the penalties set forth in the Articles of Founding."

The guards behind the gate looked to each other nervously, and then one, clearly in charge, said "He is not here."

"Then open the gates and let us search for him."

The guard shook his head. "I can't do that without permission, Lord General."

"You could lose your head if you don't get these gates open."

"Let me go find my Captain, then."

"Do that."

The soldier raced away through the snow, up the stairs and into the mansion.

"Spread out, surround the building. No one comes out," ordered the Lord General. The soldiers split into two groups, heading in opposite directions around the home.

Nina said to Gerard quietly, "He won't come out."

"I was thinking something similar, but what if the guard is correct? What if he's not here?"

Nina laughed. "Then we go find him. It's what you want, anyway, don't you?"

He couldn't deny that. He wanted to do more than observe Orliss's capture. He wanted active retribution for everything he'd been through the last several days.

He brought his horse up beside Demetrius, and Nina followed him.

"Do you see anything, Gerard," Demetrius asked.

Gerard looked for Weave's, which he realized he should have done as they first approached. He'd seemed left out of it all, though. "I don't see anything obvious on the outside. Orliss could have tied Weaves inside, or on other parts where I can't see. How long are we going to wait for him to come out?"

Demetrius chuckled. "I see you don't believe the lie, either. The

Lord General's hands are tied somewhat. He's prevented by the Articles of the Founding from preemptively entering the abode of a wizard. He has to wait for Orliss to come out, or for someone inside to allow him in, or for Orliss to run."

"Orliss will run."

"Without doubt. He hasn't expended all this effort to give up without a fight. I have two worries. The first that he will fight here. The second is that he is already gone, and will take the fight to the Conclave. If he can manage to become invested as Senior Wizard, there is little that the King will be able to do to him until he is replaced."

"Why is that?"

"The writ for his arrest is based on inference and supposition. That works as long as he's not Senior Wizard. If he becomes Senior Wizard, the Articles provide that the King cannot imprison or remove him. Only a majority vote of the Conclave could do that, and the Conclave wouldn't likely vote that way without solid proof, which we don't have."

"So, basically, we need to catch him using proscribed magic, or with letters written by him to someone in Mrongil detailing the plot."

"Right. Or, stop him from becoming Senior Wizard. Oh, look. The Guard returns."

Gerard looked up, and saw the guard emerging from the home. When he reached the gate, he opened it and stepped aside.

"Enter if you must. He's not here."

The Lord General rode through, followed by the ten of his men that had stayed with him. When they were all through the gate, Demetrius said, "Let's go," and followed them through the gate. Gerard followed him, as did the rest of their group.

"Search it top to bottom," the Lord General commanded, and the ten men quickly entered the house and disappeared.

Gerard itched to join the search, but Demetrius stayed where he was, and Gerard decided to follow his lead. He could hear furniture being tossed, items moved, doors crashing open.

"You know," he said, "it's likely that there are proscribed Works in his laboratory."

"Damn. I should have thought. Lord General, a moment."

"Demetrius?"

"You need to stop your men from entering Orliss's laboratory."

"Why?"

"If you were hunted and guilty, what would you leave behind for your pursuers?"

His eyes grew larger as the implications dawned on him.

"Sergeant," the Lord General yelled to a soldier standing near the door of the home. "Tell them not to enter the Laboratory."

Gerard spoke up. "Tell them not to even touch the door."

The sergeant turned to head into the home, but even as he did, Gerard felt a burst of energie rip through the building. It knocked him from his horse, and he fell hard on his shoulder. A sharp spike of pain hit him and he cried out. He managed to get his head up to look around, and he saw Demetrius on the ground.

His horse had run in fright, several of them had. He was lucky not to have been crushed under hoof.

He tried to push himself up, but his injured shoulder couldn't take the weight. He rolled himself over in the snow, and saw Nina just getting up from where her horse had tossed her. She didn't appear hurt, which somehow made the pain in his shoulder less.

He managed to maneuver himself into a seated position, and got, for the first time since falling, a look at the house. It looked sturdy for a moment, and then he could see flames flickering deep inside, and growing rapidly larger.

Some of the Lord General's soldiers came stumbling out of the house, but not all of them. Within moments, the flames spread throughout the first floor.

A soldier jumped through a window on the second floor, pursued by gouts of fire. He landed awkwardly in the snow and cried out in pain. His leg had bent at a strange angle. Gerard had to look away. He felt sick to his stomach, but maybe that was the pain in his shoulder.

Soon, the house was entirely engulfed in flame, and the heat was overwhelming the cold air. Nina helped him to his feet and they moved away from the inferno. Their backs were against the gate that encircled the property before the heat from the fire was bearable.

Demetrius soon found them.

"What happened?" Nina asked.

"A trap," Demetrius said.

"How?"

"He made a Weave," Gerard said, "that triggered when the soldiers tried to go somewhere Orliss didn't want them. Probably the lab. Any evidence of proscribed Works is likely gone."

Demetrius nodded.

"So what now?" Gerard asked. He knew what he wanted to do. Go find a bed and a healer.

"I think we go back to the inn at the ferry. We know at least two of Ivron's men are there, and with luck, Ivron will stop there."

At that moment, Georg and Horuth came over, leading their horses. Somehow, in spite of the confusion, they'd managed to round them up.

Gerard, unthinking, tried to reach for the reins of his horse with his injured arm, and found he couldn't lift it at all. He was rewarded for the effort with more pain, instead.

"Are you hurt?" Nina asked.

"Fell on my shoulder." He was surprised she hadn't noticed while pulling him away from the burning home.

Her hands went to his shoulder and felt around. She was gentle, but it hurt, and he pulled it away.

"Stop being a baby. Let me see it." And she worked her fingers into his shoulder again. The tip of her tongue was visible between her lips. Her eyes rolled up and hid behind her eyelids while she dealt him more pain.

Demetrius stepped over. "How is it?"

Gerard grimaced. If it didn't hurt so much, he thought he might enjoy Nina touching him.

"Seems like it might have dislocated," Nina said.

"Get him up on the horse and strap it to his side, then. You think you can make it to the ferry, Gerard?"

Gerard didn't know if he could make it anywhere, but he was not about to be left out of anything if he could help it. "I'll manage."

"Wait for me. I need to let the Lord General know what we're planning." Demetrius mounted his horse, and rode off through the confusion that still reigned in the courtyard.

"C'mon, Apprentice," Nina said. "Let's get you up on your horse. Georg, help me out."

Soon, they had him up on his horse, and his arm strapped to his side with a thong from one of the saddlebags. Every movement caused more pain, though it was better with the arm no longer hanging from his shoulder.

About the time he was ready, Demetrius came back.

"The Lord General wanted us to stay and help figure out what happened."

Gerard couldn't believe it. "We're not staying, are we?"

"No. I convinced him it would be futile. Orliss is gone, and we need to find him. We know where he will be, so we just need to find our way there."

"Do you really think they'll be at the inn?"

"I think it's the best place to start looking. Georg's friends did say they went west from there, so it's on our way in any case." And then he seemed to look more directly at Gerard. "Are you sure you're good to ride? I'd rather not take the time to stop and get your shoulder taken care of if we can wait until we get to the ferry."

"If I start to pass out, strap me on. What's a dozen miles of riding a horse in the dark?" He already felt a bit dizzy from the pain.

Nina pulled her horse up next to his and leaned over to whisper in his ear. "You're not being brave for my sake, are you?"

"No." But part of him thought *yes*.

"Let's ride," Demetrius called out, and they fell in behind him as he rode through the gate.

Gerard tried to keep from grimacing too often. Nina stayed abreast of him as they rode, and he didn't want her to see how much it really did hurt.

✹ ✹ ✹

A HARD KNOCK at her door roused Angela from a troubled sleep. Over and over, she had dreamt of Wallace and his last moments, the threads from the Weave taking him, killing him.

"Angela, wake up, you need to come downstairs." Ivron was at her door.

"I'm awake," she called out.

It must have been good enough. She heard his footsteps echo down the hall, and knocks on another door.

She slipped out of bed. For a moment, she thought she was having trouble opening her eyes, until she realized that it was still dark outside the one tiny window in the room. *What time is it?*

She put her clothes on as quickly as she could in the dark, and opened the door to find Robert in the hallway. He looked as sleepy as she felt.

"Hi," he said.

"Why are we up? Is it morning yet?"

"Let's go down and find out."

He held out his hand and she took it. It felt so good to hold his hand. She still was having a hard time believing the past didn't matter to him. He hadn't brought it up, though, since that night. He didn't seem to care about it, and that made her as happy as just about anything else could. Now that they'd found Monteous, everything would go back to the way it had been. Everything but her and Robert. And Wallace.

She wondered if she'd ever get over Wallace's death. Robert felt it was his fault, but she thought it just as much her fault. If she could have seen the Weave, she could have unraveled it, she felt sure. It helped, a little, knowing that she couldn't see it because she hadn't yet been taught how.

They navigated the staircase hand in hand, she followed Robert down. And following him, she didn't see the reason Ivron woke them until after Robert said, "Gerard."

Instinctively, she tried to drop Robert's hand, but he held onto it, and pulled her into the room, where she got her first look at him.

She could see the pain in him almost immediately. His arm was strapped to his side, and next to him, with a cup in her hand, sat a red-haired girl. As Angela watched, the young woman held the cup up to Gerard's lips and he drank.

"Gerard!" Robert called out, and the cup came away from his lips.

"Robert, Angela," he said. The girl looked at them, and Angela saw she was older than a girl. Maybe fifteen or sixteen.

"You're hurt, what happened?"

"Fell off a horse when Orliss's home exploded."

Robert dragged her across the room. He pulled some chairs out and sat down. Reluctantly, she sat down next to him. She didn't want to have the conversation she knew was coming, even if Robert knew the truth. Even if he said it wouldn't matter. She couldn't bury the idea that it must matter.

"Exploded?"

"We went to the King, and Demetrius explained the situation. Then we ended up following the Lord General to Orliss's home. The guards there said he was absent, so the Lord General had his men search the place. In the search, they must have tripped a Weave. A huge wave of energie knocked me off my horse. When I looked up, the house was on fire and my arm was useless."

"Did you see Orliss at all?"

"No, which is why we came here. Where's Wallace? Is he here, too?"

Robert shook his head, but didn't say anything.

"He's not here? Where is he?"

Angela decided she'd answer, rather than make Robert talk about it. "He's dead."

"Dead?" There was shock on his face, and the girl next to him immediately reached her arm out to comfort him.

"We found where they were holding Monteous. We entered the house, where there were two wizards. The first one died quickly, but the second one was in a room with Monteous. There was a proscribed Weave over the door that neither I nor Robert could see. Wallace could see it, and he tried to unravel it. When it came apart..." She couldn't finish. Tears were returning to her eyes.

No one said anything for a moment, and Angela was glad. She didn't want to answer any more questions about Wallace.

Then Gerard leaned over to the girl and whispered in her ear, and she got up and left. "Robert," he said. "May I talk to Angela alone for a minute?"

Angela looked to Robert, and she tried to plead with her eyes for him not to leave, but either he didn't see it, or... or she didn't know what.

"Right," he said, then got up.

He leaned down and whispered to her, "I'll get you something to drink. Don't let him bully you."

Don't let him bully me? How am I supposed to do that? But Robert's confidence in her had already given her some support she didn't think she'd ever get.

When Robert left, she said, "So, Gerard. What do you want?"

"You and Robert, huh?"

"Yes. Don't you even think of telling him that stupid lie."

He leaned forward, and the movement caused him obvious pain. "That's actually what I wanted to talk to you about. I..."

"What?"

"Look, I'm sorry I told you I'd do that. Robert was Monteous's favorite, and when I figured out I couldn't have you, I didn't want him to, either."

"It wasn't right, Gerard."

"No, it wasn't right, and I truly regret it. I'm glad to see that you two are together."

"No help to you." Now, she was angry. "Why didn't you tell me this long ago? Is it that girl?"

A smile crossed his lips, absently. It didn't look like he knew it was there. "Nina? No. I decided before we ever left Monteous's laboratory. I just couldn't find the right time."

"And this is the right time?"

"No, but I figured it's better than not telling you at all and having you hate me forever."

Angela relented. He deserved to suffer, but she couldn't do it. Not with everything else going on. "Apology accepted. Is someone out looking for a healer for your arm?"

"Demetrius is."

"Good, then tell me about Nina. I need to know whether I should warn her about you."

Gerard laughed. "Somebody should have warned me about her."

From across the room, Nina said, "I heard that."

"To be fair, Gerard," said Demetrius as he entered the room, followed by a middle aged woman bundled up in a winter coat, "you were warned more than once."

Angela laughed. "Maybe you'll get what you deserve, after all."

Gerard rolled his eyes. "I said I was sorry."

"And you'll need to say it a couple more times to make up for your mistake."

She stood and got out of the way as Demetrius brought the healer over to Gerard. Robert handed her a cup of tea. "Everything all right, then?"

She kissed him. "Yes, everything is exactly right."

CHAPTER 25

ROBERT WOKE IN the morning, and found himself generally happy, despite the hard stone of sorrow in his gut over Wallace. Gerard had apologized to Angela, and she felt good about it. Monteous was alive and with them. And he was going to a Conclave today, where he would see the end of Orliss.

It turned out that he and Angela had only been asleep a couple hours when Demetrius had brought Gerard and the girl Nina into the inn. After the tea, they'd stayed up a little longer while the healer worked on Gerard, and then Ivron had recommended they go back to bed.

He put his clothes on quickly, picked up his staff, and went down to the common room of the inn. The innkeep greeted him as he emerged from the stairs, and seemed far less surly than he'd been the previous day. Robert guessed the prospect of having his inn full in the middle of winter helped him surmount his earlier indignation.

Robert found Ivron, Demetrius and Monteous seated at a table near the hearth, eating. He walked over to the table, and Demetrius pulled out a chair for him. "Join us."

Robert took the chair, and sat down.

Monteous looked much better, Robert thought. The bruises and cuts were still there, but his eyes were brighter, and the energie that always surrounded him seemed more focused. "You look better," Robert said.

"Thank you, I feel much more like myself."

The innkeep showed up then with a plate of bread and soup of some sort. He set a cup next to it and filled it with tea.

"When do we go to the Conclave?"

"Soon. We'll wait until everyone wakes and is rested. It won't begin for another few hours."

"How do we get there? I've heard it's never in the same place."

Monteous laughed. "That's the secret. It's never in the same place because it's always nearby. As a Guild member, you're taught how to create a special Weave that will allow access to a gateway, a portal if you like. All you need to get there is a hidden place to work the Weave. A room in an inn will work just fine."

"What will happen when we get there?"

"I should hope nothing as exciting as the last few days, but it is hard to know. We do not know how many of the members are in on this plot with Orliss. I hope that it is not too many. The implications, if there are more than the few members we already know about, are appalling."

Monteous looked up, then, at something behind Robert. "Ah, Angela. Sit down and eat."

She pulled a chair over and sat next to Robert, and smiled at him when he looked up. The innkeep soon placed food in front of her as well.

"Monteous!" Gerard's voice came from behind Robert, and Gerard followed close behind it. The girl, Nina, came to the table soon after. Robert snickered to himself. She wasn't letting Gerard out of her sight.

"Good to see you Gerard. I trust your shoulder is better?"

"Much. She said I shouldn't do anything strenuous with it for a few weeks."

Gerard pulled up two chairs, and sat Nina in the first, taking the second for himself. The table was getting crowded.

"And Nina. I'm pleased to see you again. How is your father?"

"I'm sure he's dancing in the fields now that I'm gone."

Monteous laughed. "I wouldn't be so quick to think that. Your father has been trying to push you to be more than a farmer's daugh-

ter for more years than you can remember. He loves you dearly. If
there were any way to push you up without pushing you out, he would
take it."

She looked down.

"Well, now you're here with us, for good or ill.

"And since you are all here, I think we can begin our preparations.
Eat, you two. The day will be long, and I'm afraid there won't be much
food in the middle of it."

Robert finished the his meal, using the last of his bread to swab
out the remains of his soup. When it was in his mouth, he pushed the
empty dishes to the center of the table.

"Monteous," Ivron said. "Are you expecting me to go with you?"

"No, dear friend. I don't think so. I think only Demetrius and my
Apprentices. It will be — difficult to explain any more. It'll be difficult
to explain these four before the time comes to accuse Orliss."

"How so?" Robert asked.

"It's simply not done. There's no specific prohibition against bringing guests, but in general, Guild members expect to see only Guild members at the Conclave. I cannot remember a time when even one outsider
was brought in, let alone four. I do wish I had a staff with me, though."

"You could use mine."

"May I see it?"

Robert passed it to him, and Monteous took to examining it with
vigor.

"This is a nice staff, though not one of mine."

"I took it from one of the wizards that were holding you captive."

Monteous ran his finger along the carvings, and Robert looked at
them closely for the first time. The top was carved in the shape of a
hawk, its mouth open. Hawk feathers were carved into the body of the
staff. Several bands of metals, engraved with various runes, wrapped
each end of the staff as well. Robert had seen most of them before in
the various books in Monteous's laboratory, but he couldn't place all
of them at the moment. Each of the runes enhanced some property of
the staff.

"I couldn't take this staff," he said, handing it back. "It is yours, won in combat. I think it will serve us better if you carry it. The wizard who carried it before you, he stood high in the Guild. Those who recognize it will be, perhaps, more careful."

"I have a wand, too, if you would like that."

"Yes, I think that will work fine."

Robert pulled it from his coat pocket and handed it across.

"You could use my staff," Gerard said.

"No, I think not. Your skills work much better through a staff than a wand." Monteous examined the wand Robert handed him. "Yes, this will work fine."

When Gerard was done eating, Monteous led them all to a private room in the rear of the inn.

"Ivron, once we're gone, you can set those men free."

"You think so?"

"They will be unable to affect the outcome, and you can't just keep them in the cellar forever."

"I had thought to keep them until you return. I don't want them going directly to Orliss if things go awry."

"I see your point. Do as you will. Now, get behind me." He waved everyone back toward the door so that he had an open space in front of him.

He pulled out the wand Robert had given him, and used it to draw a Weave in the air, but it was like no Weave Robert had seen. None of the threads connected, but they hung where he placed them. They should have fallen apart. Monteous placed one last thread, in a sort of curl around the others, then pulled it tight and the threads snapped together. He drew them out, one by one, into a shape similar to a portal. When he placed the last thread into the new shape, the area between all the threads grew dark.

"In," he said, pointing to Demetrius. Demetrius stepped forward and into the black void hanging in front of them. He disappeared into the blackness. "The rest of you, get in there, quickly."

Robert took the lead, grasped his staff tightly, and stepped forward and through. A sharp slice of cold slid through him, where he contacted the void, but as he stepped beyond it, he found himself in a solid stone room, empty of all furniture. Demetrius was in the room ahead of him, and already guarding the lone door.

"Step out of the way," he said, and Robert quickly obeyed, then turned around to see where he'd come from.

Two thin, iron poles rose from the floor, and in between, a silvery flat surface hung between them.

As he stared at it, Angela emerged from it, and stepped into the room. She came over to stand by Robert. "That was odd," she said. "Where are we?"

"We're in some sort of arrival chamber, I think. Where that is, I really haven't any idea."

Gerard came into the room, followed quickly by Monteous. As soon as Monteous was through, the shimmery surface disappeared.

"How does that work?" Robert asked. "That Weave was strange."

"The Weave takes little power, and is just a signaling mechanism to the Work that creates the gateway."

"The iron bars?"

"Exactly."

"What happens if two wizards try to signal it at the same time?"

"Whoever completes their Weave first gets to go through. The other Weave will fall apart and they will have to try again." He stuck his wand in a pocket, and then walked to the door. "Follow me."

The door opened on its own, and Monteous went through. Demetrius followed right after, and then the rest of them.

They came out into a hallway that curved away from them in opposite directions. Several wizards were in the hallway, eying the group as it emerged. Three of them approached Monteous immediately, still eying the rest of them.

The first one to speak, short and fat with unkempt hair, said, "Monteous. Good to see you."

"Umbror, good to see you, too."

"There was a rumor you wouldn't be here this year."

Monteous opened his arms wide. "It was rumor in truth. Why would anyone think I would be absent and let Orliss take my seat unopposed?"

A second one, taller, but with a beak of a nose said, "You look like you were attacked."

"I was, and you'll find out once the meeting begins exactly how and why."

"And these others?" said the third, a stooped, older man, his head bald.

"My evidence."

"Evidence," he spat. "Outsiders are not to be brought to a Conclave."

"There is reason, Wendell, and there is nothing in the bylaws that prohibit it."

Wendell eyed Robert, and Robert didn't like it. The gaze slid from his face and focused on the staff he held. "Explain that," Wendell demanded, pointing to the staff.

"Explain what?"

"The staff. That's Uden's staff. How did this — this apprentice — come by Uden's staff?"

"I believe he took it from him."

"So you've brought a thief with you? You sink lower and lower, Monteous."

Monteous rose to his full height, his eyes flashing. "Spoils of combat, Wendell. Robert is no thief."

The other two were obvious in their reappraisal of Robert. But Wendell carried on. "No apprentice could defeat Uden."

"Have you really looked, Wendell? The only thing separating him from being an apprentice, and being ranked quite highly, I should think, is a matter of passing the tests. Truthfully, if you persist in your questioning of my decision to bring them here, I will have no choice but to suspect you have other motives, and are perhaps, surprised I am here at all."

"You just be careful, Monteous. Outsiders have no place here," he said, and walked away.

"How much of that will we run into?" Demetrius asked.

"I hope not too much. As a whole, the Guild and its members are supposed to wait until they judge, but I fear many would prefer things to remain unchanged."

Umbror came up to Robert. "Did you really wrest that staff from Uden?"

Robert didn't know what to say. He looked to Monteous for help, who just waved at him, which was no help at all. "I had help."

"Help?"

"I held him in place, while one of the soldiers rushed in and used a sword to behead him."

Umbror smiled. "That is no small feat, holding Uden in place."

"It was luck."

Umbror laughed. "He's humble, too, Monteous. Are these others of similar quality?"

"They have their qualities. Most important, though, they were all instrumental in my ability to be here today. Now, if you'll excuse us, I really need to find them seats."

"Of course, of course. My respect, apprentice. May you find success when you take your tests."

The two wizards backed away into the crowd that Robert noticed had gathered. It was a bit disconcerting. Everywhere he looked, he could see the energies around the gathered wizards, and they were all organized and coherent. A signature, of sorts, that identified each wizard. He knew that before, but he'd never really understood what it really meant until seeing the group of them, together, each easily identifiable by the pattern and motion of their energie.

"Come," Monteous said, "let's seat ourselves." He started off down the hallway, and the rest trailed after, finding their way through the dispersing crowd.

He led them through a doorway into a bowl-like room. There were seats for several hundred people surrounding a platform at its center.

"There are so many seats," Robert said.

Monteous kept walking down the steps toward the center of the bowl. "Early in the life of the Guild, there were many more wizards."

"What happened to them?"

"The Guild decided there were too many, and put restrictions on the number of apprentices that were allowed to be trained. Slowly, the Guild membership fell to what it is today."

Robert looked around. Other wizards were trickling in through other doors, some of whom saw Monteous and hailed him, others who saw him and tried to pretend he did not exist.

Monteous stopped them while they were still several rows from the platform. "Seating is somewhat assigned, in that the various factions generally tend to sit together, and older, more powerful wizards generally sit toward the front."

"Where do you sit," Gerard asked.

"Typically, I sit up front, but not today. I'll sit with you, until it's time to start." He looked around. "Whatever happens, remain quiet until I call on you. I expect Orliss to be here. Some of his supporters are here already. We don't need you getting tossed out before I've had a chance to bring the discussion around to exposing him.

"Demetrius, you're here, in part to testify against him, but primarily for an extra set of eyes. I expect Orliss or his supporters to try something, and I need you to watch for it."

"What would they try?" Robert asked.

"I don't know, but duels and outright fighting between factions have been known to erupt in the past."

Monteous went and sat in a seat behind them.

Robert took the time to look around him. Light filtered into the room through stained glass panels in the ceiling, and was supported around the walls by lamps lit from within by a Weave. The wizards filtering in were of many ages, some ancient, some not much older than himself.

Several wizards stopped to chat with, or at least greet, Monteous as they made their way to their seats. Robert assumed they were members of Monteous's own faction. A couple even greeted

Demetrius, which surprised Robert until he thought about it and realized that many of them would know Demetrius from the work he did for Monteous.

At the point where the lower portion of the bowl, from the row in front of them to the rows up against the platform, was nearly full, a wizard stood and took the platform. Monteous leaned forward and spoke quietly. "That's the Master of Gatherings. He's appointed by vote each year for the subsequent Conclave. He will direct the order of things."

The noise in the room fell almost to nothing as the Master stood in the center of the platform. When it was quiet, he spoke. "Masters, welcome to the Conclave. It seems that this may be an interesting event as we have some guests."

"Send them away," and "No guests," were shouted from various points around the room, but most often from the other side of the platform.

The Master raised his arms in a request for silence. After a few moments, the shouts subsided. "I have researched this, as soon as I was made aware they were here, and there is no prohibition against guests in these meetings. And, since it appears the Senior Wizard brought them, he must have a purpose. I, for one, would like to hear that purpose."

"First, we must attend to the succession. Any who wish to be eligible or wish to vote, and are not in the Citadel, please take your seats. The doors will close in two minutes."

Feet could be heard in the hallways outside, and several more wizards entered the Citadel. Among the last, entering from the far side, was Orliss.

"Damn," said Monteous. "I was hoping he'd just run."

Orliss found them and glared across the room, then he smiled, and took a seat in the front row on the other side of the platform.

The Master of Gatherings stirred again. "The doors will shut," he said. The doors around the Citadel shut of their own accord, locking with a Weave. Robert could see it was a simple Weave, more symbolic than anything. Any of the wizards here could unravel it.

"Senior Wizard, please approach the platform," said the Master of Gatherings.

Monteous stood, then leaned over them. "Stay vigilant."

He moved into the aisle and down the steps, and took a place on the platform next to the Master of Gatherings.

"Senior Wizard, do you recognize this body?"

Monteous turned in place, looking out into the gathered wizards. "I do."

"Do you recognize that it holds the right to choose a new Senior Wizard as it wishes?"

"I do."

"Will you accept challengers?"

"I will."

"Gathered wizards. Now is your opportunity to lead this body for the next biennium. If you so wish, step forward and be recognized as a candidate."

A few moments passed with only some rustling as wizards looked around to see who might rise, until Orliss finally did rise from his seat and step forward, onto the platform. Robert thought he looked confident. He didn't seem to be bothered that Monteous was on the platform with him.

After a few more moments of rustling, but no one else stepping forth, the Master of Gatherings said, "Are there no more who wish to challenge?"

He waited a few moments, then said, "Standing for the challenge are Monteous Roarke and Orliss Kilore. Bring forth the Challenge Orb."

The three wizards on the platform stepped back to the edge, and from the center, emerged a solid crystal orb a foot in diameter. It was pushed up by a wooden pedestal, intricately carved with a thousand runes.

It came to a stop, about waist high.

Robert said to Demetrius, "How does it work?"

"I don't know, exactly. I've never been here before, either. I gather from discussions I've had with Monteous that they both place their hands on it, and the last one to remove their hands wins the challenge."

There had to be something more.

"Before we begin the challenge, are there any that object to any of the challengers?"

I object, thought Robert.

"Why doesn't Monteous object?"

"Challengers don't object to those challenging them," said Demetrius. "It's just not done."

"How do you know?"

"I've asked Monteous before."

One of the wizards in front of them turned around and glared at them. Robert decided to stop asking questions.

A wizard near where Orliss had been seated stood up. "I object to Monteous Roarke."

A collective gasp came from the rest of the room.

"On what grounds, Silas?"

"His apprentices murdered three members of this Guild just last night." His eyes were looking right at Robert and Angela.

All of the heads in the room turned to look at them.

"What proof do you have?"

"Does anyone see Trilech, Pruitt, or Uden here?" He waved his arms around the room. "You don't because they're dead. That apprentice, there, murdered them."

"How can you say it was murder?"

"He has Uden's staff."

The eyes really focused then on the staff. The whispers and murmuring grew louder. Robert didn't know what to do. He could feel their eyes, their energie directed at him.

"Quiet!"

The chatter and whispers slowly dissipated.

"What, Monteous, have you to say about this?" asked the Master of Gatherings.

"I had hoped to leave this matter until after the Investiture. It would have made certain procedures easier to follow."

"Monteous."

"Robert, stand up." commanded Monteous.

What? He stood. *Why does he want me to stand up?* He wanted to shrink back into his seat, but he fought that desire and remained standing.

"How did you obtain the staff?"

Flies buzzed in Robert's stomach. "While trying to rescue Monteous from the wizards that held him, I used my wand to hold the wizard in place. One of the soldiers killed him. I took the staff."

"Lies!" came shouts from the other side.

The Master of Gatherings turned to them. "Quiet!"

Monteous spun slowly. "Masters, how do I look? Do I look like I spent the last three days being pampered like the women in Lord Brendel's court?"

Spots of laughter could be heard throughout the room.

"No, I do not. What I look like is how one looks after you've been beaten and tortured for five straight days. Robert saved my life, rescued me in time so that I could be here to face the one who perpetrated this crime upon me. Some of you know who that is."

More shouts. "Who?" "Lies!"

Again, the Master of Gatherings shouted above the din. "Quiet!"

When silence ruled, he asked Monteous, "Who did this, then?"

"Why don't we wait to get to that part? Before I reveal who I think is to blame, you must know that there is more at stake than my well-being and the deaths of the three wizards who held me captive.

"Robert, would you kindly bring the staff here?"

Robert eased his way into the aisle, then started down the steps. Every footstep was loud in the silence. He looked up to see Orliss watching him, appraising. He had to know they suspected him, but he was standing there with no emotion on his face, as if this didn't concern him at all.

When he got to the platform, Monteous stepped forward and took the staff from him. Robert turned to go back, but Monteous said, "No, stay."

Then Monteous held up the staff.

"Are we all in agreement that this was Uden's staff?"

The wizards assented that they agreed.

"Master Brin, would you kindly step up here?"

An old wizard, twice Monteous's age, or so he looked, stepped up from the first row.

"What do you need?"

"Would you please examine this staff and tell me what you find?"

The old Master took the staff from Monteous, then started brushing his fingers along it, turning it in his hands, examining every detail. "It's an exquisite staff. The detail, the metals chosen for the binding, the..." The old wizard trailed off.

"Master Brin?" Monteous said after a few moments had passed.

"There is something bound into the staff, I hesitate to say what it is."

"Why do you hesitate?"

"It cannot be. Uden was a well-respected wizard. Powerful. He wouldn't need to do this to his staff."

The Master of Gatherings said, "Do what?"

"There's a proscribed Work bound into the staff."

Bedlam erupted throughout the hall. Wizards calling for someone else to examine the staff, disbelieving cries of shock. The wizard who had objected to Monteous stood and shouted, "You planted it!"

This time, Monteous's voice erupted into the din. "Silence!" When the room quieted, he continued. "You all know that a Work cannot be bound into a staff after its creation. Quit being foolish. One of my apprentices died trying to remove a proscribed Weave from the door to the room where I was bound. These three wizards were parties to abomination, and they deserved their fate."

Stunned silence. Robert could feel the tension in the air, the disbelief. If one wizard was using a proscribed Weave, well, it had happened occasionally. But three, three was something more significant, almost inconceivable.

"You think that's all?" Monteous asked.

No one said a word. Orliss stood near the crystal, resignation apparent on his face, but Robert didn't believe it. For Orliss to have shown up here, he had a plan. He had to have known of Monteous's escape.

"Who would benefit from my abduction? Those three? How far does this reach?"

What benefit would Orliss derive from showing up? What could he do to accomplish his patron's goals? The accusation of Monteous, of himself, it seemed too simple. Robert wished he could talk to Demetrius.

He looked to see them, Demetrius, Angela, and Gerard. Demetrius was watching everything, it seemed, eyes moving in never flagging patterns. Gerard was focused on Orliss and Monteous. And Angela, her eyes were on him. It gave Robert comfort, but it wasn't what he was looking for.

"I'll tell you, if you cannot guess. I was abducted after stepping through a portal at the rear of an estate. I had taken a job to retrieve something of value from this estate, only the job was a ruse and I did not see through it."

Robert looked toward the wizards Orliss had been seated with. His faction, his supporters. Each gripped his staff tightly, knuckles nearly white for some of them. *What could Orliss do? Five of them. What could five of them do?*

"Who should I find to greet me on the other side of this portal, but Uden, Trilech, Pruitt, and one other."

Certainly, they could kill Monteous, but Robert didn't think killing Monteous would solve Orliss's problem at this point. What was Orliss's problem? What did he need? What did Mrongil need? Robert wished he had Uden's staff in his hand, but Brin still held it.

"Who was the other, Monteous?" asked the Master of Gatherings.

Monteous held out a finger, pointing it unerringly in Orliss's direction. "Our colleague, Orliss Kilore. The man who stood to benefit the most were I to be absent from this assembly."

Nearly every wizard in the hall rose from their seats upon hearing the accusation. Shouting rang from wall to wall, some voices outraged at the idea that Orliss could possibly have anything to do with it, and other voices calling for Orliss's immediate expulsion.

"You think this will stop me," Orliss said, low enough that only those on or immediately near the platform could hear.

Orliss raised his hands, motioning for quiet. "Masters! Masters!" he called out. Eventually, the shouting subsided. "Monteous's accusation is absurd. How would I personally benefit beyond having the Senior Wizard position available unchallenged? Of course I would like that position, but to resort to proscribed Weaves?"

He turned to Monteous. "You injure me Monteous. We have always been rivals, but to stoop to spouting this slander."

Monteous stood and listened. Robert couldn't believe Monteous didn't respond immediately.

"Masters, it is known that those three rogues were against the measures we all know Monteous will bring to a vote if he is again invested as Senior Wizard. Is it so hard to believe that they abducted Monteous on their own initiative?" Orliss looked around the room, almost daring them all to contradict him.

"My colleagues," Monteous said, "There is an easy way to settle this. We'll put it to the Challenge Orb. There is no other way to tell, in this room, the truth of the matter. I know Orliss was central to my abduction, and I have reason to believe he is intimately involved in the use and construction of proscribed Works and Weaves. But that certainty lies only in my mind, where you cannot see. Let's put it to the Challenge Orb, and we shall find out who is telling the truth."

"How does that work?" Robert asked aloud.

Master Brin apparently heard him. "The Challenge Orb will adjudicate any question put to it that is in contention between two people. The one who is wrong will be unable to endure its touch."

"Orliss? Do you agree?" the Master of Gatherings asked.

Robert was struck with a thought, then. "Master Brin, what would happen if it were destroyed?"

Master Brin's head came up sharply and looked at the Orb, then at Robert. "Why, the Guild could not govern itself. All manner of disputes are submitted to it. The Guild would fracture. No one would risk that."

Orliss was still looking around the room.

"Master Orliss?" The Master of Gatherings sounded agitated.

Orliss looked right at him, then at Monteous. Robert saw his hand move in an odd, fluttering motion. "I think... not."

Then he dove off the platform.

Robert shouted, pointing at the wizards. "Monteous! They're going to destroy the Orb!"

They were already Weaving something.

Monteous turned toward the five, but he only had the Wand. Robert reached to grab the staff out of Master Brin's hands, but he was too late to have done anything, even if he'd managed to wrest the staff away.

The Weaves of the five Masters hit the Challenge Orb as one, enveloped it, then penetrated its shell. The Orb glowed red momentarily, then burst, sending shards in all directions to slice faces, arms, and anything exposed. Robert felt a stabbing pain in his forehead and blood quickly flowed into one eye.

He pulled the staff free from Brin, and then used his sleeve to try to wipe the blood from his eye. The blood kept flowing, so he just shut that eye, and used the other to look around for Orliss. He couldn't find him, though. *Where did he go?*

His eye fell on Monteous, lying on the platform, fragments of the Orb embedded in his chest and neck. The Master of Gatherings was attending to him, despite his own gashes.

Orliss. Where is he?

Robert spun around again. He could see Weaves flying everywhere. *Where is Orliss?*

Some wizards were racing up the aisles, heading for the doors. Momentarily, he wondered where Angela was, but he shook that thought away. He had to concentrate on finding Orliss.

There. Heading up one of the aisles, Robert caught sight of him as he turned to survey the carnage he'd wrought. A Weave struck Orliss, but he shrugged it away, then turned and strode up the steps.

Robert ran after him, pushing people aside in his effort to get to the aisle Orliss had taken. Strangely, Orliss didn't seem to be hurrying. Robert had made it probably a third of the way up the stairs when Orliss stepped through the door into the hallway, and the door shut behind him.

When Robert reached the top, someone pulled on his arm, preventing him from following Orliss through the door. He tried to pull away, but couldn't. He had to get Orliss. If Monteous was dead, he couldn't let Orliss escape.

"Robert!" Demetrius's voice.

Robert faced him. "What?"

"You're going to need to be able to see in order to confront him." Demetrius pulled a strip of cloth out and wrapped it around Robert's head and tied it tight. He took another one and used it to wipe the blood from Robert's eye. Finally, he could see again.

"Thanks."

"Right, let's go."

Demetrius pulled the door open and raced through it. Robert followed. It was easier with two unobstructed eyes. After several steps, he heard footsteps behind him, and looked to see Angela and Gerard on his heels. *Orliss will pay.*

Ahead of him, Demetrius leaped over the bodies of two wizards, and then turned into one of the entry chambers. Robert looked down as he jumped over the bodies, and saw they were empty and shriveled. He had no idea what could have done that to them, but he didn't have time to think on it. He followed Demetrius into the room and came to a halt. Demetrius hung in the air, feet above the floor, kicking violently.

Without hesitation, Robert wove a razor-thin Weave and sliced it between Orliss and Demetrius. Demetrius fell to the floor, holding his neck and gasping for breath.

Orliss smiled. "Well, Monteous's prodigy comes to save the day. Do you really think you can keep me from leaving, Robert?"

Robert threw a Weave at Orliss, the one that had worked on Uden. Orliss brushed it away.

"You'll have to do better than that, Robert."

Angela and Gerard came through the door, then, and stood one to each side.

"You brought help. Good thinking."

Orliss gestured and Weave's wrapped around both Angela and Gerard.

"Now, I think we can talk. Do you know why you're still alive, Robert?"

Robert shook his head. *What can I do?* He'd managed to sever the one Weave that held Demetrius, but the other Weave he'd tried, Orliss had shrugged it off like it Robert had tossed a skein of yarn.

"I *let* you live. I do regret not taking you when I came to Monteous's Laboratory that day. It would have saved a great deal of hassle, and I'd be invested as Senior Wizard right now. But this works just as well."

"What are you talking about?"

Orliss laughed. "I believed what I'd always heard about you. That you had great potential. Monteous despaired, though, when he talked about you, that you would ever live up to it. You still have great potential, and if you are smart, you will come with me and put that potential to use. There are great changes coming, Robert. In part, they've already arrived."

"No."

"Oh, yes. Do you think the Guild will survive this day? Its destruction was always part of the plan. If I could not be invested as Senior Wizard, we planned to destroy the Guild. The Seven Kingdoms rots from within, and I mean to see it remade. Monteous's plan would have maintained the current separation between the Rulers of these lands and the Guild. You could be a part of the remaking."

"I will not help you. You killed my friend." He couldn't allow

Wallace's death to mean nothing. And Monteous, Monteous was down on that platform, possibly bleeding his life away.

"Then join your friends." Orliss gathered a Weave and threw it at Robert.

It skirted the edges of his vew, but Robert saw it, and wove a barrier. Both Weaves fell apart.

Robert threw a fireball at Orliss, but it burst around him without effect.

A Weave wrapped around him, and he felt himself flying through the air, weightless for a moment, until his back smashed hard against the stone well, and he slipped to the ground. Monteous's crystal fell from his pocket, and he stared at it. Something was different, and it took him several moments to determine what it was. It no longer pulsed. The light in it had faded.

He looked around the room and saw Orliss had turned to the gateway and started forming a Weave. Demetrius lay on the floor, still having difficulty breathing. Angela and Gerard were still immobile. And the light had gone out on Monteous.

Monteous is dead.

All the rage from Wallace's death he'd directed at himself, the pain from losing his parents, and now Monteous, he gathered it all together, and directed it into the staff. He took everything he could from everyone around him and poured it into the staff. And he found that proscribed Work embedded in the staff and incorporated that, somehow, into the Weave he hurled at Orliss.

And this time, it stuck, and it burned, and it drained, and it fed on itself, on Orliss. Orliss screamed a sound no human voice should utter. Robert had no idea what the Weave was, or what it did, but he kept feeding it every bit of energie he could find. Orliss's skin shrunk around his bones, and then began to smoke. Flames burst out from his extremities, and quickly grew to engulf him.

The stench of Orliss's charred flesh filled Roberts nostrils. The smoke, he could see, began to fill the room.

Robert tried to end the Weave, but he couldn't. The Weave kept draining him, feeding on his energie. Robert fell back to the floor. The smoke started to fill his lungs as he breathed, forcing him to cough.

His last vision, before the Weave drained his remaining energie, was of Monteous's crystal, lying on the floor, dark and lifeless.

✻ ✻ ✻

WHEN HE WOKE, it was in a room he recognized. He lay in a bed at Ivron's estate. The room was warm. He tried to sit up, but a throbbing in his head caused him to lie back down.

"You're awake." Angela's voice. He couldn't see her yet.

"How did we get here?"

He heard her footsteps, and then her face hung over his. "One of the wizards brought us through the gateway back to the inn. Do you remember what happened?"

"Is Monteous..."

"He's gone, Robert. A shard from the Orb slit his throat." A tear fell on his hand.

Robert turned away from her for a moment, thinking back to how Monteous had taken him in, trained him — to how Monteous was ripped away so soon after rescuing him. He couldn't hold back the tears he felt forming. *But I have to move on, again.*

"How about Demetrius?" Robert asked, still facing away from Angela. He didn't want her to see the tears.

"He's fine. He's out helping build the pyre. There will be a funeral soon for Monteous and Wallace and the others."

"You know, I killed Orliss, but I wonder if it was too late."

"What was that Weave, anyway?"

Robert heard the door open.

"The Weave was something that should never have been used." Robert turned to see who had entered, ignoring the throbbing it brought, and saw it was Master Brin.

"I remember pouring everything I had into the staff," said Robert, "and sending that Weave at Orliss."

Master Brin nodded. "The Weave came from the Work embedded in it. You are fortunate that it did not kill you, as well."

Robert turned to look out the window.

"What now?"

"The staff has been taken, and will be studied, and likely destroyed."

"No, I mean, what now for us? For the Guild?"

"Oh. The Guild is broken. Fortunately, it is not completely shattered, but we lost a good third of our members, either to death in the fighting, or to flight. I am charged with completing your training." Master Brin patted him on the shoulder. "You, young wizard, when you are recovered, will take your tests. Your friends will finish their apprenticeships with me."

"Angela and I are..."

"Yes, she has informed me of that complication already. You will be allowed to visit, but if you pass your tests, and I fully expect you to do so, you will have duties to the Guild."

"But how can the Guild continue with the Orb shattered?"

"We will find another way. Demetrius explained Orliss's intentions, and those of us that remain, we shall not allow Mrongil to succeed. Monteous's measure passed. The Guild will have far more wizards in the future, as well as a school. We just have to hope the Seven Kingdoms survives until then."

Robert found some comfort in Master Brin's assertion. Monteous's wishes would at least be fulfilled. He closed his eyes. A moment passed. He felt Angela's lips brush his, and then he slept.

ABOUT THE AUTHOR

Mark Fassett lives in western Washington with his wife and children. He delivered pizza, measured rocks, played guitar in an early 90's metal band that almost went somewhere and programmed multiple video games and other pieces of software before settling down to write.

FIND ME ONLINE

Blog - http://www.markfassett.com
Twitter - http://twitter.com/mark_fassett

Shattered: A Wizard's Work Book One was written using StoryBox, software designed for writing novels. You can try it for free at http://www.storyboxsoftware.com

www.ingramcontent.com/pod-product-compliance
Lightning Source LLC
Chambersburg PA
CBHW021505240626
47154CB00002B/517